THE RANGER'S SORROW

The King's Ranger Book 4

AC COBBLE

Cobble Publishing LLC

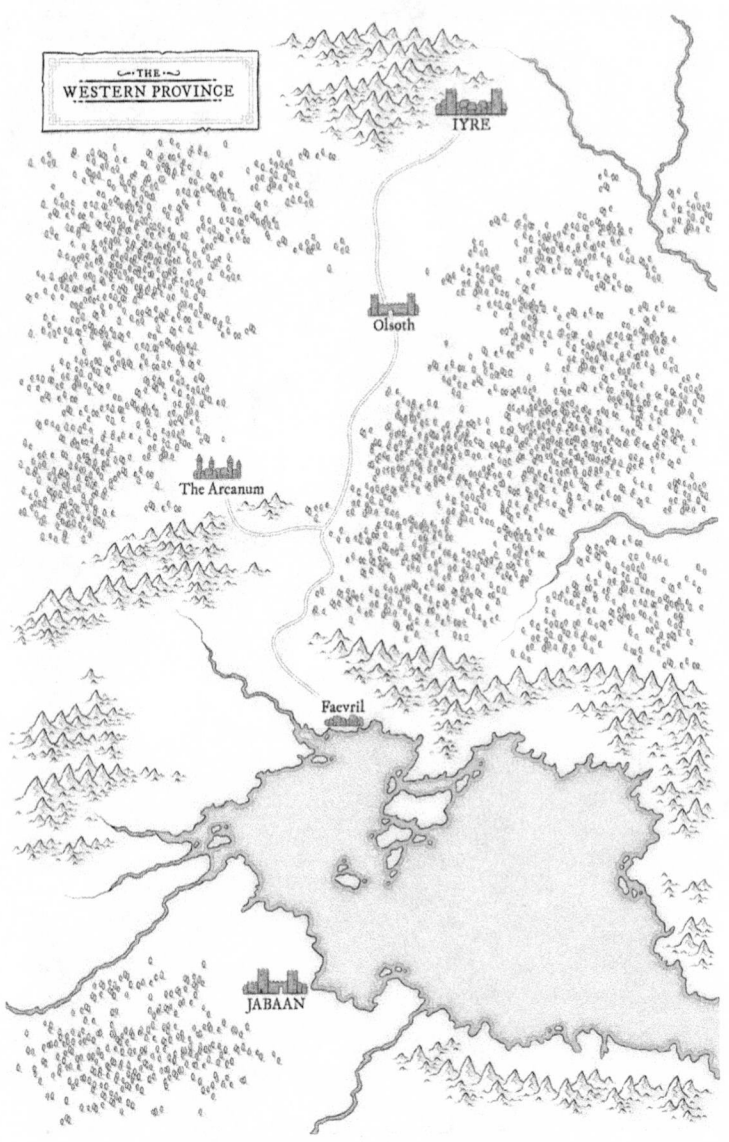

THE
WESTERN PROVINCE

IYRE

Olsoth

The Arcanum

Facvril

JABAAN

Keep in Touch and Extra Content

Y ou can find larger versions of the maps, series artwork, my newsletter, and other goodies at accobble.com. It's the best place to stay updated on when the next book is coming!

Happy reading!
AC

Chapter One

Blood dripped from the dagger.

Shaking his hand, flinging the crimson liquid in a fan across the room, Raif barked, "King's Sake, Kallie!"

Snarling, the nobleman's older sister lunged at him, swiping her hand-length blade at his face.

Raif leapt back, his greatsword lying on the plush carpet two steps behind his sister.

"Stop!" bellowed Cinda, and to everyone's surprise, they did.

Kallie stood, panting, her dagger held threateningly in front of her. She was garbed in a fine dress like that of a minor noble. Her hair was bound atop her head, and she wore blush and lip paint. If it weren't for the blood-stained dagger grasped in her hand, she would've looked as if she were on her way to a formal dinner party.

Raif gripped his bleeding hand and scowled at Kallie. His armor was dented and scored. Blood, sweat, and dust clung to him like water on a cool mug of ale. A moment before, he'd been in Carff in the midst of a battle with a throng of imps, dozens of spellcasters, swordsmen, and Prince Valchon himself. An hour before that, they'd witnessed the destruction of Stanton. Raif had been flung through the air into a portal and had appeared on the opposite side of the kingdom. Now, he was facing his elder sister, who'd cut him with a dagger.

The fighter's bewildered, stunned expression showed he was having some difficulty coming to grips with the change in circumstances.

Rew turned slowly, appraising the place they'd portaled into. It was a well-appointed sitting room adorned in intricate tapestries and finely-made furnishings. Wide, heavy glass windows were on the wall behind him, but they were thrown open, revealing a large body of sparkling water far below. It was a little cooler than Carff, but not cold. The open window brought the sounds of giant, gray birds that drifted on the wind and called to each other in high-pitched, mournful cries. Rew could see little but the water and the birds and hear nothing but the birds and the wind.

"Rew," hissed Anne, "where are we?"

"Jabaan. We're in Jabaan, in Prince Calb's palace," he murmured, turning to face Kallie Fedgley. "Alsayer brought you here to meet the prince, didn't he? What did he tell you his plans were?"

Kallie spit on the carpet and raised her dagger without answering. The side of her face was red, and Rew guessed Raif had smacked her. Had the fighter done it before or after she'd cut him? The lad had been holding his greatsword, so either way, he hadn't tried to kill her. What did Raif think was going to happen here?

Sighing, Rew glanced around at the others. "We have several minutes, I'd wager, until Prince Calb returns, and then we're in a great deal of trouble. We need to get moving. Quietly if we can, but quickly for certain."

"There's the door," said Zaine, pointing behind Kallie.

"You aren't going anywhere," snapped the noblewoman.

"Don't be foolish, Kallie," retorted Cinda. "We have you outnumbered, and we're armed. Get out of our way, and—"

"Come with us," interrupted Raif, taking a hesitant step

toward his older sister, his hands raised as if to show he meant no threat. "Come with us, and we'll get you to safety."

Kallie stared back at him incredulously.

"What happened in Spinesend... Father... We're all that we have left, Kallie. We need to talk, but not here, not now. You're our sister, and we won't leave you in this place with these people. You're safe with us."

"You really don't get it, do you?" Kallie asked Raif, shaking her head in disbelief.

Rew asked her, "When were you meeting with Calb? Were you going to him, or was he coming to this room?"

Kallie would not look at him, and Rew scowled. She was to meet Calb in the room, then. That bastard Alsayer had set the entire thing up. He'd placed Kallie as the bait and timed it so that Rew and the prince couldn't help but stumble into each other. What had Alsayer told the prince? What would Calb be expecting when he entered the room?

In other circumstances, Rew would have been impressed with the complexity and ingenuity of the spellcaster's plotting, not to mention the fact that so far, it had worked. But now, it just made Rew angry.

Alsayer had manipulated them as easily and callously as the carved, wooden pieces on a game board, and he'd put them right in the path of danger. They only had minutes to get away, if any time at all. Or... they could follow Alsayer's plan. Rew seethed at the idea, but Calb would be weakened from his attempt at Valchon and surprised to find Rew standing inside of his palace, waiting for him.

Would Rew get a better chance than the one Alsayer had given?

But the room was small and led to nowhere but the open air. If Calb put up a fight, it would turn ugly, and Rew wouldn't be able to protect the others and strike at his brother. Even weakened from his fight against Valchon, Calb would still be dangerous. He would have armed soldiers with him, and maybe spellcasters and imps. Calb and his minions wouldn't know what they were facing until someone opened the door, but the palace would be thick with reinforcements. It occurred to Rew that it might not even be Calb who came. After a tussle with Valchon, would the prince come directly to see Kallie, or would he send someone else to fetch her? What sort of clues and tricks had Alsayer used to ensure Calb would come? He hadn't told the truth to the prince. Rew could be sure of that much.

"We have to go," said Rew, deciding that surviving was more important at the moment than the slim possibility they might get a jump on Prince Calb.

Raif took another step toward his sister. "Kallie, they're tricking you into—"

"Into lying and telling everyone that I'm the one with Father's powers? No, Raif, that is you. You and her," cried Kallie, spinning and slashing her dagger in Cinda's direction. "I know it all. You've been walking around, convincing everyone that it's me they should be looking for. Pfah! You set me up as bait and then tell me I am family? Alsayer shared all of your little secrets with me, Raif. Prince Heindaw and the king himself are hunting me because of your lies. I may not have Father's talent for necromancy, but I have something just as powerful—the truth."

"No!" snapped Raif. "Kallie, we can talk about this!"

Kallie shifted in front of the door, holding her dagger menacingly, blocking the only exit from the room. "It's Prince Calb I'll be talking to, and then, I won't be the one in danger." She grinned wickedly. "I think the prince is going to be quite pleased to find you here."

"We have to go," repeated Rew.

"We're going to take her with us," growled Raif, and he charged his sister, his arms wide to engulf and presumably restrain her.

While Raif had learned much in their years apart, Kallie hadn't been idle, and she did what any attractive young noblewoman was taught to do when a suitor was dangerously aggressive. As her brother wrapped his arms around her, Kallie slammed her dagger into his bicep then whipped it across his face as he staggered back, drawing a long, bloody line across his jaw.

Raif, perhaps acting on instinct, dove for his greatsword, and Kallie went after him. Rew surged toward them, but he was still on the opposite side of the room where the portal from Carff had closed. He was going to be too late.

A burst of pale white-green light blasted into Kallie's side, and she was flung against the wall beside the door.

"Cinda!" cried Raif, staggering to his feet.

Wailing, Cinda rushed forward, her face locked in horrified shock at what she'd done to her sister. She knelt beside Kallie, picking up the older girl's head in her hands, looking at her closed eyes. "Oh, no. Oh, no—"

Kallie swung with her dagger, catching Cinda in the side once, twice, and three times before the younger sister fell back. Kallie's eyes flicked open, and a smile curled her lips. She crawled onto her knees and raised her dagger above Cinda for a killing blow.

Raif reached his greatsword and reared back to swing at his older sister.

Rew, knowing he couldn't make across the room in time to stop the dagger or the greatsword, flung his longsword. The steel, dark from the blood of the imps they'd faced back in Carff, flashed across the room and skewered Kallie through the chest. She flew back from the force of the blow, slamming against the door. Anger twisted her face until her mad rictus fell, and her features went slack.

Cinda, lying on her back on the floor, coughed, spitting crimson blood that leaked down her cheek.

"Anne," barked Rew, kneeling in front of Kallie and putting his back to Raif so he could draw his longsword from the girl without the fighter seeing. Somewhat less than gracefully, Rew shoved Kallie's body out of the way to the door.

"I-I don't know what... I was going to..." stammered Raif.

Rew stood and put a hand on the big fighter's shoulder. "You were going to do what you had to do."

"But I didn't," muttered Raif. "I was too slow. Cinda—"

His eyes widened and he spun. Anne was kneeling beside the novice necromancer. The empath's expression was grim. Raif croaked, "Will she…"

"I don't know," responded Anne.

"Calb is coming. We have to leave," said Rew.

"If we move her, she won't make it," murmured Anne. She looked up at Rew, stricken. "I need time."

The ranger nodded and glanced at Zaine. "Keep an eye out, will you?"

The thief, her bow clutched tight in her hands, only two arrows left in the quiver, nodded.

Rew moved to the door and opened it, stepping out onto a long gallery that overlooked the foyer to Prince Calb's palace. It was a massive hall, the length of a city block but several times wider. The open gallery was on a second floor and ran the length of the foyer. Across from it was another gallery, dotted with rooms where visitors could be kept until the prince or his administrators were ready to see them. Below was the huge marble floor of the entrance hall. It was filled with hundreds of soldiers who appeared to be returning from the conflict in Carff.

"Blessed Mother," grumbled Rew. Then, he adjusted his grip on his longsword and prepared to fight.

THE SOLDIERS WERE GOING TO BE A PROBLEM, BUT A MORE IMMEDIATE concern was the two hulking imps that bounded up the grand, marble staircase. The creatures were thrashing their heads, sniffing the air. Evidently, they'd caught the scent of an intruder. Rew looked down at himself, at his torn, bloody, and sweat-stained clothing. He scowled. Imps were known for poor eyesight, but they had good noses and other supernatural senses as well.

Calb could have trained his summonings to detect someone who did not belong, but Rew had to admit, he probably smelled something awful.

On the floor below, Rew heard shouts, and people turned and followed the path of the monstrous imps to where they saw Rew, standing at the marble railing of the gallery, with a longsword in his hand, looking as out of place as anyone possibly could look. The soldiers didn't have the senses of the imps, but it didn't take extensive training as a guard to identify Rew as a threat. Maybe he should have just poked his head out first.

Slavering growls preceded the imps, the sounds of their vicious hunger bouncing off the marble and filling the huge foyer with their bestial rage. Muscles bunched and claws scraped on the floor as they rushed toward him.

Rew stepped back and kicked open the door to the room the party was in. "We can't stay here."

"Rew," snapped Anne from inside. "I cannot move her."

"It's not a choice," argued Rew, glancing over his shoulder. "Raif, Zaine, make a stretcher or something we can carry her on. We have to go, now!"

The two imps had reached him. There wasn't time to say anything else, but it seemed the arrival of the imps made the point well enough as everyone started scrambling to get going.

Down the long gallery, the imps skidded and leapt, their clawed feet sliding on the polished marble floor. It gave Rew a precious opportunity. He ducked close to one of the imps that was flailing off balance in its eagerness to reach him. The other creature's taloned hand whipped over Rew as he crouched beneath the blow.

Rew lashed out, taking the first imp along the side with a brutal, raking cut that opened the flesh across its ribs, shoulder to hip. The imp wailed as Rew's enchanted steel sliced cleanly through skin and muscle, cutting the creature to the bone and sending a shower of blood and gore spraying across the white marble floor and the tapestries that hung alongside the wall of the gallery. Below, in the open foyer beneath them, Rew could hear shrill calls and gruff instructions being issued.

He knew his time was limited, but those below had been frozen in surprise for a moment watching the imps attack. It gave him a chance to formulate a plan, which was going to be difficult because they were stuck in the center of Prince Calb's palace in view of hundreds of the prince's soldiers. Rew wasn't sure there was a plan that could address that complication.

It didn't help that his planning window was being encroached on by the two imps that had spun around and were coming back to finish him. The wounded one was dragging one leg and moving slow, but the other jumped into the air in a springing attack, its arms and jaw spread wide.

"King's Sake," muttered Rew, ducking again and thrusting up with his longsword to stab the creature in the chest.

He lost his blade as the imp's heavy body tumbled past him, wrenching his arm around and jerking the wooden hilt of his sword from his grip. Moments before, while still back in Carff, he'd snapped that arm back into the socket following a fall from Prince Valchon's throne room. His shoulder throbbed with pain, and his arm spasmed at the stress of his movement. His fingers trembled helplessly as the sword was yanked away.

The second imp reached him and grasped at his head with a clawed hand. Rew got his left arm up to block, but then, the imp simply closed its hand around his forearm and yanked him toward its maw. He tried to reach across his body to awkwardly draw his hunting knife from behind his back, but it was positioned to be pulled free with his off hand, and he couldn't move his injured arm far enough to reach. There wasn't time to fumble with it. He kicked up with his feet, launching his lower body toward the imp and wrapping his legs around its neck.

The imp looked at him with large, yellowed eyes, startled.

Hanging from the imp's neck by his legs, Rew locked his ankles and squeezed with his thighs in a move which could choke the air from a man, but the creature's neck was three times the size of a man's, and Rew didn't have the strength to crush its throat.

The imp tried to bite him, but with his legs wrapped around it, the creature couldn't get close to him, so instead, it roared in frustration, drenching Rew's trousers and tunic with its rancid spittle.

One of his arms was clutched tight in the imp's grasp. The other was injured. His hunting knife hung from his back, the hilt on the wrong side of his body. His throwing knives were in his boots, on the opposite side of the imp's head. His longsword was lodged in the body of the dead imp behind him. It left Rew with few options.

The imp, gnashing its teeth fruitlessly at him, evidently came to the same conclusion, and decided to rip Rew's arm off of his body.

His muscles and ligaments strained as he fought the impossible strength of the conjured beast. Rew punched with his free hand, his fist bouncing harmlessly off the monster's head. He tried digging his thumb into the imp's eye. It roared, filling his face with the sound of its anger and the stench of its foul breath. Rew pushed deeper, jabbing into the imp's eye socket with his thumb.

The imp flung him away.

Rew hooked his thumb and tore the creature's eye from its skull before he went tumbling to the marble floor. Flicking his hand to dislodge the eye, Rew lurched toward the dead imp, wresting his longsword from its chest and spinning in time to skewer the second creature as it fell on him. The steel plunged to the hilt, killing the imp, but the imp continued its momentum and knocked him down. Rew fell to the floor, pinned beneath the dead body.

"Blessed Mother," grumbled the ranger, wriggling beneath the bulk of the imp. His arms were smashed beneath it, and he had no leverage to shift the weight on top of him.

Then, the imp moved, rolling off of him, and Raif was there, looking a combination of impressed and horrified.

"Are you all right?" asked Zaine, peering around the big fighter.

"No."

Raif reached down and hauled Rew to his feet. The nobleman glanced down at his hand, now covered in the imp's blood and saliva. In a voice carrying the sort of disdain that only a nobleman could summon, Raif remarked, "That is disgusting."

"Yeah, well…" muttered Rew. He found he didn't have the energy to complete the thought.

"We need to go," said Zaine, staring toward the stairwell where the imps had come up to the gallery. From the distance, they could hear the clamor of armored men running. The thief had one arrow nocked on her bow and one left in her quiver. It sounded like a lot more than two men were charging up those stairs. In a high-pitched plea, she added, "Right now. We need to go right now."

"That's what I've been saying," snapped Rew. He glanced at Anne where she crouched on a makeshift stretcher inside the room, straddling Cinda's prone body.

Anne, tending to Cinda and not looking up, allowed, "If we have to go, let's go."

Rew started a lurching run down the open gallery, heading away from the stairwell. Behind him, Raif picked up the handles of the stretcher and began to drag it. Anne, still kneeling over Cinda's bleeding body, worked feverishly to heal the girl as they slid out into the open. The fighter winced at the weight of the two women, but did not complain, and doggedly hurried after Rew, the back end of the stretcher gliding smoothly over the marble floor. Zaine brought up the rear, but after several updates that the soldiers were on the stairs, that they'd ascended to the gallery, and that they were coming, she stopped sharing what she saw.

Rew frantically glanced at the doors they passed along the gallery, struggling to recall the layout of Calb's palace, fumbling for ideas of how they could lose what sounded like half the prince's army crashing after them.

A green-robed spellcaster bolted out in front of Rew, a hand clutched to a talisman on his chest, an arm raised, and arcane words bubbling from his lips.

Without pausing, Rew swung a left hook and caught the man full in the face, ending the conjurer's ritual and preventing him from casting his spell and summoning whatever imps the man had at his command.

As the conjurer fell, Rew shoved by him, and snatched the talisman from the conjurer's neck. The ranger flung it over the edge of the gallery, hoping that if it shattered on the floor below, it might release whatever was trapped inside of it. With no guidance, any conjured imp would be just as much trouble for Calb's men as it would be for Rew and the party.

Grimacing, Rew realized none of Calb's spellcasters would have returned to the palace much before the prince himself. Was Calb down below or somewhere else in the sprawling grounds of the palace?

A junior conjurer and a handful of imps, Rew could handle, but Calb himself would be a problem. The prince would be weakened from his effort against Valchon, but Rew had taken thumps and cuts back in Carff, including dislocating his shoulder, and the fight with the imps had aggravated the injury. Rew's right side throbbed in agony, and already, he could feel painful swelling in his shoulder tightening his range of motion. The others in the party weren't in much better shape, and Cinda was completely incapacitated.

Rew shook his left hand. His knuckles felt bruised from punching the conjurer in the face. He didn't want to fight Calb left-handed, but he switched his longsword to that hand and whispered a hope to the Blessed Mother they would find a way out. Rew was well-practiced with his hunting knife in his off-hand, but without his longsword in the other, it wouldn't be the same balance. He felt inadequate and wasn't sure he trusted his skill to compensate for the heavier blade in the opposite hand he was used to. But he didn't want to give up the improved reach of the longsword, either. He knew it was only a matter of time until his injured shoulder gave out.

He glanced back and winced. Raif was staring ahead, focused on following Rew. Past the fighter, Rew could see Anne perched on the stretcher, her expression set, her arms covered in Cinda's blood. Zaine brought up the rear, an arrow still nocked, her face panicked. Behind her, two dozen armored men were racing after them along with another green-robed conjurer and several dog-sized imps that leapt and bounced along the gallery like coursers on the hunt.

Ahead of them, the gallery extended several hundred more paces, but in the center, a marble bridge crossed over the expansive floor below. Rew hissed a warning and took a turn, streaking across the bridge and the open air. Raif cursed, trying to follow the ranger on the tight turn without spilling his sister and Anne off the stretcher.

Down in the foyer below them, Rew heard frantic shouts as the soldiers followed their progress. It occurred to Rew that some of those men might be carrying bows, but it was too late for that. He tried to hurry across the wide-open bridge. Cutting perpendicular to the gallery, he saw the closest pursuit was just fifty paces behind and coming fast. The soldiers weren't close enough that anyone below would stay an attack, but they were close enough Rew and his bedraggled companions weren't going to win a foot race.

Ahead of him, the gallery extended in both directions over the giant foyer, but instead of turning, Rew ran to the closest door he could find and yanked it open. It didn't matter what was behind it. Injured and carrying Cinda, they weren't going to out run anyone. They had to find somewhere to block pursuit.

Two servants looked up in shock and terror. Beyond them, Rew saw the sharp-peaked roofs of Jabaan through an open window. Cool air blew in, and a fierce grin lit Rew's face. He spun just as Zaine slammed the door shut and found a bolt to lock it. Rew rushed to her side and put his left shoulder against a heavy dresser, the wooden legs scrapping until he maneuvered it in front of the door. A breath later, a desk joined it, pushed in place by Raif, who turned and found another sturdy piece of furniture to add to the barricade.

"It won't slow them long," murmured Rew.

Ignoring the two servants who stood speechlessly on the side of the room, a duster in the hands of one, a cloth and crystal bowl in the hands of the other, Rew darted to the open window and peered out. There was a steep slate roof, a sheer drop, and the tangled streets of Jabaan half a dozen floors below the window.

He turned to Anne. "Can she move?"

"No," hissed the empath.

Rew held her gaze.

"She might not make it."

"The only other choice is to allow ourselves to be captured. I'm sorry, but we've got to risk it." He looked to Zaine. "Tie up the servants."

Raif returned from stacking more furniture in front of the door and picked up the stretcher again, dragging it and the two passengers toward the window. He peered out. "Ah, Rew, that goes straight down. I don't... We can't survive that fall."

The ranger nodded and then clambered outside the window onto the slate tiles. They were dry, thankfully, but sloped at a treacherous angle. He called back inside, "Raif, hand me the end of the stretcher."

Muttering foul disparagements on Rew's name and all of his ancestors, Anne climbed out first to join him, looking down nervously at the city of Jabaan which spread out in jagged rooftops and towers like a field of broken glass. None of those towers reached the height of the palace. If they fell, it would be a long drop before they hit something.

Whispering, the empath worried, "Raif is right. That's a fatal drop, Rew. How are we going to get down from here?"

Rew shushed her and accepted the end of the stretcher from Raif. With Anne's help, they carefully pulled it outside and laid it on the roof, Cinda's feet pointing down at a sharp angle, Rew's boot wedged beneath the end so the stretcher didn't slide off into the void.

Raif came next and then Zaine. The thief offered only a shrug when Rew inquired whether the servants were securely bound.

"All right," Rew declared loudly, raising his voice so all could hear, "down we go."

He then gestured up, toward the top of the roof, and the party's eyes brightened. They weren't going down. There was nowhere to go that way, but perhaps the captive servants had heard and believed the ruse. Perhaps that would give the party a few extra steps to escape their pursuit, which, as they crouched on the slate rooftop, Rew heard was already smashing against the door.

The imps he'd last seen in the gallery were of the smaller variety and wouldn't have the strength to batter down the barricade or furniture they'd thrown against the door, but it wouldn't be long before the soldiers got through the door and shoved away the furniture or until the conjurer summoned something bigger.

Rew sheathed his longsword, awkwardly because his right shoulder was nearly useless now, and grabbed the end of Cinda's stretcher. He began scuttling higher toward the peak of the roof. Raif easily lifted the bottom half of the stretcher then slid and nearly went plummeting down and off the edge before he caught his footing again. A single slate tile broke loose and skittered away. It fell out of sight. They couldn't hear it land. Raif offered a sick-looking smile, and with Zaine's help, they started inching higher. Anne stayed by Cinda's side, putting her hands on the girl, pouring what empathy she could into the injured necromancer.

Below in the palace, there were thuds and crashes as Calb's people tried to break down the door. Alarm bells rang, and Rew wondered if Calb would come straight away or if he would try to learn the nature of the threat to his palace before he showed himself.

It was their only hope, that the prince was weakened enough by his run at Valchon that he would be afraid. Calb might worry it was Heindaw or some other powerful enemy, and he might not expose himself until he learned different. The prince's fear gave them a chance, but it would last only as long as it took for Calb's soldiers to inform him of what they'd seen. Whether or not they could describe Rew to the prince, when Calb learned it was a small group that hadn't cast a single spell, he would come.

They reached the top of the roof, and Rew took them over the peak, balancing carefully as he descended the other side. His shoulder was on fire, and he wondered how much longer he could risk carrying Cinda's stretcher. If he stumbled, if he lost her even for a moment, she would have a short roll and then a long drop.

"Where, ah…" murmured Raif, looking out at the expansive view.

Jabaan was situated hundreds of paces above a massive inland lake that extended as far as the eye could see. The palace was perched on the edge of a cliff that loomed over the water. The rooftop of the palace ended, and then, there was nothing until the deep waters of the lake far below. Rew guessed that Raif had not imagined a fall from the other side of the building could be even worse than crashing down half a dozen stories into the city, but it was.

If they slipped and fell, there was no hope of survival.

Rew turned. Walking parallel to the drop and the peak of the roof, he led them toward the rest of the palace. Beyond the massive entrance hall they'd been running through, the structure sprawled out into a warren of towers, courtyards, and blocky stone buildings. There were places to hide there, if they weren't seen before they made it.

Faint voices reached his ears, and Rew guessed that their pursuers had breached the door and climbed out the window. Hopefully, they wasted precious time peering over the edge and wondering if anyone could have survived the fall to the streets of the city.

"Just a little bit longer," murmured Rew. Then, he glanced up and saw a soldier peering out an open door twenty paces in front of him.

"Duck," hissed Zaine.

They did, and she released her arrow. It thumped into the startled guard, and the man pitched backward out of sight.

The party hurried and found that the guard had been standing inside of a steep, spiral staircase. They heard the crash of his body rolling down the stairs and saw blood smeared along the wall where he'd tried to stop himself from toppling down. The trail of blood continued out of sight, and they didn't have time to try and clean it.

Rew glanced behind them, looking at the steep slate roof. The soldiers chasing them hadn't appeared yet, but there was nowhere to go. Nothing but roof and open air. The only exit was the narrow door the soldier had opened, which must have been access for maintenance. Rew had no idea where the stairwell went, but it was the only way forward.

He entered the tower. As he did, the sounds of the soldier falling down the spiral stairs finally stopped. There were shouts coming up from the bottom where someone must have heard or seen the man.

Rew glanced at the others and shrugged. "Up, I guess."

Chapter Two

"An arcanist's lair?" wondered Anne when they entered the room they'd found at the top of the tower.

Rew tried to scratch his beard but couldn't reach as his throbbing and stiffening shoulder limited his movement. He cringed. Stuck in a tower in Calb's palace and unable to use his arm. That wasn't good.

Zaine slipped a small pouch back into her belt and grinned. "I knew that set of lock picks would come in handy."

"You picked the lock all right, but next time, try disarming the trap as well, eh?" complained Raif, touching a dent on his armor that had been left by a thin, steel dart. "That thing would have stung fierce if it'd hit one of us."

"Not for long," said Rew. "It was poisoned."

Raif looked at him, aghast, and even Zaine swallowed uncomfortably before opening her mouth, probably to attempt some quip to distract Raif from the fact that she'd nearly killed him.

"How long do you think we have, Rew?" questioned Anne, interrupting Zaine.

The empath was crouched beside Cinda where they'd left the stretcher on the floor. Anne's hands were covered in blood to her elbows, but she'd lost the panicked look in her eyes. Cinda wasn't going to die, yet. Instead, Anne looked resigned. The spiral stairwell led up from the roof to the room they'd found and nowhere else. If they left the room, their choices were back onto the roof or down below where the dead soldier had fallen and been found. Staying in the room wasn't a good option, but Rew wasn't liking any of their other choices, either.

"We don't have long," responded Rew, looking around the chamber, hoping for inspiration. "Zaine, that cloak there, help me tie it into a sling."

The thief assisted, and in moments, Rew's sword arm was bound to his side, his shoulder immobilized as best as he and Zaine could manage. Anne, in between her ministrations of Cinda, observed their efforts grimly.

Raif was poking through the chamber, trying to find something they could use, but he looked up shaking his head. "It's all worthless. Just books and... experiments, I guess. I don't know what any of them are supposed to do."

Rew grunted. He went to study the various decanters and burners that Raif had found on a wide, heavily scarred wooden table. Without the knowledge of an arcanist, none of it looked particularly useful.

"I don't imagine it will take long for whoever found that soldier to call for some more of them," remarked Zaine, looking ruefully at Cinda's unconscious body. "Will she be all right?"

"She'll live for now," murmured Anne. "If we had several days and a quiet, safe space, I'd have no worries about a full recovery, but as it is... She lost a lot of blood, and I had to put most of my energy into repairing her lungs where her sister— where Kallie—stabbed her. I'm still working, but after such an abrupt surge of empathy, her body needs time to adjust. Too much empathy in some circumstances is almost as bad as none at all."

"How long until she's stabilized?" asked Rew.

"A few hours until she's hale enough to get through this without my help?" speculated Anne. "Even with my help, at least a full day until she's back on her feet. Maybe two."

"We're not going to have that," mentioned Rew.

Wordlessly, Anne turned from him and went back to work on Cinda. Rew and Zaine tried to patch up the various cuts and scrapes Raif had gotten between the battle in Carff and the attack by his sister, but when the fighter began to remove his armor to give them a better access to a laceration on his side, Rew shook his head.

"Lad, you're going to need that."

Wincing, Raif gripped his greatsword and let them work.

On the stairwell outside the room, they heard the racket of armored men moving about, but it was a quarter hour before someone finally pounded a heavy fist on the door. "Open up or we'll break it down!"

"And why should we save you the effort?" Rew called in response.

There was a pause, as if the speaker was thinking that one over. Then, the voice answered, "Because if you open it up, I'll walk you down nice and easy. If I have to come in there, I'll lock a chain around your neck and drag you to the dungeons like a goat to slaughter."

There was a commotion on the other side, and Zaine pressed her ear to the door to listen. "The arcanist, I think. He's coming up. He says he has a key."

Bellowing, Rew called out, "If you put a key into that door, I'll start putting these books into the fire. Go fetch the prince. I want to talk to him."

"What?" came a startled response from the other side of the door. "The prince? You want to see the prince?"

"First book is going into the fire now. Every few minutes, I throw in another," warned Rew loudly. "Get the prince, and I'll stop."

There was another sound of commotion. An old man's voice called, "Hold on. Hold on, those are invaluable tomes. The knowledge in them is irreplaceable. I don't know what sort of game you think to play, but the prince doesn't—"

"Four more minutes, then another book," shouted Rew.

There was a curse, and a hurried discussion, then the other side of the door went quiet except for the clank and shuffle of steel as the soldiers tried to get comfortable in the narrow, spiral stairwell. Evidently, they were going to wait right there while the arcanist fetched the prince.

Rew looked to Anne and Cinda, but the empath stayed focused, and the noblewoman hadn't regained consciousness. It was hard to tell if her condition was improving or not, but her chest rose and fell with breath. She still lived.

On the mantle above the arcanist's fireplace there was a mechanical clock, and it ticked through the minutes with gleeful viciousness. Rew didn't know how many soldiers might be crowding the stairs below, but it was enough. He peeked out a window. The tower was four stories above any of the rooftops below. He figured he and Zaine might be able to make the climb, if it wasn't for his wounded shoulder. If they tied together some linens perhaps the others... He looked at Cinda and sighed. Trying to climb down was likely to kill the lass, and it might get the rest of them killed as well if the soldiers had bothered to station someone to watch the outside of the tower.

They could split up, but what good would that do them? If Calb learned who Cinda was and what she was capable of, the adventure was over. The prince might attempt to use her, kill her, or gift her to the king along with warnings of what his brothers were attempting. Rew didn't like the odds of a rescue in any scenario. If they were going to face capture, it was best to do it together and hope to the Mother an opportunity would arise.

Rew waited impatiently. The guards might not know who they were, but they weren't going to let the party walk out peacefully no matter what Rew told them. They'd killed Kallie, a soldier, and a pair of Calb's imps. There wasn't an explanation for all of that which anyone was going to believe. Attempting to fight their way out would be worse. He could only guess how many of Calb's men were packed into the stairwell, but by the time he got through them the rest of the army and the prince's spellcasters would have had time to arrive. Even uninjured, it was an impossible idea.

He paced the room, his mind racing. The fact was they were trapped and there was no way out of it. He tried rolling his shoulder and then stopped. King's Sake, he would have trouble feeding himself supper, much less effecting an escape from an isolated tower while Calb's entire army surrounded it. All they could do was wait and hope that when Calb found them, he'd make a mistake and give them an opening.

While Rew paced, Anne knelt beside Cinda, and Raif crouched next to them, his greatsword at his side, his face stone-still. Zaine moved from window to window, peering down fruitlessly, mumbling under her breath, evidently trying to calculate the odds of survival if they hit a rooftop at an angle or if they could somehow fashion a swing from the arcanist's bedsheets. Periodically, she would glance at Cinda and change course to begin muttering about some new, even more outlandish plan.

Then, the thief let out a startled shriek and stumbled backward.

Rew spun. Sitting on one of the narrow windowsills was a small imp, no taller than the ranger's knee. The tips of its stubby wings poked above its back, and when it saw him, the imp licked its teeth and chortled. "Rew. What are you doing here?"

The ranger blinked back at the imp. Its voice was high-pitched and guttural, like breaking glass, but it was unmistakably the king's tongue the imp was speaking. An imp that could talk? He swallowed. An imp that knew his name?

It stretched, thin limbs extending, its pudgy belly jiggling with its mirth. Behind small, sharp teeth, it croaked, "You don't recognize me?"

"Calb?"

The imp winked and then frowned. "Wait, what about this body makes you think of Prince Calb?"

Shaking his head, Rew studied the imp nervously. "How are you doing this?"

"I've been experimenting," claimed the imp. Its fat head turned to survey the others in the room. The imp sniffed the air, eyeing Cinda and the blood pooled around her on the stretcher. "What happened to her?"

"She had an accident."

"Her blood smells the same as Kallie Fedgley's. Sisters?" The imp sniffed again.

Rew struggled to move his right arm, bound in the makeshift sling, then gave up and rubbed the top of his head with his left hand.

"You're hiding something," accused the imp. "You always do that when you're hiding something."

"I do that when I'm thinking," protested Rew, forcing his hand back down by his side.

"Exactly," declared the imp. "Why don't you join me downstairs? We can talk, catch up. Face to face. Ha. Not this face, my real face. It's been awhile, Rew. You can tell me I've gotten fat, and I'll tell you that you've lost your hair."

"We, ah, we have to be leaving," muttered Rew, recoiling at the casual words squeaking from the imp's foul mouth. Its yellow eyes glittered, as if it knew the effect it was having on him.

"Come now, let's not pretend. We found Kallie Fedgley's body. My soldiers saw you fight my imps—the bigger ones. There's another body down at the bottom of this tower with an arrow in its neck. Surely you don't think I'll let you just walk away? I have more soldiers, and I can summon more imps, but I needed Kallie Fedgley. She... was going to tell me something. I have to know why you killed her. Why you came to Jabaan. Come downstairs and let's talk like old times, Brother."

"Brother?" hissed Zaine.

Ignoring her, Rew glanced at Anne.

The empath, without looking up, stated, "I need at least two more hours."

Turning back to the imp, Rew said, "Two hours. You can give us that, can't you? We're not going anywhere, and after two hours, we'll come and talk."

The imp, its large, gleaming eyes on Anne and Cinda, shrugged. Then, it sat down on the windowsill to wait.

Scowling, Rew began rummaging around the arcanist's rooms, looking for something to drink, trying to distract himself from the feel of the imp's gaze on his every move.

———

TWO HOURS LATER, A VERITABLE ARMY OF PRINCE CALB'S MEN marched them down from the arcanist's tower. Rew noted as they went that it was largely armsmen who escorted them and not the spellcasters that clustered in the royal palaces like flies around offal. Had Calb committed all of his high magicians to the attack on Prince Valchon? Had they been lost, or were they merely exhausted? Rew had seen at least two of Calb's conjurers alive, but he hoped he'd punched the one hard enough the man was going to need a few days recovering.

The ranger had little time to consider the implications of the missing spellcasters. In moments, they were escorted to a bare-walled room beneath the base of the tower. It wasn't exactly a dungeon, but it wasn't exactly not a dungeon, either. It had no windows, for one, and the only door was a hand-width thick steel barrier that it took three guards to shove closed once they were inside. On the outside of the door, Rew had seen massive bolts that could be slid across to lock it and then an imposing portcullis which could be lowered from the ceiling. On the inside of the door, he saw evidence of the futility of trying to break out. Long, deep grooves had been clawed into the steel, presumably from imps who were unexcited about confinement in the depths of Calb's keep.

Prince Calb was there to greet them, along with two score armed guards and a pair of young-looking invokers. Rew smirked. So the prince had lost spellcasters during the assault on Valchon. If he had more talented high magicians available, he would have them with him. Even if they were too exhausted to cast, Calb would have wanted to make a show of it for Rew.

Calb saw the ranger's look and grimaced. He was a short, portly man, and his bald head gleamed in the light of the torches hanging from the walls. Rew glared at him. Calb had accused the ranger of losing his hair? The prince's cheeks were bright red from years of drink and hours of the exertion he would have put into attacking Carff and then fleeing. He wore rich green velvet robes, signifying his talent as a conjurer. Like Valchon, he did not wear any other luxury accessories his station and wealth could have bought him. Both princes, all of the royal family, did not care for visible expressions of power. They wanted power itself.

"I use this chamber for experimentation," remarked Calb, gesturing around the empty space. "It's secure enough to keep even the angriest imp inside of it and will serve just as well as your home until I'm satisfied with the explanations you give. I'll have some beds and chairs brought down."

"You're too kind," grumbled Rew.

Calb tilted his head, studying the ranger. He asked, "Why are you here, Rew?"

Rew did not answer, and Calb shrugged. He left without speaking, and his men filed out after him, swinging the giant steel door shut and locking it from the outside.

For a moment, the crackling of the torches was the only sound. Then, Zaine asked, "What did he mean by brother?"

"It's complicated," muttered Rew, turning away from where Zaine, Raif, and Anne were all looking at him curiously. "Very complicated."

Shaking himself, Raif began prowling around the edge of the room, looking at indentations and scars on the walls and peering up narrow shafts in the stone which must have been built for ventilation. The openings were covered with metal grates, but even if they weren't, none were wide enough that a person could crawl up. Not even the small imp they'd seen in the tower would fit into the narrow chutes. The room was long, wide, and completely empty. The door was as sturdy as any Rew had seen, and all Rew had were his fists.

Calb's soldiers had searched them and removed their weapons before taking them from the arcanist's chambers. There hadn't been anything to do about it, except to fight, and he'd decided that was suicide. Maybe that would have been better than captivity.

Down below the tower, there was an entire palace of stone surrounding them, now. Force wasn't going to get them out, and Rew couldn't think of a plan at the moment, so he decided to lay down and rest.

"What are you doing?" asked Raif.

"Taking a nap," replied Rew. He could feel the boy staring at him, unsatisfied with his answer, so he added, "It's been a long day, Raif, and if we do find a way out of this, the days will only get longer. Get some sleep while you can."

"Should we, ah, keep a watch?" wondered Zaine.

"We'll hear them opening that door, don't you think?"

With that, Rew rolled onto his good side, his injured shoulder throbbing in agony, and ignored the sounds of the others as they clustered by Anne. The empath checked them over, granting some small healing, then told them to rest.

There was little she could do after putting so much energy into Cinda, but Rew didn't ask for even that.

Brother.

They'd all heard it. His secrets were spilling out like ale from a tumped-over mug. Most of his secrets, that was. He still had a few. Rew still had his reasons to refuse Anne's help.

As he lay on the stone floor, he worried the pain in his shoulder would keep him awake, but he was wrong. Within minutes, he fell asleep, but true to his prediction, the clank and scrape of the steel door woke him when they arrived.

MOST OF PRINCE CALB'S SPELLCASTERS MIGHT HAVE PERISHED, BUT IT seemed he still had a pocketful of arcanists at his disposal. Ten of them came to visit, accompanied by four times as many guards and three imps, including the small one Calb had made his famil- iar. They all crowded into the room, and then the door was shut and locked behind them. Rew felt some satisfaction, that even visibly injured and unarmed, he still drew such caution, but his satisfaction was doing little to get them out of Calb's basement, and it seemed the prince himself was avoiding them.

The arcanists were led by a man who was slender and tall, and who spoke with a crisp lilt that sounded more of Iyre than Jabaan. Arcanists traveled in pursuit of knowledge and power, so that was little surprise, but Rew noted it all the same. Anything might help. And if they found nothing...

"What happened to the lass?" asked the thin arcanist, peering down at Cinda.

"She was stabbed."

"I know that," muttered the man.

Before the arcanist could add another comment, Rew retorted, "Then why did you ask?"

The arcanist clasped his hands in front of his chest and remarked, "I see you are intent on making this difficult."

"You've locked us in a dungeon with no food, no chairs, and no beds. Not even a proper drink. This is uncivilized, which is to say it's not us who is making it difficult. You want to talk, I under- stand, but let's do it upstairs after we've eaten and had a dram to settle our nerves and lubricate our voices. We can explain every- thing, but not while we're being treated like this."

"You know very well why the prince has sequestered you here," snapped the arcanist. "You are dangerous. Dangerous to the prince and to his people. That's why he's locked you up, and you'll stay locked up until we understand why you're here. You want to leave, to feast and drink from the prince's larder, then answer my questions."

"Dangerous to one of the most powerful spellcasters in Vaeldon?" scoffed Rew, peering around the arcanist at the silent form of Calb's tiny imp familiar. "I hardly think that's true."

The arcanist released a slow, frustrated breath. "I heard it from the prince, and if you'll pardon me, I'll trust his word and not yours."

Rew crossed his arms over his chest. "What else did he say? Did he tell you who I am?"

"The King's Ranger of the Eastern Territory, which begs the question, why are you here in the west?"

Rew pursed his lips. So Calb hadn't told his men everything. Was there a way to exploit that?

Suddenly, one of the other arcanists stumbled backward. "Is-Is she a necromancer?"

Rew turned and saw the man backing away from Cinda. The girl was still lying on her back, blinking her eyes sluggishly. In the torchlight, those eyes had a distinct green sheen. The ranger cursed to himself.

"But we were told only one of the girls had a talent for necromancy," babbled the lead arcanist. "She was... the one you killed! Kallie Fedgley. She was to meet with Calb and explain... But she wasn't the necromancer. That one is!"

Rew's shoulder ached from where it'd been dislocated and then wrenched again. Cinda lay on her back, barely alive after being stabbed by her sister. Raif and Zaine were banged up and tired. Anne wasn't much of a fighter in any circumstance. None of them had any weapons. The things Calb would want from them weren't things they would be willing to give. In short, they had no good options, so it was time for some strategic recklessness.

Rew glanced at the small imp that was standing at the back of the crowd. He cleared his throat and said, "Yes, she's the necromancer. Kallie Fledgley had no talent for it. Heindaw wanted the Fedgleys because he's plotting against the king. He and Alsayer are working together, and they believe the lass has the power to overthrow Vaisius Morden. Valchon is working with Alsayer as well and knows all about it. Everyone knows about this but you, Calb."

The room was silent. Then, the arcanist cackled. "Plotting against the king? What kind of fool would plot against—"

The rest of his statement was broken off when the imps in the room suddenly turned against the men, and all around Rew and the others, Calb's soldiers and his summonings churned in a vicious, bloody brawl. With only three imps, including the small one, it could have been an even fight, but the men were unprepared, and half of them were dead before they realized what was happening. When they did figure the situation out, to their credit, they felled one of the larger imps, but it wasn't enough, and in short time, they were all dead.

The arcanist and four others were the sole survivors. Most of them cowered in the corner like frightened kittens, but the leader still stood in the middle of the room. He hadn't moved at all during the fight. He was a tall man, though now his shoulders were hunched like he carried a great burden, and he trembled like a newly born bird. Was he braver than the others, or simply too scared or stupid to have moved?

His voice was plaintive and hesitant. He babbled, "But no one could face..."

"I need to think," declared the small imp, its thin, grating voice sharing Calb's thoughts, interrupting the arcanist.

The imp hopped up beside the arcanist for a moment, studying Rew and the others, then it turned and retreated to the wall. The terrified arcanist slowly followed it, cringing when the larger of the surviving imps turned to look at him.

"I didn't see that coming," quipped Zaine in a low voice, watching the two imps as the small one sat against the wall and the larger one prowled in front of it. The arcanist collapsed a dozen paces down the wall from them, his face blank, his eyes glistening. The other esteemed scholars had mostly closed their eyes, and were whispering prayers to a goddess that moments before they would have scoffed at.

Zaine stepped forward and toed one of the broadswords Calb's men had dropped in the process of getting killed by the imps. She shot a glance at the arcanist and then raised an eyebrow toward Rew.

The ranger nodded to the locked door and shrugged. Even armed, they weren't getting out of there. He told Zaine, "I would rather have not shared that information, but it didn't seem we were getting anywhere otherwise, did it? We should be quiet while the imp thinks."

The thief snorted, but the party fell silent, watching the imps and the arcanist. Rew considered laying back down to finish his nap, but he knew it would only be a show. The larger imp had been blooded, and while he guessed Calb's control over his summonings was superb, one never knew. Just in case the conjurer decided the easiest way out of the potential predicament of learning about a plot against the king was to kill everyone involved, Rew stayed awake, watching the imps warily and waiting.

Chapter Three

I t took one day, which was how long Rew estimated Calb's spellcasters needed to recover from their assault on Carff. During that time, the party was kept in the dungeon, fed regularly, and the torches were replaced, but the promised beds and seating never arrived. Worse, there was no ale. They tried to rest, but they'd left their packs and most of their supplies in Valchon's palace. They had their cloaks and clothing, and that was all. It made for uncomfortable sleeping conditions, though Rew made the small protest of putting out several of the torches when he estimated it was night.

In the belly of the palace, locked in a room of stone and steel, he tried vainly to extend his senses, but he found nothing. His power, low magic, was rooted in his connection to the wild world, and they were about as far as one could be from the untamed places. He could not replenish himself, could not gather the ancient magic that flowed through the world. All he could do was wait.

But while far from the wild, they weren't as far from death. In whispered conversations with Cinda, Rew asked her to feel for what power she could draw. He'd told Calb who she was and why she was wanted, but the prince knew none of the details.

Calb might overestimate or underestimate what Cinda was capable of, and they could use that.

Anne spent her time trickling empathy into Cinda. She was careful not to surge too much power toward the girl, but with a full day and nothing else to do, Anne was able to meter the flow until Cinda was up and walking around with hesitant, slow steps.

Raif and Zaine loitered, too tired and frightened for their normal banter.

The empath offered healing to them, but Rew suggested she save her strength. He imagined the rest of them might need more than a little bit of Anne's care soon enough. She shrugged but did as he asked.

Rew's own cuts and abrasions were more annoyances than anything, but his shoulder was a problem. Without his pack, he had no herbs to reduce the swelling or mask the pain, and he wouldn't have let Anne tend to it even if he wasn't trying to conserve her energy.

She did assess his shoulder. She found nothing was permanently damaged, and advised, "You need to rest it. Two weeks."

He rubbed his head, and she gave him an apologetic, tight-lipped look.

"If I have to fight..."

"If you have to fight, we don't really have much choice, do we? Everything you do, you risk further injury, but even I have to admit, that's the least of our concerns right now. Hearing you complain about your shoulder a week from today is a luxury I hope we have."

When Calb's people finally came for them and brought the party before the prince, Rew was stunned to find the nameless woman and Ambrose present. The nameless woman stood with her head held high, portraying bold bravado, but Rew had gotten to know her well enough to see through the facade. She was nervous. He wondered what she'd told Prince Calb.

He really wondered how she'd gotten there.

Ambrose, compared to the woman, looked quite a bit worse

for wear. Rew didn't know if it had happened in Valchon's or Calb's care, but someone had thoroughly beaten the necromancer. The forlorn-looking man barely spared Rew a glance when they were brought in, and Rew guessed that whoever had questioned Ambrose had learned everything the man had ever known and probably some things Ambrose didn't know but said just to make the violence stop. Luckily, Ambrose had few details to share which Rew hadn't already blurted out in front of the prince's familiar.

His arm recently freed from the sling, Rew scratched his beard and eyed the woman and the hairless necromancer. They hadn't gotten to Jabaan on their own, had they?

Prince Calb cleared his throat and stopped the procession bringing Rew and the others while they were still thirty paces away from his throne. A pair of soldiers scuttled forward, laying out the weapons and gear they'd stripped from the prisoners before they'd left the arcanist's tower. Rew regretted not hiding any of his daggers, but the guards had been thorough in their search, and Prince Calb wasn't going to fall to a dagger thrown from thirty paces away, anyway.

His longsword, knife, and daggers were laid beside Raif's greatsword, Zaine's bow and daggers, her single remaining arrow, a variety of utilitarian belt knives, the nameless woman's bronze scimitar, and Vyar Grund's gleaming, silver falchions.

Surprised, Rew glanced at the nameless woman. The falchions had been in Carff, left in the party's sitting room when they'd accompanied Valchon to Stanton. The nameless woman must have slipped them out when the prince was distracted from the aftermath of the battle. It gave Rew hope as he knew Valchon wouldn't have volunteered to give the swords up. The nameless woman wasn't working for Valchon, and it didn't make much sense she would be working for Calb, either. The nameless woman gave Rew a pained smirk, as if to say she'd tried.

"You travel with odd companions, Rew," said Calb, looking at the weapons from several paces away.

"That's what everyone keeps telling me," agreed the ranger, studying Prince Calb, wondering what the man's intentions were. The prince hadn't killed them yet, but that wasn't necessarily a good sign. Rew held up his arms. "A hug for old times' sake?"

"I don't think so, Rew," responded Calb dryly. "I wonder, is there a collection of enchanted weapons this extensive outside of Mordenhold or our brother's court in Iyre? Pfah. Our brother. You never thought of us that way, did you? All of those years in Mordenhold, growing up in the creche together, and you never thought of us as family, as your blood."

"Do you think of us that way?"

Calb laughed. "I do, but I suppose that means something very different for us than it does the rest of Vaeldon. No, family is not a calm harbor for us, a place of safety and succor. Family is competition. Family is the enemy. We were raised to kill our family. So yes, Rew, I do think of you that way."

"Best get on with it, then," drawled Rew.

Calb raised an eyebrow, as if he'd expected Rew to beg for his life.

Rew waited.

"M'lord?" asked one of the spellcasters standing to Calb's side. In his hands, he was building a small blue ball of intense flame. Rew wondered if the spellcaster thought he would be able to strike down a king's ranger with such a paltry effort.

Calb scowled at his spellcaster then began to pace, shooting looks at Rew then at Ambrose and the nameless woman. Rew's lips curled into a grin.

"What?" demanded Calb. "Something funny? Are you that eager to die?"

Rew gestured around the room. "Kill me if you want. I'm unarmed and surrounded by your people, so you certainly could, but what then? What did you learn in the creche, Calb? One does not win the Investiture through strength of arms alone. One wins through strategy and cunning. You're falling behind, Brother. You failed against Valchon and allowed him to prove his resilience. I imagine allies are flocking to him as we speak. And through it all, Heindaw went untouched. You sacrificed your resources and gained nothing for it. I'd bet my longsword you'll be the first to fall."

"Shut your mouth!" snapped the prince.

"And you don't even know what the other two are plotting, do you?" asked Rew, shaking his head and smiling. "Alsayer must have told you something, hinted at what Kallie Fedgley would share with you, but I don't need to tell you how little you can trust our cousin. Kill me, and you'll die not knowing the truth."

Calb licked his lips. "Tell me the truth, then."

Rew returned his brother's look and did not respond.

"I could have you tortured, but I won't waste my time. I bet you'd hold out longer than I have patience for," admitted Calb. "You always were stubborn, but what of your friends? How long will you wait while I work through them one by one? I've been experimenting, Rew, and I think you'll be surprised at what my conjurings are capable of. Hmm, where should we start? Not the Fedgley lass, we may need her, but what about the empath? She'll be used to pain. As difficult to break as you would be, but perhaps a challenge is what I need. She'll stomach the pain, but can you stomach the mutilation and disfigurement of one of your friends?"

Rew stared at his brother, stone-faced.

"The other lass?" asked Calb, twiddling his thumbs and smiling. "She looks terrified, already on the verge of breaking."

"Don't give into him, Rew," cried Zaine, her voice tight with fear.

The tall arcanist, the one who'd quizzed them below, sauntered closer. Now that he was out of the dungeon and had a dozen spellcasters behind him and the prince himself in the room, the man was a lot more confident than he'd been below. His eyes were harder now, but he seemed to have dismissed the horror he'd seen when the prince's imps turned on his companions. He stopped in front of each of them, studying their faces. Rew winked at the man, but the arcanist ignored it and moved to stand in front of Cinda. A smile grew on his lips as he assessed the necromancer.

"M'lord, I've been thinking about this plot," he called to Prince Calb, "and I believe it has something to do with my brother, Salwart. You recall he works for Heindaw? My brother was researching the boundaries of necromancy for the prince, and he traveled east in recent years and attached himself to Duke Eeron's court. He believed the secret at the heart of his theories was in the east. What if it's this lass? The spellcaster Alsayer hinted something similar about Kallie Fedgley, did he not?"

"You're Arcanist Salwart's brother?" demanded Rew, surprised.

"Half-brother," answered the man, brushing a bit of imaginary dust from his shoulder. "We share little other than a mother and a devotion to the arcane."

"Nothing but lies come from Alsayer's mouth," snapped the prince. He paused, then questioned, "Can we trust what your brother told you?"

"Of course not," said the tall arcanist, "but we don't need to. Before he joined Heindaw's cause, Salwart shared his theories with me. I thought them outlandish. I suppose he believed if he could convince me, he could convince anyone. I... I borrowed some of his research material, and I read it think I may use... Pfah. At the time it was like reading a fever dream, but it matches the story the ranger told us yesterday. My brother believed he learned a way to defeat King Vaisius Morden, but he didn't have the resources to do it. I think the girl is the key."

"What use would Heindaw have for a method to face my father?" barked Calb. "As soon as the Investiture ends, one of us will be crowned king. Why fight the old man when he's prepared to step aside? Valchon and I are Heindaw's real enemies."

"Information has power, m'lord. Or perhaps, your brothers aren't content to wait for the end of the Investiture?"

"If you become king, then this information is just as great a risk to you as it is to Father," Rew pointed out helpfully. "Methods that could topple one king might topple any king."

Calb blinked at him in confusion.

Rew asked the arcanist, "Do you have your brother's materials, still?"

The arcanist smirked. "Do I carry around documents purporting to be the secret of overthrowing the king? I'm not a fool. But," the arcanist tapped his head, "my memory is sharper than ever. I believe with a little time, I can put together what my brother and Prince Heindaw were going to attempt. Now that I've seen the picture, it makes sense in a way it did not before. With the girl in my custody, I just need to—"

"Come close, and I'll tell you what you need to know," offered Rew. "I'll tell you exactly how Heindaw plans to use the lass."

"You'll tell me, will you?" snickered the tall arcanist. "Why do I need to come close?"

Rew turned his head slowly, looking over everyone in the room. "Don't you think this is a secret that you should keep… secret?"

The soldiers in the room and the other spellcasters shuffled, as if it suddenly occurred to them just how dangerous it might be overhearing the discussion Rew and the arcanist were having.

"Hear what he has to say," barked Calb. "I want to get this over with."

The arcanist stepped toward the ranger.

Rew thrust out a hand, his shoulder protesting at the motion, and he called to one of Vyar Grund's falchions. The blade twitched, and then it flew in the air, streaking across the throne room. Rew caught it and spun, bringing the blade against the side of the arcanist's neck and decapitating the man cleanly with one blow.

Bands of crackling energy snapped around Rew from half a dozen spellcasters. Several of Calb's imps lurched closer, putting themselves between the ranger and the prince, but Rew's work was done. The arcanist was dead. The moment Rew had seen the falchions lying there, he'd planned to pull the stunt on Calb himself, but his brother wasn't a fool. If he wasn't going to step close to hear that secret, he wasn't going to come close for anything. Besides, if the arcanist knew what he'd claimed to know, then he couldn't be allowed to live.

The spells around him tightened, and Rew dropped the falchion. Even with the enchanted blade, he couldn't face the full force of Calb and his men when they were ready for it. Best to stay alive and hope he got another chance.

He cleared his throat and asked, "Shall we start over?"

THEIR SECOND ROUND OF CONFINEMENT WAS SIGNIFICANTLY LESS pleasant than the first. Instead of the dungeon at the base of the tower, they were chained outside, their arms stretched above their heads, clapped in thick manacles. The chains were raised, so they were forced to stand upright against a stone wall, but there was enough slack they could move about a little, which meant the heavy links hung uncomfortably on top of them. It was a position meant to allow little chance of mischief and impose a great deal of discomfort.

Rew looked up, thinking perhaps he could climb the chain if there was a time no one was looking, but the sturdy steel links disappeared into a hole above his head in the bottom of an over-hang. There was room there for the chain and nothing else. He wouldn't even be able to fit a hand into the hole. He wasn't sure it'd do him any good if he could.

Besides, the chances of no one watching were nil. Calb had stationed fifty armed soldiers in the courtyard, a dozen of them clutching crossbows, and half the prince's spellcasters were on duty as well. It was almost laughable, as chained to the wall and weaponless, they really weren't much of a threat.

But it wasn't for Rew, he didn't think, despite what he'd done in the throne room to the arcanist. Calb knew that Cinda was the key to Heindaw's plot against the king, but he didn't know what that plot was or what she was capable of. The prince must have considered whether Cinda could cast powerful magic but simply hadn't yet because she'd been injured or for some other reason. That was why the crossbowmen and spellcasters were there. They were spread out in a fan, so if she did release an attack, she wouldn't be able to get them all, and Calb's people could retaliate before she managed to escape.

Evidently, Calb didn't have any of the magic-dampening devices that they'd seen in Falvar and Spinesend, which meant there was only one way for him to keep a spellcaster prisoner—with a veritable army of guards on duty at all times. Did Duke Eeron not tell the prince about the devices, or had Calb simply not thought he would need them? Either way, the lack of preparation didn't bode well for Calb's chances in the Investiture.

Not that it did them any good.

Rew figured they had as much time as it would take for Calb to try and locate Alsayer. The prince wouldn't want to execute them until he heard from the spellcaster or realized he couldn't find the man and thought it was too much a risk to keep Rew and Cinda alive. Information had power, but keeping an enemy necromancer nearby and alive was a dangerous way to try and get it. Even if Calb believed Cinda was the key to defeating his brothers or had value he could extract from the king, he would be nervous every moment she was imprisoned within his palace. They had a day, thought Rew. Calb would have been suspicious of Alsayer from the beginning, so given reason to distrust the man, he would. Calb wasn't that big of a fool.

Rew shook his chains. He wondered if Cinda could summon enough energy for her funeral fire to snap the links? The fire she called did not have the heat of natural fire, but it did have force. If the metal was cold enough, it would be brittle and prone to breaks. He'd never actually tried breaking frozen steel. He was pretty sure it was possible, but he wasn't completely sure. There was also the problem of what they would do if she freed them.

She couldn't face so many spellcasters at once, or even one on one, given her condition and recent brush with death. His own odds, empty-handed against fifty armed men and the spellcasters, weren't worth considering.

But they had to get loose. That'd be the first step in any plan. The second step would be getting his longsword. With it, they might have a chance.

Zaine was hanging beside him. Once they'd been there for hours and their captors had gotten comfortable, Rew turned to the thief. "Can you, ah, pick these locks or something?"

She rolled her eyes at him.

"You're a thief, it's what you do. You got us into the arcanist tower easily enough," he hissed. "Don't you practice for this sort of thing?"

"I got us in and almost killed Raif," she responded. "And yes, in a sense we do practice this sort of thing. When a thief is taken in, we practice abandoning our guildhall and fleeing to a more secure location. We practice hiding all those who might know the thief and presenting distractions to guards coming our way. We don't even bother trying to rescue the person taken captive, and to my knowledge, no one ever escapes if they're given the sort of attention we're getting now. If anything, the thieves would try to assassinate compromised members instead of freeing them. It's safer that way."

"Well, that's a pessimistic way to look at the world," complained Rew. "What about the locks? Can you do something with them?"

"They took my lock picks, but even if I did have them, do you think I'd have a chance to use them with half the palace watching us? Face it, Ranger, we're stuck here."

"Well, I don't know about you, but I plan to escape."

"How?"

"I'm working on that," muttered Rew. "It would have helped if you could pick the locks."

Zaine shook her head. She seemed unable to find words to

respond, so he leaned out as far as he could, looking down the line of his companions where every six paces, one of them was chained to the wall. Calb had strung up the nameless woman and Ambrose as well. It gave Rew a little pleasure seeing the sour-faced necromancer there. Ambrose looked like his favorite dog had died, assuming the necromancer had ever loved an animal. Rew cringed when he saw Anne, who was looking back at him with an accusatory glare. Rew considered whether he'd be better off with Calb or with the empath.

Cinda was on the other side of Zaine, and when she saw Rew peering down the line, she scuffed her feet on the stone below them and said, "Was that wise? This is going to get extremely uncomfortable later this evening when we're tired of standing."

"Was it wise to kill the arcanist, or—"

"Telling him all of our secrets in the first place," snapped Cinda. "The arcanist wouldn't have put it together if you had kept your mouth shut. Our only advantage was secrecy and, with it, surprise."

"Shh," Rew told her. "They can hear us."

She looked back at him incredulously.

"Right," said Rew, coughing slightly. "They know our biggest secret, but Calb doesn't know all of it. He'll be nervous and uncer-tain now because he realizes the ground is covered in caltrops and hidden pits. Each step he takes may put a spike of steel into his foot or cause a fall into the unknown. I bought us time."

"For what?"

"We need my longsword."

"What are you going to do with your longsword, Ranger? Did you forget you're currently chained to a wall? Unless you've a plan to free yourself, you're not going to do much with that blade."

"I'm going to need it when I go after Calb," hissed Rew, lowering his voice so only Cinda and Zaine could hear him. "I can't face him unarmed."

The two girls blinked back at him as if he was a dog that had suddenly decided to talk. He thought about reminding them that the blade was enchanted, that it had properties which could help them, but there were some secrets best left unspoken.

"We're in the courtyard Calb uses for executing prisoners," he told them instead. He nodded toward a nondescript doorway set in a plain stone wall to the side. "That's the mortuary, where they keep the palace's dead until a burial can be arranged or until the bodies are collected by family."

The girls' looks did not change.

"The forty men we saw killed in Calb's dungeons ought to be in that building. Thirty-nine of them are going to cause a distraction. One needs to go get my sword."

"What in the Blessed Mother's Grace are you talking about?" asked Zaine.

On the other side of the thief, Cinda paled. She knew.

"Remember the opossum," said Rew quietly after glancing to make sure no one was overhearing them. "You were in the room when those men died. The connection is there. You're asking them to do what I believe most of them might like to do already, if given the chance. Revenge is powerful motivation, and it was Calb who caused their deaths. You were close to death yourself, Cinda, and that familiarity will cling to you. It will help. You can do this."

"I-I don't think I can."

"If you bind them, that fool Ambrose can command them, but we need your power to make the binding."

"I can't do it."

"Then I suppose we can all stand here until Calb gets around to killing us," growled Rew. "You thought this would be easy, that challenging the king wouldn't require sacrifice, that it wouldn't take all you've got and then some?"

"I don't have the—"

"Death clings to this place, lass. It permeates the courtyard. Can't you feel it? If you can cause a big enough distraction and collect my longsword, I can get us out of here."

Zaine, spluttering, said shrilly, "Hold on. Are you planning—"

"Quiet," instructed Rew as one of the guards approached. The ranger met Cinda's gaze one more time. He told her, "I'll get you started."

"Captain told us to make sure you weren't talking to each other," roared the guard, pausing a dozen steps from them. "So shut yar traps."

"No," said Rew, grinning at the man.

"Ya shut yar jaw, or I'll come shut it for ya."

"Nah, you won't."

"Don't ya tell me what I will or won't—"

"How about I tell you what your mother did last night? Or maybe it'd be quicker if I just said what she didn't do."

The guard charged, and Rew hauled himself up, pulling on the steel manacles encircling his wrists, ignoring the ache in his injured shoulder at the strain. He wrapped his legs around the guard's neck. The man, rushing in a surge of anger, hadn't expected the move and didn't react in time to stop Rew.

"Last time I did this," Rew told the man, squeezing with his legs, "it was to one of Calb's imps. I've gotta say, your breath isn't much better."

The man pounded ineffectually against Rew's thighs then tried to pry the ranger's legs apart. Rew shifted, curling his body and wrapping the chain that hung from above around the guard's neck. Rew dropped his legs, letting his full weight rest on the chain, crushing the other man's throat with the steel links.

The soldier's eyes boggled and he flailed frantically. If he had a knife or a dagger and had thought to draw it, he might have stabbed his way free before Rew got the chain on his neck, but he didn't. Now, he was too close to do anything but land ineffectual punches against Rew's arms and back.

Slowly, the man was choking to death.

His companions raced closer then paused. The captain appeared and screeched, "Stop that!"

Rew simply smiled around the shoulder of the dying guard and did not respond.

The captain, evidently too nervous to approach the ranger, watched from a distance as his man died. The soldiers must have been warned about coming close to Rew and the others. Some of them clutched crossbows, but they'd either been told not to use them, or they didn't want to hit their own man, even if he was dying.

The guard grew still, and Rew held him until he was sure the other man was dead. Then, he unwrapped the chain and kicked the guard away before resuming his previous stance. His shoulder throbbed from being twisted above his head and carrying his weight as he'd wrapped the chain, but he could live with that pain for now. Like Anne said, if they were alive in a few days, he'd grouse about it then.

"No food and water for you, you fool!" yelled the captain. "If it's up to me, we'll all stand here and watch you starve to death!"

"It's not up to you," replied Rew calmly.

The captain grasped the hilt of the broadsword hanging on his side and looked as if he was considering using it. He didn't get the chance, though, as the door to the mortuary slammed open. All of the guards looked confused as a man shambled out of the dark room and approached one of the spellcasters.

"King's Sake, lass," hissed Ambrose into the quiet of the courtyard.

The new arrival showed injuries of a brutal attack from Calb's imps. Its face was ravaged, half the skin on its skull hanging limply. Its color was that of curdled milk. Its motions were stilted and strange, and its eyes glowed a wicked green. It emanated hatred, and as Rew had suspected, it had a powerful thirst for revenge. The first person it reached was a spellcaster garbed in the green robes of his profession. The corpse Cinda had animated wrapped its cold fingers around the spellcaster's neck.

Rew, trying to pitch his voice an octave lower than usual, cried out, "Quick, they're trying to rescue the prisoners. Get them!"

Everyone in the courtyard was looking at the corpse attacking the spellcaster, so he hoped someone might think his voice was that of a guard. Sending the soldiers toward the open door would make it that much easier for Cinda's animated corpses to get to them.

More of the shambling wretches were shuffling out into the open, and as each new one appeared, they were sent after a target. The guards were rooted in place, stunned and confused about what was happening.

Rew wondered how many years it'd been since a necromancer had been in the Western Province with the strength to animate a corpse. Outside of the Fedgley's line and, of course, the king himself, there couldn't have been many necromancers in the kingdom who could manage the feat.

Rew watched in morbid fascination as more of the undead appeared from the mortuary. It occurred to him that as a son of Vaisius Morden, he was one of the only people in Vaeldon who had seen something like this before. The soldiers in Calb's employ very well could have believed that raising the dead was a myth. To Rew's knowledge, only the king had done it at scale over the last two hundred years, and Vaisius Morden typically left no witnesses.

The spellcasters had known Cinda was capable of necromancy, and they should have been prepared, but like everything Rew had seen of Calb's efforts, the prince and his men were a step behind. The prince's people never had a chance.

"What are you doing?" cried the guard captain, spinning and yanking his sword from the sheath.

The captain took two steps toward Rew before the dead man at the ranger's feet, the one Rew had choked, rose and began to grapple with his former captain. To his credit, the captain did not panic. Instead, he forced the corpse away and slammed his sword into its middle. It would have been a terrific blow, if the guard wasn't already dead. Instead, the dead soldier tore the sword free of its own guts and, holding on to the edge of the blade, brained the frozen-in-shock captain with the hilt.

"Don't push me away," called Ambrose over the tumult of the guards rushing to confront their former peers. "If you don't fight me, I can give instructions. You deal with the other. I... That one is beyond my talent to control."

Cinda did not reply. She was hanging motionless from the chains, her face obscured by dark hair that hung over her limp neck. Some of the soldiers nearby glanced at the prisoners, but they didn't understand what Ambrose was saying. Once they got over their surprise, they did understand that a company of undead was filing out into the light and attacking them, so they did what they could to defend themselves, which wasn't much.

Finally regaining their wits, the spellcasters began to fight back as well, and blasts of heat, cold, and electrical charges began to sizzle across the open courtyard. The corpses were mauling their brethren, impervious to further wounds from blade or crossbow, but the force of the spellcasters' attacks shattered the slow-moving wave of undead. Bodies were engulfed in liquid fire and fell to the cobblestones, popping and sizzling. Spears of ice crashed in torrents and tore through flesh, shattering bone and dropping the undead where they could only claw their way forward with broken hands. The spellcasters advanced, pushing the undead toward the mortuary doors where presumably they hoped to seal them inside.

Until the imp joined the fray.

That gave even the spellcasters pause.

The undead imp, moving more comfortably than the animated humans, charged out of the open doorway of the mortuary and immediately set on a spellcaster, tearing into the man with horrific zeal. Rew watched, impressed and appalled, as the thing flung aside the body of what had once been a man and bound after another.

Several of Calb's soldiers began to run away.

Staggering out of the madness, a man, freshly dead and

missing one arm, teetered toward Zaine, fumbling at his belt with a fat ring of keys. The corpse's hand trembled, and it didn't have the coordination to find the right key and fit it into the lock, but Zaine was able to grab the key ring. She said to Cinda, "I, ah, I can open the lock if you can get that thing out of my face. Quickly, please."

The corpse, mouth open, blood dripping down its side, green fire burning in its eyes, turned and sought one of its fellows who was retreating from the undead imp that was rampaging through the pack of soldiers. The key-bearer grasped the back of its fellow soldier and then smashed its forehead into the skull of the living man, battering him over and over again, cracking both of their heads in the process.

Zaine stumbled forward, looking a bit green herself as she turned from the melee. She came to Rew and climbed up his side to where she could start trying keys in his manacles. Her weight hung on his injured shoulder. He gritted his teeth but did not complain.

Somewhere within the palace, they heard a terrific concussion, and Rew guessed Calb had joined the fight. He frowned. Fighting what? There were dozens of undead rampaging in the courtyard, but surely none had time to get...

Unless they'd raised more of them.

Zaine found the right key and freed him.

Rew called to Cinda, "I'm going to need that sword soon."

"It's coming," she hissed, not looking up. After a pause, she added, "Ranger, I think we've made a mistake."

Rubbing his wrists and working his shoulder, trying to force the ache away through will alone, Rew asked her, "How so?"

"It's not just the mortuary. There are... more of them. More than I can control."

"What? What do you mean, more of them?"

"She's raised half the corpses in the city," called Ambrose from the other side of Cinda. "So far, that is. Ranger, the whole crypt has risen. There's... there's got to be thousands of them already coming out, and they're not under her command. I don't... I don't even know how many are down below. My senses are full of them. I don't have the strength for this, Ranger, and she doesn't have the control."

"Oh. That's not good. That's not good at all."

In moments, a dead maid, with the desiccated mien of a raisin, came tottering into the courtyard. Ignoring the fury of the battle happening around her, the undead maid stumbled toward Rew, all of their weapons clutched clumsily in a bundle.

Rew wondered where Cinda had sensed and found a long-dead maid stuffed somewhere within the palace, and still wearing her livery, but he gratefully accepted his longsword from the cold, dry hands. Zaine took her weapons as well and scowled at her quiver containing just a single arrow.

"Well, she tried, I guess."

Rew grinned at the thief then instructed, "Free the others and take them to—Pfah. None of you know the palace."

The buildings around them rumbled as concussive blasts of high magic were unleashed inside. Calb and his other spellcasters were battling the legions of undead that had been released by Cinda's necromancy.

The spellcasters in the courtyard were nearly finished. Every time they struck at one of the corpses from the mortuary, more rose from the freshly killed soldiers. As long as Cinda's and Ambrose's strength remained, fighting the undead was a battle that could not be won. Calb would be facing much the same, except he would know that the only way to defeat an army of the undead was to slay the necromancer who had raised them.

Fighting the corpses themselves was a fool's errand. Calb would figure out what had happened and would be coming for them any moment. They'd have the greatest advantage near the crypt, where Cinda's corpses could help in the fight, unless she lost control, and then...

"King's Sake, I'm going to need you all, and we're safer together. Come on, let's get them out of these chains."

The battle in the courtyard was finished by the time they'd freed the others. Rew instructed Raif to carry his sister. Then, the ranger shook off Ambrose as the necromancer tried to lean on his shoulder.

"I'm nearly spent," moaned the man. Sweat ran in rivulets down his bare scalp. He was stooped like a worker in the fields after decades of labor, and his face was twisted in fear. The older necromancer shuffled away from Cinda, like he couldn't bring himself to touch the noblewoman. "Her strength…"

"Can you seal the doors to the crypt?" Rew asked the nameless woman. "They ought to be similar to those in Iyre."

She looked uneasy but nodded. "Yes, if the doors are the same. All adherents to the Cursed Father are taught—"

"I know," snapped Rew. Around them, corpses were lurching aimlessly. Rew turned to Ambrose and waved his hand around. "Can you, ah…"

"I've already released them from my control, but their final instructions were to leave us alone. We're somewhat safe," muttered the necromancer, "from these at least. I can't do more. I told you. I'm almost spent."

"You've got until we reach the crypt to find your spine, Ambrose. There's going to be… King's Sake, there's going to be a lot of them."

"The crypt? She needs to release the bindings, or we need to flee the city," warned Ambrose. He shivered. "Not the city, the province. We can't go deeper into this morass, Ranger. It's certain death. We can get out while they're all distracted. Once we're outside of the city, she can release the bindings."

"We're going to the crypt, and you're coming with us," snapped Rew. He put a hand on Cinda, not sure if she could feel it or not. "Hold the bindings, lass. We're going to need them a little bit longer."

"This is madness, Rew," worried Anne.

"Just wait until you hear my plan."

Chapter Four

T hey ran through the chaotic corridors of Prince Calb's
palace, dodging soldiers that they saw but not seeing many
of the palace's other denizens. Most of the staff had wisely gone
into hiding, and all of those in the halls were heavily armed. The
guards were running, their eyes panicked but alert. Rew doubted
any of them knew where they were running to.

Those who did know what was going on would no longer be
in the palace. If they had any sense at all, they'd be fleeing out
into the city and then into the countryside beyond. One did not
stand against a legion of undead with only armor and a sharp
sword at your side.

The soldiers paid little attention to a small band of people who
looked to have been on the wrong end of a battle. Rew and the
others weren't the only ones traipsing through the corridors with
weapons drawn, speckled with blood.

Periodically, they would pass a hallway or a room where
sounds of fighting and screams of terror bounced along the
marble walls and floors. The undead had risen, and they were
slowly filling the building like an irresistible tide.

Rew didn't know if Cinda had instructed the creatures to
attack or if there was something inherent in the nature of an

animated corpse which caused it to strike out against the living, but it seemed the corpses were acting with single-minded determination to bring down anyone they found who still breathed.

Fighting the things was a futile act. The undead did not require the beat of a heart or the inhale of breath to sustain them. Their brains did not need to function. They could not be killed through normal means. The undead were basic matter, and the souls bound to them were able to manipulate that matter through magic. They could be damaged and broken, but as long as the magic infused them, they would keep coming. Raised by magic, they had to be destroyed by magic.

Or, while not technically destroyed, they could be stopped by other extraordinary means.

They passed one corpse which had been hacked and trampled until it no longer resembled anything that had once been alive. It was a smear of blood and pulped flesh and no longer a threat to those living. Rew wasn't sure if the soul tied to that body had fled again or if there was simply nothing left to move. He supposed if you chopped the things into small enough pieces, it didn't really matter.

But while you could hammer the undead hard enough that they were no longer a threat, the problem was that if anyone fell during the fight, they'd rise again and turn on the living. Cinda had unleashed a torrent of magic, and it grew stronger with each new death, feeding upon itself, raising more corpses, who caused more dead. The raging storm of necromancy had whirled beyond her control.

The girl lay limp in her brother's arms, and Rew offered a hope to the Blessed Mother that she would have strength for what was coming. For now, she was a conduit, channeling the incredible power that was rising as more and more of Calb's people died, but she was no longer able to direct that power.

Rew felt guilty every time they passed a stricken-looking soldier or member of Calb's staff. These people were innocents, for the most part. They weren't responsible for the destruction of

Stanton and the tens of thousands of people who died there. They didn't have a part in Calb's machinations. No, most of them would be normal folks who'd thought they lucked into a job at the palace. They weren't mass murderers who—

Stumbling, Rew swallowed. Tens of thousands died in Stanton when Valchon had unleashed his maelstrom, but how many were dying now? How many would die so Rew could strike at the prince? They were no different than...

He let the thought go. He couldn't think that. Not now. Tomorrow, they would grieve for what they'd done, but in the middle of Calb's palace there was no time for regret, no time for sorrow.

"Hurry," he barked to the others, forcing himself to move rather than think. "Come on, we need to hurry."

He led them down into the bowels of Calb's palace, ignoring Raif's complaints about what sort of terrible architect had placed the crypt so far from the mortuary. Rew didn't bother to explain that it was because the bodies in the mortuary were those of men and women who had family, who had someone who would come looking for them to conduct a burial. Those in the crypt were the forgotten, looked after only by the priests of the Cursed Father.

Rew wondered how mad the king was going to be when he found out what they were doing with all of the bodies he'd been hoarding.

"What are you planning?" asked the nameless woman, her bronze scimitar held in front of her, her gaze darting down each passageway they crossed. "I can seal the door to the crypt, but you do realize what's going to be coming out of it when we get there, right?"

Rew nodded. "I'm hoping the necromancers can keep them off our backs until we do what we need to."

"The lass is unconscious, and Ambrose looks like he wants to be. If you're hoping they'll face Calb for you, I don't think that's going to happen."

"Let me worry about the prince."

She eyed him skeptically but fell silent.

After several more turns, Rew skidded to a halt. In front of them, a shuffling column of the undead marched down the hallway. These were not the same as the corpses of the guards they'd seen in the courtyard. These were the long dead. Their flesh, when they still had it, was dried and tattered. Many of them had no flesh at all, just skeletal remains with ancient burial shrouds clinging to them like spiderwebs. Several of them carried weapons.

"That madman!" said Rew, nearly choking on his words. "He armed these things. Blessed Mother, he's always intended this as an army, and he's been gathering it for centuries..."

"That army is coming toward us," mentioned Zaine, stopping beside Rew and the nameless woman.

"The stairwell to the crypt is at the end of this hallway. We, ah, we need to get through here." Rew turned to Ambrose. "Can you...?"

Pale-faced, his mouth hanging open, the necromancer shook his head. "I might be able to repel a few, but... we need Cinda, Ranger. Only she has the strength to command these things."

"We won't waste her strength," said Rew, shaking his head. "She has to hold the bindings on all of these souls until we finish. Zaine, Anne, carry Cinda between the two of you. Raif, I need you to take my side. We'll force our way through the crowd. We've got to reach the stairwell and fight our way down into the crypt."

"And why, exactly, do you want to go into the crypt when an entire damned army of undead is walking out of it?" snapped Raif, horror in his eyes.

"Because it's the only way to sever the bindings the Investiture has tied to us. I don't have time to explain, but if we don't do that, the king can find us, and I don't need to tell you how angry he'll be when he hears of this. If we mean to see the sunset tonight, we've got to make very sure Vaisius Morden has no idea where we are."

"Oh," said Raif. He voiced no other arguments, but he didn't look pleased at the notion.

The big fighter handed his sister to Anne and Zaine then drew his greatsword and took Rew's side. The nameless woman took his other. The wave of the undead were halfway down the hall, shuffling ever closer.

"Don't try to kill them. That's a waste of time, obviously," ordered Rew, "but make sure we knock them back enough that the others can follow behind. Ambrose, you take the rear and keep them off our backs! Come on, the longer we wait, the more of them there'll be."

They weren't going to get any more ready than they were, so Rew led them forward, and when the first skeletal remains lurched at him, raising a cutlass that was brittle with rust, Rew kicked the corpse in the chest, shattering bone and sending it flying to the side.

The nameless woman raised her left arm and used the bronze bracer encasing her forearm as a battering ram, smashing into the undead, pushing them back. They gnashed their broken teeth at her, and some swung swords, but she beat their strikes aside with her own blade and forced her way down the hall. Dead fingers clawed at her armor, but they found no purchase on the gleaming bronze.

Raif, with little room to maneuver, waited until Rew had hammered several of the macabre creatures back. Then, the big fighter rushed forward and swung a sweeping, horizontal blow that crashed through half a dozen of the undead and sent their bones flying like a child's game of jacks. The sword and Raif's targets crackled with vibrant, sickly green bolts of energy. Acrid smoke boiled off the fallen remains, and none of them moved from where they fell.

Everyone paused, mouths agape.

"W-What..." stammered Raif, staring down at the greatsword in his hands.

"Attack again!" bellowed Rew. "The enchantment on your sword, lad! It must have the power to release the souls from their bodies. Lead the way, quickly, and we'll follow."

Shrugging his armored shoulders, Raif charged, smashing his way down the hall, battering the undead out of his path, leaving a trail of desiccated flesh, broken bone, and eye-watering smoke.

The undead showed no fear at the boy's terrific attacks. They kept marching into the path of his greatsword, their own weapons raised, but they were slow and unskilled, and Raif was young and full of fear. It spurred him like wind in a sail, and at a jog, he barreled his way down the hall, his huge greatsword cleaving the masses before him, dead bones cracking beneath his feet. Rew and the nameless woman chased after him, smacking aside any of the creatures Raif missed, clearing the way for Anne and Zaine to drag Cinda between them.

They reached the end of the hallway and found a giant chamber. It was a perfect circle, a domed ceiling capping it, and aside from the hallway they entered, there was only one other door, a yawning archway that led to a stairwell and down toward the crypt. In the room, the press of the undead lessened as the creatures were not forced together to lurch down the hallway.

It gave them a little space to breathe but increased the chances of attack from behind. Rew urged Raif to hurry, and the boy led them toward the stairwell, smashing undead into lifeless piles of bone as he went.

Rew marveled at the way Raif waded through the terrifying creatures and was struck by the simple fact that Raif's weapon was the Fedgley family's chief heirloom. For generations, the most powerful necromancers outside of the royal line had been passing down a greatsword that felled the corpses their magic animated. How many members of that line, like Raif, had no talent for necromancy? Were the children of that blood always in opposition, or were they meant to work together? It meant something, but Rew didn't have time to ponder what.

They fought their way into the archway then started down the stone stairwell beyond it, Raif stooping and chopping at the undead below him.

"Ranger," he called, "I'm not sure how much longer I can do this. The sword is… tiring me, more than it should."

"It's not much longer," responded Rew, walking the stairs easily behind Raif. "You can hold on."

They forced their way down the long, broad staircase and then at the bottom found another perfectly circular room, this one smaller than the one above. Like above, there was only one other opening in the circle, a narrow doorway braced by two, tall copper doors. They were flanked by the masked priests of the Cursed Father. They, unlike all other living souls they'd spotted since Cinda began her magic, were standing calmly beside the doors as a host of their charges marched out of the crypt.

Evidently, the undead recognized something of themselves in the priests of the death god and ignored the pair to march out into the palace. The priests' faces were covered by masks, but Rew could see their eyes turning in curiosity to the newcomers.

"We must go inside," said the nameless woman, calling loudly above Raif's exertions against the undead.

"It is forbidden," intoned one of the priests.

The nameless woman barked a command in a harsh language that Rew did not understand. The priests turned to each other.

"It is forbidden," the second one repeated.

The nameless woman released another string of commands in the strange language, and the priests kept eyeing each other. Then, as one, they drew long, curved daggers from beneath their vestments and plunged the blades into their stomachs. They wrenched the steel to the side, spilling their guts. Wordlessly, they collapsed. Unlike the other corpses in the palace, they did not rise again.

"Blessed Mother, what did you tell them?" asked Zaine.

"I told them that they'd failed, that these souls had been bound by another and were no longer in the domain of the Cursed Father," the woman responded. She punched a skeleton that had stumbled close to her. "There's only one punishment for failure within the Cursed Father's priesthood."

"The corpses weren't attacking them," murmured Zaine, glancing at the bodies of the priests. "They're not moving like the soldiers did when they died."

"They still harbor in the Father's grace," explained the nameless woman.

"Grace?" choked Anne.

The nameless woman shrugged. "They're not rising again, are they?"

"How come these things are attacking you, then?" questioned Anne. "Aren't you supposed to be a follower of the Cursed Father?"

Cinda stumbled, and Anne and Zaine struggled to hold her upright. The nameless woman's lips twisted into a sour grimace, but she did not respond to Anne's comment.

Rew stared at her then shook himself as a corpse teetered toward him. He grabbed it and flung it aside. He pointed to the two copper doors. "In there."

The nameless woman darted ahead, and while unable to kill the undead, she could knock them down or push them aside. She set to it with a fervor, as if to lose herself in the fight and forget Anne's observation about the corpses ignoring the priests.

Raif joined her, and together, they cleared the doorway of the undead.

"What's the plan?" demanded Anne, staggering beneath the weight of Cinda's limp body.

"I think I know how to sever the king's connection to me and break the tug of the Investiture. Ancient magic. A soul for a soul."

"What?"

They stumbled into the antechamber of the crypt, finding a huge copper altar in the center of a bare, stone room. The walls were studded with hollow openings that led down and away. Only the antechamber was lit, and into that light, filed legions of the dead.

"There!" called Rew, pointing to a niche in the wall that did not open to a tunnel and the burial chambers. "We make a stand there."

Raif fought through a crowd of the undead, and they reached the wall and spun. Ambrose, finally proving some worth, knelt in front of them and whispered, "I'll hold as long as I can."

Rew stood over the necromancer, looking around the room. "But the copper? Your spells won't work in here, will they? I, ah, I'd hoped—"

Ambrose grunted, waving a hand dismissively and interrupting Rew. "I can't cast through the barrier, but the power of death is vibrant inside of the crypt. I can use it. You're right, Calb will be as helpless as a babe in here. That's your plan, isn't it? He won't have the benefit of his magic, but for us, it's like a dam that Cinda pulled down. I-I don't know how she did it. She shouldn't have been able to reach inside of this place."

"Does that mean—"

Ambrose hissed, cutting Rew off. "I need to concentrate."

Rew looked at the back of the man's bald head and fell silent. The undead stumbled closer, but two paces away, paused and moved on. The necromancer had erected some sort of invisible barrier that shielded them from attack. Already, Rew could see beads of sweat forming on Ambrose's smooth skin. Rew guessed Ambrose wouldn't be able to hold the protection for long and that it would be best to let the man focus on his work.

"Rew," said Anne, propping Cinda in a seated position against the wall, "what did you mean, a soul for a soul?"

"I think that's how her father freed her," said Rew, nodding toward the nameless woman. "At least, it gave me the idea. He sacrificed himself to loosen the king's binding on her. I think it will work for me as well."

"You think?"

Rew shrugged.

Raif leaned heavily on his greatsword. Drawing ragged, gasping breaths, he rasped, "Ranger, who is it you're planning to sacrifice?"

Zaine pointed at Ambrose's back and shrugged silently. At their expressions, she asked, "What? Who were you thinking?"

Rew shook his head. "It's not so simple. A soul for a soul, but not all souls are equal. The king's connection to my soul is strong. It will take an equally strong connection to break it. I'm going to use Calb."

"How does that work? Are you going to cut his heart out or something on the altar?" wondered Zaine, looking torn between discomfort and interest in the idea.

Between them and the altar, a handful of undead milled about, as if eager to fall upon them but unable to pass through the magical barrier Ambrose had erected.

Rew shook his head. "No. This is ancient magic, natural magic. It's the only thing that can counteract the pull of the Investiture. There's no ritual, no proscribed series of actions to enlist it. It's about seizing power and bending it to your will. There will be a surge of that old power when the sacrifice is made, and I think I'll be able to use it. I hope I'll be able to."

"That's a lot of think, Ranger."

"You have a better idea?" asked Rew, gesturing at a particularly tall skeleton wielding a spear that was looming over Ambrose, as if waiting for the man to fail, so it could plunge its weapon through the offending necromancer's bald head.

"How are we going to draw Prince Calb here?" wondered Anne.

"If he wants to face me, he'll come," said Rew, "and if he doesn't, then we don't stop Cinda, and we're going to find out how many more of these skeletons the king has accumulated over the last two hundred years. There's no way to stop these things unless Calb comes for Cinda."

"The longer this goes on…" warned Anne.

"I know," responded Rew, a surge of sorrow filling him. "I… Maybe we shouldn't have done this, but we did. It's too late to turn from it now."

Anne stared at him, and Rew looked away. He could feel her

gaze, like a dagger, pressing against his flesh. How much of a connection to the people in the palace did Anne have? What could she feel of the madness happening in its marble halls?

Rew blinked and then smiled.

"You hear that, Calb?" he called loudly. "Come and face me, or these damned things are going to keep marching on you until there's nothing left of Jabaan but the undead. It's only a matter of time then, until one of our brothers finds you and ends it. You'll be finished. Your only hope is to face me and to salvage what little you can of your strength. You see me. There's no trap here. We're injured and alone. Come and let's end this."

"Who are you talking to?" whispered Zaine.

"Your bow," requested Rew, and when she handed it to him, he added, "and that last arrow."

He nocked it and pulled the arrow back to his cheek and then released it, sending the shaft streaking a pace above the entrance to the crypt. There was a startled squawk, and the small imp that Calb had been using as a familiar fell off the wall where it'd been lurking, covered by a glamour.

"I wonder if he felt that?" Rew said, handing the bow back to Zaine, who looked at it askance as she no longer had any arrows. Rew told the others, "When Calb gets here, he's going to come with a lot of soldiers at his back. We've got to draw him inside then fight our way through those doors. After we're outside, we've got to close the doors on him. The sacrifice is locking Calb inside of this place. Only when those doors are sealed can we have Cinda release her binding on all of the corpses."

"King's Sake, Rew," muttered Anne.

He grinned at her and adjusted his grip on his longsword.

"Is Prince Calb much of a fighter?" wondered the nameless woman, peering at the doorway, waiting restlessly.

"He's not," assured Rew, "but I imagine his elite guard is reasonably skilled."

"Of course."

"Then there are the imps."

The nameless woman scowled at him.

"He won't be able to summon more of them once inside the crypt. I don't think he'll be able to issue new commands, either, but he likely can instruct them outside and then send them in."

"Why come himself, then?" demanded Zaine. "Did we just trap ourselves inside of here?"

Rew shook his head. "Remember, all he knows of Cinda is that Heindaw believes she can overthrow the king. He has no idea what she's capable of. For all he knows, we will continue marching these things into his city at her direction. He has no idea we're also in danger from the corpses. He's got to come himself and finish it quickly."

"I can't hold much longer," grunted Ambrose. "A minute, maybe less."

"When this begins, watch out for the undead," warned Rew. "They won't like us any more than they do Calb's men."

"I'm not sure if you need me to tell you this, Rew," complained Anne, "but this is the worst plan you've ever had."

"Ready..."

Outside of the crypt, they heard the angry sounds of fighting and the bestial roars of summoned imps tearing their way through ranks of the undead.

"Ah, you know," said Rew, rubbing his hand rapidly on top of his head, "I hadn't really considered what might happen if those imps are killed and then get animated. That one in the courtyard was a terror. Maybe we should just... wound them."

He thought he could hear Anne rolling her eyes.

The light from outside the crypt was blocked by a giant, hulking creature that rose twice Rew's height and stretched four times his width. It had to duck and turn to wedge itself inside of the doorway to the crypt, but it did so without pause. All around it, the undead swarmed, hacking and stabbing with their crude weapons.

This imp, though, was covered in glimmering, gold-colored scales. They reflected the light of the torches in the crypt and made the thing seem as if it were on fire. On its head, two massive horns curved back behind it, twisting into sharp points. Its hands were capped with heavy claws, its feet with talons like a bird, and on its heels a single spike which looked as stout as a ballistae bolt.

The attacks by the undead bounced off its scales harmlessly, and the imp ignored them except to casually brush a handful of undead aside as it rose to its full height. The skeletons it struck went flying across the room as if they'd been launched by a trebuchet and burst against the stone wall in a shower of bone fragments.

"R-ranger..." stammered Zaine.

"Leave that to me. The rest of you... just try to stay alive." He stepped around Ambrose and put a hand on the man's shoulder. "Well done."

Then, he ran toward the copper altar, jumped up on it, and launched himself toward the giant imp.

Chapter Five

The creature looked as it'd been fashioned from metal. It was like a living statue, but it moved as if it was fashioned of lightning. As Rew soared through the dim air of the crypt's antechamber, his longsword raised above his head to strike, the imp swept an arm at him.

It caught the ranger dead center, the width of the imp's forearm the length of his torso. Rew went flying back, and only a wrenching twist in the air allowed him to land feet first instead of on his head. He collapsed into a roll, tumbling into the skeletal remains of several of the undead, their bones splitting and clattering around him like lawn bowling pins.

It hurt a great deal, but Rew sprang to his feet and drew a hesitant breath, hoping his ribs weren't broken. He'd underestimated the speed of the imp, and if he did it again, he wouldn't survive.

Before any of the undead standing around him had time to start toward him, the giant imp was on him again, and Rew darted to the side, narrowly avoiding a massive clawed hand that slapped down on the stone right where he'd been standing.

He flicked his longsword at it as he ran away, and the tip of the steel parted the imp's sturdy, scaly hide. The creature bellowed, the sound of its cry ricocheting around the stone room, threat-ening to deafen them all. The enchanted steel of Rew's blade had done what the lesser weapons of the undead could not.

The imp's cry rolled around the room and down the passages that led deeper into the crypt before echoing back, sounding worse than it had the first time. Rew wondered if the creature had ever been wounded before. He spun his longsword, preparing to charge in again while the imp was still in shock over the injury, but out of the corner of his eye, he saw a flash of movement and ducked.

A man, clad in tight-fitting leather armor, went soaring over Rew's head, a short spear in his hands thrusting right where Rew had been standing. The man landed lightly and spun, prepared to come at Rew again, but one of the undead shambled up behind him and buried a hatchet in the back of the man's head. The man had a thick thatch of hair standing up in a narrow shock with crawling blue tattoos inscribed on the sides of his head.

He looked like Mistress Clae. King's Sake, had Calb hired the entire clan? Did they know Rew had thrown one of their own off a ledge to fall ten stories where she splattered like a rotten apple below?

Another of the spear-wielders darted in, and Rew turned to face him. Then, he ducked and was nearly knocked over by the wind of the imp's giant arm passing overhead. The spearman wasn't as quick and was blasted away and out of sight.

So far, none of the foreigners were faring much better than Mistress Clae had, though Rew had to credit their bravery and willingness to fight through the horde of undead and attack him so close to the massive, golden-scaled imp. Calb must have been paying them a fortune.

The first warrior, a hatchet still embedded in the back of its skull, rose tottering to its feet. Its eyes glowed with ethereal green, and its teeth clacked as the animated warrior snapped its jaws shut. Perhaps bravery wasn't the right word.

More of the spearmen were pouring into the room and instantly becoming embroiled with a surge of undead trekking up from the bowels of the crypt. Blood and bones flew, and in the center of it, the huge, golden-scaled imp spun in confusion, looking for Rew. The ranger, for his part, attempted to duck around behind it, keeping from the horrible creature's view and out of the way as men and undead fought ferociously around him.

The nameless woman darted in, swinging a vicious strike at the back of the imp's leg, trying to hobble it. Her scimitar carved into the imp's flesh, but the tough scales prevented the blow from doing more than irritating the creature.

"How…"

"Stay back!" shouted Rew. Then, he lunged in and thrust upward, stabbing his enchanted longsword shallowly into the imp's thigh.

If its first cry had been terrific, then Rew didn't have words for the onslaught of sound that burst from the imp now. He wondered if outside the stone chamber of the crypt, the entire palace would be shaken down by the incredible roar.

Rew was deafened by it and didn't hear a man approach him from behind. He didn't sense the man at all until the sharp point of a spear plunged into his shoulder. His right hand twitched as the spear pierced his skin near where he'd dislocated his arm. He dropped his longsword and fell to his knees.

His hearing gradually returning, Rew heard a man laugh. "That was easier than I'd expected."

Rew turned and looked back to see Prince Calb standing there, raising one of his men's spears, preparing for a killing thrust. Spinning on his knee, Rew kicked out with his other leg, connecting with the prince's knee, and sweeping Calb's feet out from under him. The prince yelped in surprise and tumbled down beside the ranger.

Rew snatched the spear from his brother's hands and

slammed the butt of it into Calb's stomach. He used the weapon to push himself to his feet. He spun the shaft and bashed an approaching skeleton over the head with it as well then tossed the spear aside and stooped to collect his longsword.

Calb spluttered and gasped on the floor behind him. Inside of the copper-lined crypt, the spellcaster wouldn't be able to use his magic. Only necromancy, borrowing from the power entombed within the space, would work, but King's Sake, Calb's attempt with the spear had nearly ended it.

Staggering away, Rew caught Zaine's eye and pointed toward the exit with his longsword. Then, he scrambled away as the massive imp finally found him in the confusion and came rushing closer, crushing undead beneath its clawed feet with each step. Rew gave up any pretense of grace or professionalism and ran, scampering around the edge of the room like a frightened child.

He shouted toward Ambrose, "The lights, can you put out the torches? Give us that, and then it's almost over."

The necromancer, cowering beside Anne and Cinda, nodded curtly and closed his eyes. The light of the torches flickered out, the living flame drawn into a spectral, white-green funeral fire that burned atop the copper altar and then that went out as well, casting the room into darkness, only the light from the entrance illuminating the battle between Calb's men, the undead, Rew's party, and the huge, hulking imp that dominated it all.

Unable to wield his longsword in his right hand, Rew turned and darted back toward the imp, hoping to the Blessed Mother what he'd heard was true and imps couldn't see well in the dark. He stabbed his longsword down with his left hand, impaling the imp's foot.

It howled at him, and Rew ran, pelting toward the exit, smashing through undead and spearman alike. He shouldered into a smaller, softer form and grabbed it, guessing correctly it was Zaine. He hauled the thief to the doorway and flung her through, glancing around wildly to see who else made it.

Raif lumbered out of the darkness a breath after Rew, Cinda

clutched in his arms, Anne grasping the back of his steel back-plate. The nameless woman was already outside, facing off against several dozen of Prince Calb's men, who looked as if they had no idea what was going on, so they were making the assumption that anything that moved was an enemy. Several skeletons teetered about as well, lurching toward Calb's men who surrounded them and hacked at them relentlessly.

"Ambrose?" called Rew.

Anne gestured behind them, back inside the crypt.

"King's Sake, we don't have time for this," muttered Rew.

He turned and went back in.

THE IMP, AS BLIND AS ANYONE, LAID ABOUT IN FRUSTRATED ANGER, smashing and killing anything it could reach. The men, while impressively loyal to Prince Calb, had evidently decided enough was enough, and were fighting and forcing their way toward the exit. The undead, seeing quite well in the darkness, had no trouble chopping them down.

Rew, with a ranger's senses, could not see, but he could feel. He darted amongst the fighting men and the undead, staying well clear of the rampaging imp. He headed toward where he'd last seen Ambrose and was startled when the prone form he thought was the necromancer lashed out with a foot, kicking him squarely in the groin.

Crippling pain pulsing from between his legs, Rew slumped over. The form rose, raising a femur it must have stolen off one of the undead. Prince Calb. The prince limped forward and began raining blows with the bone club down on Rew, who in the darkness and without the use of his right arm, was having a terrifically difficult time defending himself.

One strike caught him on his injured shoulder, freezing him with pain. The next blow struck his head, splitting his scalp and sending a stream of blood trickling down his face. The next swing missed, and Calb stumbled off balance on his injured knee. Fighting the pain from the stab wound in his shoulder and the throbbing agony in his head, Rew grasped the prince's tunic and yanked him down to the floor.

They fought, rolling and kicking. Rew smashed his forehead on Calb's nose, shattering it. Calb lunged as if to bite Rew, and the ranger gripped his brother's head and conked it against the stone floor. The prince, apparently feeling the blood on Rew's shoulder and remembering what it was from, battered his fist like a hammer, sending spasms of pain through Rew's entire right side. Rew wrapped his left hand about his brother's throat, but his palm was slick with blood, and as they flailed on the floor, he lost his grip.

The undead lurched after them, stabbing and slashing, catching them with glancing cuts, unable to land one of their clumsy blows with accuracy because the two men fought and thrashed so violently.

Then, Calb dug a finger into the spear wound on Rew's back and tore at the injured flesh like a beast. Ripples of pain from the damage coursed through the ranger, and he arched his back and twisted madly, trying to wriggle away from his brother.

Calb staggered to his feet and slammed one foot down on Rew's longsword, pinning it to the ground. He stomped on Rew's injured shoulder with his other boot. Rew's breath caught, and he quaked with pain. In the dim light from the doorway, the prince raised his bone club, prepared to bring it down in a final blow on top of Rew's skull.

"Father always wanted you to be a part of this, Rew," snarled the prince, his giant, golden imp suddenly looming behind him, brushing half a dozen undead away from them, protecting its master. Calb glanced over his shoulder then turned back, the dim light in the room barely illuminating his predatory smile. "He wanted you to accept the mantle instead of Heindaw. It was your right, as the eldest, but ever since you were a child, you turned your back on what you were, what you could be. We never understood. He never understood. I think he wanted to hate you for it, Rew, but Vaisius saw something in you. I didn't know what. I still don't. Was it a plot for us to weaken each other and then you'd strike? The old man would appreciate that. Were you in the Investiture all along, hiding and biding your time out in the wilderness? Whatever your plan, it failed."

"I wanted nothing to do with the family, and I still don't. This is about stopping you, not being one of you," growled Rew, lying still beneath his brother.

Calb had slowed, confident with his imp at his back. He slapped the femur in his hand then raised it above his head. "I'm glad I'm the one who gets to do this. I'm glad it's your heart that will be the first to stop beating. I can't wait to walk out of here and announce that it was I, Calb, who killed the first son of Vaisius Morden. I'm glad it's like this—personal—instead of by one of my imps. Goodbye, Rew."

Fighting an ocean of agony, Rew lurched off his back and swung as hard as he could, catching Calb on the side of the knee with a balled fist. Bone cracked, and Calb shrieked. He fell beside Rew.

"Try walking out of here now, Bastard."

Rew staggered to his feet, longsword in hand, and looked up at the imp looming above him. It had a huge fist raised to smite him, but he was standing atop its master. If it struck him, it would injure Calb as well.

Rew kicked Calb's broken leg for good measure then sprinted beneath the imp's wide legs.

The gargantuan creature wailed and tried to bend down to grab him, but it had expected him to run the other way, and he was a step too fast for it. He darted out of the shaft of light bleeding in from the doorway, dodging between undead that were a thinner crowd now, thanks to the imp. Then, he almost tripped over Ambrose.

"You came back?" whispered the necromancer as Rew tucked

his longsword beneath his bad arm and reached down to grasp the back of the man's crimson robes.

Rew started dragging the necromancer toward the door, shushing him as the imp spun, unable to see them in the dark with its poor eyesight, but it could hear them. Undead began to shuffle after them as well, and Rew hurried.

"You should have left me," lamented Ambrose. "Don't you understand, you fool? You should have left me. I've been seen in Valchon's court and now Calb's. If I walk out of here with you, the king will know. He'll take me. Don't you understand what he can do? Death is not the end, Ranger."

"Shut up!"

"Don't you understand?"

"I do," growled Rew, steering the man around a pack of slow-moving undead. "I do, which is why I don't plan to die in here."

"Leave me," snarled Ambrose, suddenly finding some energy and beginning to struggle to get himself free of the ranger's grip.

Rew smacked him and then kept dragging the hapless man to the door.

Half a dozen steps from the opening, the nameless woman and Raif appeared, and the big fighter sent the undead scattering. Rew made it to the doorway of the crypt and stumbled, cursing. For the first time, he was looking closely at the incredible copper doors. They opened inside. They had no handles. There was no way to pull them shut.

"Oh no," hissed the nameless woman, seeing Rew's look. "I... Those have to be shut. I can't seal the crypt unless they're shut. I forgot—"

"Someone has to shut it from the inside," said Rew, his spirits falling.

"Me," said Raif, swinging his greatsword and crashing it through a pair of undead who shambled out from the crypt. "I'll do it."

"No, you idiot," snapped Rew. "We—"

The golden-scaled imp was coming toward them. It looked too

big to fit through the doorway, but it'd managed to get inside well enough, and without the use of his right arm, Rew didn't like his chances outside the crypt any more than he had inside of the crypt. They had to close the doors before that thing came out. If the imp got to the door, it could stop them from sealing Calb inside. They had to close the door. Someone had to stay inside to do it.

"I'll go," said Rew, but even as he said it, he knew how ludicrous it sounded. If he died, no one else knew how to face the king. He might be able to break the king's magical hold on them before he fell to the undead swarming inside, but what then? Where would the others go? What would they do? Cinda wasn't ready to confront Vaisius Morden. None of them but Anne knew the ways of the world. They would be hunted by every power within the kingdom, and he didn't doubt they would quickly be caught. If the king found them, he would imprison their souls. They knew too much to be safe, but they didn't know enough to continue the fight. If Rew died in the crypt, the others would have no hope.

"I... I'm the only one who can seal the door, and I have to do it from the outside," murmured the nameless woman. "I'm sorry, but it has to be—"

Raif put a hand on Rew's arm. "Valedon needs you. Cinda needs you. It has to be me."

Then, they both squealed and jumped out of the way from one of the huge copper doors. It slammed with finality, and standing in the doorway, they saw Ambrose reach for the second door. He told them, "I wish you luck, but against the king, I'd rather die in here."

The necromancer grabbed the second door, and without word, he swung it closed. In the breath before the door slammed shut, Rew saw the imp catch the necromancer. The ranger looked away.

The nameless woman stepped forward and placed both her dark hands against the gleaming copper. She fitted her fingers into the intricately etched, whorled patterns and murmured under her breath. The copper doors began to glow, like molten metal poured from the forge, but there was no heat, just the light. The etchings in the copper writhed, crawling across the metal like snakes climbing over each other, and then she stepped away. The light faded from the doors, but they were no longer a pair. It was now one solid barrier of gleaming copper, impervious to magic.

The doors were magically sealed by the king's own enchantments. Opening those doors took involvement from the king himself, or more force than even Calb's imp could muster. The imp and the prince were sealed inside forever.

Rew turned, seeing all of the remaining party there and half a dozen undead beyond them. Calb's soldiers were gone, evidently fleeing from the imp as it had approached the doorway, and they'd drawn many of the undead after them, but half a dozen foes was a lot when your opponent couldn't be killed.

"King's Sake," hissed Rew. "They'll be scattered all through the palace now."

"Cinda!" cried Raif, shuffling in between her and the undead, raising his enchanted greatsword to defend. "Cinda, we need you to release the bindings!"

"She can't hear you," worried Anne, still holding the girl upright. "She's completely unresponsive. She's caught in the flow of the power, so much of it, so much death. She's not going to be able to—"

"Raif, look at that," said Rew, pointing up the stairwell they'd originally entered through.

The fighter spun, searching for the threat. Rew stepped forward and punched Cinda in the side of the head, knocking her from Anne's arms, knocking her unconscious.

"Blessed Mother, Rew! Why did you..." began Anne before trailing off.

Around them, the undead were collapsing.

"I hoped that would work," muttered the ranger.

"What did you do to my sister?" demanded Raif, stepping toward Rew.

"Let's talk about it over a pitcher of ale when we get out of here, eh? These corpses aren't a threat anymore, and Calb's imprisoned in a copper tomb that he can't portal out of, but there's an army of soldiers in this palace whose last instruction was to execute us. We've got to slip out before things calm down, you understand? When we get to safety, you can pound me like iron on a blacksmith's anvil, but until then, we run."

Chapter Six

R ew reached out for his ale mug, cringed, and then switched hands and lifted the wooden tankard with his left. He tilted it awkwardly and gulped thirstily. A few more of the frothy pours and he thought he might be able to ignore the ache deep in the socket of his shoulder and the sharper pain where Calb had rammed a spear into him. The bastard.

Of course, Rew had left Calb sealed in a crypt filled with undead and not much else. The entire structure had been encased in copper, rendering Calb's magic impotent. The prince had his imp with him, though. The imp had likely kept him alive long enough that the bindings were broken and the animated corpses collapsed, but that wouldn't be much better. The prince would be stuck in the dark with the desiccated bodies and his conjuring. Were imps good company? Probably not. Food and water were going to be problems soon enough as well. Would hunger break Calb's command over the imp, or was his control strong enough that they would both starve to death, sitting beside each other and a pile of broken bones?

Would Calb eat the imp?

Could you eat an imp?

If Calb's control broke, the imp would definitely eat him, and that might be a mercy.

Rew shuddered. A chill breeze gusted off the lake, but it wasn't the cold that affected him. He'd been sitting out on the rooftop porch of the tavern for hours, and the cold felt good. It kept him awake. Gave him something to think about other than the last few days.

He regretted that he hadn't killed Calb himself. It would have brought him a measure of pleasure, and it was the merciful thing to do, but it hadn't felt right. That was the core of ancient magic. It had no procedures and no rituals. It was about finding circumstances with potential and utilizing that potential to enact one's will. It was similar to low magic, where the caster could lean on connections, and far from high magic, which involved bending specific science to specific ends.

Ancient magic was something everyone made a little use of but never understood, except for old men and women whose children and grandchildren had stopped listening to them. Sometimes, ancient magic manifested in lucky totems and omens, or other times in mantras passed down through centuries until the origination was lost. Bold proclamations that came true due to sheer force of will were the fruit of ancient magic. It was ephemeral, but when one paid attention, one could harness it to great effect.

Most hadn't heard of ancient magic or, if they had, thought it was an ignorant explanation of low and high magic. It was the sort of thing that was discussed in the past. Always history. Of course, most people weren't the son of the king. Most people couldn't feel the pull of the Investiture tugging on their soul.

Rew rubbed his chest. He had felt it, but he didn't now. Sacrificing Calb must have worked to sever King Vaisius Morden's connections to them. Not feeling the tug was one sign. That they were alive still was the other.

The king, of all people, would recognize what had occurred inside the crypt in Jabaan. He might not fully understand the sort of threat Cinda posed to his reign, but he knew they'd raised the corpses he'd been accumulating for almost two hundred years and that they had drained much of the power which had been stored there. From that alone, the king would understand enough to see Cinda as a threat. Through Vyar Grund's dead eyes, the king had seen her with Rew and the others. He'd have all the pieces he needed now to put the puzzle together.

Rew lifted his ale mug again. Had they destroyed the crypt? Perhaps the king could force his way inside and salvage some of what was left. It was impossible to tell how much of the stored necromantic power Cinda had tapped into or how many more corpses had been held below in the depths of the place. Rew wondered if you could reuse a corpse. He'd never heard stories about such a thing, but a dead body was a dead body.

Sealing the doors might have damaged the delicate balance of power which formed the crypt. Fashioning such a device wouldn't have been easy even for Vaisius Morden. If it was easy, someone else would have done it. But there were too many unknowns to be confident they'd destroyed a significant portion of the king's power. Rew figured they'd done some damage, though. Vaisius Morden would be less than he was before they'd arrived in Jabaan.

Rew finished his ale.

The king had been building what was housed in that crypt for two hundred years. He'd been building it in Jabaan and every other major city in Vaeldon outside of the east. The king had access to a trove of stored power that Rew struggled to fathom. What Cinda had accomplished was a tiny fraction of what the king had planned, and she was untrained, a novice. In the hands of a two-hundred-year-old practitioner? It was strength Rew knew they would never be able to face directly. No one could.

Not head on. Not out in the open. They had to start knocking out the legs which Vaisius Morden stood upon. Take away his support. Remove the tools he used to oppress Vaeldon and the power he could summon to squash them like ants. Before Jabaan,

Rew had pondered going directly to Mordenhold and casting the dice and letting the pips decide their fate. After Jabaan, he had a better plan. They would go to the other capitals, confront the princes, and do what they could to destroy the king's crypts in the process.

Stealth warfare, a battle of attrition. With each strike they executed successfully, the king would be less. It would give them a chance. Maybe. Maybe not. Rew grunted and peered into his empty ale mug. However it went, it felt right. The ranger's path was a circuitous one, but before they began, they needed time to recover. Even if it wasn't a fight with the king himself, they needed to be at their best for what was ahead.

While they rested, Rew thought he would drink some more ale. He needed it to drown the sorrow of Jabaan. The legions of undead that had marched from the crypt were bad. Dried, time-ravaged corpses. The scores of fresh dead were worse. Men and women who'd been alive the day before were dead because of his actions. He tried to tell himself it was a necessary bargain. They did what they had to do to kill Calb. Perhaps. There could have been another plan, another way. Rew hadn't known the crypt would rise, but he wouldn't blame it on Cinda. It hadn't been her fault. He was the leader. He'd suggested she do what she did, and he'd taken advantage of it the moment he'd known it was happening.

There'd been hundreds of dead that they'd seen. There must have been thousands of dead throughout the palace and the city that they had not. A terrible bargain.

He would get more ale soon, he decided. A lot more.

He told himself he was better than his brothers, more honorable, that he cared for people. That care cut deep now. He didn't know if he was better than them or not. Did the hurt make him better than Valchon? Was that his quality, his sorrow?

His body hurt something fierce, a small echo of the storm that raged inside. The thought of getting up and walking to collect another mug was too much. A temporary situation, he imagined, but for now, he sat quietly on the rooftop deck of the tavern they'd settled into and looked out over the lake. The wind whipped the water against the rocky shore, stirring the fishing boats there and churning the dirty, shallow water at the foot of the village into a froth.

Had he thought about it, he might have compared the look of the water to freshly poured ale, except the water was filthy with the refuse of the village and the detritus of generations of fishermen unloading their catches along that rock-studded muddy beach. It smelled rank, man's imposition on the wild world. When it lapped against the shore, the water hid the filth for a brief moment and brought respite, but the brief moment was all it brought.

Like ale, he might have thought, but all that crossed his mind was that he needed another. When he accidentally put his right hand on the table to push himself up to get it, a lance of pain stabbed into his shoulder, and he sat back down glumly. He would let the pain fade and then he would go.

Moments later, salvation arrived in the form of Zaine. The thief came bustling out of the interior of the tavern with a full pitcher in one hand and an empty mug in another. She sat down across from him, putting the drinks on the splintery table and pouring his mug full before topping up her own.

"Anne wouldn't like you drinking," remarked Rew before taking a sip of the fresh ale.

Zaine snorted. "That's the thanks I get for bringing you a pitcher? I don't think she'd much like you drinking either, in your condition. Or in any condition, I suppose. You've just worn her down over the years, while I'm only getting started."

He chuckled and nodded in acknowledgement. "Fair enough."

"Feeling better?"

"Not really," he admitted. "It'll be another week before I think we ought to move on. Before I can move on, I should say. That gives Cinda and me time to rest, and you and Raif time to train."

"You could accept Anne's healing."

He shook his head.

They sat together for a spell, looking out over the massive inland lake that spanned much of the Western Province. Out beyond the haze coming off the water, perched on towering cliffs that overlooked the lake, was Jabaan. Rew had been told that on the right day, the cliffs of the far shore were visible, but he'd never sat still long enough to see them. He hoped they wouldn't see them now, during their stay in the humble village of Faevril.

It was a comfort, not being able to see Jabaan, knowing that no one in the city could peer across the lake and see them.

Not that he thought anyone would be looking very hard. When they'd fled, they'd found passage on an open-topped fishing boat that was pushing away from the docks. Rew had thrown a handful of coin at the captain, and the gruff man had allowed them aboard with no questions and little curiosity. After all, just about everyone else in the city of Jabaan was fleeing as well.

It'd been the perfect cover. All of Jabaan's fishing fleet had taken to the water for safety. Thousands of boats darted off in every direction, skimming across the smooth lake, overloaded with panicked passengers. Someone might guess their party had taken a boat rather than escaping on land, but not even the king would be able to sort out which boat they'd taken and where it'd gone.

They'd disembarked on a barren stretch of shore and hiked a day west to Faevril. It was small enough that Rew had been surprised it had a name, but he declared it the place they would lay low until they recovered. Until he recovered, really. Everyone else had accepted Anne's empathy, and the empath herself, while tired, was already regaining her vigor. Even Cinda seemed to have recovered from unleashing the torrent of power she'd pulled from the well within the crypt. She was getting stronger, building a tolerance for the virulent magic she could cast. She'd changed in other ways as well. It wasn't just Rew who noticed the ethereal green burning deep in her eyes, and he didn't think she'd slept since the first night out of danger. The others could see those tangible differences, but she'd changed more than they realized.

He stretched and winced. Earlier that morning, Cinda had told him she was ready to travel, but he wasn't. There were dangers on the road, and he thought it simple common sense he be able to hold his longsword before facing them. The young necromancer had glanced across the room at Anne during the conversation, but Rew hadn't commented. Cinda didn't say anything, either. Now she understood more about secrets and the pain one might endure to keep them. When you hurt enough, what was a little bit more?

Rew wondered whether it was habit or sensible protection of his few remaining secrets that spurred him to refuse the empath's care. The rest of the party had already learned more about his past than he'd intended them to. That was why Zaine was there, he figured, trying to suss out more details, trying to peer into the darkness he held close, though she couldn't have known how dark it got. He could feel her beside him, waiting impatiently for the right opportunity to broach the subject. He sipped his ale, and she sipped hers.

Finally, she got bored. She noisily slurped her ale and then asked, "So... Prince Calb was your brother?"

Rew grunted and did not respond.

"Does that mean, ah, that Valchon and Heindaw are your brothers as well? And that... the king is your father?"

Rew looked over the fishing boats bobbing at the foot of the village. Just ten of them, built to hold one or two men and a parcel of fish. The boats had short sails, furled in the gentle, late afternoon breeze. Their owners would be sleeping now, preparing to leave hours before dawn and be on the water when the sun rose. It was a simple life those fishermen led. They had little concern for what happened outside of the village, outside of the weather and the runs of fish that swam through the great, inland lake. Even when refugees from Jabaan began to arrive, the fishermen showed little interest. They were uninvolved and wanted to stay that way. It was safer. Like the fish they sought, they sensed danger instinctively and knew it was best to swim away. Didn't matter what the danger was. It was safer to swim away. Ignore the hooks and the nets and stay below the surface.

"Rew…"

"Aye, he's my father, and they are my brothers," admitted the ranger. He cleared his throat and sat back. It felt strange to say that.

Slowly, he stretched his right arm, feeling the tension as the stitches in his back pulled. He stopped before he went too far, merely testing his range of motion and wondering how much longer it would take to fully heal.

"Why aren't you a prince, then? If the king is your father…"

"The king has a lot of children. Dozens, I'd guess. Had dozens, I should say. Most are dead. Life in the creche can be as dangerous as life outside of the creche for the king's children, though actively conspiring against one another while there is discouraged. Doesn't stop some from trying, of course. That is the point, after all, to pit sibling against sibling, and may the strongest inherit the throne."

Zaine didn't speak, but he could feel her question hanging in the air.

"I was a prince, but I chose a different path. I abdicated my title, my responsibility, and that horrible future. Some of my brothers thought my path was cowardice, and others thought I'd understood something they did not. I'm not sure whether it was wisdom or folly, but I ignored the blood flowing through my veins. I didn't accept the perks of my station. I didn't study the high magic I'm capable of. I turned my back on all of that and tried to forge my own way."

"As a ranger?"

"Eventually."

"You were something else before?"

"Allow me a few secrets, lass. Yes, I was something else before. I decided that wasn't my path, either, or Anne decided. You know how she is. I met her. We traveled for a time, and then I sought the wilderness outside of Eastwatch. The king knew where I'd gone, and he appointed me his ranger after I got there. I didn't say no. For the first time, it seemed his desires and mine were aligned. And of course, he was still my father and my king. I'd meant to find my own path, and being his ranger was close enough. It had to be. I'm not sure if I could have said no and remained within Vaeldon."

"So what now?"

"For a long time, I hid from what I was, and I pretended it wasn't true. But it is true. I'm the king's son. What I learned after meeting you children was that while maybe I'd started my path with the right intentions, the way had become one of cowardice. I decided after meeting you that it was time to take a stand, and take a stand we will. Nothing has changed, except now you all know. Calb was the start, but we've much to do to finish this."

Zaine tilted up her ale and then poured herself another.

"You could turn from it, you know?" he said to her. "It's not your blood that created what we saw in the crypt. It's not your responsibility, lass. No one can ask this of you."

"Aye, and if I ran, would it be any better than when you ran ten years ago?"

"It's not your blood."

"Not my blood, but my family," retorted Zaine. "At least, if you listen to what Anne has to say. She claims we're family, Ranger, and while I only have spotty memories of what my family was like, I think it was something like this. We stick together, and every person's fight is all of our fight."

"Family... That wasn't what mine was like. My family was nothing but fear and pain," he retorted. He softened his tone and added, "I know yours was the same, lass. It wasn't your fault. My family wasn't my fault. Doesn't mean I can turn from it, not anymore, but their actions are not my actions. Your parents... that's not you."

"Aye, but fighting together, rather than against each other, that's what I wish it'd been like," mumbled the thief. "A lot of families are like both of ours, I guess. More hate than love. But not all. Not even most, I like to think. As you say, it doesn't matter. But we chose this family we're in now. We can choose what to make of it."

"You're a good lass, Zaine," he said with a grin. "You're better than your circumstances. Better than me. And maybe you're right. Maybe we can choose how it is."

"The child is always better than the parent, right?"

He frowned at her. "That's not exactly—"

She shrugged and stood, moving to slap him on the shoulder but then pausing, apparently recalling his injury. "It's close enough. I'm going inside now. I'll leave the pitcher. I'm sure the others will ask me what you said."

"Tell them so I don't have to say it again."

"Cinda will have questions," mentioned Zaine. "You know she will."

Rew grunted and did not respond.

Zaine ducked inside the tavern, leaving him sitting on the open rooftop, staring out at the water.

THE NEXT WEEK PASSED IN COMFORTABLE SECLUSION. THE FISHING village emptied as those who'd fled Jabaan either kept running or returned once it was clear the undead had suddenly dropped, leaving corpses scattered around the palace and the city but ending the threat. The fisherfolk had initially asked questions but soon realized they didn't want to know the answers, and after that, they left Rew and the others alone.

The party spoke to each other about mundane matters; when to meet for supper, how long the weather would hold, different techniques to vary their arms training, how the bread had been fresher the day before, and other safe topics. After the conversation with Zaine and what she'd relayed to the others, it seemed they were all afraid of what else would be said.

The reality of their task had sunk in following Jabaan. They'd seen first-hand what they were facing, and every one of them must have understood they were not strong enough to face it directly. Even Calb, weakened from his efforts against Valchon, had summoned a creature that was beyond them. They knew, finally, why Rew had hesitated to tell them all of it to begin with.

Rew didn't have the heart to tell them that he considered Calb the weakest of the three princes. Heindaw did not exceed Calb in high magic, but he was cunning. He would not have been fooled into entering the crypt as his older brother had been. He wouldn't have left Rew and the others alive long enough to pull the stunt that they had. Valchon was worse. He was both cunning and strong. He commanded magic second only to the king himself and, with that power as an advantage, had amassed a larger contingent of allies than the other two brothers combined.

Of course, the three princes even together paled in comparison to the king. Vaisius Morden was a two-hundred-year-old necromancer who'd spent that entire time accumulating unimaginable power. He had the full strength of Vaeldon's military behind him as well as its spellcasters, its spies, and its assassins. Beyond that, he commanded legions of undead that were nigh unstoppable. Hundreds of thousands of them. Millions? There was simply nothing they could do to fight against such an army. No one could fight against that. It was inconceivable power.

But the reminder of the difficulty of their task was also a reminder of how necessary it was. They'd seen what the king was doing, and they knew he would continue until someone stopped him. There was only them. No one else had the knowledge or the skill. If they didn't make a stand, if they weren't successful, then a nearly immortal necromancer would continue his atrocities forever. It was heavy stuff, and it took most of the week for them to sort through their varied emotions and reactions.

Anne, in particular, gave everyone their space. She told Rew one night, "It's an important step for them to fully understand what we do and to come to terms with that on their own. They were like children when we met them, unaccustomed to the world outside of their keeps and their minders. They've grown since then."

"Aye, I've noticed."

"They can make their own decisions, but in truth, the decisions were made before we found ourselves in Jabaan. Cinda had some idea of what was coming and was already committed, and the others will follow her wherever she goes. Still, it's best to let them figure that out themselves."

"And you?"

Anne smiled at him. "I've followed you since the day we met."

He snorted. That wasn't exactly the way he remembered things. In his recollection, he'd spent a good bit of time chasing after her, though she'd agreed to come to Eastwatch once she'd finished talking him off the path he'd been on.

"Now that we have that settled," continued Anne, "what's next? Do we return to Carff? The nameless woman told me it was Ambrose who managed to open the portal stone and slip through once the excitement had died down, but you could do the same, couldn't you? Valchon wouldn't expect it."

Rew rubbed his freshly shaven head. "No, I don't think he'd expect to see us back so soon. I've considered it, but he'll be watching the portal stones, particularly now. I'm sure he was before, but Calb overwhelmed his guards to break through without tripping Valchon's wards. He won't let that happen again. Even if it wasn't for us, he'd be protecting himself against Heindaw. No, if we appear through a portal stone in Carff, I expect we'll find an army waiting for us."

"How did Ambrose get through, then?"

"My guess... Valchon let him through," said Rew. "Maybe he thought the necromancer and the nameless woman would help us in the fight against Calb, or maybe he had other reasons. What did that bastard Alsayer whisper into Valchon's ear? I worry about that."

"Whatever Valchon's reasons, Ambrose is dead now."

"He's dead," agreed Rew, "but the nameless woman is not. We have to consider that her goals aren't ours. I wouldn't think Valchon would allow her to take Grund's falchions, but maybe he did. She could be working for him or for Heindaw. Anne, I think it likely she's a dagger poised at our backs."

The empath pursed her lips. "If the woman was planning to harm us, she already could have. She's had access to us sleeping and could have slit our throats almost any night since we've met her."

Rew shook his head. "It's not just a physical threat I worry about."

Anne tilted her head, signaling her confusion.

"I've been thinking about it. The nameless woman came from Iyre. Heindaw is in Iyre. Maybe that's the connection. She could have come to us in Jabaan to make sure we faced Calb. Killing him did as much good for Heindaw as it did Valchon—or for us. We're helping the princes as much as we're helping ourselves, and that could be why she hasn't attacked us."

"So, what do we do?"

Rew shrugged. "She might be working for Valchon or for Heindaw—or neither of them. King's Sake, she could be playing the same game as Alsayer and is getting in bed with everyone, but it doesn't matter. The point is, we don't know, so we can't trust her."

Anne sighed then looked into his eyes. "I'll ask again, what do we do?"

He looked back at her, waiting a moment before saying, "Cinda proved she's capable of handling immense power, but she lacks control. Her father is dead, and the king won't teach her. There's another place, though, where they understand her art, a place we might find a guide for her."

"We said we'd never return there, Rew," muttered Anne.

"Things change. Are you willing to face that again?"

"Do I have a choice?" asked Anne loftily. She pulled her shawl tighter around her shoulders and scowled at him. "I was a child when I left that place with you. I'm a woman now. I'll be fine."

"Then that's where we'll go."

"If we're going to do it, should we move along the lake shore to a bigger settlement? Perhaps we can find a place with horses for sale. We have funds now, don't we? It'd be faster."

"We do have funds," conceded Rew. "Zaine managed to steal enough for months on the road before we left Calb's palace, but ah, I think horses will be too conspicuous. We're better off on foot. No one will suspect that."

Anne looked at him quizzically.

Before she could question him, he declared, "I think one more day of rest, then we travel. We should get to bed so we're ready."

Chapter Seven

The next morning, they were served heaping bowls of steaming porridge, which they'd ordered instead of the tavern's usual fare—leftover fish stew. Between mouthfuls, Rew told the others that they would leave on the morrow. Looks of relief and trepidation passed over their faces. They'd known since they'd arrived at the small village of Faevril that they wouldn't be staying long, and the place had few luxuries to recommend it to anyone who wasn't interested in taking up a career as a fisherman, but it felt safe.

Since they'd been there, there had been no attacks, no searchers, no spellcasters, no Dark Kind. After the first days, when the narrow mud streets had been filled with refugees from Jabaan, there'd been hardly anyone in the village except them and the fisherfolk. Those now-departed refugees had supplied all of the cover their group needed to be seen and forgotten. What was one more party of injured people recovering slowly when the entire city had emptied out and thousands had died?

But they had to move on. Their path was not one of safety, and they knew that. It didn't make it easier, though, to embark from shelter into the wild of a looming storm.

For a time, they lingered over breakfast. Then, they scrambled about, finding small chores to occupy themselves. Anne and Zaine visited every shop in the village, purchasing every conceivable good they thought they might need on the next stage of the journey despite Rew's warning that he would toss half of the gear they'd purchased. He knew Anne well enough to guess who she expected to carry all of that extraneous equipment.

Raif and the nameless woman, on the other hand, tended to their weapons and armor. It was an equally frivolous exercise as Anne's purchase of a new sewing kit. The empath wasn't going to find time on the road to mend torn garments, and the two fighters' gear was enchanted. Their blades did not need the same care and attention that normal steel did, and if it did require repair, they didn't have the skill to do it.

But fighters relied on their armor and weaponry for protection, so no one said anything as they polished, tightened, unbuckled, buckled, and adjusted. From another group of refugees who'd decided it was too heavy to carry over land, Raif had found a fresh set of front and back plate, along with dull steel pauldrons and gauntlets, which he laid over a motley of leather hauberk and chain that he'd patched together. The nameless woman offered him advice on strapping it all into a cohesive shell then spent hours rubbing oil and a cloth over her own armor. The bronze gleamed as freshly as it must have the day it was forged.

Rew, uninterested in shopping or giving his own gear more attention than it deserved, lurked nearby, curious. They'd finally discovered the enchantment annealed into Raif's greatsword. The giant blade had the power to sever the bindings a necromancer used to animate a corpse. If Rew had to guess, he imagined it would also serve the same purpose against wraiths, banishing the spirits from this life to the next. He mentioned it to Raif, and they'd both been silent a moment, realizing that they hoped to never test that property. The damage the wraiths had done to Duke Eeron's men in Spinesend was still vivid in their memories.

But what to make of the nameless woman's gear? It didn't have the same properties as Raif's sword, which was unfortunate since they were aiming toward a confrontation with Vaeldon's preeminent necromancer, but what would a priest of the Cursed Father have considered worthy of passing down to his daughter? Had it been her father at all who'd gifted her the equipment?

The armor and the scimitar the woman wielded would have cost as much as a minor noble's landholding. Forging it in secrecy would have only increased the price. Rew smirked, wondering just how much coin the king was funneling through the temple of the Cursed Father in Iyre. For that outpost to have such a treasure horde was impressive. That the nameless woman's father had been able to siphon off enough to pay a talented enchanter with no one noticing—

Rew blinked.

The nameless woman rapped her knuckles on the bronze armor. "Go ahead and ask, Ranger. You're wanting to know the properties of this suit, aren't you? I can see it in your eyes."

Mutely, Rew nodded.

She grinned, showing her bright white teeth. "The truth is, I'm not certain. The armor is nearly impervious to damage, and the scimitar cuts better than the finest steel. I've never had to conduct repairs on either. Not even a nick on the blade after a tussle. But there's more, I think. When, ah, my father gave me this, he told me it was unattuned. He claimed that this gear would bond with an owner, and it would feed off that person's natural talent. That sounds like a lot of mushy talk to me. If one has a fiery temper, does the sword light on fire? I don't know. But that's what he claimed, and I know he believed it. He, my father that is, would know."

"But it's never activated for you?" questioned Raif from across the table. "You think you haven't... bonded to it, or maybe it just doesn't have additional properties? Could it be like your sword, Ranger? No magic, but a finer piece that's ever come straight from a forge?"

Rew grunted. His longsword had magical properties, they

were just too dangerous to use. He didn't fancy getting into that explanation with the young fighter, so he didn't respond.

The nameless woman shrugged. "I'm not sure. I've been wearing this kit for the last four years, ever since I left Iyre. I've been giving it attention like it was a newborn, but aside from being the highest quality metal I've encountered, it's never done anything else for me. I haven't tried to make it do anything, though. Not sure if that means I'm not bonded to it or if it's bunk, or maybe I'm just ignorant. What do you think, Ranger? You know more about this than the rest of us, don't you? Is there a way to test what properties an enchanted item has? Could it be doing something I'm not aware of? Influencing me… somehow?"

Rew frowned. Magical properties or no, how had the nameless woman's father come by such fine armor?

"What is it, Ranger?" asked Raif. "Is that the way enchanted gear works? Does it bond to an owner? Makes some sense, I guess. My family, with necromancy in our blood, would have had good use for a sword that combats the undead."

"Yes, it can work that way," said Rew slowly. "Enchantment, like all magic, has to draw from somewhere. It can either pull from the talent of the enchanter or from the wielder of the item. There is a… bonding. That bonding typically occurs during creation of the artifact, but I suppose there are stories of it happening during use."

"Does it take four years?" asked the nameless woman. "Four years of regular use?"

Rew shook his head. "Not that I've heard, but enchantments are rare, and the men and women who conduct them are secretive. I don't claim to know all of the possibilities, but I do know this. Only an enchanter can be certain if an object has properties or not."

The woman frowned then shrugged. "Well, it's served me well enough. I was told there was nothing more to it, so I hope if there's anything else surprising about this suit, it doesn't come out at the wrong time, eh?"

"Aye, bursting into flame at the wrong moment could be rather awkward," jested Raif, grinning at the woman.

She winked back at him. "I don't need armor to do that, lad."

Raif flushed.

Rew cleared his throat. "Your father gifted you this set, yes? Who was the enchanter?"

The nameless woman's gaze fell down to the gleaming bronze, and she was silent a moment before answering. "I don't know. My father never told me."

Quietly, Rew turned from them and walked outside. The woman's armor and sword were worth a literal fortune. A duke might be able to afford such a thing for an eldest child, and there could be half a dozen merchants in the kingdom with enough wealth, but that was it. Lesser nobles or merchants would be bankrupted attempting to finance that level of enchantment, and that's assuming one was able to find an enchanter with time to do the work for any price.

Enchanters had no need of patronage like the other spellcasters, and they could be a fickle bunch. Sometimes, they worked for strictly economic purposes, sometimes political. Frequently, it was for protection. It wasn't unheard of for an enchanter to be assassinated by a rival before they could finish a piece, giving them good reason for secrecy. Rew doubted there were more than a dozen in the kingdom capable of enchanting an entire suit of armor, and most of those worked for the king in Mordenhold, and they exclusively handled projects for Vaisius Morden's most loyal supporters.

Rew rubbed a hand over his scalp, glad he'd found time to shave before they left, though the cool air on his head made him shiver.

He frowned. Vaisius Morden wouldn't have found it necessary to direct so much treasure into a small cult of warrior priests, and if that much money had gone missing, it would have been noticed long before the equipment was finished. Except, it seems no one had noticed. At least not before the nameless woman had walked off with the armor. The armor had been fit just for her. Could that have been done without her ever meeting the enchanter? Whatever other properties it had, it was a finely wrought set, and he'd seen its efficacy in Jabaan. She was right. It was far superior than any mundane steel.

Someone with true skill had created the piece just for her. How? Why?

The nameless woman had claimed to have been born and raised in Iyre, never straying far from the city until her father burned down the temple of the Cursed Father. The Cursed Father, she claimed, was Vaisius Morden the First, who Rew knew was the same soul as Vaisius Morden the Eighth.

Burning the king's temple was more than a simple distraction by a father trying to buy time for his daughter to slip away unnoticed. It was a declaration of war against the king. For someone who understood the king's power and ability to reach into the underworld, it was a bold act. Beyond bold. It was foolhardy. Clear insanity. Who would challenge the king himself?

That thought elicited a bitter chuckle. Who was as reckless as he was? Rew could only think of one man—Prince Heindaw. The Prince of the Northern Province, the Prince of Iyre, the nameless woman's home. An unparalleled enchanter.

Prince Heindaw wasn't bold in the same sense Rew was, but he was arrogant. Only he might believe he could outmaneuver the king. He was the sort of man who thought six or seven moves ahead on a Kings and Queens board. He marshaled his resources and played with precision. He could have set a plan in motion four years prior, but what was the play with the enchanted armor?

Rew didn't know, but the string of coincidence was too much. He was growing certain that Heindaw had been the one to enchant the woman's armor, but why? Why would a prince of the realm have spent time crafting armor and a scimitar for an adventurer who'd been roaming Vaeldon directionlessly for years? Even for one with the prodigious skill of the prince, enchantment was a delicate, time-consuming art. With the Investiture looming even half a decade ago, Heindaw would have only invested his time in projects which would bear fruit in the fight against his brothers or against their father.

There were properties to the woman's armor. Rew was certain of it. Heindaw had imbued something into that gleaming bronze, and he'd done so with a clear purpose that, according to the woman, he hadn't shared. He'd aimed the nameless woman and her armor at a target, and had let her fly, but where was she directed?

Even before Rew had turned his back on the Investiture and the privilege of the royal family, Heindaw had known it was coming. He'd known he would have an opportunity to ascend to the throne, and he'd been planning. How deep did those plans run? How far had he expected the nameless woman to fly?

Her presence in Spinesend so close to Rew's own time in the city was no error. Her move to Stanton just ahead of him wasn't a mistake, either. She'd been placed in his path. Why? Anne was right. The nameless woman could have killed them dozens of times over by now, if that's what she was sent to do. There was something else…

Shaking his head, Rew considered her arrival in Jabaan after they'd been taken prisoner. That couldn't be a coincidence either, and as he mulled it over, he realized her story did not make sense. She couldn't have known where they'd portaled to unless someone told her. That someone had sent her to help, not to hurt. Had she come to assist them killing Calb? If that was all, why hadn't she left, or slain them in their sleep afterward as Anne had mentioned?

The nameless woman acted as if she was only with them to save her father, but there was more to it. Rew felt in his bones there was more to it. Her patron had further plans. What Rew couldn't decide was whether she knew those plans, or if she was as ignorant about it as the rest of them.

HOURS LATER, REW WAS ON THE ROOFTOP DECK OF THE TAVERN which abutted the inn. It was his favorite place in the village, a quiet spot to drink and look over the still fishing fleet tied to the shore and the ever-changing lake beyond. With the wind rippling the surface of the lake, stirring the reflected light, the water showed him a different face each time he looked. It was both change and the illusion of change. The surface shifted, always moving, but beneath it was always the same. The water had lapped against this shore for centuries or perhaps millennia. It was permanence, but its color was a mirage, just a reflection of what shone upon it. The water had no color. It looked different, but it was always the same.

Was he like that? Changing but always the same?

He was drunk. He knew that much.

One last day in—well, not civilization, the village of Faevril didn't quite live up to that grand title, but something like civilization. One last day to sit in the quiet storm of his own thoughts instead of the storm of the Investiture. He worried it would be his last chance for a while to dip into a full ale barrel and savor a tankard in quiet. He was taking advantage.

The sun was getting close to the horizon, and he knew soon the others would come looking for him. They would dine together at a proper table with someone else doing the cooking, though the tavern's cook was a far cry short of Anne's skill in the kitchen. Still, eating under shelter at a table would be a ritual before they left. Ancient magic suffused Vaeldon—the pull of the Investiture, grand sacrifices, and small motions like breaking bread before a journey.

Rew turned up his tankard, letting the frothy ale spill down his throat. Did she know? Did the nameless woman know what task Heindaw intended for her? Was she a blind pawn or a knowing agent? Did it matter?

"Rew," called a soft voice.

He turned and blinked.

Cinda, garbed in the crimson robes of a necromancer, stood in the doorway to the tavern. In the shadow the building cast, her eyes glowed crisply green. Her hair shone, freshly washed, and her skin was pale. Her color had been like that following Jabaan. In the week since, it hadn't regained the youthful glow she'd once had. She was beautiful in the moonlight, frightening, too. No longer the child he'd met in the jail cell in Eastwatch. She was a woman now, and she knew where she was going. She smiled at him, and he suspected she knew exactly what he was thinking. She picked up her robes and twitched them in mockery of the flighty young noblewoman she'd once been.

"What do you think? Does it suit me?"

"Everyone who sees you wearing those robes will know exactly who you are, lass."

"Yes, I think you're right," she agreed.

"Cinda... the king—"

"Do you think there's any chance the king doesn't know exactly who I am already? We raided his crypt for corpses and power, Ranger. Whatever shroud Alsayer threw over his eyes to fool him into thinking Kallie was the necromancer has been ripped away. He knows exactly who I am and what I'm capable of. Dressing me like a fishmonger's daughter won't fool the king, so I'll not hide who I am from anyone."

"The king knows who you are but not where you are," reminded Rew. "Why make it easy for him?"

"Jabaan taught me much, Ranger. It taught me what I'm capable of and what your father is capable of. It taught me that the time for hiding is over. It's time to stand up to him, so I will."

"I'm not suggesting we turn from this fight, just that we select our ground and don't shout to anyone and everyone who sees us who we are and what we're doing. You have no idea what the king is capable—"

"What I am capable of!" interjected Cinda. "I bound those souls to those bodies, Ranger. I heard their pleas. I felt them. I felt those they killed as well, and I raised them too. I know what the king is capable of because I am capable of it as well. I know better than anyone how horrific that is, but I won't hide from it. You've been hiding for ten years, and where has that gotten you?"

"It's kept me alive," suggested Rew.

"For now," retorted Cinda. "You're alive, but you have not won. You have not overthrown the king. You have not—"

Rew stood, jabbing a finger at the girl. "We beat Calb!"

"Not through careful planning and stealth," argued Cinda. "We beat Calb because we accepted who we are. What happened in Jabaan, Ranger, is who I am. Our only success so far has been because I embraced it."

"Aye, and if it gets you killed?"

"Won't it?"

Rew blinked back at the girl.

She gave him a sorrowful smile. "Ranger, we know how this story ends, don't we? You won't say it to me, but I have guessed. How does an untrained girl stop the king? This isn't a story about me living happily ever after."

"You won't stop him if you make it easy for him," grumbled Rew.

"We are in this fight, and there's only one way we're going to win it. I have to embrace who I am and what I have to do. We have to fight to win. There's no other way."

"You've been spending too much time with your brother," complained Rew.

"Maybe my brother has known something that I've just realized," countered Cinda. "When the stakes are high enough, you cannot allow yourself to be held back by fear. You have to plunge in, to fight to win. There's a reason berserkers are feared in battle. For us, it's the only way."

Rew rubbed his face with both hands, unsure of what to say to the girl.

"Come on, Ranger. Supper is ready, and the others are waiting. One last meal before we go back into the storm."

Chapter Eight

The next morning, they set out from the village, leaving the lake, the gently rocking boats tied to the shore, and the dilapidated wooden structures behind. They followed a dirt tract that led north, cutting across sloping hills for half a league and then entering a forest of thin-trunked pines. The wood was thick with lush bushes and tangled branches. It would have been terrible travel off the path, but there was a path, and while there must be times it became overgrown and difficult, Jabaan's refugees over the last week had beaten the trail through the woods. The party found it easy walking.

Rew waited until they were in the cover of the trees to broach the subject of where they were going. No one had asked. He imagined because they all thought they would take the shortest path possible to the northern capital of Iyre so they could confront Prince Heindaw just as they had Calb. But the difference between the princes was that they would have no opportunity for surprise with Heindaw. The prince already knew of Cinda and what she was capable of, and now that Rew had openly confronted Calb, Heindaw would be watching for the ranger's visit. Heindaw was a cunning strategist, so he would be prepared.

They had to be prepared as well. They had to find a way to

unlock Cinda's talent. There was a place on the western fringe of the kingdom in which Rew thought they could find help. So once within the cover of the trees, he raised his voice and declared, "I think we should go to the Arcanum."

"Tell me that's where they train arcanists," interjected Zaine, grinning at him in the dappled light of the wood.

Rew snorted. "Yes, that's where they train arcanists. There and Mordenhold. As you can imagine, there's a bit more freedom outside of Vaeldon's capital. The arcanists at the Arcanum have a reputation for... ah, creative thought. If someone is studying necromancy and is open to helping us, that's where we'll find them."

"They're all lunatics," muttered Anne.

"You know the place?" the nameless woman asked the empath, sounding surprised.

"I do. There's a women's colony nearby which helps support the Arcanum. I... lived there, for a time. My mother brought me as a child and raised me there. Much of my early work, how I learned empathy, is thanks to the women's colony and, while I hate to admit it, the Arcanum."

"Interesting," remarked the nameless woman.

"Why did you leave?" wondered Raif.

Anne offered a wan smile. "I left because of Rew. I met him there, and we ran off together. Not like that, Zaine. We spent the next few years wandering Vaeldon before we found homes in Eastwatch. You know the rest."

"Not like that, huh? What were you doing in a women's colony, then?" Zaine asked Rew innocently. The mischievous twinkle in her eyes belied her intent, though.

"Ranger." The nameless woman laughed. "I wouldn't have thought!"

Rew rubbed the back of his hand over his mouth and didn't respond. It hadn't been like that. It hadn't been like that at all, but he didn't want to tell them the truth, so he let them think what they wanted to think. Anne, perhaps recalling the bloody night they'd first locked gazes, remained silent as well.

FOR THE FIRST TIME IN WHAT SEEMED MONTHS, REW FELT AT EASE. IN the back of his mind, he knew they were marching toward danger, and he knew that chances were they wouldn't be successful, but there, at that moment, he felt like he was home.

He was stalking through the forest, Zaine's bow in his grip, his eyes restlessly scanning the undulating grass in a clearing in front of him. It was half a league from their campsite, the farthest away from the others he'd been willing to go, even though the morning and the forest seemed peaceful enough.

A brace of fat rabbits hung from his side, enough to supplement their breakfast, but he was enjoying himself so he kept going. It'd been too long since he'd been alone in the forest, and he wasn't yet ready to break that spell.

The branches in the wood were bare in the tail of winter, but the grass in the clearing had come back and grown thick. Rew smiled, listening to the wind rustle the emerald blades. He was still as the birds called around him, and then, a deer stepped cautiously from the trees opposite of him, walked forward, and ducked its head, drinking from a tiny band of water hidden in the grass.

Rew glanced down at the arrow nocked on Zaine's bow. It was a straight, ash shaft topped by a sharp steel arrowhead. It was a surprisingly well-fashioned arrow, though he supposed Faevril had its share of hunters as well as fishermen.

Looking at the deer across the clearing, Rew couldn't have asked for a better shot, and for a moment, he pulled back the arrow, feeling the tension bend the bow. He sighted on the deer and breathed slowly. Then, he released the tension while keeping his grip on the arrow and lowered the bow. He watched for several more minutes until the deer drank its fill and meandered back amongst the trees.

Rew withdrew into the forest as well, moving silently, and crept back toward their camp. He smelled the woodsmoke from a quarter league away, and as he got closer, he detected the low murmur of conversation. If someone was out there looking for them, the party wouldn't be difficult to find. Then, Rew smelled freshly brewed coffee, and any thoughts about going without fires fled. Sometimes, the risk was worth it.

"Any luck?" Anne asked him as he appeared in their camp, startling Raif, who was supposed to be on watch.

Rew unhooked the brace of rabbits and laid them beside the fire. "Took a couple of them early, but it's quiet out there. Too close to civilization."

Anne poured a mug of coffee and nodded toward the fire. "I found enough quail eggs for us to share, though I couldn't get my hands on any of the birds. The rabbits are nice. It will be good to have something other than smoked fish to pair with the eggs. We've plenty of salt, and there's a patch of mushrooms a hundred paces east, if you want to go collect them for me. I can fry the mushrooms in the rabbit's fat. They ought to crisp up nicely."

Nodding, Rew headed back into the forest, sipping his coffee and looking for Anne's mushrooms. They had far to go and much to do, but for the moment, he was at peace.

THE ARCANUM AND THE WOMEN'S COLONY THAT SUPPORTED IT WERE situated north of Jabaan and along the southern boundary of a vast plain. The settlements were nestled along a string of hills. The women's colony clung to the side, and the spires of the Arcanum stabbed skyward from the top of the hills as if they wanted to become mountains. The arcanists loved their towers, maybe because they granted a better view of the surrounding area, but Rew thought more likely it was because they caught better wind to blow away the noxious fumes that sometimes resulted from both failed experiments and successful ones.

As the sprawling compound came into sight, Rew wondered who had built all of those towers. The arcanists themselves had a tendency to abhor manual labor unless it was directly related to some dangerous magical experiment, and the women in the colony certainly had no interest in constructing such impractical buildings.

Those women barely had any interest in providing their services to the arcanists at all, but the learned men, with fat purses from the king's coffers, paid far too much for the women to ignore the opportunity.

"The king funds all of this?" wondered Raif, observing the top of the hill where the Arcanum perched. Three dozen towers stuck up erratically from the lower stone buildings at their feet. There was a low wall surrounding it all, capped with a forest of black iron spikes. It hid much of the lower buildings except several large structures that had the blocky look of soldiers' barracks, though Rew knew those buildings were designed to house the sometimes-voluminous apparatus the scholars used to conduct their research. From at least one of those structures, slender curls of vibrant purple smoke drifted into the air.

Rew nodded his head. "Aye, it's all funded by the king. He, of course, gets the first look at any research they produce. If it's good, he'll keep it for himself. If it's not, they're allowed to share it with the kingdom, though realistically, that just means with all of the arcanists scattered around Vaeldon in the nobles' courts. No one else has time to read all of that feverish scribbling."

A quarter league from the Arcanum, halfway up the hill it crowned, sat a neat-looking village comprised of hundreds of small cottages and dormitories. It was poised close enough to the Arcanum to make travel between them easy, but far enough below that it would be out of the blast radius of any experiments gone awry.

Farther below the colony and hidden by the surrounding folds of land, at the base of the hill, were twin towers and a massive gate that guarded the path to the Arcanum. The paired forts looked like nosy siblings, thought Rew. They were fashioned of dark stone, nearly black, and were spanned by a gate that would be difficult to storm even with several hundred men and a battering ram. It would be far easier to simply walk around the towers, but Rew supposed the fort had been placed there as much for the message it sent as the practical defensive nature of the structure. The towers and gate were meant to show the Arcanum was protected by the king, and anyone who went around them to attack the scholars faced the consequences of crossing Vaisius Morden.

"Do you think we'll be able to talk our way inside?" asked Raif, looking at the dark stone of the fort. "Are we in the Western or the Northern Province? If it's Calb's men, they may not yet know—"

"These are king's men, lad, and as long as the king hasn't given instructions to arrest us on sight, we'll have no problem at the gate," replied Rew. He began fishing around in his pouch for his documentation. "No king's man will deny the passage of a ranger."

"What was that you said?" asked Raif, suddenly turning to Rew. "Instructions to arrest us?"

"Cinda did raise thousands of corpses and marched them out of the king's crypt," reminded Rew, "and then we killed one of the king's sons. I'm not sure if there's a law specifically codified to forbid the raising of corpses, but surely killing a prince is not legal."

Raif blanched.

"We're better off finding out now if the king has put a price on our heads," claimed Rew. He gestured to the twin keeps in front of them. "There are certainly more men in there than I'm interested in fighting, but it's better than facing the king himself, eh? If something happens, shout if you see anyone headed toward the

Arcanum. They have portal stones to Mordenhold and elsewhere, and that's our true worry."

"This is seeming like a worse and worse idea," mentioned Zaine.

"We all agreed that Cinda needs to learn, and where else but the Arcanum? We're running out of friendly necromancers to recruit."

REW FELT THE TENSION RISING AROUND HIM AS THEY WALKED CLOSER to the paired forts, but it was only relief he felt rush through his own body when they finally made it in front of the imposing structures and saw the two men standing in the open gate that led between the stone towers.

Anne let out a wordless cry of glee and ran forward, scooping one of the two men in her arms, hugging him tight enough his eyes seemed to bulge out. Then, she shoved him away, as if looking him up and down as if to check for injuries or see how tall he'd grown. Over his objections, she granted the second man the same treatment.

"Twins," murmured the nameless woman, watching the display curiously.

"Ranger, are those…" began Cinda.

"Aye," confirmed Rew. He strode forward and grasped the first man's forearm, giving it a firm pump. "Good to see you."

The second man, free of Anne's clutches, leaned forward and slapped Rew on the shoulder. "Unexpected, but good."

Rew gripped that man's forearm as well and replied, "Unexpected. That goes for both of us. What are you doing in the west?"

"Are you not going to… hug or something?" interjected Anne.

The three men turned to her, shifting uncomfortably. The movement brought with it the rustle of steel, and Rew noticed that beneath black tunics, the two men were wearing dark gray chainmail.

"You're soldiers now?"

The first man turned, displaying a crimson badge of rank on his shoulder. "Captains."

"Co-captains," added the second man, grinning. "I don't think this garrison has ever had co-captains before, but we told them we operate as a team and would rather stay in Eastwatch if they thought to split us up."

"We'd have rather stayed in Eastwatch regardless," murmured the first man quietly, "but when the king asks, you go. It didn't feel much like asking, if you know what I mean. We spent what leverage we had gaining a posting together and were glad they listened to that small demand."

The two men, twins, were quiet for a moment.

Finally, the first asked, "You heard about Vyar?"

"I did," said Rew. He paused then asked, "What are they saying about him?"

"Said he ran afoul of the king…" murmured the second man, studying Rew's reaction. "Tensions were high, and then he was killed. The story is that no one knows what happened to the body, which means everyone can guess what happened to the body. The rangers had already been muttering amongst ourselves. That didn't help, and the king must have felt the heat rising. He shook things up, and… well, we're here, now."

"Ang and Vurcell," burst Cinda. "The two brothers from East-watch! I knew I recognized you. The armor and tabard threw me, but you haven't changed a bit otherwise."

"Aye, lass," said Ang. He tapped his chest and said his name then indicated his brother.

"You can tell them apart from their weapons," said Anne.

"Other ways as well," declared Vurcell, winking at the empath.

"My girls back at the inn told me," remarked Anne drolly. "I don't think we need to get into that, do we?"

The twins grinned and nodded. The nameless woman looked interested.

Ang wore a swordstaff slung across his back. It was the height of a man, a third of its length sharp steel, the rest a wooden haft. Vurcell carried a falchion on his side. Well made, but no frills or ornamentation. Both twins had glossy black hair bound into buns atop their heads, and they looked as comfortable in the black livery and armor of the king's legion as they had in the soft brown and gray of the king's rangers.

Ang tilted his head, studying Cinda, then drawled, "You, on the other hand, have changed quite a bit. You've the eyes to match those robes."

Ang glanced at Rew, suddenly less at ease than he had been before.

Vurcell spoke up for the both of them. "It appears we need to talk."

"We do," agreed Rew. "About Vyar. About… a lot. Best if it's just us, you understand? Not all of the king's men will appreciate what I have to say, and I'd rather they not get a look at our faces up close."

"It's never easy with you, is it?"

"Blessed Mother, I've missed you two," cried Anne. "I can't tell you what it's been like traveling with this man and without another soul to complain to."

Smirking, the twins turned and led the party through a narrow stone arch and into one of the two towers. Rew and the others followed, the ranger privately grousing about Anne's last comment. No one to complain to? From what he remembered of their journey, she'd certainly had no problem with that…

Ang took them up several flights of stairs and down a bare hallway to a large room which appeared to be the twins' office. There was little in the way of decorations, but it had two small desks with chairs beside them and narrow windows looking up at the women's colony and the Arcanum beyond. There was a long, ancient table which Ang explained was where the officers took their meals and conducted meetings, though there was little to discuss except training, organizing provisions, and keeping the men from visiting the women's colony and bothering the residents at night.

"Not many dignitaries here," said Vurcell, apologizing for the utilitarian furnishings. "There are portal stones in the Arcanum, and most arrivals from Mordenhold or the provincial capitals stay up there when they visit. Since we've been here, we've only seen the Lieutenant General twice, and one of those times was when he dropped us off. We appreciate our independence, but he's not the leader you are, Rew."

"Was. The leader I was," corrected Rew.

Vurcell shrugged. "Times are changing, but if you ask, we'll follow."

"How did you end up getting posted here?" wondered Rew, ignoring the comment and taking a seat at the table opposite his two former rangers.

"When Blythe received your letter in the post, she sent to Mordenhold requesting replacements for you and… and for Tate and Jon," said Ang, leaning back in his chair and rubbing his eyes before continuing. "We got the replacements and a bit more. Blythe was named Senior Ranger, and they gave her half a dozen fresh recruits yanked from the king's forces. Vurcell and I were taken to Mordenhold and told we were joining the king's army. It wasn't framed as a question. As I said, we pressured them to post us together, and that was that. I'd have rather have stayed in Eastwatch, but it's quiet enough here. Better than remaining in Mordenhold, which is where they're keeping most of the rangers at the moment until they figure out new assignments."

"Most of the rangers? New assignments?"

"Been a lot going on, Rew. The rangers are talking. The king's trying to tamp it down without causing too much obvious disruption."

"Why'd they put you here?" wondered Rew.

"Don't think we deserve the captain's shield?" asked Vurcell with a wink.

"I know you deserve it, but the Arcanum? No one's attacked

this place in centuries. No one's attacked it ever, I guess. There's no threat of Dark Kind, nothing. It's a waste of your skill."

"A different kind of skill," responded Ang, touching the side of his nose. "Things have been strange up at the Arcanum. You know we've a sensitivity."

"Part of why I recruited you," responded Rew, frowning. Things had been strange?

"They had to put us somewhere," added Vurcell. "We'd been sent to Mordenhold first, and it was getting uncomfortable there. We weren't sticking our noses out too far, you understand, but the other rangers had questions, and we gave honest answers. They were upset about Vyar. Thought you ought to be his natural replacement. No one could find you, but there were rumors. We were told to keep quiet, to not comment, but that only made everyone more curious. We tried to walk a straight line and didn't do anything leadership could complain about, but we were becoming a focus of dissent. The king didn't want more martyrs, but he didn't want us hanging around any longer, either."

"Tell me more about this," asked Rew. "The rangers are discontent?"

Despite sharing a commander, the men and women in the king's rangers were a loose collection of individuals more than they were a cohesive team. They were scattered across the kingdom, faced different challenges, and held different responsibilities. Most of the time they had no contact with each other. When they did, it was brief and usually only at some ceremony or another. The only things they had in common were incredible skill and the courage to face whatever the world threw at them. In the spoken histories they shared when they did meet each other, there'd been other times they'd been… discontent. It had never ended well.

"More and more often, the rangers have been asked to do things they aren't comfortable with," explained Ang. "We were lucky in the east because of you, I suppose. Elsewhere… they've been asked to move against political enemies, and their warnings about rising threats of the Dark Kind and other dangers are being ignored. It's the worst it's been in two hundred years, according to some. The rangers started talking months ago. In response, Vaisius Morden has been moving us around like pieces on a Kings and Queens board. He's taken rangers out of the field and moved us to remote postings. He put a few people behind desks. You can guess how everyone felt about that. It's not the same as when we began. I worry it's the end of us, truly. For some, Rew, that can't come soon enough."

Frowning, Rew scratched his beard. That sort of talk was dangerous. "If the king is trying to break up the rangers, and you've been the focus of some of it, I'm surprised he agreed to let you two stay together."

"Pfah, we haven't been the focus of anything. You've been the focus, Rew, but they all think we know what you've been up to," responded Ang. "Besides, there's a bit of a unique situation here. There is more to the posting than just trying to shuffle us out of sight, though I can't think they were sad about that bit."

Vurcell nodded his head toward the window that overlooked the Arcanum. "Told you it's been strange up there. Soldiers have gone missing. The king's own legion, Rew, vanished inside of those walls. The previous captain went inside to investigate, and now, he's gone too."

Rew blinked at the former ranger. "The king..."

"I imagine the king's aware of what's happening in there, though he hasn't shared that with us. No, we're here to monitor the situation and let 'em know back in Mordenhold if anything changes. Our sensitivity, you see. That's what drove us out of Mordenhold and into Eastwatch all those years ago in the first place. Couldn't stand the feel of the capital, like spiders crawling over our backs every time some spellcaster in the creche started flinging spells. During this last stretch in Mordenhold, it was worse. The king's arcanists were constantly fiddling with magic they didn't understand and couldn't control. Between that and everything else going on with the rangers, we were ready to leave, one way or the other. This posting was a compromise. King got the use of our sensitivity, and we didn't have to worry about executions for deserting."

"It's not the wilderness," said Vurcell. "The quiet there was like a balm on our souls, but this place isn't Mordenhold, either. It worked out, in a way."

"So... you're watching and waiting?"

The twins nodded simultaneously.

"The king's eyes, eh," said Rew.

"Come on now," protested Ang. "What else were we supposed to do? We're in the king's service still, and far from retirement. There's only one way out of that contract. With the others constantly asking us questions, I've no doubt we would have ended up dangling sooner or later. Besides, it's not like we're being asked to do the things the others are being asked to do."

"The things you used to do," added Vurcell pointedly.

Rew grunted and cleared his throat. "So, ah, what is going on up there?"

Ang pursed his lips and folded his arms over his chest. "We haven't been inside the compound. Our instructions have been to monitor from afar. There's a darkness over that place that never brightens. I don't know what exactly they're doing, but it's not high magic. Not like we know it. It's something different, something I haven't felt before. Necromantic... but different."

"And all the king is doing is having you watch the place?"

Shrugging, the former ranger responded, "Aye, as far as we can tell. He knows something is happening up there, or we wouldn't have been stationed in this place, but aside from bringing us here, I don't think he's done anything about it. Maybe he's too busy with the Investiture. We were told to report if that sense of darkness leaves the compound or swells for more than an hour or two. It... comes in bursts. Sometimes, nothing for days, but then there'll be a time with quarter-hour surges. It's gotta be some experiment they're conducting that flares enough we can feel it all the way down here."

"How do you report back?"

Vurcell stood and moved to his desk where he pointed to a small mirror resting on a stand. "It's enchanted, a paired set with one in Mordenhold. Once a week, it flickers to life, and if necessary we can light it up the other way and talk to whoever is on that side. We haven't had to use it except for the scheduled visits, but we've only been here a month."

Rew grunted. He stood and walked to the window, peering up at the Arcanum in the distance. "It's not high magic you feel?"

"It's got the flavor, but it's off," answered Ang. "Like biting into a piece of spoiled meat."

"It's curious the king lost most of a company up there and hasn't sent anyone to investigate."

Vurcell laughed. "We haven't argued about that. They told us to stay away, so we'll stay away and be happy doing it. Whatever is going on up there isn't natural."

Rew, still looking at the Arcanum, cracked his knuckles. "Well, no one's told me to stay away."

The twins shared a look then asked, "Are you sure?"

"We don't have much of a choice," replied Rew. "We need help, and I don't know where else to get it. It's worth the gamble to go inside."

"Rew," said Anne, shaking her head. "Instead of smashing our way in like drunken louts, why don't we go see the women first? Whatever is happening in the Arcanum, they'll know about it. If we go in, let's go in with eyes open."

Rew rubbed his mouth with the back of his hand. "Ah…"

"I'll talk to her," assured Anne.

"Talk to who?" asked Zaine. "Is anyone else as confused as I am?"

"Mother Solomon," said Anne. "Last time he visited the colony… Well, Rew killed her predecessor."

"Oh," murmured Zaine.

Vurcell cleared his throat then mentioned, "We've told our story, but I'd like to hear yours. Last we heard anything from you,

Rew, you were still on the run with the children, which doesn't seem to have changed, but we heard the commandant was chasing you personally, that he'd gotten involved in the Investiture, and now he's dead. We heard what happened in Spinesend, and rumors are flying about Carff and Jabaan. The king and his advisors haven't said anything officially, but to the rangers who knew you before Eastwatch, all those sound like your work. Did you kill Vyar? Did you... Rew, I'll just come out and ask. Are you a part of the Investiture?"

Rew strode toward his pack and removed a leather-wrapped bundle. He placed it on the table and looked between the twins before unwrapping the package. Ang and Vurcell stared open-mouthed at the two enchanted falchions.

"We've got a lot of ground to cover," said Rew. "I don't suppose you keep any ale around here?"

Chapter Nine

The last time he'd seen Mother Solomon, her face had been a visage of horror. She'd been shocked and terrified at what he'd done. She was a decade older now, and only echoes of that horror showed in her eyes when she saw him. The decade had softened her stare, but the rest of her was as hard as always. She still had the same steel-colored hair twisted into a tight bun, and he imagined she hadn't let it down since he last saw her. Her skin was kissed by the heat of the sun, wrinkled around her lips where she frequently pursed them. Perhaps those furrows were a little deeper? Her back was as straight as an ice sickle, and the hands clutched in front of her still looked strong.

She was toughened by the labor of the colony, but when Rew held her gaze, he saw lingering pain. It was holding that hurt which had softened her. Her pain was her own burden, and she had carried it before Rew came into her life, but he had to acknowledge he'd added his share to the weight on her shoulders.

She turned from him and blinked slowly. She asked, "You want to go into the Arcanum?"

"We do," confirmed Anne.

Mutely, Mother Solomon shook her head. Unconsciously, her

gaze drifted to the northern wall, where a quarter league beyond was the Arcanum. She shuddered.

Anne frowned. "In my time, the Arcanum was not a place to fear."

"Aye, but that was a different time. For years now, the Arcanum has been… odd. The experiments have gotten darker."

Crossing her arms over her chest, Anne arched an eyebrow and commented, "I wouldn't be here today if I didn't know how to step around the explosions and fumes those men release."

"Like all men release," quipped Zaine.

Anne scowled at the thief and might have been fighting to hide a smile, but Mother Solomon leaned forward and pinned Zaine with her gaze.

"It's not a matter for jesting, girl. What goes on in there… I heard you know the new captains down at the fort? Surely they told you about the missing soldiers? Some of my women have gone missing as well. Ever since that man from the east, Arcanist Salwart, began his—"

"Arcanist Salwart?" burst Anne, letting her hands drop to her side and shooting a quick look at Rew. "Did you say Salwart?"

"You know him as well?" queried Mother Solomon, frowning. She sat back, suddenly appearing frightened. "We have a history, and I owe you, but Anne, in the Mother's eye, there are unforgivable sins. That man—"

"We know of him," clarified Anne. "I've never met him and wouldn't recognize his face if I saw it. We're not his friends, and we will not be."

"What is Arcanist Salwart doing here?" asked Rew. "He was assigned to Duke Eeron in Spinesend and was involved in a terrible conspiracy. I'd never heard of him until several months ago, but it seems he's been busy since then."

Mother Solomon hugged herself as if trying to stay warm. "He's been showing up here for about four years, if I recall correctly. At first, I thought he was quirky like the rest of them, if a bit more demanding. Arcanists get like that in their later years, but then he began requesting women—girls—and when some of them did not return, I realized it was not for the usual reason."

"The usual reason?"

Mother Solomon snorted. "Aye, the usual reason. This is a place for women who, for whatever reason, no longer want to be within the confines of Vaeldon's society. Sometimes, it's because they prefer a simpler life. More often, they're running from something. We, and the king's men, keep them safe. They never have to fear harassment from a man while they are here, but some of the women aren't entirely done with men. They may want company for a night, or they may want a more permanent arrangement. It's natural. It's going to happen whether or not I approve, so I facilitate. Matchmaking, they'd call it in the noble's courts. No one is forced, but if that's what the woman wants... The arcanists, of course, are like all men."

Shifting in her padded chair, the older woman continued, "In truth, most of the arcanists are not bad men, they are just distracted and reckless. They spare little thought to the women here except when they need something or they're aroused. I personally don't appreciate such a base, transactional relationship, but some of the women do. Who am I to judge? Arcanist Salwart was different. When he first inquired, I wrote him to say we were not a brothel, and our women aren't here to lay with a visitor at his whim. He came to see me in person the next day and said that he wasn't going to sleep with the women. He needed them as assistants in his lab, he told me. It's traditional for younger men, arcanists in training, to serve that purpose, and I told him as much. He claimed his experiments required a woman and that he would make it worth their while. He badgered me until I agreed to ask if anyone was willing. Some were. He was offering gold... I saw them over the next months when I was in the Arcanum, and they seemed like different people. Then, I never saw them again."

"Years before the king's soldiers went missing," murmured Rew, rubbing his hand over his head, thinking he needed a shave.

"I reported the missing women to the old captain of the king's legion here, but he did nothing," continued Mother Solomon, her voice bitter. "I don't have any vested authority from the king, but I did what I could to keep my women from entering the Arcanum, and most listened. We lost some more over the years, but as I was told, we've always lost some. Things changed again a few months ago. All but a few of us were barred from entering the Arcanum, which was fine by me. I told you, the experiments were growing darker up there."

"Darker," mused Rew. He glanced at Ang and Vurcell who were standing behind them in a corner. He raised an eyebrow.

Ang shrugged.

Her eyes on the captains of the guard as well, Mother Solomon continued, "But then, half a company of the king's legion went inside and never returned. The king has to know what is occurring but does nothing. I cannot decide if that gives me comfort or makes it worse."

"Worse," said Anne. She turned to Rew. "These dark experiments, do you think…"

He nodded. "Aye, but four years back? Cin—ah, she was no more than a girl then, still in her father's home. Could Salwart have been plotting since then?"

Anne shrugged. "Maybe the experiments he was conducting here led him to the east."

Raif, who had been silent up until that point, cleared his throat and asked Mother Solomon, "Ah, can you not write to the king? Or use the mirrors the captains have down in the fort? Surely if someone in Mordenhold understands… Have you even tried?"

Mother Solomon turned to Rew and remarked, "The king's attention on this place has never been benign. There are those who recall the last time we called to our liege. It will not happen again. Not in my lifetime."

"I-I don't understand," stammered Cinda. "Was Salwart running experiments to… To serve the prince, as we suspect? If he, ah, if he was attempting what we suspect of him, then I believe the king would oppose his… research."

Mother Solomon's eyes darted between them, clearly under-standing Cinda was speaking around her point but not knowing what the girl was getting at. The older woman looked curious, but she didn't pry. She'd been around the arcanists enough to know that there were some secrets she was better off never learning.

"There's only one way to find out," said Rew. He frowned. "If we should find out, that is."

The Arcanum being sealed from visitors was an unexpected complication. He'd intended to find an arcanist who studied necromancy and to beseech their help in training Cinda. Even if they had no magical talent, the arcanists would be familiar with the various spells which could be cast, and they would be a better guide than no guide at all. There were few talented necromancers in the kingdom, so going to the Arcanum had seemed a better option than wandering the countryside looking for people wearing crimson robes.

For the arcanists, the chance to closely observe a talent like Cinda would be all the encouragement they needed. It's not like the king was going to agree to them watching his foul casting. Rew had hoped it would work. He'd thought it would work.

But just because the place was closed, did that mean they should turn away? They might not find help for Cinda inside, but if they found Arcanist Salwart or what he was working on... The man had been in the employ of Heindaw, and he'd been behind the plot against Baron Fedgley. Salwart had been involved from the start—King's Sake, all of it might have started just up the hill from them. Rew didn't think they could turn away from the opportunity to question the man about both the plot against the Fedgleys and anything they could learn about Heindaw's current situation. Information on either topic could be invaluable.

"If we go in, how do we do it?" asked Anne, apparently thinking along the same lines as Rew.

Mother Solomon frowned. "You don't. You shouldn't, at least."

"We need to."

"Lass, I don't remember you being so bullheaded when you lived here."

"Then you don't remember me well," retorted the empath.

"It's dangerous to—"

"What do you remember of my time here?" demanded Anne.

Mother Solomon glanced at Rew.

Anne gave her a bitter smile. "Before that."

Clearing her throat uncomfortably, Mother Solomon looked down at her hands.

"You and your predecessor pressed me to work healing the injured and the sick of this place," reminded Anne. "I was only eight winters, the first time. I took the pain of this entire colony for a decade. My childhood was spent absorbing the agony of you and the rest so that no one else had to feel. I felt it all. After that, do you think I'm scared of getting hurt?"

Mother Solomon's hands clasped tighter together, but she did not respond.

"And then you assigned me to those upstarts, those rebels against the king." Anne sat forward and jabbed her finger at the older woman. "I was barely more than a girl, left alone in a sea of hundreds of men. You claim to protect women? What about me when I was a girl? What do you think would have happened to me if I wasn't so valuable to those men? Pfah. Instead, all that was required was sharing their agony as the king crushed them under his boot. I wonder if the king knows you supported the uprising?"

Mother Solomon bolted upright and hissed, "Quiet! That was a long time ago, and things have changed. I didn't... I don't—"

"I felt a thousand beatings, accidents, assaults, and deaths when I was a child. I didn't have a choice. You put that on me."

"We needed you," whispered Mother Solomon.

"And I need you now," declared Anne. "This won't balance the ledger. That can't be done, but it's something."

The older woman, evidently unable to meet Anne's look, turned to the back corner where Ang and Vurcell were sitting. She flinched.

Ang raised a hand and said, "Don't mind us."

Anne glanced at the two captains of the king's guard and grinned. Then stiffening her expression, she turned back to Mother Solomon. "When I was younger, when you forced me to join the rebellion, I was not strong enough or confident enough in myself to say no. I went along with your demands despite what it cost me."

"It wasn't like... We weren't a part of it. We just... They needed healing and a place to hide. Food..."

"What was it like?" questioned Vurcell. He leaned forward, his armor rustling and drawing Mother Solomon's eyes to his black tabard.

Shushing him, Anne continued, now addressing her comments to the rest of the group, "I had little choice in the matter. Once I knew about it, it was go along, or they'd kill me. I went along, if only for a brief period. Rebellion against the king is a dangerous art. They lasted two seasons before they were snuffed out. I can't imagine it caused much of a stir in Mordenhold, and I doubt there was even a ripple in the rest of the kingdom. Still, a rebellion must be dealt with. Someone has to pay, and the king's black legion was marching to the colony to collect the price. That's when I met Rew. Both the colony and I were spared, but someone had to pay. Baroness Solomon became Mother Solomon that night, following the death of our previous leader. Levies were raised, there was a probation which lasted years. I was forced to flee the only home I'd known. Everyone paid some price, except for her."

"And now you'll have your revenge," cried Mother Solomon, her eyes darting between Rew and his former rangers, Ang and Vurcell. "Under the guise of asking for my help, you've sought my blood."

Anne shook her head. "I don't want your blood. I'm merely setting the terms for us to bargain. You're going to give us what we want, and in exchange, these men will not chop your head off."

"Lass, you're a fool," cried Mother Solomon, standing from

her chair and backing away from Ang and Vurcell. "You've implicated yourself as thoroughly as you have I. You marched with the rebellion! You aided them with your healing! You think the king will forgive either of us?"

"The king isn't here."

"Those two are king's men."

"They wear the black of the king's legion, but they are mine, my friends, my family. That's a bond that will not be broken. Not by you. Not by Vaisius Morden. We saw signs of life inside of the Arcanum. People are still there, and they have to eat. Someone from the colony is going up there. Get us inside, and do it with a guide who knows their way around."

Caught between a glare at Anne and hooded looks of fear at Rew and his former rangers, Mother Solomon nodded curtly. She rasped, "There is a woman, but I don't know if she'll help you. I cannot speak for her, but I will arrange for you to meet. Come here tomorrow morning shortly after dawn."

With little else to discuss, they all stood and left.

On the way back to the fort, Ang slung an arm over Anne's shoulder. "Rebelled against the king, did you?"

"It wasn't much of a rebellion, and it was never going to work. Live and learn, and do it better the next time, eh?"

"The next time?" asked Vurcell, taking her other side. "Is there a little more you want to add to your story from earlier? What's Rew up to that he isn't telling us about?"

Rew coughed into his fist. "It's not your fight, and it's dangerous."

Ang laughed. "We're members of the king's rangers, Rew. If something has got to be done about the old man, then we're the ones who ought to do it."

"It's very dangerous," added Rew. "It's… it's beyond our skill, both your skill and mine."

Vurcell looked over his shoulder at Cinda. "I see. You think she—"

"Not here, not now," interrupted Rew. "Some things are dangerous to discuss even away from others and out in the open."

"Rew, we want to help," said Ang. "Not just us, but the other rangers, too. They all know the stories, even if the rest of the kingdom has forgotten them. We know what price Vaeldon pays for Morden's rule. You cannot do this alone. Let us walk this path beside you."

Rew scratched his beard. He glanced between the twins. They were earnest, and he knew they understood what they were offering—risking—but could he accept?

"You're going to take help from the children but not us?" barked Ang. "Blessed Mother, Rew, you're strange. Tell us how we can help, or we're going to follow you like motherless ducklings until you do."

"LUCIA," MURMURED ANNE.

They were standing upon the wide front porch of a humble cottage. The awning that covered the porch was as large as the roof that covered the rest of the building. The cottage had an impressive view, looking over the fort below and across the broad expanse of the plains. The sides of the porch were lined with heavy wooden troughs filled with herbs and flowers. It was like the backyard of the apothecary's cottage in Spinesend, thought Rew, though the woman in front of them didn't have any of the tenderness he'd seen in the apothecary. It was like the empathy had been boiled off of her.

"Anne," responded the woman, inclining her head slightly, her expression unchanging. Rew didn't think the woman was pleased to see Anne on her porch, but she was too careful to show it. Instead, she remarked flatly, "I didn't think I'd ever see you again."

"I didn't believe I'd ever return," replied Anne. "I didn't want to return, but here I am. We have need of your help. Mother Solomon says you still enter the Arcanum?"

"You want inside?"

Anne nodded.

The woman scowled and shook her head, her glossy black hair shimmering with the motion. She wore a set of coal gray robes, like those worn by spellcasters, except in the king's drab colors instead of those worn to proclaim a particular form of magic. She was tall and thin and had the look of a person who was rarely pleased. "I encourage you to forget going into the Arcanum. You will not like what you find."

"You work for the king?" asked Rew. "What, ah, what capacity do you serve him in?"

The woman glanced at Rew and then turned back to Anne. "You should leave this place. Go to wherever you've been hiding and stay there."

"She works for the king," said Anne, speaking to Rew but her eyes still on the other woman. "She came here shortly after the rebellion, shortly before you, Rew. She's the king's eyes and ears in this place."

Lucia snorted then declared, "You're better off not knowing what is happening within that compound. The king knows, which should be good enough for you. Tell them, Captain."

"I don't actually know what's going on in there," admitted Ang. "We were told to stay away."

"As you should."

"We're not asking," said Anne.

Lucia laughed. "You can threaten Mother Solomon, but you cannot threaten me."

"Rew," said Anne, turning to the ranger. "After you came here the last time, in the days that followed, Lucia was blamed for what happened to the previous Mother. Some of the women were quite cross with her and expressed it physically. Those women were escorted to Mordenhold and never heard from again, and Lucia almost died. It was my healing that saved her and my word that protected her after that. You and I left before Lucia had the chance to thank me."

"Hear me now, then," said Lucia. "This is my thanks to you. I advise you to avoid the Arcanum. You will regret going there."

"Perhaps. You are obligated to me, though, and we need to get inside."

Lucia grunted, shaking her head. "I am obligated to the king as well."

"Was it guilt that kept you here? I thought someone of your talent would have moved on now, found a more prestigious posting. You wanted to die, didn't you, when I saved you? Payment for the suffering you caused with your arrival."

"I am sorry, Anne, but—" The woman snapped her mouth shut.

Rew blinked at her then turned. The children, accompanied by Vurcell and the nameless woman, had just rounded the corner of Lucia's cottage. The former ranger was giving a tour of the colony, though there was little to see.

"They're with you?" asked Lucia.

Anne nodded.

Sighing, the gray-clad woman said, "One last warning, because I am obligated to you—you should turn from this, but if you insist, I will accompany you. Not all of you, though. Too many and… there are things inside of the Arcanum, now. It is unwise to enter with too many people. It's still dangerous with just a few, but more than a few and it will mean our lives."

"I'll stay behind," said Zaine quickly, walking up to the foot of the porch, evidently having overheard Lucia's comments.

Rew snorted then looked around the group. "Ang, Vurcell, your place is out here. You've work to do, like we talked about. Raif, stay with Zaine."

"Hold on—" began the fighter.

"The other girl?" interrupted Lucia.

Rew frowned at the grey-clad woman. "She'll go."

"Very well."

"Ranger, if it's dangerous inside..." said Raif, trying again.

"When the twins have done what we've discussed, I want you to train with them. There are some skills they can share with you which I haven't found time to. Besides, Lucia seems to think the more people we bring, the more dangerous it will be. You're helping protect your sister by staying behind."

Raif looked skeptical, but Cinda gave him a nod, and with Zaine's encouragement, he agreed to return to the fort.

"I'll stay as well," said the nameless woman.

Rew shook his head. "No, we need you to come with us."

She frowned at him, but he remained firm. He hoped she thought he wanted her expertise on the Cursed Father, but the truth was they simply could not trust the woman. If she was working with Heindaw, then Rew wasn't going to let her slip away and alert the prince of what they were finding, and whatever they did find, Rew wanted to see the woman's reaction to it. He didn't know if she was complicit in the prince's plans, but he hoped to find out.

Lucia eyed the nameless woman silently. Rew had expected an objection, but it didn't come. Anne looked to Rew, and he opened his mouth to tell her to stay as well.

"You should come," said Lucia, staring at Anne. "We might need you."

Cringing, the empath nodded.

Lucia declared it was best to go right away, if they were set on doing it. Rew shrugged, so she led them from the women's colony up the hill toward the looming walls and towers of the Arcanum. The jagged thrusts of stone stood out like teeth when looked at from below. Rew swallowed and kept following the gray-clad woman, hoping it was just his imagination granting the place such an ominous aspect.

The nameless woman marched beside Lucia, and Rew studied both of their backs as they hiked the quarter league it took to come to the rambling walls of the Arcanum. The two women wore their attire like badges of allegiance, but allegiance to what?

Rew wished he had time to conference with Anne, to learn what she knew of Lucia, but since they met the woman, there'd been no chance to break away and speak out of earshot.

Rew sighed. He yearned for the simplicity of facing his brothers with his longsword in hand, like when he'd tried to strike at Valchon in Carff or when he'd fought Calb in Jabaan. He needed that—unambiguous combat, simplicity. As they stood before a small entrance into the side of the Arcanum's sprawling compound, he realized he would not have that, not here.

The wall around the Arcanum was built of large blocks of granite quarried somewhere in the mountains beyond. It was sturdy, but it had no battlement, and none of the normal defensive features of a serious fortress. The wall was built to keep out stray travelers who might have wanted a peek, not to withstand a siege. It seemed to have grown organically, crawling over the hills and cutting through the foot of the mountain as the Arcanum had expanded within its confines. Towers and halls, storerooms and workshops sprouted randomly like mushrooms after a storm. They'd grown as needed, with little planning, and had gnawed across whatever space the arcanists required. With no significant bodies of water and nothing but open plains beneath it, the Arcanum could spread unbound.

Rew frowned. Why was there no water nearby? Who built a city away from fresh water? He'd never considered it, but why was the Arcanum perched on the far fringe of the kingdom? It was as remote as Eastwatch, except outside Eastwatch, there was nothing but wilderness. Eastwatch had no visitors from the capital. No one ever had a reason to go there, but the Arcanum was a vital piece of Vaisius Morden's power base. The arcanists there developed the tools and weapons he used to rule. Why was it so far away? It was as if it'd been placed there to make it difficult to visit.

Rew had little time to wonder as Lucia paused in front of a blank steel door. It was set discreetly in the wall, only a slender dirt path through the grass giving away its presence. She removed a short iron club from her belt and rapped sharply on the steel door. She repeated the sequence, and Rew realized it was a code.

In moments, he heard a scrape of steel, and the door swung outward. In the entrance was a man clad in the black tabard of the king's legions. He had a short sword on his belt and clutched a gleaming, black steel crossbow. His face was covered by a sturdy helm, and in the shadows of the doorway and the armor, Rew could not see the man's eyes.

The ranger was taken aback. Ang and Vurcell had told him that none of their men were stationed within the Arcanum. No one from their command had ventured inside of the place for a month. Who was this man? Was it one of the missing soldiers?

After evidently recognizing Lucia, the guard wordlessly stepped out of the way. The woman led them inside of the Arcanum. Then, the guard slammed the steel door and turned a crank, locking it. Rew glanced behind them as they walked through a tunnel in the wall and saw the silent guard facing the inside of the steel door, standing motionless in the dark. Rew shuddered. They'd expected it, but now, he could feel it. Something was wrong.

He regretted not insisting either Ang or Vurcell accompany them, but both of the twins had tasks to do back at the fort—work for the king and work for Rew.

The tunnel through the wall was thick with shadow. There was no light except for the opening at the far end. The guard evidently spent his entire shift in that darkness. Why didn't he come out on the street where he could still hear the clang of Lucia's club but enjoy the light of the sun?

The tunnel was longer than Rew would have guessed, looking at the wall from the outside of the Arcanum. It was darker as well until, in the palm of Cinda's hand, a pale white-green glow emanated, casting its light in front of them. Even her funeral fire seemed wan inside the tunnel.

Lucia eyed Cinda but did not comment. She led them out onto a broad, dirt street. It was as wide as one might expect to find in a medium-sized town, but instead of hard-packed soil or mud, the way was filled with grass that grew tall beside the buildings, and only a small strip was worn bare in the center from the irregular passage of feet.

The street twisted languidly, curving around buildings and towers, flowing naturally deeper into the compound. The thrusting towers had been raised with little concern as to what was around them, simply stabbing upward where they were to suit the esoteric needs of the arcanists. In the distance, Rew saw the one tower which leaked tattered purple smoke, and he heard a rumbling nearby coming from some contraption hidden within a building. And that was all. There were no people on the streets, no one peeking out of the nearby windows. No animal sounds, not even birds. There was also no damage that he could see to the place, no bodies in the streets or charred rooftops which indicated an attack. The Arcanum was just empty. It was like the place had been abandoned.

But that wasn't it either because they'd seen the guard at the door, and Lucia regularly came to visit to keep an eye on someone. Mother Solomon said she had other women bringing food and supplies periodically. To whom?

Rew stepped toward Lucia. "Where are the people?"

"Gone," she declared. "I warned you. You shouldn't have come here."

"We had to," retorted Anne.

Shrugging and giving the empath a sour look, Lucia turned to Cinda. "Allow me to guess why. This is the girl responsible for Jabaan?"

Rew coughed, suddenly regretting allowing one of the king's spies to lead them.

"Pfah, you didn't think word of that event would spread like wild fire? Blessed Mother, the girl is wearing the robes of a necromancer. Do you take me for a complete fool? I knew what you wanted the moment I saw her."

"You're right," said Cinda, her voice cutting like a knife. "I was responsible for Jabaan. It... We want to make sure that does not happen again. We thought that here, in the Arcanum, there may be someone who can help me... help us, that is."

"There's no one here, lass," said Lucia, some of the ice melting from her tone. "The arcanists who could have helped you are gone. Dead. You will not find what you are looking for."

"Someone is here," said Cinda, pointing up toward the tower where the purple smoke spilled out. "Perhaps they are not who we came for, but—"

"That is not someone you want to see," declared Lucia. She crossed her arms over her chest and said, "There is something you can see, a place I can take you. You may... learn something there about yourself, about what you're capable of, and about what happened to the Arcanum. Some things are better left unknown, but you are here, and this place has some of your answers."

"Let's get on with it," said Rew, tapping his foot impatiently.

Lucia continued, "Anne, I will take you, but not because you helped me in the past. Instead, because you helped me, I'll offer you one last chance to turn from this."

"Well, after all of these dramatics, you have to take us now," quipped Rew. He offered, "Bring us to someone, or somewhere, that can be of help, and then you may leave."

"I don't work for you. I can leave anytime I want."

"Take us to this place, and then, your obligation to me is completed," said Anne.

Grunting, Lucia picked up her gray skirts and began walking confidently into the Arcanum at a brisk pace. The dark granite was silent around them except for occasional muffled sounds that even Rew found difficult to source. He spied a few additional streamers of smoke from towers in the distance, but the street looked abandoned, with scant evidence of regular traffic. Lucia strode with purpose, though. She knew where she was going.

"Does the king know the state of this place?" asked Rew, thinking back to how bustling it'd been years ago when he'd last visited. It'd been a grim place, dangerous, but it'd been alive. Now...

"Of course the king knows what happens inside of his own Arcanum. The king's coffers support the work that occurs here."

"And what does he say about it?"

"The king does not explain his plans to me. I report what I see and what I know, and he does what he pleases with that information. He... His plans are not for me to know."

Lucia turned and began a brisk walk down the weed-strewn street, and Rew and the others were forced to scurry in her wake without further questions. Before she'd moved on, Rew had caught her look and saw that beneath her exterior, which was as hard as the granite walls of the place, she was disturbed. She must have known what Arcanist Salwart was working on and had told the king, but why hadn't Vaisius Morden done anything about it?

Or had he? It was one of his legion who'd been guarding the door.

The last time Rew had seen the Arcanum had been a decade before, and then, it'd been a noisy, thrumming hub of activity. Dozens of arcanists had lived there, supported by ten times as many assistants. They'd had others who tended to the place and cared for their mundane needs. Women from the colony were frequent visitors, and it was common to see guests from all over the kingdom coming to inquire about esoteric knowledge or to commission research.

The occupants of the Arcanum had been feverishly plumbing the depths of possibility. They studied ancient texts and conducted new experiments, all striving to be the one who wrote the next tome which would be enshrined in their libraries. It was all that such men cared about, understanding what others had discovered then adding their own contribution to the repository of human wisdom. If they could do so while disproving some theory laid down before their time by another arcanist, all the better. Something had interrupted that work. Something had caused those men to flee.

It wasn't uncommon for arcanists to be maimed or killed during their experimentations. They pushed the boundaries of what was safe, or sensible, in a gamble to unearth the next major leap in understanding. Usually, they managed to ensure it was their assistants who bore the brunt of experiments gone afoul, but even in the worst cases, the largest explosions or the more virulent releases of trapped magical energy, it was only a handful of people and a few buildings that were destroyed. There was a reason even the meanest structures in the place were constructed of thick granite blocks, but it didn't appear anything had been destroyed. Each building they passed was perfectly intact, if uncared for in some cases.

Lucia knew. She had to know.

They passed the slender, pale-stone tower where the wisps of vibrant purple smoke blew off into the breeze far above their heads. It was the place they'd seen from outside of the walls.

Rew caught up to Lucia and asked, "Can we... Should we stop here and speak to whoever is inside? Perhaps they can tell us—"

"This tower is Arcanist Reynald's abode," explained Lucia, cutting Rew off. "He rarely leaves his tower, and he doesn't know much more of what's going on in the Arcanum than you do. He's dangerous, and we're all the better for the fact he rarely ventures out. He's a madman, and even I avoid him as much as possible."

"What's he working on?" questioned Rew, pointing up at the trailing smoke.

"Chemical combinations which could be used in warfare. Poisons," responded Lucia with a wicked smile. "He intends to bottle the concoctions and have soldiers throw them at their enemies or perhaps fling them from some device. If he's successful, it could harken a new era of warfare."

"Chemicals that would... poison the enemy?"

"Yes, but on a mass scale. Clouds of toxic vapor, like some spellcasters can unleash, except every soldier in an army would be capable of it."

"That's horrific," said Rew, unconsciously taking a step back from the tower, looking nervously up at the smoke drifting innocuously on the wind.

"Don't worry, Ranger," assured Lucia. "The man has been working on it for the last two decades, and he's yet to perfect his mixture. He's also yet to kill himself during the process, which makes him rare amongst practicing arcanists. I'm not certain if that's due to uncharacteristic caution or a lack of skill in mixing the potions to be deadly. Not that he never stumbles across something lethal. You can see the buildings around his tower have been unoccupied for years, long before the current troubles. Trust me, there's a good reason. It's best to stay clear of Arcanist Reynald."

"How many others like him still reside within this place?"

Lucia shrugged. "I'm not a tour guide, Ranger."

"You're being rather obtuse…"

"There are some," admitted Lucia. "Most who have stayed are as bad as Reynald, or worse. Here, this building here, this is where you'll find your answers."

The place had the look of a warehouse, except it was constructed of thick blocks of granite which could have served as the foundation for the wall around the Arcanum. There were no windows, just an impressive steel door. The door was bound by chain as thick as Rew's wrist and clasped by a lock as big as two of his fists.

"King's Sake," muttered Rew, looking at the device. "We should have brought Zaine."

Lucia raised an eyebrow.

Shrugging, thinking it did no harm to share with the woman, and that maybe it'd incline her to share as well, Rew explained, "She's a thief."

"Ah," acknowledged Lucia. Offering him a wry grin, she produced a fat steel key and said, "I brought something better."

Chapter Ten

Lucia stepped forward with the key and hefted the lock. She tried to fit the key inside of it then scowled. She fiddled with it for another moment then dropped the lock and punched the door. Hissing and clutching her fist as if surprised it hurt after striking the steel barrier, she asked, "Someone else want to try this?"

Rew took her place, but the key did not fit. "What's inside of here?"

"You want to know what happened to the Arcanum? You want to know more about necromancy? You'll find the answers." She looked at the key then at the door. "Of course, we've got to get in the door first…"

Rew rattled the chain. Nothing happened. "Who put this lock here? Could they have known you had a key and changed it?"

Shaking her head, Lucia replied, "No, there's no way they knew I had a key. If they even suspected I knew what was inside of here, I'd have bigger problems than them changing the lock. It's, ah, possible I took the wrong key."

"Is there another key back in the colony?" inquired Anne gently. "Maybe one that works?"

Shaking her head, Lucia explained, "This isn't my lock. I stole the key. I thought this was the right one. It was the biggest, but it was on a ring of keys and... I didn't have much time, and I haven't been inside of here since my last attempt failed. We can't just go and steal another key, so we've got to figure something else out."

"Zaine?" asked Anne, glancing at Rew. "We could be back here in an hour."

"You remember what happened last time she picked a lock?" asked Rew, thinking of the poisoned dart which had nearly stuck in Raif back in Jabaan. Eyeing the heavy fortifications of the building, he didn't doubt this place could have its own traps embedded in the door.

He peered down at the key in his hand, frowning. Along the length of it, there was a thin cerulean band of color. It was dark, but it reminded him of something he'd seen before. "This key seems a finer thing than the lock."

Lucia shrugged.

The nameless woman approached and fiddled with the lock and chain, bending down to examine both. When she stood, she was staring at Lucia.

"Let me try," suggested Cinda.

She stepped forward, and a pale glow built around her hand.

Lucia watched avidly, ignoring the nameless woman's look. She asked Cinda, "Can you feel it?"

Frowning, Cinda nodded, and her hand brightened until it was difficult to look at. Then, she thrust it toward the door and released a wailing blast of wind and cold. It was like funeral fire but dense, and when it hit the steel door, it did so with the impact of a giant sledge hammer. The door crumpled, flying open, and links of chain burst as the steel barrier swung inward. Crackles of energy sizzled in the freezing air, but in a breath, it was over.

"That was impressive," remarked Rew.

"There's power inside of this place," responded Cinda. "It's strange, though. Not like I've felt before. It's like an echo."

The interior of the building was dark, with only several paces of stone floor illuminated from the open doorway. There were no windows and no lights.

"There's a lantern to the left of the door," offered Lucia.

Rew gestured for her to lead the way.

Smirking at him, the woman shook her head.

"I don't think… I don't think I should light our way," said Cinda, her voice tight, her eyes wide as she studied the darkness. She was holding her hands together at her waist, clutching tightly the one she'd used to cast her funeral fire.

Throwing up his own hands, Rew stepped inside and fumbled around in the dark until he retrieved a copper lantern with clear glass walls. He shook it and heard the slosh of oil in the basin. There was a striker hanging beside it, and after a moment of struggling with the device, he got it lit. He held the lantern high and let out a whistle.

In the center of the room was a giant wood, rope, and iron contraption. Above it hung glass globes of liquids and gases. Some of them appeared to be warmed while others boiled with freezing clouds of multi-colored smoke. Ice clung to the exteriors of several, and others appeared empty. Rew saw no obvious sources for the heat or the cold, except for nondescript boxes hanging beneath some of the glass orbs. Could they be enchanted, or was it a chemical mixture the arcanists had devised? There were tubes strung around and through the contraption, moving liquids with a rhythmic pulse like a heartbeat.

The thing was shrouded in gloom, and Rew began walking the edge of the space, finding more lanterns hanging on delicate stands. He used the striker to light them. A warm glow from the copper and glass devices spread through the room, though what he saw only gave him chills.

The room was mostly empty, aside from the giant contraption in the center, but against one wall was a huge, copper-bound glass container, like a giant version of the lamps. It was constructed similar to an oversized wardrobe, but inside of it, spectral mist swirled constantly. The mist seemed to pick up and reflect the light of the lanterns, and to Rew's eye, it burned with a pale shimmer.

Cinda stood, transfixed by the glow that emanated from the cabinet.

"Rew," said Anne, looking at the massive construction in the center of the room.

He followed her gaze. It took him a moment to realize that the body of a man was suspended in the middle of the strange apparatus. The man was shirtless and barefoot, wearing black wool trousers. His head hung limply, and he was pallid in the lantern light. On the man's shoulder, Rew saw a tattoo signifying membership in a company in the king's black legion.

Across the man's chest, there were a number of tubes and leads sunk into his flesh and sealed there. Needles sprouted from his arms like the quills of a porcupine, and as Rew followed the path of the tubes, he saw they came from the containers hanging above. The liquids that were flowing to and from the containers were passing through the man's body. Rew gaped at the giant device and the dead man, confused.

"King's Sake," muttered the nameless woman. "What is this?"

"It's… It's doing something to that man, I think," stammered Rew.

"Necromancy," said Cinda, her gaze turning to the man. "He's dead. They're… resurrecting him, or at least trying to. That cabinet is filled with the essence of souls—the power of their departure. This device is pouring that essence, along with a lot of other substances I don't recognize, directly into the dead man. They're trying to animate him. It hasn't worked, at least for him. I don't know if it's possible…"

Rew swallowed and didn't know what to say.

"This might work, Ranger," declared Cinda, taking a hesitant step toward the contraption. "I don't understand the science, how they are doing it, but I can feel the power radiating from that vessel against the wall. It's true power. They've manually captured the same source I use to cast my spells. It's… not strong,

I don't think, not efficient or pure. It's just an echo of the real power that spills out when someone dies, but I can feel it. This is the power I was drawing upon when I cracked open the door. I don't know if they can apply what they've gathered, but they have manually captured peoples' souls!"

"What do you mean when you say echo?" asked Lucia, tilting her head slightly and looking at Cinda's back.

Appearing to ignore the other woman, Cinda approached the wardrobe, her hands clasped carefully behind her. "It's hard to describe. Drawing power from death feels like… the wind against my face. This is like the wind stirring distant leaves. I know it's there because I can see it. I know what that breath of air would feel like if it touched me, but it's not there, present against my own face. It feels like I could reach out and touch it, but it's not touching me. Do you understand?"

Frowning, Lucia began a slow circuit of the room, her eyes darting between Cinda and the device in the center. Rew began to get an uncomfortable feeling about the way the woman was discussing the device with Cinda. Lucia had known this was here. It must be why she warned them not to come to the Arcanum. But she'd also claimed it would give them answers.

Now, it was as if… as if she was soliciting Cinda's opinion, but Lucia was a servant of the king. If he wanted to know about the device, he could portal to the Arcanum in moments. The arcanists worked for the king, after all, and no one had more talent at necromancy. Was it possible the king did not know about the device? The ranger shared a look with Anne and could tell she was wondering the same thing he was.

Cinda held a hand up toward the wardrobe, careful not to touch it. The mist swirled, distinct patterns curling and uncurling against the frosty glass. The necromancer's eyes rose, and her gaze followed a series of copper piping that ran up from the wardrobe, across the ceiling, and then dropped down into the tangle of tubes, glass globes, and metal boxes above the wood and rope contraption.

"What does that do, do you think?" asked Lucia, pointing to the copper pipes.

"A conduit for the souls?" wondered Cinda. "They draw them out somehow with this machine and store the power in the wardrobe. I think... I don't know if it would work, but it looks like whoever built this is trying to put a soul back into that dead man."

"That's horrific," muttered Anne, staring aghast at the corpse suspended in the center of the contraption.

"I believe one can turn the machine on with that lever," said Lucia, nodding toward a heavy metal switch on the side of the device. "You should try it."

Cinda walked toward the switch, and Anne barked, "Why would anyone want to turn this infernal thing on?"

Lucia shrugged, her face blank. She held up a book that she'd produced from within her robes. "I found this in the room. The artificer who built the device was using it. It's about necromancy, but I have no talent for the art. I don't understand a fraction of what is in here. There's nothing useful for me in these pages, but perhaps you can find some answers, some explanation of the device?"

Cinda took the book and opened it. She frowned.

"Anything useful?" asked Rew.

Not looking at him, Cinda responded, "I'm not sure. Maybe."

Rew scratched his beard and left her alone. It looked like a thick book, and he supposed there wouldn't be much she could tell him until she'd had time to read the thing.

"Blessed Mother!" cried the nameless woman, staggering away from where she stood at the back of the room.

Rew darted to her side and saw she'd opened a discreet door in the back wall of the building. She was shaking, and he saw grave discomfort in her eyes. He steeled himself then looked through the door.

A body was stretched out on a table, its chest cut wide open, only an empty hollow where its organs had been. The eyes had been plucked from the head, the tongue ripped from the mouth. The dead man wore black trousers and had a tattoo on his shoulder from the king's legion.

"Blessed Mother," croaked Rew, unconsciously repeating the nameless woman's curse.

He looked around the rest of the room and saw a pile of dead bodies stacked like cordwood in one corner, a barrel like one that would catch rain near the table. From the putrid odor wafting from the barrel, he guessed where the dead man's organs had gone. There was a pile of discarded clothing and other debris which must have been stripped from the bodies before they had been mutilated.

Soldiers from the king's black legion, some of the missing men, had been... Pinching his nose, Rew entered the room and circled the table. The bodies in the pile had all been sliced open and crudely stitched back together. They'd been tossed there with no more care than sacks of beans, and it'd happened some time ago, judging by the state of them. Most wore the trousers of the black legion, as if it'd been too much trouble to remove those when the body parts beneath the trousers would remain intact, but some were naked or only in underclothes.

Rew adjusted his belt, glad that not all of the soft organs had been removed. These men hadn't suffered that indignity, at least.

He knelt. Two bodies had been leaned against the bottom of the pile, and they were still fully clothed. Rew raised his lantern and grimaced. The fabric was covered in char and blood, but the pair wore the crimson robes of necromancers, and their deaths were more recent than the others. It was as if they'd been dragged there just to get them out of the way. Had they been the ones responsible for this awful experiment?

Seeing nothing else of interest and unable to force himself to study the corpses any longer, Rew hurried out of the room and kicked the door shut. He rubbed his hand across his nose, wishing he could scrub the stench from his nostrils. Lucia was watching him.

"Do you know what's in there?"

She nodded affirmation.

"Explain yourself."

"You wanted to know what happened to the Arcanum." She raised her hands and gestured around the room. "This is what happened."

"People were... fed into this thing?"

"Not many, relative to how many used to live in the compound," she responded. "Several score. Maybe one hundred over time. Most people were wise enough to leave once things got uncomfortable. Arcanists can always find a position in some nobles' court or in Mordenhold if they don't mind being so close to the king's grasp. Some weren't as quick to leave and paid the price. You saw the bodies of the legionnaires? They didn't have the choice to leave and suffered terribly for it."

"The king did this!" snapped Rew. "He sacrificed his own men?"

"He did not," replied Lucia, her lips set in a sour grimace. "The king has nothing to do with this. He, ah... I lied to you earlier. The king doesn't know what's happening here."

"He doesn't know?" demanded Rew, glancing at the contraption. "You're his spy, aren't you?"

"When I report to him, I want to do so with complete information. I... I need to know what exactly this device is capable of. It can kill a man. That was easy enough to learn. But... does it work? It appears it can extract the soul from a body, but as the lass wondered, I need to know if it can raise the dead. The truth, I don't know. I have to know before I speak to the king."

"I don't understand," murmured Anne. "You're wanting... You want us to try it for you?"

"Not you," answered Lucia. She pointed to Cinda. "Her."

"There are dead necromancers in that room," said Rew. "You put them there? They tried to work this thing and failed?"

"Yes." Lucia began circling the room again, studying the device. "Evidently, this machine is rather dangerous to operate.

It... has a kick." She glanced at them and, seeing their expressions, explained, "It's been my role to monitor the Arcanum, to ensure the king's coin is well spent and all discoveries are known to him. I failed. This... thing, was created under my nose. I fear it's been used. The king has a particular interest in necromancy, and... Do you understand the implications if this device works? It could shatter Vaeldon, and it happened on my watch. I have to know if it works before I inform the king. If I inform the king. Maybe I could... Pfah. I have to know if it works before I do anything."

"But..."

"You're a ranger, yes? You know the price of failing the king. The creation of this abomination is my fault, I admit that, but the punishment for failure is severe. I'd... end it, but the end is not always the end. You know his reach goes beyond this world. I've monitored the building, but when the arcanist arrives, he's always careful to shut the door behind him. I can't risk a confrontation until I know more. My only hope is for a necromancer to discover the truth."

"You expect Cinda to try and activate it?" scoffed Rew. "Why would we agree to that?"

Lucia removed the short iron club from her belt that she'd used to gain entry into the Arcanum and rapped it against the stone wall. She beat out a distinct pattern and then waited.

"That's a signal," guessed Rew. "To the king's legion?"

Nodding, Lucia glanced at the door where an armored man stood. "They serve at my command."

Rew drew his longsword and set his feet. "The missing soldiers? You'll need more than that to threaten us."

"Will I?"

"Ranger," warned Cinda. "That man is dead."

"The king doesn't waste resources feeding men when he can utilize those that don't eat, sleep, or breathe," said Lucia. "Before you do something rash, Ranger, think about whether or not you really want to test your might against the king."

"I can't break the binding," said Cinda, scowling at the shape in the doorway. "That corpse is in the king's thrall tighter than I've ever felt. It's not like when I... Ah, I can't break the binding. And there are more of them, gathering outside."

"Blessed Mother," grumbled Rew.

"Those dead necromancers in the back room understood what the lass does," said Lucia. "Attempting to use this device is a risk, but defying the king is worse than death."

"It'll be your death and worse if the king finds out what's going on in this room."

Smirking, Lucia nodded in acknowledgement. "If the lass was responsible for Jabaan, she doesn't want the king's attention any more than I do, but I have to know, does this device work? Has it been used? Don't you realize there is nothing you can do to me worse than what the king will do if he finds out about this and blames me? If it doesn't work, I can destroy it, and I will be safe. The king may never know. If it does work—"

"Who built it?"

Scowling, Lucia spit, "Arcanist Salwart."

Rew shifted his grip on his longsword, unsure what to do. Could they let Cinda attempt to operate the device, even though there was ample evidence it might kill her? He didn't fancy the alternative—fighting an entire company of undead which he could not kill and Cinda could not release.

"We should have brought Raif," muttered Rew, glaring at the legionnaire in the doorway. Quickly, he added, "Don't tell him I said that."

"I told you to turn away," mentioned Lucia suddenly, speaking to Anne. "I'm sorry it's come to this, but we are where we are. It's not just my life, you understand? For a failure of this magnitude, the king will follow me into death. I have to protect myself—my soul. I have family, friends, as well. I have to under-stand and make this right before the king finds out."

"Where is Salwart now?" growled Rew.

Lucia shrugged. "I don't know. If I knew that, maybe there'd be a way out of this."

"Well, we're not going to let Cinda try and turn this horrific thing on," declared Rew. "I don't care what you threaten us with. That's not going to happen. You can try to fight us, but I'll tell you, I'm coming for you first. I may not survive against a company of undead, but you won't survive against me."

"A false threat, Ranger," retorted Lucia. "The king has ties to my soul. If I die, he'll feel it. You can't kill me without drawing his attention. To be frank, that's why I haven't killed myself. When he feels me die violently, how quickly do you think he'll be here?"

"Is that true?" asked Anne when Rew did not respond to Lucia's threat.

"It could be," admitted Rew. "The king is capable of it, though he doesn't bind every one of his minions."

"You don't have any choices," suggested Lucia. "You cannot kill me without bringing the king. You can't fight against an entire company of his dead. You can't even get out of this room without facing them. I didn't want to drag Anne into this, but you forced my hand, so let's be done with it. Lass, summon your strength, and flip the switch. We'll find out what Arcanist Salwart has accomplished here. Are he and Prince Heindaw able to raise the dead?"

The nameless woman gagged and coughed.

Lucia gave her an exasperated look.

"You shouldn't have said that," growled the nameless woman.

"Shouldn't have said what?" questioned Lucia.

"There are, ah, enchantments I have heard of," stammered the nameless woman, "where one can detect when one's name is spoken. You said the prince's name. If he's behind the construction of this device, then you may have drawn his attention."

"How do you know that? What did you see?"

"You're working for Heindaw," snarled Rew, spinning to face the nameless woman. "I knew it."

"Don't be a fool," she snapped.

"It's too late for that," replied Rew, raising his longsword. He paused. "Wait, that didn't come out the way I meant it." He shook himself. "If you're not working for the prince, then how do you know about his enchantments?"

"You're being naive," retorted the nameless woman. "You think they'd put a lock like that upon the door and not inscribe an enchantment to know when it was shattered? Look at it, what's left of the back. That sigil is—"

"Why didn't you say anything?"

"I didn't think anyone would be stupid enough to say the prince's name," growled the nameless woman. Her eyes grew distant and then hard. "Did you hear that? Arcanist Salwart is here, in the Arcanum."

"Salwart?" gasped Rew, his thoughts spinning. "How do you know? Hear what? Why would Salwart be here?"

"He's here."

Rew scowled at her.

"If the prince was coming, he would have come right into this room. Salwart, though, would have had to use a portal stone. Ah, I see. No one wants to be associated with this, in case the king finds out. That's why Salwart came without the prince. Like Lucia, they understand the danger of the king learning of what happens here."

Rew shifted his stance and held his longsword ready. Half the time, it felt like the nameless woman was talking to herself or to someone they could not see. The other half of the time, she wasn't making any sense.

He stepped closer to her. "What is going on?"

She turned to him. "Arcanist Salwart has arrived in the Arcanum by portal stone. Can't you hear? It has to be him."

Rew quieted, and his heart fell. The nameless woman was right. Somewhere out there, he heard the distinct clash of steel on steel.

"What's going on out there?" asked Rew, spinning to Lucia.

Gripping her iron club tightly in frustration, Lucia replied, "I don't know. I'm not… I didn't bind these soldiers. I'm not a necro-mancer. I was just taught the means to control the company here using a pattern of sounds. I can't sense what they're seeing any more than you can."

Rew glanced back at the nameless woman.

"Salwart would rather die than see us leave here. He'll be a victim of the same fear Lucia has. I believe he'll have the Sons of the Father from Spinesend with him. He might have enchanted devices. I don't know."

"How could you possibly know—" began Rew.

"We don't have time to talk," said the nameless woman. "Lucia, can the black legion defend us?"

"Against what?" snapped the king's spy. "I can't direct them to attack what I cannot see. If I'm not careful, they'll turn on us. The commands I can give are limited, and it's dangerous to guess. I need to see what we're up against."

"Blessed Mother," said Rew. "Outside, then. Let's go outside and get this over with."

Chapter Eleven

T he black-clad legionnaire in the doorway turned when Lucia approached. They followed the silent shape outside. It'd grown dark while they had been inside of the building, and only a handful of lights were visible in the Arcanum, all too far away to provide them any illumination.

Lucia drew close to Rew, and against his drawn longsword, she rapped out a pattern with her iron club. From the shadows, shapes began to emerge, and men garbed in the king's colors began to form a circle around the party.

"They'll defend us against anyone who approaches," explained Lucia. "They're terrifically difficult to kill, but they're slow to respond, and they won't be aggressive unless I can see a target and direct them to it. It's more elegant when a necromancer can control them, but this is better than nothing."

"These are the missing legionnaires?" asked Rew, studying the backs of the forms nervously.

"Some of them," replied Lucia, peering into the dark around them. "I… was given these resources by the Lieutenant General. He, ah, recruited these men for me from the existing allotment at the fort, and added some of his own… men. He's become embroiled in politics and is aware of what's happening here."

"We need to talk," said Rew. "The king's Lieutenant General is aware of this, and hasn't told the king?"

"A friend of his, are you?"

Rew grunted and did not respond.

"These were given to you? How long does the king bind them for?" wondered Cinda, clinically studying the dark forms around them.

Lucia shrugged. "As long as he needs them. Fresh bodies are the strongest. They have the most material to animate, but there's a period where they can be unpleasant to be around. The odor, you understand? After that, the bodies have deteriorated physically so they are weaker, but don't smell as strongly of rotting flesh. This company has been beneath the Lieutenant General for some years, I imagine. They could have been used for a guard detail in Mordenhold or something like that. Not even the king wants his hallways to smell of the freshly dead."

"The king binds the souls for years at a time?" choked Cinda.

Giving the young necromancer a tight smile, Lucia replied, "You use the tools you have available the best you are able. This is who you are, lass. Best get used to it."

Down the street, they heard another clash of combat, and everyone turned. They couldn't see anything, but there were heavy crunches and thuds from impacts. There were no shouts, no cries of pain.

"The dead don't voice their wounds, but..." murmured Cinda.

"But their opponents should," agreed Lucia.

The woman clutched her iron club like she meant to use it against someone's skull. Cinda stood close, trails of vapor building around her hands. Anne had her arms crossed over her chest. She looked scared and disturbed at everything she'd been hearing. The nameless woman came beside Rew, her scimitar held ready.

"Ranger, the Sons of the Father are as talented as I, and they have no more fear of death than the legionnaires. These men worship the Cursed Father, and they think they'll find comfort in his embrace. Dying in battle isn't something they'll try to avoid."

"Great."

"Don't get me wrong. They're still going to try and kill us, but they'll have no fear. They'll sacrifice themselves if necessary. Be wary of rash attacks at your front. They'll give up one of their own to leave you exposed on the side or back."

"How do you know all of this?" growled Rew, half an ear cocked to the approaching sounds of fighting.

"The Sons of the Father trained me. I told you that."

"You told us a lot of things," said Rew, glancing at the woman from the corner of his eye. "I'm questioning how much of it was true."

"Trust me on this, at least. It is the Sons of the Father we will face, and they will not fear death."

She gave him a toothy smile, and he was about to reiterate just how trustworthy he found her, but out of the darkness came a low whistle.

"Duck!" shouted Rew.

A spear swished overhead and thumped onto the weed-strewn street behind them. In front of them, the dark shapes of the king's black legion lumbered about, some apparently trying to position themselves in front of additional attacks, others vanishing into the gloom, heading toward whoever threw the spear.

Over the clank of the legionnaires armor, Rew barely heard the next incoming missile and yanked Cinda out of the path of it at the last second. Another came right behind it, and Rew stumbled, cursing.

"They can see your casting, lass. You've got to release it or use it. Sooner or later, one of those is going to hit us." He called to the nameless woman, "No warning about the spears?"

She shrugged.

"Use my spell against what?" Cinda snapped. "I can't see a thing."

"Just fling it down the street," he ordered.

"I'll hit the legionnaires."

"They're already dead," he reminded her.

Her eyes sparking with a green glow, Cinda raised her arm and hurled the vapor of death's breath down the street. It boiled over the backs of the legionnaires, leaving them unharmed, and then vanishing into the dark.

Another spear came flying out of the gloom in response, but from a different angle, and it smacked harmlessly into the torso of one of their undead guards. Rew thought that, with luck, Cinda had hit someone. The legionnaire turned to face the direction the spear had come, a pace-long shaft of wood sticking straight out from its center.

"We've got to find cover," snarled Rew, crouched down, ready to spring out of the way of more spears. "Back, everyone. Fall back."

They began moving the way they'd come originally when they'd arrived at the Arcanum. Rew thought that if they could gain the wall with its long tunnel, they might improve their chances. The sluggishness of the dead legionnaires wouldn't matter as much if they didn't have a lot of ground to cover. It would also limit the sight lines of the spearmen. With their backs against solid stone and steel, Rew would feel better about fighting blind.

A man, dressed entirely in black, including a hood and mask, burst silently from the dark and struck at one of the shambling legionnaires. He punched the tip of his spear into its side then yanked it free. He twirled the weapon and swept the legionnaire's feet out from under it.

The legionnaire crashed to the ground, and the man stepped over the body, raising his spear. Rew advanced, putting himself between their attacker and the others.

"Be ready to dodge," he warned, hoping the spear didn't come at him and Cinda or someone was stupidly standing right behind him when he jumped out of the way.

The masked man, evidently understanding Rew's warning to his companions, aimed the spear as if taking Rew's advice.

Rew growled, ready to try and knock the weapon down, but before he could, and before the spearman could make his throw, the fallen legionnaire reached up and grasped the spearman's belt. The spearman looked down, surprised that the legionnaire wasn't dead, and then the spearman caught the point of the legionnaire's broadsword in his face. The man died silently and quickly.

"Blessed Mother," said the nameless woman as the legionnaire clumsily clambered back to its feet.

"I told you. You don't want to fight these things," said Lucia.

"Come on," barked Rew.

He turned and started jogging down the dark street. He made it two blocks before he stumbled into three more men carrying spears. They were as shocked as he was when Rew came jogging into their midst, but none of them took long to react.

Rew lashed out with his longsword, the steel barely visible in the low light. A spearman raised his weapon in defense, and Rew's blade slammed into the wooden shaft. The weapon was torn from the spearman's hands, but the other man dodged away from Rew's follow-through swing.

A second spearman lunged forward, thrusting with the sharp point of his weapon. Rew twisted, and the spear tore into his cloak, causing him to stumble to the side, which helped avoid the third man who came crashing into his back.

The third man grappled with Rew and grunted, "I'll hold him still."

Rew grabbed the man on the back of the neck and tore him away, hurling the spearman toward the first man and then spinning and stabbing his longsword into the second, who was still trying to recover his spear from the tangle of Rew's cloak. That man grunted but did not scream or cry out as Rew's steel found him. The ranger darted after the other two, lashing at them, striking flesh but unable to see well enough to deliver a fatal blow.

Cinda's light flared for a moment, and Rew saw startled eyes. He stabbed them.

"King's Sake," muttered the nameless woman. "I can't see a thing. How'd you—"

"I can't see either, and neither could they," interjected Rew. "It was luck. Could go the other way next time. We can't keep stumbling through these streets hoping we get a jump on everyone. It's blocks to the doorway in the wall, and I get the feeling the Sons of the Father will be scattered all throughout the city. They're certain to hear us coming…"

Rew waved around them, where more of the king's black legion were shuffling into place in a defensive position, their shambling lope finally catching the party's quicker pace, their armor and weapons clanking with their disjointed movements.

"I can't get them to go any faster," apologized Lucia, "and they definitely won't understand the idea of being quiet."

Rew looked around, hearing the sporadic sounds of battle all through the arcanum. "How many do you have under your command?"

"One hundred," answered Lucia. "There's another hundred that are, ah, on standby. I don't know if they're in the fight or not. They're well on the other side of the compound."

"We've got to find cover," said Rew.

The battle was too spread out, too random. They couldn't risk one of those spearmen getting a lucky thrust or one of their party catching a spear hurled out of the dark.

He spun and spied a single light high in the air. "That's the arcanist who was making the poisons to use in battle?"

"Arcanist Reynald. He's crazy."

"Can't be worse than what's going on out here. At least we can defend the tower."

Lucia rang her club again, and the king's legionnaires formed up and began marching toward the tower. She told the others, "At least in the midst of them, we've got bodies to block any attacks from the dark."

Thinking that the noise of the soldiers outweighed the benefit of their cover, Rew made as if to hang back, but then behind them, they heard another clash of fighting, and the voices of their attackers drifted on the air. The Sons of the Father had found the trail and were calling for help. Rew sighed and hurried after the legionnaires.

THROUGHOUT THE ARCANUM, CLASHES OF VIOLENCE RANG THROUGH the night, but there were no screams of pain or men crying out in the throes of death. The participants in the battle were either already dead or eager to reach that purported exalted plane.

Twice more, they encountered the black-garbed Sons of the Father. The spear-wielding men emerged like wraiths from the night, but they were living souls powered by breath and blood. They had no advantages at night except for their numbers.

The king's legion, however, was dead, and they saw the world with the senses of those pulled from the spectral beyond. They could sense the approach of the Sons of the Father, and soon, Rew and the others were able to detect the change in stance of the undead moments before their assailants arrived. It gave them the edge they needed.

The Sons of the Father were competent fighters, and like berserkers, they had no fear. They were fast, but trying to force their way through the undead left the Sons exposed, and they were quickly dispatched by Rew or the nameless woman.

"Pathetic," she spit after killing another of the men. "Definitely from the Spinesend temple. They wouldn't last a day in my father's command. If these men were from Iyre, we'd be in trouble."

"I thought you said the temple in Iyre was destroyed?" questioned Rew.

"The building but not the mission."

The ranger frowned at her. She'd spoken about her father in the present tense.

"Hurry, Ranger."

"If they were from Iyre, wouldn't they know you?"

The woman smiled at him, only her gleaming teeth visible in the dark. She slashed her scimitar in front of her, flinging the blood of one of their assailants into the night. "What makes you think they don't know me now?"

"When this is over, we're going to talk," declared Rew.

"There," interrupted Lucia, pointing with her iron club to a tower ahead of them.

It was the tall, slender structure they'd seen the purple smoke drifting away from earlier in the day, the one Lucia claimed was occupied by a man formulating poisons to use in battle, a man who had the door of his tower open.

Round like a mouse locked in a grain silo, the arcanist squinted at them as they came rushing out of the dark. He raised a trembling arm, holding a flask filled with a clear liquid. He cocked back his arm as if to throw.

"Reynald!" snapped Lucia, rushing to the front.

The arcanist faltered then lowered the flask. "Lucia, is that you? What is happening?"

"An attack, I'm afraid." She stepped beside the man and rang her club against the side of his tower.

All around them, the king's black legion clustered into a defensive formation in front of the door to the tower. Arcanist Reynald backed slowly through the doorway, and they followed him inside, turning and quickly locking the door.

Rew grimaced.

The king's black legion was arrayed outside, and now, they were locked behind a sturdy door and stout stone walls, but surely Salwart would have considered that possibility. The Arcanum was full of towers, which, while not designed to be defensive, would do the trick just fine against a cadre of spearmen. Perhaps Salwart had hoped to catch them unawares, but he was an intelligent man, a learned man, and one who was intimately familiar with the Arcanum. He would have planned for this contingency.

Arcanist Reynald was busy babbling and demanding Lucia tell him what was going on. The woman herself was scowling, and the nameless woman looked nervous.

Rew strode toward her and jabbed a finger in her face. "What will he try next?"

"How should I know?"

"You knew he'd bring the Sons of the Father," accused Rew. "You knew which temple he collected them from. King's Sake, it's obvious you know the man! Tell us what he'll do next. Those spears could have taken your life as easily as ours."

Scowling, the nameless woman glanced away.

"How did you know Salwart was coming?" demanded Rew.

"Salwart, you say?" asked Arcanist Reynald, peering at Lucia like she was a particularly convoluted passage in one of his books.

The man's chins wobbled, and his breath was coming in short, exasperated huffs. He wore thick velvet robes embroidered with stars and moons. The robes might have been the height of fashion for an arcanist in a noble's court three decades earlier. The robes were wrinkled and in disrepair, but it was the man's hands and face which caught Rew's eye. Reynald's skin was stained with a myriad of colors, like a rainbow had vomited on him. Amongst the colors, white splotches stood out where he'd been scarred. The results of his failed experiments, presumably. It wasn't for lack of trying the man hadn't discovered the secret formula he'd been working on.

Rew asked him, "You know Salwart?"

"Of course," snapped Reynald, scurrying to the side of his tower where a profusion of cloudy decanters, flasks, and beakers was spread on a battered table like the leftover results from a cohort of apprentice glass blowers. The arcanist unstopped the flask he was holding and began rooting through his collection, pulling out colorful potions and arranging them in a line. "The prince? Will he bring the prince?"

The nameless woman shifted nervously before quietly answering. "No."

Rew glared at her.

"We must get ready," mumbled Arcanist Reynald, focused on his work, not looking at any of them.

"Ready for what?" asked Rew, glancing at the locked door of the tower. The clashes of battle had faded. What did that mean?

"Salwart is a fool, which makes him dangerous," claimed Reynald, who was furiously dumping liquids to and from various containers, not pausing to measure and creating a frothing, multi-hued mixture that seemed to shimmer in the light of the lamps hanging around the room.

"What is that?" asked Lucia, peering quizzically at the man's work. She leaned closer.

"Don't inhale the fumes," warned the arcanist. Grimly, without turning, Reynald added, "This is a way to stop Salwart dead in his tracks."

"I thought your potions didn't work."

Reynald paused and glanced over his shoulder. "They work all too well. If the king or the princes knew what I'd developed, can you imagine the carnage…" The man huffed and turned back to the mixture. "My research has led me to understand there are some fields of knowledge which are too dangerous to be shared with the political set, so I continue my charade, pretending I don't know what I know and making sure that any other searchers into the realms of chemical warfare are led astray. It's a quiet life, one I'm proud of. It's unfortunate Salwart didn't follow my lead and keep his foul speculations to himself."

"I see."

The arcanist spun around, two half-full flasks in his hands. "How long do we have?"

Rew and Lucia looked at each other then both turned toward the nameless woman.

"How should I know?" she snapped.

"Salwart must be here," said Rew. "He would have come along with the Sons of the Father. We haven't seen him, but perhaps he's preparing… whatever it is he's planning."

"We don't have much time, then," grunted Arcanist Reynald. He pursed his lips, lost in thought, the two flasks held carefully in his hands. He shook himself then continued, "Salwart is a fool, and his experiments were failures. It won't be his own strength he brings to this fight. If he attacks, he'll have some sort of device from Prince Hein— Ah, the prince. Is that what I think it is?"

Rew looked between the nameless woman and the arcanist. The old man was studying her armor, and she simply shrugged.

"Salwart is here. We're sure?" asked the arcanist quietly.

The nameless woman sighed and then responded, "He arrived in the Arcanum with the others. I don't know where he is now or what he may have planned."

"So what do we do?" asked Anne.

The arcanist poured one of his flasks into the other and then the contents of both back into the first container, mixing the liquids thoroughly. Rew blinked. The contents were clear, like water, but they bubbled as if being boiled. The arcanist stoppered the mixture then strode forward and handed the flask to Lucia. "Instruct the king's black legion to find Salwart and then shatter this glass at his feet."

"The legionnaires—"

"They're already dead," interrupted the arcanist crisply. "Hurry now. Time is a factor."

"I'll need to—"

"Go outside, yes, of course."

Reynald strode to the door, listened for a moment, and then unlocked and opened it.

Lucia held up the flask she carried and peered at the clear liquid inside.

"Don't drop it," Reynald warned.

Stepping quickly, Lucia walked into the night, tapping her club against the exterior wall of the tower.

Arcanist Reynald slammed the door of the tower shut and locked it, trapping Lucia outside.

"What's this!" cried Rew.

"There's a trapdoor beneath my dining table," said the arcanist. "We have thirty heartbeats to get into it. Give or take a few."

Rew's mouth fell open, but the arcanist looked as serious as death itself.

The gaudily robed man cleared his throat and said, "I'm not a young man. That table is too heavy for me to move."

Cursing, Rew spun, darted to the table, and flipped it out of the way. The glassware atop it shattered against the wall and the floor, acrid smells and popping and hissing filling the room. The arcanist was beside him, fumbling at a small hole on the floor then getting his finger beneath it and shifting a section of the wood. Rew grasped beneath the rim and tore the trapdoor open, revealing a narrow chute down into darkness.

"Fifteen heartbeats left," said the arcanist. Then, he put his hands at his sides and jumped into the hole, disappearing with a swish.

"Go!" barked Rew.

Anne jumped into the hole right behind Reynald then the nameless woman vanished as well. Cinda hesitated for a second, looking at the door Lucia was trapped behind. Then, she jumped into the hole. Rew followed a blink after, his instincts screaming they needed to protect Lucia, that something was wrong with this, but he'd seen the urgency in Reynald's eyes. Rew fully believed the man had activated some terrible weapon, and that if they dawdled, they would die.

The hole dropped into a narrow chute lined with smooth stone. It barely would have been big enough for the arcanist to squeeze through, and had Raif been with them, he wouldn't have made it in his armor. Rew popped out the bottom and landed right on top of Cinda, about twelve paces below the floor of the tower. Cinda squawked, and Rew apologized, but their fall was cushioned by the nameless woman, who was lying beneath Cinda.

Rew thanked the Blessed Mother they hadn't landed on Anne.

"I could use your help," mumbled Arcanist Reynald. He was a dozen paces away, limping down a short hallway, shaking a vial and causing a chemical reaction with the contents. The vial began to glow, bathing his face in a low, red light. He hooked a thumb over his shoulder and said, "The ladder is broken, and I think I twisted my ankle..."

Grunting, Rew moved forward and knelt, providing a platform for the arcanist to climb. The nameless woman scrambled up Rew's back first, to a ledge the broken ladder was leaning against. The ledge was only the height of Rew's head, but the short, pudgy arcanist couldn't make it without help. Rew boosted the man over the lip of the ledge then helped Anne and Cinda right after him, the nameless woman gripping their arms and hauling them clear.

"Blessed Mother," groaned the empath. "What is this?"

"A tunnel to safety," came the muffled voice of the arcanist. Already, he was speaking between shortened breaths. "You, fighter, there's a chain hanging on the right. Pull it when you're inside the tunnel."

Rew easily ascended behind the others and found they were crawling into the tunnel. It looked like an ancient, abandoned aqueduct that had once brought fresh water to the Arcanum. It was made of close-fit stones, and it was a tight space. As the others moved deeper, Rew could barely see Arcanist Reynald's light. The bodies of the others cast jagged shadows as they crawled after him.

The ranger rubbed his face with both hands then looked back into the pitch black behind him. Could whatever Reynald released be worse than the tiny, cramped tunnel?

"If he doesn't pull that chain, someone else do it," instructed Reynald. "If the vapors get inside of here, this tube will be our tomb."

Grunting, Rew felt around and found the chain. Then, he pulled it, and a series of sharp cranks and grinding of gears followed. There was a rush of water, and a waterfall of liquid poured down from somewhere above. Rew gaped, astonished. He couldn't see a thing behind him, but he could feel the hole filling with water, the spray billowing up to kiss his face. Then, he felt the water spilling over the edge of the ledge, wetting his boots and his knees.

"King's Sake, how much water is coming down?" he cried.

Arcanist Reynald, either unable to hear him or choosing not to, didn't respond.

Rew figured that regardless of the answer, he was better off moving. He scrambled into the tunnel, cracking his head on the ceiling as he went. His skull throbbing, rising water splashing as he went, he crawled behind the others into the dark.

THEY WEREN'T IN THE TUNNEL LONG, BUT IT FELT LIKE THEY WERE. The rush of water from behind had slowed, but it was still rising up the sloped tunnel. It made the stale air in the narrow space humid, and Rew felt like he couldn't get a breath. It didn't help that they were in near black, and only the feel of Cinda's boots when he got too close and the muttered curses of the others assured him he wasn't lost in some nightmare.

They crawled for a dozen city blocks, Rew figured, until they exited the tunnel into a circular room which he realized must be a cistern. Reynald's light bathed them all in its hot red glow. Rew stretched, looking up at a trapdoor far above and steel rungs sunk into the wall they could use to reach it. His gaze dropped to the arcanist.

"Care to tell us what that was about? You left her to die."

Clearing his throat, Arcanist Reynald said, "I, ah... We had no choice."

Rew waited.

The arcanist shifted, his sodden robes clinging to his legs, his chest rising and falling from the exertion of crawling through the tunnel. "I don't have the craft to stand against any enchanted artifacts the prince may have gifted Salwart, so I felt it best to take decisive measures. That preparation I handed the woman is toxic. Within moments, it would shatter the glass, and the fumes would spread over half the Arcanum. By my calculations, even now, we are just outside the reach of the cloud. Ah, depending on which way the wind is blowing, that is. Do you happen to recall before you came to my tower which way—"

"No, I don't recall," snapped Rew. "That flask was going to shatter on its own?"

Reynald nodded.

"Then why not let Lucia set it down outside the door and come with us? King's Sake, man, you've killed her for no reason!"

The arcanist coughed. "Perhaps setting it down would have worked. I didn't consider that. I just thought… It had to stay safe until the solution was fully mixed. A single drop spilled, and the composition would be off, and those legionnaires are as fumbled-fingered as children. I thought the woman holding the decanter was the best way. With hindsight, I'll concede things could have been done differently…"

"That's awful," stated Rew coldly.

The arcanist puffed up like a pastry in the oven, his face glowing red from his light. He claimed, "Scholarship is about efficiency, boy. Having the woman carry the solution was the easiest, quickest way. A better way, I might add, than anything I heard you offer when you came panicked to my doorstep. Besides, she was an agent of the king."

"What does that have to do with it?"

The arcanist fell silent, and Rew squinted at the man. An agent of the king? Why would… Reynald didn't want his secrets known. Whether Arcanist Reynald killed Lucia because of laziness or to cover those secrets, Rew wasn't sure. Eyeing the man, he thought it could be either. He resolved to watch his back around Reynald from then on. Rew, after all, had heard the same secrets Lucia had, and he was an agent of the king as well.

Shaking himself, the ranger turned to Cinda. "Can you confirm Lucia is dead?"

"Of course she's dead," muttered the arcanist, but they all ignored him.

Nodding, the necromancer closed her eyes, her lips tight. "She and dozens of others. I don't know Salwart well enough to identify his… flavor. If he was close enough, I imagine he met the same fate they all did."

Smiling, the arcanist crowed, "Thanks to the Mother's Grace."

"I'm not sure she'd be happy about her blessing being used this way," commented Anne.

"Well, yes, you're right," said the arcanist, hugging himself and jostling the vial of light around his neck. "I'm just grateful we escaped. I'd planned this route out in case there was ever trouble, but I've never had the need to test it. The water… Much could have gone wrong. The liquid barrier was the only thing which prevented the fumes spreading into the tunnel, and it worked! My own design. I thought it would work, but it always feels good to prove a theorem correct, don't you agree? Now, another minute or two to make sure whatever vapors are left have a chance to blow away, and we can emerge onto the street. The preparation is designed to fade quickly, but I'd avoid any tight spaces with poor ventilation over the next hour, just in case."

Rubbing his hand over his head, Rew looked around the cistern they were in. It had very poor ventilation.

"Lucia's dead…" murmured Anne, shaking her head. "She was no friend of mine, but I feel awful she died this way. She didn't deserve that. If you'd told us, if we'd known… We could have done something different."

The arcanist shrugged, his arms over his chest.

"Lucia is dead," repeated Rew, feeling like his heart just leapt into his throat.

"What?" asked Anne, sensing something in his tone.

"She claimed the king had bound his awareness to her soul," said Rew. "If he did, he'll have felt her death. Blessed Mother, the king may have felt her die!"

"What's that, now?" queried Arcanist Reynald.

"We need to go," said Rew. "Right now."

"Another minute for the solution to dissipate—"

"Right now," said Rew, and he rushed to the steel rungs in the wall and started to climb. "We have to get out of the Arcanum."

"I'm afraid I don't understand," called Arcanist Reynald, wringing his hands and backing toward the tunnel they'd emerged from. "You're taking a terrible risk, going up there. My plan is that I stay here, to make sure... I—I'm going to stay here."

Rew reached the top of the cistern and leaned over, tugging on a wheel that released a mechanism to open the trapdoor. He pushed the trapdoor open and saw the night air above. Climbing out, he leaned down and assisted Anne, who was coming on his heels. As he was pulling the empath free, a booming voice reverberated through the compound.

"REW, I KNOW YOU ARE HERE."

Under his breath, the ranger muttered, "Let's hope that's not true."

There was a pause while the voice echoed through the streets.

"I SET A TASK FOR YOU. FIND ALSAYER, BRING HIM TO ME ALIVE. FIND KALLIE FEDGLEY, BRING HER TO ME DEAD. I FELT HER SOUL WHEN SHE DEPARTED. I FOUND HER. I FOUND YOU TRICKED ME. IT WASN'T HER I NEEDED. HOW LONG HAVE YOU KNOWN?"

Thinking it best not to answer even quietly, Rew helped Cinda and the nameless woman out of the cistern and then began leading them down the street, staying close to the walls, hiding within the shadows.

Rew knew the voice. He'd heard it since he was a child. It was the king. Vaisius Morden must have portaled into the Arcanum the moment he felt his spy perish, and was now amplifying his words, casting them through the entire compound. Pausing, Rew frowned. Why would he do that? The king was likely telling the truth. If he'd found Kallie Fedgley's soul, he could have learned everything that she knew. The king knew it was Cinda, now. The king wasn't the type to ruminate on such things once the circumstances changed. He acted decisively. He acted quickly.

Pointing to a building, Rew led the others silently into an abandoned tower.

"YOU LEARNED THE SECRET OF THE SWORD? BE WARNED. MY FATHER WILL USE YOU TO HIS OWN ENDS. YOU CANNOT TRUST HIM. THERE'S A REASON I LOCKED HIM AWAY. DO NOT LISTEN TO HIS HONEYED WORDS. HE'LL USE YOU TO ESCAPE. DO. NOT. TRUST. HIM."

The old man had a point, but that's not why he was speaking. He was trying to drive Rew out of hiding. The sacrifice in Jabaan had worked. Rew was no longer bound to the king, but a company of the black legion were. They wouldn't have been affected by Reynald's poison. Even now, they could be moving through the Arcanum, hunting.

Rew wouldn't risk explaining that to the others. He didn't know how well the undead could hear or if the king had some other means to ferret them out. Fortunately, after listening to the king's booming voice, it seemed they all agreed that hiding was the thing to do.

They crouched down in the tower, leaving the door open but finding the deepest shadows. Rew drew more darkness about them. He gathered it like a cloak and spread it over the others. They must have felt what he was doing. Anne and Cinda had felt it before. They scooted closer, all pressed together in the corner of the empty tower, their eyes gleaming with fear.

There was a distant wail. Arcanist Reynald? Then nothing. Then the crunch of boots and armor. A shadow passed across the doorway. One of the black legion? It was impossible to tell in the dark. Rew held the pall of darkness, his illusion, hoping it worked as well against the undead as it did the living. He'd never needed to test it before.

The shadow moved on. A minute later, two more passed.

Rew and the others sat in silence, too terrified to even consider moving. Lethargy weighed on the ranger. It'd been a long day. Even lying prone, it was difficult to maintain the shadow around all of them, but he did. He had to. They weren't ready to face the king. Not yet. If they were found, it would be over.

The king's voice periodically called out, offering forgiveness, a chance to explain, warnings about Erasmus, and then taunts. Had the king known a little bit more of his son, he could have descended to the fort at the base of the hill. He could have forced Rew and the others to make a difficult decision, but evidently, he didn't know that half their party was down there. The king didn't know what levers he could pull, who he could hurt to get to Rew, or perhaps it hadn't occurred to him. Vaisius Morden would let his own sons murder each other so that he could take the strongest of their bodies. Maybe after so many years, so many deaths, he no longer understood remorse, how one person could care for another.

And then it was over.

The echoes of the voice faded. No more figures stalked by outside.

Had the king left? That didn't seem—

Rew grimaced. There was a tugging on him, like a fish hook sunk into his skin. He looked at Cinda, but she stared resolutely at the doorway to the tower. If she'd felt necromantic magic, she would have shown it. It was low magic, ancient magic, largely forgotten over the last two centuries. The king's binding to Rew's soul was severed, but they were still of the same blood.

Vaisius Morden couldn't work such magic from afar, but he was near them, somewhere outside. He might be able to find Rew.

The ranger let his thoughts drift, and he pushed, stretching with his mind to the land beyond the Arcanum. The compound was old, stable civilization, but the area around was wild. Rew gathered himself there, filling the space with himself. He spread, his consciousness swelling outward along the lines of the ancient magic that coursed through the world. The king would feel it. He'd know Rew was near, but not where. Vaisius Morden wouldn't be able to pin them down unless he brought more men, enough to blanket the entire compound. What would he do?

"Ah, Blessed Mother," whispered the ranger.

Rew grabbed the others and clutched them tight, rolling so that his body was over theirs. He flung himself out, riding the course of his own low magic, running adrift along the veins of power and clutching at the king. The old man might destroy the Arcanum, but he would shield himself first. If Rew could use the connection to bridge to the king, to wrap them in the king's high magic—

There was a roar. There was light. There was dark.

There was silence.

Chapter Twelve

W hen he opened his eyes, vibrant color filled his vision. Was he dead? Was this the afterlife? It was a lot bluer than he would have expected.

Then, Zaine's head popped into view as she leaned over him. She told him, "You look rough."

He wasn't sure if he was moving or speaking. He couldn't feel anything.

Vurcell joined the thief, frowning at him. "Aye, I haven't seen you this bad since after that night in Carff several years ago. You remember? Probably not. That woman wagered you couldn't drink the entire jug, and—"

"Now isn't the time," chided Anne's calm voice.

Calm.

Why was she calm?

The king had just blown up... Rew wasn't even sure. He couldn't summon the ability to turn his head and look, but he guessed the king must have blown up the entire Arcanum, if not more. King Vaisius Morden had tried to kill them. That he'd evidently failed wasn't reason for calm, it was reason for panic, and that wasn't even getting started on the fact that to the best of his recollection, they'd been inside when the explosion happened.

Blessed Mother, what had happened?

Anne, pushing the others aside, leaned into his view. She brushed her hair back. Her eyes were sunken, and dark semi-circles hung beneath them. Her lips were parched, and even her hand seemed thin, skeletal. She did not smile, as the others had, but her eyes had the same calm acceptance he'd heard in her voice. She'd healed him. King's Sake, she'd healed him. He wanted to fight, to thrash, to scream, but he couldn't move. He couldn't do anything. He saw, beyond the calm, the darkness in her eyes. She finally understood.

"I'm sorry, Rew. For what it's worth, you will live, but you need to rest."

Anne's hand, warm, the first sensation he'd felt since waking, brushed over his face, and he slept.

WHEN REW RETURNED TO CONSCIOUSNESS AGAIN, HE REGRETTED IT. Not just because Anne had healed him, but because every part of his body was aflame with pain. His skin felt blistered and raw, his muscles wrenched and torn, his bones hurt with a fierce ache he'd never known before. He hadn't thought bones could hurt, but they did. His skull roared in time with the beat of his heart, each new surge of blood vanquishing thought with a wave of agony. He would have cracked his own skull to end it, if he could summon the energy. His jaw quivered. Had he been clenching it for hours, for days?

Long enough that he'd been moved. He no longer saw blue sky above his head but canvass. It was lit by what looked to be natural light. The same day, the next day? His stomach rumbled at the thought.

He heard a rustling, and then Anne was above him again. "Let me help you up. I think you can take some broth now."

He didn't see as he had much choice in the matter, and before he could work up the ability to respond, Anne had put her hands beneath him and shifted him, putting something soft behind his head to prop him up.

Opening his mouth, he began to work it slowly. It felt numb, like a stranger's lips and tongue. He could move his eyes and glanced around the tent. He was sprawled out on a mat, a thick wool blanket over his body. The tent flap stirred from the air outside, and he could see it was day. There were several other empty pallets in the tent and Anne, who was leaning toward him with a bowl and a spoon.

He practiced swallowing, then managed the slightest nod to her. She began trickling the broth into his mouth, and at first, he felt nothing, but as more of the rich liquid dripped down his throat, he felt the warmth. She must have just taken it from the pot. Had that woken him? He didn't think so. He couldn't hear much beyond the walls of the tent. It felt like his ears were muffled with wool.

Anne was halfway through spooning the bowl into him before he garnered enough energy to speak. "What... Where?"

"We're two hours north of the Arcanum," replied Anne. She frowned. "What is left of the Arcanum. You remember, the king?"

He nodded, slightly.

"The entire place... exploded. You dove onto us, saving our lives. We were the only things that survived. The entire complex was demolished. It was a clean, controlled blast. The damage scoured the walls of the Arcanum and nothing beyond. Whether the king was striking at us or destroying evidence of what occurred within that place, I don't know. I supposed it could be both. All I know is that when I came to, you were lying on top of me, and while we were all the worse for wear, we were intact. The others were unscathed—more or less—but you were severely drained of life. I thought you might be dead. I poured empathy into you, but... What did you do?"

"I..." started Rew. He paused, trying to gather himself. "I knew the king would shield himself, so I channeled that protection. I—I am his son. I drew on our connection."

"Surely there's more?" asked Anne. "I've never heard of anyone doing such a thing with low magic. You must have used high, but…"

"Later," he said. He shifted and aimed at what he knew would reach her. "I'm feeling weak. I should rest."

Anne nodded and began spooning more broth into his mouth.

He was bone-tired. That was the truth. His body was more exhausted than he ever recalled being, but his mind, in fits and starts, was beginning to work again. He needed time to gather strength to talk, but he also needed time to muster his thoughts, to understand what had happened.

Anne kept feeding him, and as she did, she told him of the last three days. They'd been unconscious for several hours after the explosion, long enough that Ang and Vurcell had deemed it safe, and they and Raif and Zaine had come looking amongst the destruction of the Arcanum. They'd found the four members of the party lying unconscious in the lee of a blown-over tower. With their assistance, the party had escaped the ruins of the Arcanum, but the former rangers had sent them north instead of sheltering them in the fort. The twins worried about emissaries from the king coming to search the wreckage.

It'd been a wise concern, as a party of arcanists had appeared, though they'd spent no more than a few hours perusing the wreckage of the compound. It wasn't clear to Ang and Vurcell if that was because the arcanists already knew what had happened or if they were afraid to go too close to the scene of such an incredible conflagration. It must have occurred to the learned men and women that if the king was willing to lay waste to the Arcanum, their own lives were of little value to him.

Anne had told the former rangers what she knew, and all had agreed it was best for the party to remain in hiding until Rew recovered. Ang and Vurcell had arranged supplies, and since then, they'd all been waiting.

Rew nodded and felt his eyelids begin to droop.

"Sleep," instructed Anne, putting away the empty bowl she'd

been feeding him from. "On an empty stomach, this won't do much to fill you, but I'll give you more in a few hours when we know what you can keep down. Until then, sleep, and we'll be nearby if you need us."

Wordlessly, he closed his eyes, but it was some time before he finally fell asleep. He had a lot to think about.

THE KING WOULD BE ACTIVELY HUNTING THEM. NO MATTER HOW often Rew thought it, no matter what angle he assessed their situation from, no matter how many times he tried to imagine his way out of that simple fact, it never got better. The most powerful man in Vaeldon's history—the man who had formed the nation itself—would be putting all of his effort into tracking them down and killing them. And once dead, he would capture their souls. For eternity, they would dance on strings Vaisius Morden pulled.

The situation was grim.

The others tried to stay buoyant through Rew's recovery, but they all knew the score, and they all felt it. Cinda mentioned that they'd been planning on facing the king anyway, and Raif had declared he'd been aching to make it a fight. Zaine had tried to relieve the tension with her dry humor, but her barbs landed on raw flesh, and quickly she gave up and kept quiet. The nameless woman seemed shocked, as if she couldn't decide how things had gone so wrong. She didn't come to see Rew in his tent, and the others told him she rarely spoke at all. Anne was a soothing presence for everyone, performing the same functions she always had. She cooked, consoled, and chided them to not give up hope.

It went without saying that while their challenge seemed insurmountable, doing anything possible to avoid falling into the king's clutches was worth trying. It wasn't a show of bravery or a commitment to doing the right thing. In truth, it was the only thing they could do. They had to admit that their situation was what it was. The truth wasn't pleasant, but it was motivation, and that's what gave Rew the idea which finally got him moving again.

It'd been a week since the explosion at the Arcanum, and they'd been staying hidden in the tiny encampment Ang and Vurcell had found for them. It wasn't comfortable, and boring was the most pleasant description anyone voiced for their week of recuperation, but the isolated camp kept them safe. As the days passed, their instincts to hide were confirmed as valid, and eventually, they stopped complaining.

During those days, either Ang or Vurcell managed to slip away a few times to share news, but all of it involved an increased presence at the fort, the lockdown of the women's colony, and the release of hundreds of the king's legion on the countryside to try and find trace of Rew and the others.

The best of the king's legion was out there, but not the king's rangers. The twins had obscured the signs Rew and the party had left during their flight, and no common soldier was going to be able to follow the trail. Hidden as their encampment was, the odds of random discovery were low.

"Just a few hundred soldiers?" asked Rew. "That's more for show than a real effort to locate us."

"I agree," responded Ang. "It's been a week. They probably think you've been moving since then, but the king has to put on some sort of performance for the soldiers and the women who know what happened up there. Rew, it's better than the alternative."

Rew grunted. Ang was right. The king had stayed his hand and had contained the conflagration he'd released within the Arcanum. When it came to protecting his secrets, Vaisius Morden wasn't always so considerate of those nearby.

"What about the rangers?" inquired Rew. "Has he sent anyone after us?"

"He won't," said Ang. He looked over his shoulder, as if afraid that somehow, hours from anywhere, someone might overhear him. "The rangers are… no longer the king's. He made a mistake trying to hide the truth from us. We all know the stories, what has occurred during previous Investitures. We see it happening now, no matter how hard the king pretends we do not. It's too much, Rew. None of us want to serve that man."

"I hope no one is doing anything stupid," warned Rew.

Ang shrugged. "It's too much. They'd rather follow you. Most of them know who you are, Rew."

Rew lay quietly. Finally, he said, "It's not just the king."

"The princes—"

"Ang," interrupted Rew, "I want to believe what we are doing is right, but we've brought much sorrow to this world. I'm not the leader the rangers need, that Vaeldon needs."

"Rew," replied Ang, his words tumbling slowly from his lips, "I know your sorrow. I can see it in Anne's eyes, even if neither of you will voice it. I… Rew, right now Vaeldon doesn't need a better king. One day, I hope that need will come, but today, we need to get rid of the king we have. It's going to be messy, and it's going to be painful. We know that. It's not despite the sorrow this will cause. It's because of the sorrow it will cause that the rangers will follow you. They'll follow you, knowing that in the end, no matter how painful, it was for the right reasons."

Rew let out a sharp, bitter chuckle. "Follow me to their deaths, most likely."

"Perhaps," replied Ang, "but if there's a path to a better future, they'll take it. I know you worry about putting others in danger, but we're already in danger. Isn't it safer if we walk the path together? If the rangers oppose the king alone, they're going to get killed for nothing. We both know that's happened before. He's too powerful, and the others have no skills with which to face him. If you have a way, you have to lead us."

Ang was right. The rangers, despite their collective skill, were no match for the king. They knew that, and still, they were willing. They were willing because they knew the truth of Vaisius Morden's reign. His power was nigh limitless, and he stood on unshakable ground, supported by the strength of an entire kingdom.

But what if he didn't?

The king's rule was never challenged because everyone knew how foolhardy and doomed to failure such a challenge would be. The legend of his might did as much to protect Vaisius Morden as his actual power. It was a wall that no one could fathom climbing.

But maybe they could put some cracks into that wall. Maybe, like it had done for the rangers, the truth could mint new allies. Rew, thinking it over as he spoke, told the others the beginnings of a plan.

"Hold on," said Zaine. "You're suggesting we... spread the truth?"

Cinda crossed her arms over her chest and stated, "After all of your demands for secrecy, Ranger, this seems a rather curious time to dispense with it. Are you sure about this? Sure you didn't, ah, knock your head during that explosion? If we start spreading rumors—yes, I know, the truth—if we start spreading it, won't that make it even more difficult to sneak around the kingdom? I realize the king is looking for us with all of his resources, but why encourage everyone else to come looking for us as well?"

Rew shook his head. "The point is, if we start spreading the truth, it could burst into a fire the king has to spend time putting out. And if he's putting resources into tamping down the truth, those are resources he isn't spending on finding us. And if others are looking for us, what of it? I'm not suggesting we give everyone our descriptions. Very few people in the Northern Province will recognize any of us, and the king isn't going to go pasting up posters with our likeness. Do you see? If we tell the truth, we force the king to help keep things quiet. If he gives my description to every nobleman, spellcaster, and soldier in his service, it will confirm our story! He can't show fear. The harder he searches for us, the more it validates us as a threat, undermines the myth of his power."

"Aye, but will that actually help us?" challenged Raif. "We're not afraid of his black legion or even his spellcasters. The thing we fear the most is the king himself. His power isn't just a myth. Baron Worgon was a fool, but when we fostered with him, he had a saying about not poking a sleeping bear. Telling everyone what we're doing is poking the bear, Ranger."

"The king can't want to kill us anymore than he already does," argued Rew. "I don't see us bringing any additional risk down on our heads by spreading the truth. It may force him to keep his dogs on the leash, and who knows? If the king is no longer seen as invincible, perhaps we'll gather allies we haven't expected. The rangers know, and they're eager to join the fight."

"But they are rangers. I'm not saying they are crazy, but they are wild loners who spend all of their time off in the wilderness. The king is invincible, more or less," retorted Zaine. "Without Cinda, no one else can face him, right? If we recruit allies, we'll be sending them to their deaths."

Shaking his head, Rew replied, "I don't want anyone to defy the king to his face, but they can work against him behind his back, out of his sight. Not even Vaisius Morden can be every- where. Not even he can rule this kingdom without allies and others to do his bidding."

The younglings turned to Anne, perhaps hoping she'd talk Rew out of his reckless course of action, but the empath sat studying him, her hands clasped and resting under her chin.

"Well?" asked Cinda, prodding the empath to speak.

"I think," started Anne, "that we should walk the path we were meant to walk. We should live the lives we were born to live. Maybe only Cinda has the talent to face the king, but our mission is about more than just the man. It's about the kingdom. Beyond us, beyond the king, there is the kingdom. The people of the kingdom have a right to know the truth. Rew is a son of Vaisius Morden. That's the truth. This is his path to walk."

"I can't believe I'm the one advocating stealth, but this seems dangerous to me," muttered Raif, scowling around the group. "I don't mind a fight, but if we share the truth, we lose our advantage. We might not be able to pick the place and time of the fight."

"You're growing," said Rew with a grin. "You're right. There's a time for stealth, but eventually, you've got to come out of the shadows. I think that time is now."

"Do you really think that just by telling the world who you are, you'll distract the king enough it gives us a chance?"

"Right now," said Rew, "every noble in the kingdom is focused on the Investiture. They're scrambling to realign after Calb's death, lining up behind either Valchon or Heindaw. Their armies, their spellcasters, all of them are being assembled for a final clash, but what if they have to watch their flanks? Will that freeze them? Will that force them to withdraw, to keep their soldiers off the field of battle?"

"Or force them to act immediately!" cried Raif. "Anyone who's lined up behind your brothers will have an incentive to kill you. I imagine the princes will shower wealth, land, and titles on whomever brings them your head."

Rew, drumming his fingers on the bone hilt of his hunting knife, responded, "I'm not sure you're right. The nobles of this land respect strength, and their one true goal is to end up on the winning side. We killed Calb. If you're a baron trying to decide who to support, do you throw your lot in with a prince who destroyed his own city, Stanton, and the baron of that city in the process, or do you join a prince whose only plots have failed and who hides behind his walls? Or would it be better to support the one person who's actually killed a prince? Raif, we're the only ones who've proven success in this terrible game. I think if anything, the nobles may want to join us."

"The winning side," grumbled Raif, shaking his head. He leaned forward. "The way you talk, it's like you're planning to recruit your own army. Walk your path, eh, Ranger, but that's not the tune you've been singing since we met you."

Rew laughed. "No, Raif, I don't plan to raise an army or to try and collect allies beyond what we already have. I'm not my brothers, and I won't put anyone at risk who isn't fully committed. I plan to settle things personally, but my brothers don't know that. My brothers are spellcasters and politicians. They work from afar like Valchon did against Stanton, or in secrecy like Calb did against Carff, or through intermediaries like Heindaw did against your father. They won't understand what I plan, so instead, they'll defend against what they would do in our position. We don't need Vaeldon's nobles to join us, we just need them to think about it, to undermine the trust the princes have in them. We need the nobles out of our way, and I think the truth will send them scattering."

"It is not the worst idea," said Cinda, frowning. She brushed a strand of black hair behind her ear, her eyes flashing pale green in the diffuse light of the hollow they hid within. "We're not really doing anything, really. We're just talking about leveraging rumor to force the princes and the king to defend against a position we're not taking. It's a feint, like on a Kings and Queens board. It's a ruse to trick them into watching their backs when we're coming at the front. I—as long as that's all we're doing—support it."

Raif grunted. "That gives me little choice."

"You always said I'm the strategist, big brother," replied Cinda with a wink.

"As long as Rew doesn't forget he wasn't the only one in that crypt in Jabaan," grumbled Raif. He slapped the hilt of his greatsword. "We did our part, too."

"I wouldn't have made it out of there without you," agreed Rew. Then, he glanced around the circle. "All of you. We survived Jabaan together, and we should move forward together. If you disagree and think we should continue in secrecy, we will."

Anne smiled at him. "We should live the lives we were meant to live. You're the king's son, Rew. Like it or not, this is who you are. The world should know."

Zaine shrugged. "I prefer stealth, and suddenly telling everyone who we are makes me nervous, but if I stopped following you because you'd come up with a stupid plan, I would have left long ago. I guess that means I'm in as well."

"You have my support," declared Cinda. She picked at the crimson robes she'd been wearing since the fishing village. She winked at them. "And I won't even accuse the ranger of stealing my idea."

Rew grinned, and Raif huffed, "This whole thing is about Cinda. If this is how she wants to proceed, then I'll go along with it."

The nameless woman cleared her throat, and they all turned to her. "I, ah... I know I've betrayed your trust, but I spoke true when I said I'd do whatever was needed to free my father from the king's grasp. I thought the prince and the arcanist would help me, but I can see that's not the case. What they were doing in that room, with those soldiers... My father wouldn't accept that price, even for his own soul. I cannot ask you to put your trust in me, but I will put my trust in you. I'll do whatever you ask of me, whether that means leaving you or it means my death. You're the only hope my father has, and you have my help if you can accept it."

"I don't think we need to be quite so dramatic as an execution," murmured Rew.

In truth, though, he wondered. The woman, who still had not told them her name, had betrayed them. He believed she'd been surprised at the depths of evil her allies had sunken to, but they'd still been her allies. Just because she was shocked at their actions didn't mean she'd turned from them. She'd said it herself, she'd do anything to free her father. She'd only be loyal as long as she thought they were her best hope. If she even believed that now, Rew thought bitterly. Of course a spy would lie to remain in their party. They couldn't trust her, but going to Iyre, facing Heindaw and the rest of the Sons of the Father... They could use her. Relationships had been made on less.

"So all we have left to discuss is how?" questioned Cinda. She gestured around the quiet hollow they were hidden within. "I could try yelling really loud, but I don't think that's going to do it. Deciding to spread a rumor across Vaeldon is one thing, actually doing it..."

"The rangers will help," offered Ang. He smiled. "They're aching to do something useful."

Rew nodded. "The rangers are a good start, but most of them are quiet by nature and aren't likely to generate the attention we need. It's a risk, but we could start rumors amongst the king's legion. Ang, do you think that's possible?"

"I think it will be easy," boasted the captain. "Our command is isolated, but there are hundreds of extra soldiers in the area looking for you. Every evening, those men pass through our mess hall, speculating about what happened and what it means. Vurcell and I have a few trusted people, and we can get the gossip turned the way you want it. When those men go back to their home barracks, word will spread like fire through the legions."

Rew nodded, satisfied. He turned to Anne. "What about the women's network? Those contacts who funnel women to the colony and those who have left it?"

"The women won't like it," remarked Anne. "They've developed a taste for secrecy out of necessity. If they begin spreading rumors to all of the apothecaries, nursemaids, and healers in Vaeldon, someone is going to come looking for the source of those rumors. That puts the colony at great risk, and Mother Solomon will balk at that."

"She'll like what else I have planned for her even less."

Anne frowned.

"You know her history?"

Anne's eyes widened. "I-I don't think she'll do it, Rew. She came to the colony to escape all of that."

Rew glanced at the others. "Before she came to this part of the world, Mother Solomon was a baroness in Jabaan. She was well-known and well-thought of. She outshone her husband, which may have been what led him to... That's no matter now. He's dead, and it hasn't been so long that she would have been forgotten in the city. She has children in Jabaan still, doesn't she?"

Anne shrugged. "I believe so."

"Jabaan will be the source of enormous political activity for weeks as Valchon and Heindaw scramble to collect Calb's allies. It's the perfect place for our story to spread."

"She won't lie for you."

Rew offered Anne a tight grin. "I won't ask her to. She only needs to tell the truth. I claimed to have killed Calb, and I hid at the women's colony and entered the Arcanum. It was destroyed, and I still live."

"The king will know we had nothing to do with the destruction of the Arcanum," pointed out Raif.

"The part that will matter to him is confirmation that we were there as he suspected and that we still live. By the time he hears it, I hope we're long gone from the area. But for everyone else, they'll naturally assume we did have something to do with the explosion. What is the king going to do? Tell everyone he destroyed his own compound and killed all of his own people? Between that and what everyone experienced in Jabaan, they'll believe we're serious players. Pfah, the work is already started there if anyone saw us and survived. The city could already know we were behind Calb's death. It's going to work. This is how we crack the wall of the king's mythology. This is how we plant the seeds that will grow into dissent."

"What if no one believes you're the king's son?" questioned Cinda. "He's never acknowledged you publicly, has he? We have the disadvantage of history and what people have always known. The truth won't do us a bit of good if no one accepts it."

"They may not believe that part, but I'm not sure it will matter," argued Rew. "Whether or not I'm the king's son, Stanton, the battle in Carff, Jabaan and Calb's death, and the destruction of the Arcanum are all serious events. These are things the king cannot cover up. If one accepts we were involved in them... then what else will one accept? Whether or not I am his son, the fact that we are defying the king sows doubt about him and his story."

"Fair enough," conceded Cinda.

Continuing, Rew added, "At the least, Valchon and Heindaw know I'm their brother, and if they think I'm finally a player in the Investiture, it will make them cautious. If we keep them from attacking, that could save lives."

Chapter Thirteen

Mother Solomon had been a noblewoman, a wife, a mother, a baroness, and the leader of the women's colony. She'd spent years perfecting her glare. She poured every moment of that practice into the glare she delivered to Rew, and she held it, as if attempting to wither him like grass beneath a relentless summer sun. She stared at him without speaking, her eyes and the set of her jaw communicating everything that was not being said. She looked as though, if she'd thought she could do it, she would have reached across the table and strangled the ranger with her bare hands.

He returned her look steadily, not wanting to force her if he didn't have to. He would give her time to consider what they'd said and what it meant.

Finally, she drew a deep, ragged breath and commented, "You know what that will mean for me if I turn up in Jabaan and claim I saw you? It will mean my death after a long and excruciating period of torture. If I claim to have seen you, even if no one believes I assisted you, they will think I may have some clue as to where you went. If I deny that I know anything, that won't stop them. Nothing will stop them except me calling out like a song-bird. They'll draw every bit of information from me, no matter how hard I try to stop them. Everyone breaks under torture, and I've no illusions that I'll last longer than most."

"Then save everyone the effort and tell them what you know," suggested Rew. "That's the point. Tell the truth."

"The truth? What is the truth? That you are the son of the king? I'm not sure I believe that, Ranger." Mother Solomon glanced at Anne, a worried frown on her face. "Is it true, really? You actually mean to do the things you say you will do? You don't strike me as that big of a fool."

Rew smirked at her. "It doesn't matter if you believe it or not. Tell everyone it's what I said. Tell people you don't believe it if that makes it easier, but just tell them."

"They'll press me for where you went."

"Then, tell them."

"I can't tell them what I don't know!" she cried.

"Tell them we're going to Iyre where I plan to kill Prince Heindaw," said Rew. He leaned forward, staring into her eyes. "They'll believe that, Mother Solomon, because it's the truth."

She blinked at him, her mouth hanging open.

"You're right," continued Rew. "There is grave risk for you returning to Jabaan and sharing what you know, but I don't think it's as certain a risk as you believe. The king won't act, because how would that look? His involvement would only confirm the absolute truth of what you say. The same with the princes. Denouncing you grants legitimacy to what you say. Remain in the public eye, and they cannot touch you."

Mother Solomon looked away, staring out the window. Rew followed her gaze and saw she was staring at the shattered ruins of the Arcanum.

He told her, "What happened here is not a beginning or an end. It's simply another step in a march that's been going on for over two hundred years. It's a step in a march that will go on for two hundred more years unless someone stops it. I can't right everything that is wrong in this world. I can't stop men from doing the things to their wives and daughters that drive those women here. I won't claim that if the king is dead, any of that will end. It won't. There will still be pain, still tragedy, no matter what happens. But that," he pointed out the window to the ruins of the Arcanum, "is something we can stop. It's a leap to a better world, if not a perfect one. You've devoted the last decade to making things better. Will you not help us make that big leap?"

Grunting, Mother Solomon stood and walked to a small cabinet at the side of her room. She looked inside of it then plucked a wax-sealed bottle of wine and shook it at Rew. "Years ago, do you know how I survived my husband's wrath? I nearly drowned myself in this. I drank every day, trying to numb the pain, trying to forget, I guess. I stopped drinking after I came here and rejoined the world. I forged connections—real friendships— for the first time in years. I found strength in this colony. You're asking me to leave all of that, to leave who I've become."

"What your husband did to you is like what the king is doing to—"

"Rew, that's a little much, don't you think?" snapped Anne. Shaking her head, the empath adjusted her shawl and said, "I suffered a great deal in this place, taking the pain of hundreds. I like to think it was worth it, but I don't know. That pain clung to me. I eventually found peace in Eastwatch. There was still pain and suffering, but there was also life, friendships. The people there, the wilderness, the quiet, helped me swallow the hurt and process it. I could have been happy there for a long time, the rest of my life, I think, but some things are more important than my happiness. What kind of person would I be if I'd stayed there and hadn't done what I could?"

Mother Solomon slammed the cabinet door shut with the wine bottle inside and stalked back to her desk. She threw herself into her chair and gave the party one last good glare. Then, she asked, "All right. How do we do this?"

Rew raised his hand and drawled, "If you're not going to drink that wine…"

THEY CUT ALONG A LOW MOUNTAIN RANGE EAST OF THE ARCANUM. Beyond, they would head north into a broad, flat plain. The land on the foothills of the mountains was open, dry, and cold near the tail of winter. They had exceptional visibility down below, but they were vulnerable. The elevation provided a little comfort, but with winter-bare branches on the thin trees that dotted the slope, they weren't invisible.

For two days, they would be parallel to the road that led from the Arcanum. Rew considered ascending higher into the mountains, but it was more difficult travel there and might add a week to their journey.

So they walked along cautiously, hoping that their hunters had already given up. Several times an hour, Rew or one of the others would raise his spyglass to their eye and look up and down the road which led from the Arcanum. Occasionally, they spotted movement or thought they might have, and everyone scrambled for cover. They would stand sideways behind the thickest tree trunk they could find, crouch behind boulders, or simply lie flat on the ground so they didn't present a profile.

Odds were, any travelers on the road would have nothing to do with them, but the king's soldiers had been in the area, and they would avoid those men if they could. They couldn't risk word getting back to Vaisius Morden that they were still around. Cinda wasn't ready to face the king, and after the explosion at the Arcanum, Rew was certain his instincts ten years before had been correct. He didn't have the strength to stand up to his father either. Vaisius Morden was simply too powerful.

But his minions would be another story. Rew could cross steel with the soldiers if necessary, and even the king's spellcasters would have trouble facing the ranger individually. They were talented, but mortal men like all others, and the ranger didn't plan to give them the chance of a fair fight. Worst case, if they saw a group too large to contend with, the party would run.

As long as they didn't encounter a group led by a spellcaster with the ability to portal, Rew thought their chances were good. The only portal stones nearby had been within the Arcanum, and the king had destroyed those. They were days away from major cities or fortresses, so as long as they were vigilant and did not allow any of the king's forces to get close to them, Rew wasn't overly worried. They could fight, or they could flee. The king didn't have anyone who could track him through the mountainous terrain, and there would be few in the kingdom with the speed and stamina their small party had developed after months of constant travel.

Ang and Vurcell had promised him the other rangers would support him. If forced to track him, they would make sure they didn't find him. Rew hadn't been certain about the other rangers, but he was sure of the twins. They'd reached out through their enchanted mirror and gotten in contact with the contingent of rangers in Mordenhold. The twins claimed the king's rangers had been eager to help and were already at work spreading rumors—the truth—about what was happening. The rangers were organizing at a rallying point in Mordenhold because, according to the twins, they wanted to do more than talk.

Rew had discouraged it, but the twins had minds of their own, as did the other rangers. Vurcell had curtly explained they were going to fight, so didn't Rew want to make the best use of their assistance? It was implied that if he didn't, the rangers were going to end up dying fruitlessly. It was an unfair argument, but Ang had added that life was not fair.

"We all know the histories, Rew," Vurcell had said. "We know what failure means. This is our kingdom, and it's our fight as well."

Rew had grunted and left it at that. He didn't plan to call upon the rangers, but he appreciated the twins' confidence. And, as Cinda reminded him before they left, it was sheer arrogance to believe they could do this alone. Looking past Rew, she'd instructed Ang and Vurcell to carry on and claimed that Rew would be in touch.

"Give us a week, and we'll be ready," the twins had told her. "Rew knows how to reach us through the old ways, if you can convince him to do it."

So, with the rangers at work behind them, they hiked, and they hid.

"You shouldn't have told everyone we're going to Iyre," groused Anne, two days from the Arcanum where they were turning around the tail of the mountain and facing the vast plain north of it. "They'll be waiting for us. We could have told them we were going to Carff again, you know. It would have accomplished the same thing."

"I know," said Rew with a grin. "It's part of the plan."

Anne raised an eyebrow.

"We can't portal, and we can't use the portal stones safely, so what other way do we have to be sure we catch one of the princes? They can cross the continent in the span of a breath, Anne. We won't win this chasing after them. We've got to force them to wait or get them to come to us. I figured having them wait was better, for now. By telling everyone we're going to Iyre, we make sure Heindaw will be there when we arrive. Anything else and his allies will think he's frightened of us and is fleeing."

For several hours after that conversation, Anne did not speak to him.

THE NEXT DAY, HAVING SKIRTED AROUND THE MOUNTAIN RANGE AND away from the roads, Rew felt comfortable descending onto the plains. They walked there, on the edge of the vast savannah, keeping close to the edge of the forest which bordered the western fringe. Out in the grasslands, there was nowhere to run or to hide. There were other dangers as well that he would avoid if they could.

To their left, the forest offered sanctuary, but travel through it would take them twice as long. Unlike the wilderness he'd called home the last decade, the western forest was second growth. It was thick with vegetation near its boundary. Thatches of blackberry brambles wove between slender pines, and ferns sprouted in profusions hiding the way ahead. Thin streams trickled in narrow rivulets off the plains and poured into the forest, disappearing in the green expanse.

"Are there rangers who monitor this area?" wondered Cinda, walking beside Rew and studying the wall of forest in the distance.

"There are, though they'd rarely travel the border of the wood," he said with a nod. "Strange men, out here. They keep to themselves. Care more for what's out in the forest than the people of Vaeldon. At least, they did. I thought they did."

Had the rangers not cared about the people of Vaeldon, or had they cared too much and had run away? He grimaced. Had he cared too much or too little when he'd gone to Eastwatch ten years prior?

"What about out there, on the plains?" asked the necromancer, interrupting his thoughts and gesturing to the open on their right side. "Any rangers out there?"

Rew shook his head. "There are some people who live on the plains but no rangers. The beasts that live there, well, they stay in the grasslands. They aren't the same sort of threat to men as those which lurk in the wilderness. No Dark Kind out there on the plains. Nowhere for them to hide."

"Mmm hmm," replied Cinda.

Rew snorted, hearing the sarcasm in her voice. "I wasn't hiding in the wilderness. Not exactly. I spent as much time in Eastwatch as I did the wood. Someone has to watch the wild places in the world. The beasts are dangerous, but you've seen what Dark Kind can do when they gather."

"What would these western rangers do if they did find Dark

Kind? There's no cities around here to call for reinforcements, are there?"

"There is one big city northeast of here—Olsoth. It has a portal stone connecting to Mordenhold. If they needed to, within a week, the rangers could get word to the king's forces. That's quicker, actually, than I could manage from the east. None of the cities in the Eastern Territory have a portal stone, so I'd have to rely on help from Yarrow or Falvar. Spinesend, if it was serious, though it'd be two weeks there and two weeks back."

"Should we avoid Olsoth, then?" wondered Cinda. "If someone could portal directly to Mordenhold…"

"We'll avoid it if we can," agreed Rew. "The plains… Sometimes, they are difficult to travel. There are things we don't want to meet out there, like in any of the wild regions."

"What sort of things, Ranger?" demanded Raif from behind them.

Rew waved a hand dismissively. "Odds are, with a party this small, we won't have to worry about it. I think we can easily avoid Olsoth and everything else."

"What are you not telling us?" pressed Cinda.

Rew smirked. "You wouldn't believe me if I did tell you."

Behind them, the nameless woman barked a guffaw, and both of the nobles looked back at her in surprise. It'd been a day since the woman had said anything.

She grinned at them and claimed, "He's right. You wouldn't believe it."

Rew lengthened his stride, and the rest hurried after him, muttering under their breath. He looked over the plains, thinking of what was out there and deciding the children had enough to stew over. They would be safe going this way, just along the edge of the plains. Probably.

The rest of the day passed uneventfully. The hiking was easy for seasoned travelers, and when they paused, Rew scavenged firewood from the forest and allowed them a small campfire, though buried deep in the turf to hide it. Hot food and warmth were worth the small risk anyone might see them. The fuel was dry, so the smoke was minimal, and night was coming soon to hide the rising plume of gray. They were several days from anywhere, and he thought it unlikely even the king would be able to locate them in such a desolate region.

While Anne cooked their supper, the nameless woman removed her bronze armor and began tending to it. The bronze plate and chain glistened with a light sheen of oil, and she worked a cloth over it with the familiarity of having done it hundreds of times before. Rew opened his mouth and then closed it. He wanted to question her, plumb her secrets, but he knew all he would find were lies. She'd shown her colors. She was in league with Heindaw. Was she escorting them into a trap for the prince? That was Heindaw's way, though it seemed an elaborate plan even for the prince, when the nameless woman could have simply slit their throats on dozens of nights since she'd joined them.

Closer to the fire, Raif and Zaine sat together, the nobleman telling the thief an amusing story about a time in Baron Worgon's court. Their knees touched, and Raif leaned in while Zaine lay back, propped on her elbows. Friends, but Raif would have preferred more, and now his pride wouldn't allow him to stop trying. Zaine wasn't going to be interested no matter how hard the young fighter tried, which Rew suspected even Raif realized by now, but she enjoyed the attention, and the nobleman was as stubborn as a stump. Shaking his head, Rew looked away. He supposed he'd pursued plenty of foolish things in his own youth.

Cinda was on the other side of the fire flipping pages in the book Lucia had given her. She was reading by the light of her funeral fire, the pale glow bathing the open book but not extending past it. With nothing else useful to be doing, Rew crawled over to her.

"Find anything interesting?" he asked in a low voice he hoped didn't carry to the others.

Smiling wanly, Cinda responded just as quietly. "Perhaps. I wish Ambrose had survived long enough for me to discuss this with him. The man didn't have the raw talent to ever become powerful, but he was intelligent enough and had a bit of experience. He would have made more sense of this than I can."

"Intelligent except that he locked himself in a crypt—"

"To escape a worse fate," interrupted Cinda. "Ambrose knew what we were attempting, and he knew the consequences of failure. He was driven by cowardice, true, but I'm not so sure he was a fool. We will all die, Ranger, one day. We can't avoid that fate, and Ambrose knew it. He made the choice to pass quickly into the darkness, to avoid the threat of the king claiming his soul. Perhaps he understood that a few more years of life wasn't worth the risk of an eternity of imprisonment."

"That's only a wise choice if you ignore the peril to everyone else," muttered Rew, struggling to put force behind his words.

Cinda grinned. "Ambrose wasn't a hero. He was practical. I'm not suggesting we all follow in his path, but he did teach me one thing. There is much in this world to be afraid of, but I cannot be afraid of death. I cannot be afraid of dying and do what is needed."

Rew grimaced.

"You always knew what I would have to become for us to challenge the king," said Cinda, leaning close so no one else could hear them. "It's why you were so hesitant for us to take this path, wasn't it? You knew what it'd do to me."

Rew nodded, looking into the campfire instead of the white-green mockery that Cinda's funeral fire cast.

"It's all right, Ranger. In a way, I'm already dead. My old life is over, done. Like in death itself, there is no going back to that life. It's easier to think of it that way. I've already died, so that fear no longer clutches at my soul."

Shaking his head, Rew finally turned to the girl. "Cinda..."

"Anything useful in there?" asked Zaine suddenly before plopping down next to Cinda. "I haven't done a lot of reading myself, but I've always wondered what's in books. Must be something important to spend so many hours writing all of it down."

Grinning, Cinda closed the book and declared, "Well, they wasted their time with this one. It's a philosophical musing on the nature of high magic rather than any instruction on how to cast high magic. Like a treatise on being a thief and how theft is a vital part of a city's economy, but they never tell you how to pick a lock or scale a wall. No wonder you so rarely hear of an arcanist doing something useful."

"Aye, arcanists!" barked Zaine, acting as if she was throwing an imaginary book into the fire. She pursed her lips and then said, "Perhaps I should write a book one day when all of this is over. Can't be that hard, can it, once I learn to read?"

Cinda coughed, her funeral fire flicking out and giggles bubbling from her lips.

"Maybe you could do the writing, and I could... ah..."

"Dictate?"

Zaine frowned at Cinda. "Does that mean what I think it does?"

"Unless you two plan to start writing your book tonight, I could use some help preparing the potatoes," called Anne from where she was chopping wild onions and garlic Rew had foraged from the forest.

Cinda and Zaine both rose to their feet. Whispering to Cinda, Zaine asked, "If we overthrow the king, do you think she'll stop ordering us around?"

Smirking, Cinda replied, "I hope not."

The two girls went to help the empath finish supper, and Rew flipped open the blank leather cover of the book Cinda had been reading. He winced. He'd turned to a random page in the middle of the book. Inscribed on the thin, ancient paper in spidery script were specific instructions on issuing commands to a soul which you had bound. In the seconds Rew glanced at it, it appeared the book was a practical discussion of how to animate corpses and control them. He closed the book and his eyes. After a moment, he got up and joined the others at the fire.

Chapter Fourteen

For three more days, they hiked on the outskirts of the empty plains that bridged the territory between the Western and Northern Provinces. Wind whistled over the grasses, biting through their clothes, but while it wasn't the most pleasant journey, it was easy. There were few dangers from the forest, as the barren landscape and poor soil which made it difficult for people to settle along the edge also made it difficult for the monsters of the world to survive, and they stayed well clear of the heart of the plain.

"There's nothing out there at all, is there?" asked Raif one afternoon, holding his hand above his eyes, staring out at the open grasslands.

"There are giant herds of wild cattle," said Rew. He scratched his beard. "Horses as well, I imagine, though I never much cared for them. A few settlements that are tiny even compared to East-watch. But you're right. There's little else."

"You're forgetting the land wyrms," mentioned the nameless woman from behind them.

It was the first time that day she'd spoken. Rew was content with her silence, at least until he figured a way to question her and believe the answers.

"What'd you say?" asked Raif.

"Ah, yes, the land wyrms," agreed Rew, not bothering to look toward the woman. "I don't suspect we'll see one of those. There aren't many left."

Raif laughed then stopped. He glanced between Rew and the nameless woman. "What's a land wyrm?"

"Giant... ah, wyrms," responded the ranger. "They crawl beneath the surface of the grasslands hunting the cattle. They sense the vibrations the animals make when they move as a herd. It's why there's little risk to us. There aren't enough of us to set off any tremors the wyrms could detect from afar."

"Worms hunting cattle?" asked Raif incredulously.

"I told you they wouldn't believe it," said the nameless woman.

"Big wyrms," clarified Rew, holding up his hands to demonstrate. "Well, bigger than this. Big enough to eat cattle."

"If they're no threat to us, why aren't we walking across the plain?" questioned Zaine. "It looks like easy enough travel, and a straight line is bound to be quicker than the circuitous route we're on now."

Rew snorted. "Circuitous route. I'm supposed to be the ranger here."

"I heard Cinda say it," replied Zaine. "It seemed a pertinent description."

Rew grunted. "Did you hear her say pertinent, too?"

Zaine grinned at him.

"She's got a good point," remarked Raif. "Would it be quicker to cross the plains?"

Rew sighed and told them, "I said there was little danger from the wyrms. That's different than no danger."

"If a wyrm does detect someone, it can move a lot faster than us, and it's a lot bigger," added the nameless woman. "The ranger is right. It's better to take the extra time and circle our way around."

Neither the fighter nor the thief believed them until a few days later when they crossed a broad expanse of churned-up turf. It was two dozen paces across, and it looked as if something massive had slithered below.

"King's Sake," muttered Raif.

"I told you," reminded Rew. "Big wyrms."

Shaking his head, Raif mumbled, "I've never heard of these things. They're just out here, in the grasslands?"

Rew nodded. "As far as I know. Each piece of the world has its strange creatures and its own monsters. There aren't any simians or primal sloths in this region, but in truth, I'd rather face one of those than a land wyrm. Fighting the wyrms is a particular skill, and there are those who make a career of it, but I'm afraid I never gave it much attention. Believe me, when the things find you, they can wreak havoc."

They walked on, but it wasn't for two more days until they all realized how true those words were. They came across another disturbance in the soil and quickly found signs of what had happened. At the end of a long trough torn through the surface of the plain, they found the broken hilt of a sword, the blade missing, a travel pack, and a boot. There were no bodies, but it was pretty obvious where those had gone.

"Can't detect people, eh?" asked Zaine.

"Not normally," replied Rew. He looked around and saw a low rise. He climbed it and beyond found a settlement—or what had been one. It was the remains of a village, no more than fifteen low earthen buildings, but it'd been destroyed. Rew led the party down to get a better look.

They circled the village, seeing where the wyrm had appeared, crashed through the center of the place, and then disappeared only to reemerge on the other side of the hill where they'd first found the signs of attack. A terrible bit of luck? Rew didn't think the wyrms could sense the village, or it wouldn't be there. He glanced around, wondering if something had drawn the creature.

The wyrms were voracious hunters. They lived off the wild cattle on the plain but would consume a person just as readily.

Those who lived on the plains knew that. They'd spent generations out there, hunting the cattle and hunting the wyrms as well. Their villages were always small to avoid notice.

Wyrms had dull senses, but they could follow prey once they rose above the surface. The arcanists suspected it wasn't sight or smell but some other sense that man did not have—a form of ancient magic, a connection.

Perhaps it was simple bad luck in this case.

Rew began searching in the village itself until, on the outskirts of the wyrm's path, beneath a collapsed wall of sod, he found an intact body. Clearing the dirt away, he uncovered the form of a man. He was garbed in simple clothing and soft leather boots, all made from the hide of cattle. The man's face was adorned with ceremonial piercings and dark swirls of tattoo. No doubt a resident of the village. His lips were dry, and he looked as shriveled as a rasin. Rew scratched his beard. The man smelled, but not bad enough.

The ranger stood and glanced toward the center of the wyrm's path where the crushed bodies of other victims lay. Their blood soaked the ground and had long since dried. Even from a score of paces away, Rew could smell their dead flesh. The warrior at his feet hadn't died more than a day ago. The others, the ones crushed by the wyrm, died a week before.

Rew tucked his thumbs behind his belt.

"What?" asked Cinda.

"These people were killed by the wyrm but not consumed. This man here seems to have been ignored entirely."

"So?"

"Wyrms are predators. They only rise above the surface to eat. I haven't heard of one ignoring a meal. There have to be, ah, a dozen people who died here. Why would it ignore them and consume the others? Why would it have been drawn here at all?"

Cinda shrugged.

"Can you feel their deaths?" asked Rew.

"Of course."

"What's different about this one?" he asked, pointing with a toe at the body in front of them.

Cinda frowned then shrugged. "It's more recent, from the looks of it, but that man's passing was... weak? It's hard to explain, but there is little energy remaining from his death. Why would that be?"

"I don't know," admitted Rew, staring down at the man. The dead man's eyes were still open, his expression slack. "He didn't die from violence."

Zaine, crouched atop what had been the wall of a hut, pointed down next to where Rew had excavated the body. "Is that a spear?"

"A harpoon. They use them on hunts," corrected Rew. "Strange, that broken hilt we found on the other side of the hill looked to be a scimitar. Not a common blade on this end of the kingdom."

Zaine leaned closer. "What's that, on the end of the harpoon?"

Rew knelt and saw what Zaine had seen. The end of the weapon's barb was covered in dried blood. He examined the weapon closer. There was a strand of hair caught in the serrated edge near the point of it, and the iron had cracked. The break was fresh. Sitting on his haunches, Rew drummed his fingers on the bone hilt of his hunting knife. "This man fought someone and then... then, he just laid here and died. I don't see any wounds. If I had to guess, I'd speculate he died of dehydration. Anne?"

The empath joined them, and after a quick examination, she declared, "There are no recent wounds, and you're right, it appears an advanced case of dehydration. Perhaps he was grieved about the loss of his village and family and gave up?"

"That's a pretty awful way to go if you have other means to end it," remarked Rew, "and he fought someone. That hair didn't come from cattle or a wyrm. I think maybe that's what drew the creature here. There was a battle. Someone attacked the village. It must have been enough of a struggle the wyrm sensed it, but that's not entirely right either. It's like the wyrm sensed those on the other side of the hill but not the people in the village. Strange."

"This man's body was healthy enough, except for the lack of water," said Anne, standing and brushing her hands on her skirts. "I don't know who he fought or why, but he survived whatever battle took place and the attack by the wyrm. Rew, this man could have walked away if he wanted to. You know, this is an intriguing mystery, but…"

"But we need to go," finished Rew. He waved the others on, and grimly, they left the ruined village behind.

Another half day, and in the distance, they spotted wisps of smoke drifting up. An hour passed, and the drift had turned into a fat column of smoke that Rew guessed had to be another village, except this one was burning.

"That's more smoke than a campfire would put out. It's hard to judge, but I'd guess it's at least five leagues away," surmised Rew, looking at the dark band of smoke. "Could be ten. Distances are deceiving out here."

"Is it related, do you think, to the other village we saw?" asked Cinda.

"It has to be," concluded Rew. "You saw what remained of that last settlement. These huts are built from stacked turf. They don't burn. They use manure from the cattle for fuel, but enough of it to make that fire…"

"So someone is attacking the villages, but why?" asked Raif, sweeping his arms wide as if to encompass the expanse of the grasslands. "Why would anyone attack anything out here? There's no strategic benefit, no resources valuable to an army."

"Wild cows?" speculated Zaine, "An army on the march may want them for food, but ah, I guess no one owns those cattle, do they? You could just herd them away if you wanted."

"It's not just that someone is attacking these villages," responded Rew. "They're doing it with high magic. If something that big is burning out here, it was because of an invoker."

"Rew, do you think it's related to us?" asked Anne. "Could it be the king?"

Cringing, Rew wondered. The king knew they'd been at the Arcanum and knew they'd fled. They'd planted rumors they'd go north to Iyre, but would those seeds have already sprouted? Without portals or portal stones, not even gossip could fly so quickly. And if the king had somehow heard, would he bother destroying the villages on their way? Perhaps it was an effort to prevent them from resupplying, but Rew was the King's Ranger. He could duck into the forest and forage indefinitely. Preventing them from restocking their packs in the villages was an inconvenience, but if anything, instead of slowing them, it would encourage them to move faster.

The king wouldn't hesitate to slaughter his own people, but he also wouldn't do so without a reason. Days earlier, he'd spared the women's colony and the fort, and he'd known they'd been through those places. Vaisius Morden was a cold-hearted tyrant, not a madman. Rew didn't think the king would destroy the villages just to spite the ranger, but someone was killing these people, and it was a bold act of war if it wasn't the king or the princes.

Shaking his head, Rew encouraged them to keep moving before he answered Anne. "The king has the might to do something like this, and he's never been restrained by moral concerns, but if he were out on this plain looking for us, I think he'd be… more effective. He could have tens of thousands of his black legion out here or armies of undead, but I haven't seen a sign of either. Destroying a few small villages to irritate us isn't his way."

"Who, then?"

Rew had no answer except it must be the princes. He couldn't fathom why. Raif had been right. The plain offered no strategic value to Valchon or Heindaw.

They travelled two more days, the monotonous hiking from before now filled with nervous tension. In the open plains, they were unlikely to see anyone, but if they did, there would be little chance to hide. It rubbed Rew raw. His instinct as a ranger was to move with stealth, but on an open plain, there was nothing even he could do.

Early one morning, they found a vast swath of earth that had been trampled through the grass. A herd of wild cattle, thousands of them, had trod northeast, the same direction the party was going. Rew judged it sensible to follow the trail while they could. It would be impossible for anyone to discern signs of their passing amongst the path the cows had worn, and without knowing who else was in the area, Rew would take what precautions he could.

"Do you think we'll catch up to the animals?" wondered Zaine. "It'd be something to see, wouldn't it?"

Raif laughed.

Zaine scowled at the fighter. She shoved his shoulder and said, "I've seen cows before, but thousands of cattle in a herd? You haven't seen that wandering through those keeps you've always lived in, have you? I think it would be interesting."

Rew grinned at them. The thief was right. Both her and Raif had spent their entire lives confined to the stone buildings and streets of cities. When they'd left, it'd been on the well-worn high-ways that had been there for centuries. The world, away from men, was a wild and beautiful place.

Turning from the girl to glance down at the trail the cattle had worn, Rew realized it was still a beautiful place for him, too. There was a simplicity in the animals' purpose. They wandered for food and water, for breeding and safety. They stayed in a herd for protection, just they and their fellows against the world. Cattle didn't turn on each other, didn't slaughter portions of the herd to achieve dominance. The animals were not weighed down by the concerns of men, like who would sit upon a throne.

It would be better to be like that, he thought. He had been like that, once, out in the wilderness, just him or maybe with some of the other rangers, scouting the land, looking for threats or just looking. For a time, he'd set aside his awareness of the rest of the world, and he'd simply existed. He missed that.

"Ranger?"

Rew coughed and shot Zaine an apologetic smile. "Sorry. I was thinking. I, ah, I think it unlikely we'll catch them, lass. I'd guess they're two days ahead of us, and before we find the tail of the herd, we'll need to cut north and circle wide of Olsoth. With the attacks on the villages... I worry what we'll find if we go there."

"You think someone would attack the city?"

Rew shrugged.

An hour later, they passed the site of a butchering. Several wild cattle had been brought down, skinned, drained of blood, and carved for meat.

"Narjags?" asked Raif with a gasp.

"No," replied Rew, moving delicately amongst the slaughter. "Hunters. People like those who live in the village we saw. Cattle are a staple of their diet. They'll send out men for days or weeks on hunts to bring back enough to feed the entire community for a month. This looks like their work."

"That must be some sort of hunter to take on an entire herd, eh?" asked Raif, looking over the corpses of the animals. "These things fully fleshed must be four times the size of a big man, and look at those horns. They'd rip you right in two if they got into you. I don't think my chainmail would do much to stop one of those. A thousand of these beasts turning on you, moving to protect their young? The cows in the east were slow and dumb, too stupid to even know when they were being slaughtered. To see someone hunting these wild ones would be interesting, wouldn't it?"

"What's that?" barked Zaine with a snort.

Raif offered her a sheepish smile.

They moved on, but Raif's comments stayed in the back of Rew's head. The hunters who tracked these animals would have lived in villages like the one they'd seen destroyed. Was there something about those hunters that had garnered the interest of the princes? Who would bother to kill people living out in the middle of an empty plain? There was no strategic purpose to it that Rew could divine, and those people had no resources worth fighting for.

The next day, they found another village and another clue. This village was not destroyed like the others, but it was empty. Rew called for a halt, to give him time to explore.

"Don't mess with anything you find, all right?" he asked the others. "If you see something, call out to me."

But it was quickly apparent there was nothing for the younglings to mess with. The hovels were empty of both people and many of the items Rew would have expected to find. There were no weapons, and no food had been left behind. There were no signs of struggle, either. It was as if everyone had quickly packed their lives and left. The flight looked abrupt but orderly. The buildings that had doors had them closed. The interiors of the homes were straightened, as if the occupants planned to come back, but there were some personal effects—bowls, eating utensils, tools, the sort of things that had value but would be impractical to gather quickly.

"Someone warned them," he murmured.

He walked out to the northern edge of the village and studied the earth for tracks. The way was worn near the buildings then grew faint, and then, it disappeared. There was nothing else obvious or any more clues. He peered north toward Olsoth, guessing that's where the people must have gone. There were recent signs of passage that way, and the destination made sense.

Looking back, he saw Zaine had climbed on top of one of the larger structures and was turning around with a hand over her eyes, gazing out at the empty grasslands around them.

"See anything?"

"I'm looking for the cattle."

The ranger grunted then started taking inventory of the buildings, making sure he'd checked them all.

"Ranger," called Zaine. "Toss me your spyglass, will you?"

Smirking, he pulled the device from his pack and asked, "A thousand wild cattle ought to be pretty obvious, don't you think?"

He flipped her the spyglass, and she opened it and held it to her eye. Her lips were moving. She was mumbling under her breath.

Rew ran his hand over his head. "Is it the cattle you're looking at?"

"No," she said, her voice worried. "You should see this."

Rew scrambled up the turf wall of the hovel to stand beside her on its roof. In the distance, three leagues away, was a dark smear. He frowned and wordlessly accepted the spyglass from Zaine. She crossed her arms over her chest, and he saw the worry in her eyes. He peered through the glass and in front of him jumped a company of armored warriors, clad in gleaming copper.

"King's Sake," he growled, gripping the spyglass tightly. "Those are Prince Valchon's men."

"Close to one hundred of them by my count," she said. "What would they be doing here?"

"Burning villages, evidently. I think that's... Yes, I believe they've a spellcaster leading them, though the robes look funny." Rew paused then called out loudly to the others, "We need to move."

"May I see?" asked the nameless woman.

Rew shrugged and handed her the spyglass before jumping down from the roof of the hut. Zaine followed, and he shouted for the others to hurry then led them northeast, heading perpendicular to the approaching soldiers and toward Olsoth.

The nameless woman came trotting up after them and handed him his spyglass. Her face was a blank mask.

"What'd you see?" he asked. "I think that was a spellcaster, but... I don't know. It was off."

She shook her head and did not answer.

Rew considered turning, going the other way, but he didn't know which direction the soldiers would move after visiting the village. Beyond Olsoth was Iyre. Any other way they walked, they would be going the wrong direction. They hiked for two more hours and then, behind them, saw tendrils of smoke clawing into the air. Valchon's men were burning the village.

"King's Sake," growled Rew. "It must have been an invoker leading them. There was nothing in that village which would have burned without high magic."

"Why are they doing it?" wondered Anne. "A signal to someone?"

Rew had no answer for her.

They moved quickly, hoping that Valchon's men hadn't bothered to climb atop one of the structures before they set it on fire. Without the additional elevation, Rew didn't think the party would be visible so far away, but if those men had climbed up and looked around...

An hour later, Raif broke the silence. "Where do you think they'll go after the village?"

Rew simply shrugged.

They kept walking until the sun fell below the horizon. It was a cloudy night, and there was no light of the moon, so Rew called for a halt. "No point us falling over ourselves. There, up on the hill but short of the top. If we forgo a fire, no one should be able to pick us out, and in the morning, we'll have a better view of what's around."

They settled in for the night and, unfortunately, realized most of their provisions required cooking. Ang and Vurcell had given them ample meats and cheeses, but after a week of constant travel, most of it was gone. They were left with dried beans, rice, flour, and other foods that could keep for weeks. With no heat, though, it wasn't edible. They pooled what was available and filled their bellies as best they could with stale ends of bread, a bit of salted meat, and water.

Rew shook his waterskin, grimly thinking they didn't have much more than a day of that left, either. They needed to find one of the tiny streams that crisscrossed the plains, which was more a matter of luck than of skill. There'd been a stream running near the village behind them, but they had left so quickly he hadn't thought to have everyone refill their skins. He didn't fancy going back that way. He could leave the others and scout ahead in the morning, moving several times faster than Anne and the children. They would be easy to locate once he found water as long as they headed on a steady course. He figured even the children could walk due north, and if not, he could find their tracks. Even on an empty plain, Raif left signs of his passage.

Rew winced. If he could find those tracks, they may be possible for Valchon's soldiers to locate as well.

Still, they had to have water. He mentioned it to Anne, and she looked unhappy about the prospect of splitting up, but she didn't object. Perhaps she recalled the man back at the first village who'd passed from dehydration. Rew suggested with little hope that perhaps he would find some game while he was scouting.

"A herd of wild cattle?" said Anne with a laugh. "Even if you found one, killed it, and carved off a hunk of the meat, we still couldn't cook it."

Shrugging, Rew decided to turn in for the night, letting the others take the first shifts at watch.

When Anne woke him, some hours still until dawn, he got up and began a series of stretches to get his blood flowing again. They had no fire and no food, so they wouldn't be pausing long in the morning. He had nothing to do, nothing to get ready for the others, so he merely walked broad circles around the hill, thinking.

Valchon must have unleashed his men on the fringe of Prince Heindaw's territory to either punish his younger brother or to distract him. Maybe he was trying to wound him, like Calb wounded Valchon? It didn't seem like Valchon's way, to lash out in retaliation, borrowing his brother's tactics, but it was possible. If nothing else, it was confirmation that the Investiture had not ended. If the rumors they'd tried to start didn't spread, the Investiture could end quickly now that it was between just two brothers. All it would take was one of them to slide through a fatal attack, but if Valchon's men were out ravaging Heindaw's territory, the fight was still on.

Rew hadn't considered what might happen if Valchon or Heindaw ended things while the party was traveling. During the time it would take to hike across the entire Western and Northern Provinces, Prince Valchon could move against his brother and end it, or Heindaw could enact some plot against Valchon, and it would be over. That would make things simpler in some ways.

One less brother meant one less that Rew would have to face, but once there was only one, the Investiture would end, and the brother would be brought to Mordenhold to ascend the throne. If Rew and the others hadn't given away their involvement, he would have been called to the capital as well. The king's rangers always had representatives at coronations. They were expected to pledge loyalty to the new occupant of the throne. Rew had made that pledge once, twenty-five years earlier. He hadn't been a ranger then, but he'd been a resident of the creche, and it was expected of them. It was a father or an uncle who ascended the throne, after all. None of the younglings in Mordenhold had known that they were pledging fealty to the same man who had occupied the throne before, just in a new body.

What if Rew had known it was the ancient spirit of Vaisius Morden the first instead of his blood father? Would he still have bowed and said the words? How many others through the centuries had suspected, and what had they done? He couldn't believe he was the only man to have learned Vaisius Morden's awful truth, but none of the others had made the histories, not even the spoken history the rangers shared amongst themselves.

Rew chose not to think about what that implied. It was too dark a consideration, alone in the middle of the night, far from home.

He was still wandering broad loops around the camp when the first rays of dawn spread across the plains. He paused, one foot halfway down to the turf.

Had it been his imagination, or had that early light reflected off of something?

Clouds, still thick from the night before, rolled slowly across the sky, and when the next beams of full sun peeked through, Rew saw the twinkling reflection again. He raced back to his pack and ripped his spyglass out. Slapping it to his eye, he trained it on where he'd seen the reflection, and his heart sank. One hundred men, garbed in Valchon's copper armor, were marching in formation. They were led by a man wearing spellcaster's robes that were purple. Purple robes? Rew didn't know what branch of high magic that might be, if it even represented a talent with high magic, but it didn't matter. One hundred trained soldiers were too much for the party to face.

Rew shouted to the others, waking them and demanding they get moving. Luckily, with no fire and no food, there'd been little unpacking the night before. The younglings and Anne scrambled to their feet, and Rew shouted to the nameless woman to wake her. He rushed to her bedroll, but she was gone.

Confused, he kicked her blankets, thinking she was hidden out of sight somehow, but all he found was a pile of old clothing and mounded soil. Her pack was missing as well, her armor too, but he hadn't noticed in the night. Rew spun, looking around frantically, but the nameless woman was nowhere to be seen.

Already, Anne and the others were jogging down the side of the hill, headed northeast. Raif was trotting behind the women, still trying to twirl his blankets into a wad that he could stuff into his pack.

"Rew?" called Anne, realizing he'd stopped behind them.

Cursing, he ran after her.

Chapter Fifteen

✦

An hour behind them, the copper breastplates flashed in the sun as Prince Valchon's men marched closer. Growling, Rew snapped the spyglass closed and flung it into his pack. He waved to the others, and they kept hiking. For half the day, they'd been marching relentlessly northeast, the one hundred men following behind on their tail. At first, they hadn't been sure if the soldiers were pursuing them. Those men could simply be headed in the same direction, walking toward the largest city in the region.

But after a couple of hours, it was clear it was a chase. Rew had turned the group, taking a different direction, and the soldiers had adjusted as well, gaining some distance on the party as Valchon's men got a better angle.

Frustrated, Rew turned the party back, headed toward Olsoth, the soldiers following behind. The land was open, just rolling plains and winter-dead grass. There was nowhere to hide, even if they'd wanted to risk it. There were no features nearby or anywhere on the horizon that would be defensible. Even if they had stumbled across another of the small villages, Rew would avoid the place. They'd seen the remains of one village and smoke from others. These soldiers wouldn't hesitate to kill anyone in their way, and the ranger knew there would be no one in the villages who could face a company of Valchon's soldiers.

"Why are they following us?" snapped Zaine, voicing everyone's frustration. "They can't know who we are, can they?"

Rew shrugged and kept walking.

"What if they do know who we are?" asked Cinda. "Now that Rew has killed Calb, Valchon could see us as a threat, and maybe he found out where we went after the Arcanum."

"If he kills us, Rew won't be able to take on Heindaw," argued Zaine. "Isn't that what Valchon wanted, for Rew to face the younger brothers?"

Cinda frowned, brushing a lock of hair behind her ear as she walked. "Yes, I think you're right."

"It doesn't really matter, does it?" interjected Raif. "It seems pretty clear these men have instructions to kill anyone they find. We saw evidence enough of that in the villages. We'd be crazy to think they'd do anything different if they catch us."

The girls fell silent at that, and Rew glanced at Anne from the corner of his eye. The empath marched on stoically, perhaps already having decided the point Raif was making. Whatever the intentions of Prince Valchon's men, they were unlikely to be good for Rew and the others.

They couldn't hide. They couldn't stand and defend against one hundred soldiers and a pair of spellcasters, so there was only one choice. They would run, and keep running until they somehow lost their pursuers, or they got caught.

As evening came, they hadn't paused except for brief moments to peer through the spyglass behind them or to dig food or water out of a pack. Rew was growing more and more concerned. He thought they'd gained some ground on the soldiers but not much. Their party was fit from months on the road, but the men and women behind them were keeping the pace. Both groups were in a battle of stamina, and Rew knew nothing about their opponents. He didn't know if they would stop for the evening or keep marching on through the dark. If they did keep marching at night, Rew and the others would have almost no warning until the soldiers were on top of them.

He told the party, "We've got to keep going."

There were no complaints, not even grumbles. They all knew the stakes of the game they played now, and they'd seen enough death to understand what was behind them. Wordlessly, they continued on, and the sun kissed the horizon.

"Where do you think she went?" Cinda asked as darkness fell across the plains.

Rew grunted and didn't respond.

"She must have gone to those soldiers," decided Raif. "It could be that's why they're following us."

"If she wanted to be associated with Valchon, she could have simply stayed in Carff," argued Cinda. "Remember, she came after we were thrown through the portal. No, I think whatever she is hiding, it's not loyalty to Valchon."

"She could be his spy now, even if she wasn't before," retorted Raif. "Maybe after we were gone, she spoke to him, and he recruited her. He could have promised that he'd rescue her father once he became king. She might have fallen for that, you know? She's been hiding the truth from us this entire time."

"Or she could have just gotten up to heed nature's call, and we left her," retorted Zaine.

Scoffing, Raif replied, "Gotten up and walked off so far we couldn't see her? Taking her pack, her sword, and her armor? It isn't so easy to heed nature's call while wearing several stone worth of armor, believe me. And don't forget, Rew had the last shift, so she must have left before then, unless you think she was able to sneak away while he was watching. That'd be an awfully long time to spend relieving oneself."

"Was it your shift, then, when she disappeared?"

"What are you saying, that you think I fell asleep?" barked Raif. "I didn't. I don't... I think she was there, sleeping, during my shift."

"Well, it wasn't when I was on watch!" snapped Zaine. She

crossed her arms. "The woman had her shift after mine, and I woke her up. I fell asleep to the sound of her putting on her armor."

"I don't like the way you're—"

"Wait," cried Rew, grabbing Zaine's arm. "The armor!"

The thief blinked at him.

"No way she could have snuck off wearing that armor if someone was awake," muttered Raif under his breath. He glanced around. "It wasn't me. I was awake."

"If she was planning to sneak off during anyone's watch, would she put on her armor? She took it off to polish it last night and could have wrapped it in her cloak. That would have been a lot quieter than stalking off with all of that bronze on," suggested Rew.

"So she was… taken?" asked Cinda.

Shaking his head, Rew kept striding across the grass. "Not taken. We would have seen that. But there's something about that armor. It was a custom fit for her, which is far too expensive for a priest of the Cursed Father to have paid for, so who would have done such an extraordinary deed for her? She was in Iyre, which is ruled by the greatest enchanter of our age. Years later, she just happened to be in Spinesend around when we were and then in Stanton? I think Heindaw himself enchanted the armor and set her on her course, though I don't know if the nameless woman realizes it."

No one answered, but after a while, Raif blurted out, "So she was Heindaw's spy?"

"Something like that," responded Rew. "She must have gone off to report to him, or perhaps she was compelled? Enchantments are typically designed to benefit the user, but they can trap one as well. I can only speculate about what Heindaw is capable of. King's Sake, maybe it wasn't him. I don't know."

"Why now?" questioned Cinda. "Why would she break her cover and move now? Something she saw in the villages?"

"The purple robes of that spellcaster," declared Rew suddenly.

"She could have recognized something we did not or seen something we missed through the spyglass."

"Right before we fled the village, she did look at that man longer than the rest of us," mentioned Raif. "She was upset about it. It didn't seem that suspicious yesterday, because we were all distressed, but now I wonder. Why was she studying the spellcaster so closely? It was like she knew him."

Zaine collected Rew's spyglass and, walking backward, peered through the device at their pursuers. She murmured, "Hard to see in the fading light. They're less than an hour behind us, now. No doubt they're following us. I don't see the nameless woman, for what that's worth. Pfah. The leader's robes are a different color, but he does look like a spellcaster. Thinking back to how he looked earlier, he had the same posture, same arrogance clinging to him as all of them. Reminds me of Valchon himself. I wish I could see this man's face better. I bet he looks like some sniveling worm."

"Purple robes," mused Anne. "A new strain of high magic? I don't think there's ever been one of those, has there? Even in the earliest histories of the kingdom, it was always invoking, necromancy, conjuring, and enchantment. Who would determine such a thing, what color of robes the new talents would wear? The king?"

Shaking his head, Rew replied, "I don't think the king would have anything… Zaine, you said the man looked like Valchon?"

"Well, it was pretty far away, so I can't actually see what he looks like, but he reminds me of the prince. I'm not saying… Are you thinking it's him?"

"Not him, not exactly. Heindaw was working on a new form of necromancy in the Arcanum," said Rew. "He was attempting to conduct high magic with low magic and mechanics. What if Prince Valchon had considered something different but along the same lines? Instead of low magic, he could use his own blood. In years past, the prince had a plethora of young women around him at all times. They were gone when we saw him in Carff. A lothario, I thought, but what if…"

"He was breeding a new army of spellcasters somehow?" questioned Anne. "To do that, he would have had to start decades ago."

"Aye, a few years after he left the creche in Mordenhold. He's always known this was coming," murmured Rew. "He's the second oldest of Vaisius Morden's children, right behind me. He… he knew. Twenty-five years ago, he saw what happened in the last Investiture. He could have been planning this since then."

"Blessed Mother," said Anne.

"If that's the prince's offspring behind us, we need to hurry," advised Rew.

They trudged on and, in an hour, were fully enveloped in the dark night, hardly any light from the sky falling to illuminate the way in front of them. The plains were flat, though, and at the end of winter, the grasses were small and limp. It was easy walking, if they could see where their feet were falling and hadn't been hiking all day with hardly a pause for breath and water.

For supper, Cinda trailed behind Anne, casting the glow of funeral fire into the empath's pack and rooting around for what little food they had left. They didn't stop to eat it, just kept walking. After several hours, Rew nearly fell into a small stream before hearing the gurgle of water, and he allowed a break as they crouched and refilled their waterskins in the crisp, cold flow.

He stared back the way they'd come, wondering if Prince Valchon's soldiers were still following or if they'd stopped for the night. There was no sign of a fire or any other light bleeding up from a camp, but they might have been too far back to see any glow had the soldiers made an effort to obscure it. Rew scratched his beard. He could go back, find their pursuers, and see if they were still coming. He would have no problem catching up to Anne and the children, if he could find them. He grimaced. In the dark of night, with no light from overhead, he wouldn't be able to follow their tracks. If they turned from their course, they could easily lose each other. He could catch them in the morning, but what if their pursuers kept coming and dawn found them closer to Anne and the children? No, splitting up wasn't a choice, not with enemies so close behind.

They drank their fill from the stream then started again. Without speaking about it, the whole party had decided to keep going the entire night. It wasn't a decision they would have made without complaint months ago. King's Sake, it wasn't something they could have done months ago. When Rew had first embarked with the younglings from Eastwatch, they couldn't have hiked more than two or three hours without collapsing in a heap. Now, they were going to hike the entire cycle of the sun. Hopefully.

In the dark, he could see the silhouette of Raif. The big fighter was shuffling, trying to stretch his legs. His breath was long and slow. Not quite panting, but he was wearing out. The lad might have the constitution of a bull, but he had heavy armor and a giant sword as well. He was built for fights, not flight. Raif would keep moving, though. He wasn't going to admit he was tired before his sister did.

Rew grinned, thinking of when they'd first armed themselves in Eastwatch and how he'd warned the boy about how impractical armor and a huge sword were on a long journey. Some things didn't change. Rew adjusted his pack and twisted his back, feeling his aching muscles and hearing the crack of his spine. Some things did change.

He looked up, staring at the night sky as the sporadic clouds churned slowly in front of the stars. He hadn't seen the moon yet, but at least there was some break in the clouds. They might get a little light to see if the soldiers were still coming.

He waited until he saw constellations he recognized through the cloud cover and fixed a point to the north in his head. They'd been going the right way, but in his time in the wilderness, he'd learned that even an unfailing sense of direction had a tendency to fail at the worst times. It was always wise to double-check which way you were headed.

"Everyone doing all right?" he asked quietly.

The others murmured responses, nearly whispers. Rew didn't think their pursuers could be close enough to hear them over the wind across the plain, but then again, he hadn't thought a group of armored soldiers could have kept up with them, either. He worried what it meant that there was a spellcaster back there with unusual robes. He worried that Zaine thought the man looked like Valchon. What would a child of Valchon's be capable of? More than the father?

For hours, they trod across the plains, steady steps eating ground, no one speaking, all lost in their own thoughts, or their own struggles to keep up in Raif's case. To the fighter's credit, he never complained, just kept trudging onward, one foot in front of the other.

Sometime hours after midnight but hours before dawn, Anne whispered an offer to heal any hurt they'd acquired. They all turned her down. They'd long since broken in their boots and fashioned their legs and hips into powerful tools to keep them going. They'd also learned that the empath's healing came at a cost to her. Their own pain may be lessened, but it was because Anne took it into herself. The empath sometimes seemed an endless well that could be filled with untold suffering, but they'd grown to love her and would spare her that burden when they could.

The children—he shouldn't call them that anymore—had grown. They accepted that the journey would pain them and that they didn't know what lay at the end, but they persevered. They trusted Rew and Anne to lead them to something worth their effort and that the ranger and the empath had their best interests at heart. It was a new stage of development, of maturity, but it wasn't the final stage. They'd learned to work and to trust, but eventually, they would learn their work might not mean success and that trust could be broken.

Would it be? Rew adjusted his pack so the leather straps wore on a different section of his shoulder. He hoped he did not fail them. He didn't want to, but in that long, dark night, he had to admit that he might. Rew would ask much of Cinda in the end. He would ask it all of her because that was what it would take to face the king. She would do it. She'd said she would. She would do it, but it was asking much of Raif as well to allow his sister to take those final steps. The cause was just, but the cost... The cost would be terribly high.

With such thoughts weighing on his mind, a counter to the weight of his steps, Rew greeted the sun. For an hour, they'd been traipsing through the murky pre-dawn gloom, wondering if it was getting lighter or if it was just their imaginations. Rew had trained his body for years in the wilderness to keep going, but the others did not have that foundation. He could see it in their eyes as true light finally spilled over the horizon. They were moving, but their minds had slipped into a sort of purgatory between wakefulness and sleep.

Except for Cinda. Her eyes flickered with ethereal green. She smirked at him when she caught his look and shrugged, as if to say that there were some positives to her nocturnal restlessness. A few hours' sleep was all she needed on a normal night, and Rew wondered how far she could push herself if she tried. Her body would need to stop soon, but she was growing to the point she didn't feel that need. He could see her weariness in her footsteps, but it would take time for her to recognize how she'd changed. No matter who you were, walking a day and a night took its toll, even if you didn't notice it.

They turned, letting the sun bathe their faces as it crested the distant grasslands, but no one spoke. They kept walking.

When they reached a small rise in the hills, Rew told them they could catch their breath, and he trained his spyglass behind them. The way back looked much like the way ahead, just gently undulating grasslands. And two hundred of Prince Valchon's copper-armored men, led by two men in purple robes. Rew studied the spellcasters, but he didn't have Zaine's eyesight. He knew without seeing, though. He could feel it. Those purple-robed men were the spawn of Valchon.

"King's Sake," snapped Rew, thrusting the spyglass back into his pack.

"We keep walking?" asked Anne.

Rew was silent for a moment, thinking. The soldiers were still about an hour behind them, but they'd doubled their number in the night. How had the two companies found each other in the black, and how many more of them were wandering the empty terrain? How had they kept on the party's trail? Rew, confident in his abilities but self-aware enough to admit the truth, didn't think he could have done the same.

Retrieving his spyglass, the ranger turned a slow circle, taking advantage of the slight height their hill had over the rest of the land around them. There was a smudge, which he thought might be the air above the city of Olsoth, and nothing, and then a glint of copper. He could barely see them, as the sun was rising behind them, but another company of Valchon's men were out there. There was nothing else. The land was empty. The men had to be searching for Rew and the others.

"North, and we need to make good time," said Rew.

Leather creaked as they adjusted their packs and the harnesses which held their weapons and then the low thump of boots on soft ground.

The sun was rising slowly off the horizon, and Rew was constantly looking behind them and to the side at Prince Valchon's men. His heart fell when he saw the group to the east adjust course and take an angle that would cut the party's lead in half.

"They walked all night?" complained Raif, tugging at his armor. "Pfah. Who does that?"

No one answered and pointed out that they'd also done it. Raif, through his sour mood, was voicing an insight that must have occurred to all of them. Who did march all night long? How could the soldiers behind them even know who they were, and if they did, how had their captain motivated them to continue the slow and steady pursuit for so long with no rest?

Soldiers were used to training and brutal conditions, but Valchon's soldiers were also used to the barracks. It'd been since the last Investiture when full-scale war had broken out, so none of the men following them would be veterans, used to the punishing toll forced marches took on their bodies or the alternative when fleeing after a losing battle.

But somehow, those men had kept coming. Eagerness for a reward? Fear? Rew didn't know. All he could do was to keep looking back, which was why Zaine was the first to spy a third group of soldiers in front of them.

"King's Sake!" barked Rew, adjusting course to head away from the soldiers in the distance.

"Rew, aren't we..." began Anne.

"Walking directly toward Olsoth now?" responded the ranger. "We are, but what else is there to do? If we turn any other way, these men will be able to cut a diagonal and stay in front of us. They're far enough away that they can't break into a run and make it a proper chase, and we have to keep that distance. There are three groups of them now, and we don't know how fresh they are. I don't want this to turn into a sprint. There's nowhere for us to run to. If it becomes a fight... We're finished."

"If it's going to be a fight, maybe we ought to pick our ground and give them our best. Another few leagues, and we'll be crawling on hands and knees," growled Raif. He punched a fist into his open hand. "Can you see how big their packs are? If they've got something good to eat, I'll tear through the lot of 'em. I'm right tired of our rations. No offense, Anne."

Zaine snorted, and the others laughed. It was a poor jest, but as worn down as they were, they appreciated the attempt.

Until midday, the slow motion chase continued, the three companies of Prince Valchon's men coming at them from different angles, staying apart enough to prevent the party from turning and skirting around between them.

Rew's blood was boiling. Out on the open plain, with all of the groups in sight of each other, there was little they could do. The low folds of land offered no chance of a good hiding spot. Even the streams that wound across the plain were shallow, and while they might be able to duck down and crawl along one for a bit, it would be slow going, and their pursuers would have little difficulty guessing what they were doing. If he was alone... but he wasn't. And with three different groups on their heels, there was no maneuvering to get a jump ahead of the others. Any direction they turned would give someone an angle to close the gap. He cursed. If the night before they'd taken a completely different direction, they might have shaken their tail.

But which way? They were headed to Iyre, and it lay on the other side of Olsoth. Any other direction and they would have put more distance between themselves and their goal, and given they'd already run into three groups of the copper-armored soldiers, taking another direction might have just put them into the path of a fourth. King's Sake. How many men could Valchon have put out in the middle of nowhere?

It wasn't worth thinking about. Maybe trickery would have helped them the night before, maybe not, but it wasn't going to help them now, and before darkness fell again, they would be beneath the walls of Olsoth.

"Should we..." began Anne. Then, she trailed off.

"We have to try the city," declared Rew. "It's still some hours off, but I think we can make it if we keep pushing. I'd thought about evading them under the cover of darkness, but I don't think that will work."

"Why not?" wondered Cinda, too tired to think of the answer.

"The spellcasters in the purple robes," responded Rew. "What are they capable of? Can they see in the dark or sustain those men beyond their mortal limits? I can't even begin to guess, but I know something doesn't feel right. Common soldiers deciding to march for over a day now? They'd only do that if Valchon himself was spurring them on, but if Valchon knows where we are, why not come himself? I've got to admit I wouldn't want to face the prince without a good night's sleep. And there's some way they all stumbled across us. Perhaps they're communicating or can sense us. Pfah! Spellcasters with unknown abilities. We might be better off with Valchon himself. At least I know what he's capable of."

"I agree. The city, then," surmised Anne. "With the king himself looking for us, I don't like it, but what else can we do?"

"Exactly. Unless Valchon took the city, Olsoth owes fealty to Heindaw. He's no ally of ours, but we know he's the enemy to the men who are chasing us. If we can get inside without anyone learning who we are, at least Olsoth's soldiers will defend us against those behind us."

Grimly, they continued on, and their pursuers seemed to increase speed.

"Is it my imagination..." murmured Zaine, looking behind them.

"They're only about half a league back, now," estimated Rew, shaking his head. "How they are coming faster after so long..."

In front of them, Olsoth broke the endless plain like a dagger thrust through a cloth. It was a shard of pale stone, incongruous with the land all around it. As they got closer, they saw it was not one solid piece of rock but concentric walls rising up in a spiral like a conch, and Rew knew from experience that inside of the monolith was an open well bound by the steep walls of the city. The interior of the place bled vegetation, with plants spilling from windows and the sides of the pathways that climbed from the bottom to the top. In contrast to the raw stone exterior, the inside was verdant, lush. The people of Olsoth relied on the growth. There was no farming outside of the city because of the land wyrms. Olsoth had no outside industry, the entire place was encased in the huge, hulking structure.

"The bones of Olsoth are deep enough that the vibrations of even thousands of footsteps don't draw the attention of the wyrms," explained Rew. "That's what I was told, at least. I suppose even if the wyrms did come knocking on the gates, the city is sturdy enough to survive whatever they could do to it. It was carved from living stone, a pillar of it built on a foundation that goes far beneath the surface. Olsoth is one of the most secure places outside of Mordenhold."

"Why?" wondered Zaine. "I mean, I understand you'd want protection from the wyrms, but why put a city out here in the first place? You said there's no industry. Are they digging for gold in there?"

"Olsoth is old," replied Rew. "It was here before Vaisius Morden's time, before the western forest was harvested. Who knows what was here then. Perhaps these plains were a lake, but now, the people in Olsoth are there for the wyrms. Their bodies secrete an oil which sells for a fortune. It's worth more than gold. It's supposed to make an old woman look young and beautiful. You can imagine how much aging noblewomen would pay for something like that. They're vapid, vain creatures who…"

Anne cleared her throat, and Rew decided he would leave it there.

"Does it really work?" asked Cinda. "Harvesting secretions from a land wyrm seems like an awful lot of work to stay pretty."

Rew shrugged. "I don't know if it works, but I know some, ah… I'm not talking about you, Anne, but some older women will go far to keep their man's eye."

"Worm secretions?" asked Raif. "I'm not sure a nobleman would like his wife or mistress slathering herself with worm secretions."

Grinning, Rew winked. "Gross, isn't it?"

"And I'm not sure if I'd like to be baron of a city with an economy built on that," continued Raif.

Rew laughed. "Are you unsure? There are few things more certain than the vanity of a woman."

Anne cleared her throat again, and Rew kept his eyes ahead on the towering city. Perhaps he should have kept his mouth shut.

"How many people live there, I wonder," said Zaine after a long moment of silence.

"Tens of thousands," answered Rew. "It's not a bad place to live, really. Whoever designed the monolith had more in mind than its current use. Don't get me wrong. It's a real city even now, but Olsoth was built for two- or three-times today's population. The lords of the Northern Province lure people here with the promise of free housing. A place to stay at no cost and a captive audience for your trade? People have made worse bargains."

"I'm not sure about that," grumbled Raif, looking around as if expecting one of the great land wyrms to rise up behind them.

"Hold your judgement until you see Iyre," remarked Anne. "The northern capital isn't as pleasant as Carff. It's not pleasant at all, really. Dark stone, dank taverns, everyone crowded together. I'd prefer Olsoth."

"There's something to be said for dank taverns," chirped Rew.

"I don't mean to sound panicked," interjected Zaine, "but perhaps we should run?"

Rew frowned and turned back behind them.

A thousand paces away, a company of Prince Valchon's men was jogging toward them, one of the purple-clad spellcasters leading the way.

"King's Sake," growled Rew.

He lurched into a run, and without instructions, the others started trotting after him.

Chapter Sixteen

꧁꧂

Olsoth jabbed skyward, its shadow stretching long across the plain. They ran into the gloom. A league ahead of them, the city looked silent and cold. Behind them, the copper-clad men broke into a full sprint, and Rew and the party started a harried, stumbling run. The children and Anne had passed exhaustion and were operating solely on will.

Truth be told, Rew wasn't much better. Behind them, he could see the grim, blank faces of the soldiers who chased them and the haughty expressions of the spellcasters who led them. One of the purple robbed men pulled ahead, and Zaine had been right. The spellcaster looked like a younger version of Valchon. Rew exhorted his companions to run faster.

The soldiers were a mere five hundred paces behind them, and then three hundred, and then two hundred.

Rew and the others ran, but they'd spent themselves over the last day and a half walking. They'd subsisted on bad food and quick sips of water. Even he, used to long, arduous journeys, wasn't equipped to run hard after so long on his feet.

"Hurry!" he called to the others. "Hurry!"

One hundred paces. The soldiers behind them had closed

within one hundred paces. Scimitars bounced on their sides, and their copper breastplates looked dull in the shadow of Olsoth.

"I can—" cried Cinda, her voice hollow and gasping.

"Copper, lass, they're wearing copper. It will shield them from anything you try. With enough power, you could crack that shield… but there are a hundred of them, and we can't stop for you to summon your strength."

She didn't respond. There wasn't a response.

A quarter league ahead of them, they could now make out the giant gates of Olsoth. They were closed.

"Keep going!" cried Rew, hoping the proximity of Olsoth would encourage the others to move their feet quicker, because if they didn't…

He glanced behind them and saw the simulacrum of Valchon grinning maniacally, the company of soldiers strung out behind him as they couldn't match the man's pace. A spellcaster that could run?

Rew ached to reach for his longsword, but against so many, he knew it would be suicide, but if it would save the others… Maybe he had no choice. If only the gates of Olsoth would open, if only he knew they could get inside…

A great reverberating horn called mournfully from the walls of the city. It sounded as if it was shaking the very foundation of the place, though the cry was lost in the open plains behind them. The horn's wail rose again, rolling like thunder over them, and Rew's heart leapt as he saw the gates of the city crack open.

He didn't need to shout for the others to go faster. They were putting everything they had left into a last, desperate sprint toward those opening gates.

Rew glanced back and saw that it was not going to be enough. The spellcaster was just two dozen paces behind them, and his men another two dozen beyond that. At their speed, they would catch Rew's companions well before Olsoth.

There was a streak of darkness and a huge boulder smashed

into the turf on the flank of the soldiers, rolling by them, flinging heavy clods of soil.

Nearly everyone stumbled in surprise. A breath later, another massive rock landed in the midst of the copper-armored soldiers, and that time, half a dozen went scrambling away as the rock rolled through their midst, crushing several of them beneath its weight. More huge rocks came falling from the sky with varying degrees of accuracy, but it was enough to force the soldiers to scatter in different directions.

Rew slowed and took time to draw his longsword.

The spellcaster, who'd pulled just a dozen paces away, slowed as well then peeked over his shoulder where his men were fleeing out of range of Olsoth's catapults. He glanced at Rew's longsword then up to the walls of the city. Giving a curt, mocking salute, the spellcaster turned and darted away, weaving a jagged, random pattern over the grass, dodging clear of a hail of boulders that whistled down around him.

Stumbling, staggering, Rew and his companions tottered the rest of the way to Olsoth and ducked through the slender crack in the gates. Zaine slumped against a wall. Raif collapsed in a heap in the center of the opening that led into the city. Cinda fell to her knees next to her brother, her head bowed, ragged breaths exploding from her open mouth. Anne looked to Rew and offered him a tired smile.

An armored soldier stood in a long, stone hallway. He was the only one there. He whistled, and the huge gates creaked and then clanged shut. The man surveyed them before gesturing for them to follow. His voice, echoing in the hallway, boomed, "I hope you have a good story to tell."

Rew stood straight from where he'd been leaning over, hands on his knees. "We appreciate the shelter, but there's not much to say."

His eyes flicking to Cinda's crimson robes, the soldier grunted. "We'll see, but all the same, if it's not too much of an inconvenience, my superior would like to have a word with you."

Rew nodded agreement. What else could he do? The city was obviously on war footing, and they were strangers. Refusing to meet with the man's supervisor would get them kicked out the gate, at best. More likely, they would be clapped in irons, and then the supervisor would come to them with pointed questions and hot pincers with which to pull out the answers.

The others stood slowly, clearly struggling to regain their feet and move their bodies again. The soldier, clad in a steel-studded leather brigandine, led them from the corridor to a gated stairwell cut into what looked like a mountain.

Open-mouthed, the children stared past to where the corridor they were in curved out of sight. Rew knew it was designed so that if an attacking army breached the outer gate, they didn't have a clear shot at the next one. If they'd used rams or other engines to batter their way inside, they would have hell twisting the things through the winding passage to the next gate, and all around it was solid stone, except for a handful of narrow exits which during a battle could easily be blocked by dumping piles of rubble down them.

Before they entered the stairwell, Rew glanced up and saw another opening in the ceiling of the tunnel. A murder hole where boiling oil or other terrible substances could be unleashed on attacking forces. It was dark up there, so he couldn't tell if they were being watched, but it felt like it. He sighed. Whatever was happening in Olsoth, it had to be better than being chased across the endless plain.

They climbed the stairs to another hallway, walked down two dozen paces, and found another doorway. There were several in the hall, but none had identifying features. All were shut. The soldier opened the door and led them in. It was a tight tunnel that climbed up inside of the mass of Olsoth, taking steep stairs, cutting through dark passages, and then finally exiting onto the exterior walls of the city.

They were standing on a battlement that rose in a ramp, spiraling around the monolith. There were few soldiers there.

Farther up the ramp, a catapult platform protruded from the side of the structure. Rew looked straight up, and fifty paces above the battlement, he could see the next loop of the spiraling fortification and more of the catapult platforms. They must have trained all of the giant engines on Valchon's men to frighten them off their pursuit.

Down below, the grasslands extended out from Olsoth in a broad, gentle plain. From above, they could see the scars streams cut through the land, a single stand of trees far in the distance, and several masses of men. The soldiers who had been chasing them and maybe more? Without his spyglass, it was difficult to see details, but Rew could guess well enough.

Closer to the city, there were long trenches plowed through the turf by the force of Olsoth's catapults. Some were recent. Others were older. It looked as if they collected the boulders after firing them, but they'd left the bodies of Valchon's men. Scores of them lay crumpled and smashed in the tracks from the rocks, only visible from so high up because the glint on their copper armor contrasted so sharply with the green grass.

The soldier they were following was already several dozen paces up the battlement, so Rew and the others hurried after with just a quick look around and out. The soldier led them to a catapult platform, and a broad-shouldered man turned at the sound of their arrival.

He was plainly armored, just like the one who'd greeted them. All of the soldiers they could see wore similar gear, with no designation of rank. This man wore dark brigandine studded with steel, and a simple sword hung from his belt. Unlike the other soldiers they'd passed, he had no gauntlets over his hands, and Rew saw a golden signet ring there. The baron? In case the man was the baron, Rew proffered a deep bow, and the children followed his lead.

The man grunted. "You recognize... Ah, the ring. I should have taken that off."

Rew frowned.

"Not for you, for them," said the baron, gesturing out toward the plain where groups of Valchon's men were moving about.

Rising to meet the man's gaze, Rew nodded. "I thank you, m'lord, for opening the gates for us. You did not have to do that, but it saved our lives. When I heard that horn, my heart nearly fell to my boots. May I ask…"

"I didn't do it to save your lives," responded the man matter-of-factly. Then, he turned to look out over the plain. "My name is Barnaus, Baron of Olsoth."

Unsure whether they'd been dismissed or invited to stay, Rew joined the baron at the battlement. "If it was not to save us, then you recognized who was chasing us?"

"Aye, I figured if you were enemies of Valchon's, then you might be friends of mine," responded the baron, his armored elbows resting confidently on the stone of his fortress. He glanced at Rew, studying the ranger's face, as if wondering about a stranger who was comfortable enough with nobility to question him, but after a long moment, the baron nodded as if deciding something. Baron Barnaus continued, "The horn wasn't a warning, it was a calling. Unfortunately, they're getting smarter, and the bastards understand now. See how they've scattered?"

"A calling… to the wyrms?"

The baron grinned. "So you know some of the area, then? You dress like a stranger to Olsoth, and it's clear enough it's been some time since you've been here. No one from my city has braved the plains for weeks."

"It has been some time since I was in the region," conceded Rew.

"I want to hear your story, but first…"

The man, and the other soldiers on the platform, all looked out over the plains.

Rew could see that their pursuers had scattered into smaller clumps, and now there were a dozen of them all moving away from Olsoth in different directions.

"We haven't figured out how they communicate," murmured the man. "They do, somehow, to stay coordinated out there. Pfah. Even I'd get lost in those grasses with no point of reference. Men can walk for weeks on the plains without ever finding their way out or their way back here. Valchon's men are strangers to this land, but somehow, they know exactly where to go."

"We noticed," grumbled Rew.

The baron held up a hand, raising one finger then, after a moment, a second.

Rew gasped as half a league away, he saw the soil buckling, moving like a hand beneath a sheet, and then, it burst, and one of the clumps of Valchon's men disappeared down the maw of a giant land wyrm.

The wyrm bore some resemblance to the smaller creature with a similar name, but none who saw both would think they were related. This thing was no fish bait. It was massive, its body the length of a long merchant's train, and it was as wide as two wagons abreast. Its front was all mouth. From what Rew could see, the mouth looked like a vast cavern, ringed in teeth or tentacles, and when it crashed down on the hapless soldiers, it swallowed them whole, driving them and itself down hard into the ground and then churning through the surface and plunging its front out of sight while its long, white body wriggled after it.

It moved like a snake—or a worm, Rew admitted—propelling itself down into the ground, apparently going deep as, after two hundred paces, the buckling and sagging of the soil evened, and all was still.

With a crash, two leagues east, another of the wyrms erupted into view, and the soldiers it pursued faced the same fate as the first batch.

"Two of them is good," murmured the baron. "The wyrms have been part of Olsoth's protections for centuries. It's been enough to dissuade any opposing armies ever since Vaisius Morden the First came down from Iyre two hundred years ago.

But recently... We haven't seen as many of the creatures. I haven't found evidence of it, but I believe Valchon's men are killing them. It's dangerous if you don't know the trick of it, as you can see, but it can be done."

Looking at the swathes of churned dirt where the wyrms had surfaced, where groups of men had vanished into the maws of the creatures, Rew nodded quietly.

"Come," said the baron. "The wyrms will keep feeding for another hour, but I've seen enough. The lass over there looks like she's going to fall asleep and go tumbling off my walls. Your party needs rest, but I'm afraid I need to hear your story before you get it."

That gave Rew the span between the battlement and the baron's throne room to concoct a convincing story. It wasn't enough time.

Cinda was still stubbornly wearing the robes of a necromancer. Raif, after so much time on the road, had the scruffy look of a mercenary, except for the enchanted greatsword slung across his back which was impossible to miss if one knew what they were looking at. Zaine's lithe appearance might have signaled a number of professions, but her bow and twin daggers hinted at the truth. Rew had to admit he also had the look of a man who could not be trusted, and Anne didn't look threatening at all, which would make the nobleman even more suspicious of her. Instead of letting the baron press them, Rew jumped into his own questions as soon as the man unstrapped his sword, leaned it against a heavy wooden throne, and sat.

"The spellcasters wearing purple, who are they?"

Baron Barnaus frowned back at Rew, not answering. He drummed his fingers on the arm of his throne, studying the party. His armor was the same design and quality of his men's. He wore no insignia or decoration except for his signet ring. The baron was sturdy and looked as if he practiced regularly with his sword or at some other sport, but aside from his commanding demeanor, he could have been a simple captain rather than the ruler of the city.

"You are strangers here. I'll ask the questions. Why were you out in the plains south of Olsoth?"

It was dangerous to make assumptions about nobility, but Rew guessed the baron was a practical man who cared for results and gave little thought to the frippery that ensnared most of his peers. It was likely why he'd been given the remote city of Olsoth, with its odd and uncomfortable trade.

Rew gave a shallow bow and told the baron, "We're adventurers looking to enter the wyrm oil business."

The baron frowned at him. He looked around the throne room and then called loudly for his men to exit. He gave his soldiers a pretense of checking the walls to see if more of the interlopers were coming close, but it was clear to Rew that he wanted to speak in private. Did the baron not trust his own men?

Once the room was clear, Rew nodded discreetly to Cinda and claimed, "We've a few tricks up our sleeve which I think will bring us, and you after collecting your levy, a bountiful haul."

"The wyrm oil business is a bit slow at the moment," mentioned the baron drolly.

"Ah, yes," said Rew, suspecting the man wasn't buying a bit of his story, but having no choice except to continue. "We noticed. Who, if I may ask, were those men? You said they worked for… Valchon? The prince in Carff? I must admit, as soon as we realized they were chasing us, we did not stop to ask. Whoever they were, I've found that when soldiers want you, it's best to be somewhere else."

"That happens to you often?"

Rew shrugged and smiled.

"Yes, they are Prince Valchon's men," said the baron. "He's making war on his brother."

"I've heard rumors," said Rew. He crossed his arms over his chest. "There was a spellcaster in purple robes. I've never seen one like that before."

"We're calling them hunters," responded the baron, leaning back in his chair. "It seems they command a new breed of high magic, though most of what we know of them is through investigations into the aftermath of their attacks. It's been difficult to find survivors who can tell us anything. Because of that, I'm not certain of the extent of their powers or what spells they can cast, but it's clear they're endowed with some way of tracking prey, and they can sustain themselves far longer than a mortal man, even before they absorb the strength of their catch."

"That makes sense," murmured Rew, stretching his sore legs. "They followed us well over a day. Ah, what do you mean, absorb the strength?"

The baron pursed his lips, his fingers still drumming a rapid beat on the arm of his throne. His gaze flicked toward Cinda before settling back on Rew. "You've a lot of questions for a man who showed up unannounced and in trouble at my door."

Rew rubbed his head. "Apologies. I just… I haven't seen anything like these hunters before."

"They are new," agreed the baron. "You're familiar with how other talents, high magicians, draw their power?"

"I am."

"These hunters seem to leech their strength from other people. They've been scouring the villages across the plain, draining my vassals of strength and leaving them weak and dying. I can't even begin to count how many I've lost. I worry this same method is what is killing off the land wyrms, though we haven't been able to prove it. If it is…"

"Draining?"

Barnaus nodded. "Draining. It's like they suck the life out of their victims, and afterward, the hunters have grown in power."

"Oh my," murmured Anne. "That man, back at the village…"

"I've seen things, in my time," said the baron. "Done things as well. I'll spare you the details, but I earned this barony from the king during the last Investiture, and the toll was paid in blood. I was proud of that, for a time, but I no longer am. Still, what I earned, I earned facing men like myself on the field of battle with steel and fury. It was an honest fight, and they earned an honorable death. Afterward, the king helped rebuild what was destroyed, and we moved on. This new warfare?"

The baron shuddered, and Rew shifted uncomfortably. The man's comments were unusual for a noble. As a rule, they did not reflect on how they came to power and the price that others paid to help them make that climb. The bloody road to a title wasn't a secret, but nobles did not speak this way to strangers. Rew tucked a hand behind his back to the bone hilt of his hunting knife. He was beginning to suspect that they were not strangers to this man.

"The hunters are draining the life from my people. What will be left to rebuild when they are done? The villages are empty. If Prince Valchon prevails, the entire Northern Province could face the same fate. Blessed Mother, did you hear what he did to Stanton, to his own people?"

Rew did not respond.

"Prince Heindaw isn't any better, Ranger," hissed Baron Barnaus. He watched, seeing Rew's shock, then added, "Yes, I know who you are. All of you. After Carff and Jabaan... How could you not think I'd have your descriptions, that Heindaw wouldn't have alerted his people that you would be coming for him next? One of the king's rangers, a necromancer, a berserker, a thief, and an empath. There was another, a woman with bronze armor. She is gone? No, first, tell me, Ranger, why did you come to Olsoth?"

"It wasn't my intention," admitted Rew.

"You're going to Iyre. The hunters disrupted your journey?"

Rew stared at the baron, not responding. The man was a vassal of Prince Heindaw. He ought to be clapping them in chains and shipping them north, with or without their heads attached, but he wasn't. He seemed... curious.

"Iyre is a long journey. You—and your party—need rest," said the baron. "Stay here for the night, and we will talk again in the morning."

"I don't think that's—" began Rew, tensing his body for a fight.

"I understand that given who my liege is, you will not trust me no matter what I tell you. You shouldn't. I shouldn't trust you either, eh? But what choice do good men have in this world? Pfah, not even good men. I know who you are—who you were—Ranger. We are not good men, but perhaps we are better men than others? Are we to let this happen, let the princes commit their atrocities and fill this kingdom with nothing but the dead and those who'd be better off dead, or are we to do something?"

Rew blinked in surprise.

"I don't have the strength to challenge the Mordens," continued Baron Barnaus. "I don't even want to be associated with anyone trying, truth be told, but given an opportunity to assist, I can't turn away. Did you see any of the villages out on the plains, what is happening there? They're burning most of the evidence, but not all of it. Those people are free spirits, but they are my responsibility. The same will happen if those hunters ever breach my walls. I cannot allow it. Maybe I can help you and then you help me?"

"Help you how?"

"Tomorrow we negotiate," declared the baron.

"Negotiate what?"

"The overthrow of the kingdom, Ranger," responded the baron, standing from his chair, a wolfish grin on his lips. He gestured to Rew's companions, who were swaying drunkenly on their feet from the last day and a half of flight and terror. "I'll venture to guess from the state of your companions and your history over the last decade that you've no desire to rule, but someone must. Allowing this kingdom to descend into chaos is no better than allowing the Mordens to continue occupying its highest seat. You don't want to be the one on that throne, and I don't want to be the one to face the king and his sons. You see where I am going with this?"

Rew gave a harsh chuckle. "I think I do, but I do not know you, Baron."

Baron Barnaus smiled broadly. "Not yet, but that doesn't

matter. I think you must agree we have something to talk about but in the morning, when you're rested. If nothing else, accept succor for a night, and then you may leave. I understand you distrust me, but Ranger, what other choice do you have? You cannot plan to leave here while the wyrms are hunting or Valchon's men are loitering within view of my gates, can you?"

"You make a good point, but you're putting a lot of faith in us, saying what you are saying."

Shaking his head, the man offered a hard smile and replied, "I am not. Who would you tell? The king? Speaking to you is a small risk for me, but perhaps we can turn this chance encounter to our advantage. Think about it, Ranger. If I were to turn you over to Heindaw, what good would it do me? Valchon's men are swarming the Northern Province, and Heindaw does nothing. He's weak, and he's going to lose. When Valchon prevails, what is there for me? The best case is he forgets about Olsoth, and I can finish my rule quietly. More likely, he throws me off these walls and rewards one of his minions with my barony. So, why not talk to you? As long as no one realizes who you are, I risk nothing."

Rew scratched his beard. "I see."

"It's unlikely that you'll succeed in your quest, but if you do, I hope you remember this meeting when it comes time to put someone on the throne. Perhaps you do not think I can marshal the surviving nobles to support my claim to the throne, but if I don't, you lose little. I'm no worse than any other nobleman you could turn to, am I? It might be a stretch to say we'll become allies, but that doesn't mean we are enemies. We both may give little to gain much."

"Not enemies. I've been hearing that a lot, recently," grumbled Rew.

"You'll tell me about it in the morning?"

"Maybe."

"I'll have my people show you to rooms and bring you something to eat. That hunter nearly ran you into the ground, and bold plans require clear heads. We'll talk again soon."

The baron turned and rang a small gong beside his seat. The door to the throne room opened, and he gave instructions for a valet to see to their comfort. As if moving through a dream, Rew and the others followed the servant out of the throne room.

On the way, Rew thought furiously, fighting through the fatigue that clouded his thoughts. They couldn't trust the baron, of course, but what the man had said made sense. Barnaus would give little and hope for a lot, and they could do the same.

Slowly, Rew realized their plan was working. They'd planted seeds of truth and tried to scatter them across the kingdom. Those seeds were beginning to grow in the cracks of distrust and suspicion that wracked Valedon. The nobles wouldn't support Rew outright, but all he needed was for them to get out of the way. It was something. It was a start.

A small smile curling his lips, Rew followed the baron's valet and breathed deep, for the first time in days feeling a little optimistic. He looked around, taking in Olsoth as they walked to their rooms.

The inside of the monolith mirrored the outside, with a spiraling pathway twisting its way from the base of the open well to the top of the towering walls. Lush vegetation crept up that pathway, spilling out from every opening, filling the air with a verdant scent that was as close to the wilderness as Rew had ever experienced inside of a city. They could see people moving about, performing the same errands they would in any place. Children ran and called to each other, their voices echoing within the stone confines of Olsoth. Vendors, mercifully, were quieter, and the vegetation did its part to muffle their cries. It was like a secret garden, hidden from the world. It was peaceful.

Cold meats, bread, and butter arrived along with a basket of dried fruit. Rew and the others fell on the food, famished, then quickly finished and collapsed on the beds adjacent to the sitting room.

Rew, in a sole concession to the risk he knew they were still in, fell asleep on a chair in their common space, one boot wedged against the door that led to the hallway. He knew he wasn't going to be able to stay awake long, and the others were already lost in slumber, but with his foot propped where anyone opening the door would wake him, his longsword laid across his lap, he felt comfortable enough to lean his head back. Moments later, he was asleep.

Chapter Seventeen

Terse shouts and confusion woke Rew. He yawned and blinked. The room was dim, the fire dead. An hour until dawn, he thought. He dropped his leg to the ground and rubbed it, flexing his knee, trying to relieve the ache from how it'd been awkwardly bent for hours. He cracked his neck, thinking perhaps he should have considered a different plan than sleeping in the stiff chair all night, but it was done.

The shouting continued as he pushed back his chair and began to stretch his aching body. He left his longsword drawn and luckily had not unpacked anything the night before. The sounds from outside the door were panicked, but they weren't close. Not yet.

Moving on quiet feet, he began opening the doors to the chambers the others were sleeping in and roused them. They looked tired but unsurprised at being woken to shouts. Rew gave them enough time to blink the sleep from their eyes, to check their weapons, and to relieve himself in Raif's case. Then, the ranger cracked the door open and peered into the hallway. He saw nothing, but the tone of the shouting was clear. Olsoth was under attack.

"I'd rather run than hide, and we avoid a fight if at all possible," he told the others. "But first, I want to know what's going on. Baron Barnaus seemed sincere in his offer to help."

"Help with what?" asked Raif, covering a yawn with a fist. "Sorry. It's all a blur since… uh, since we started running from Valchon's men, I guess."

"He offered to help overthrow the princes and the king—or, I should say, he offered to stand out of the way. He meant to talk further on it this morning."

"Oh, right." Raif shifted, stretching his legs, and wincing as he rubbed under his armor where it must have chaffed him the day before. "The throne room, then?"

"That's a good place to start," agreed Rew, silently wondering whether he recalled how to get there from the rooms they'd been assigned. He'd been more awake and aware than Raif the night before, but not by much.

Walking cautiously down the hallway, Rew led the others out, peeking carefully around each corner, noting that, so far, the hallway used for guest accommodations seemed quiet. Whatever was happening was happening several levels below them. The way Olsoth was designed, there were few passages that led directly up and down. As long as they didn't stumble across the wrong one, they ought to have fair warning of anything coming their way up the main corridors.

It seemed his recollection held, and Rew led them unerringly to the throne room. There, they found several dozen of Olsoth's soldiers milling about.

Rew grabbed the arm of one who was passing by, not seeming in a hurry. He asked the other man, "What's going on?"

"Who are you?" demanded the soldier.

"Does it matter?"

Frowning, the soldier shrugged and looked around as if hoping to spy a superior officer. When he didn't see one and must have realized Rew wasn't going to let go of his arm until he answered, the soldier replied, "Hunters. Several of them, we think. They broke in the lower levels. The baron and his elite guard have gone to face them."

Rew stared at the man, confused.

"You don't want to send too many against a hunter," explained the soldier impatiently. "They'll drain 'em for power. It's best to send your most dangerous men and let them deal with it."

The soldier, it seemed, was not one of the baron's most dangerous men. Rew pressed him, "What spellcasters does Baron Barnaus have in his court?"

The soldier looked askance at Rew then tugged at his arm. When Rew still didn't let go, he answered, "He's got two enchanters of decent talent and an invoker of hardly any talent at all. The baron himself knows a bit of conjuring, but he relies on our steel."

Rew released the soldier and turned to his companions as the man scurried away on whatever errand he'd been attempting when the ranger had grabbed him.

"Enchanters are next to useless in combat unless they've prepared in advance. An invoker may do quite well, depending on what these hunters are capable of, but Valchon wouldn't have risked his new cadre of spellcasters on this attack unless he thought it would be successful. Spellcasters with unknown abilities would be an incredible advantage against Heindaw. Valchon would want to keep their skills secret as long as possible."

"They tracked us here," remarked Anne. "They must be looking for us."

Rew nodded. "If these hunters have preternatural abilities to follow us, we may as well face them now. I, for one, am not looking for another endless chase across the plains. At least in Olsoth, we'll have the baron's men and spellcasters at our side."

"What are we waiting on then?" asked Zaine, drawing an arrow from her quiver and setting it on her bowstring.

Raif unslung his greatsword and stretched his arms above his head. "I suppose we're not breaking our fast until this is done, so we'd best get on with it, eh? I'm hungry."

Her eyes shimmering with subtle green, Cinda turned to Rew. "I'm not going to hold back, Ranger."

Grunting, Rew shared a look with Anne then led the others from the throne room, heading down Olsoth's long, curving passageways. The clamor of battle rang ahead of them, but before they reached it, they rounded a bend and found Baron Barnaus with two dozen of his soldiers, his invoker, and one of the enchanters.

"We need more men!" cried the baron. He jabbed a finger at one of his soldiers and demanded, "Tell the commander, Blessed Mother, tell everyone you see to get down here with everyone they can bring. I want a wall of steel blocking this passageway."

"But, m'lord," said the invoker, flexing his fingers and staring down the hall, "you said earlier we shouldn't bring too many bodies in front of these… hunters. Allow me to—"

"I don't care what I said. We need more men!" bellowed the baron. "If you were going to do something, you should have the last time we saw them."

"I wasn't ready, m'lord. My fault, and it won't happen again."

Baron Barnaus glared at the soldier he'd addressed, and the man skittered up the hallway, eyes wide, looking at Rew and the others as if wondering whether he should instruct them to join the fight, and then, he was past them. The baron was staring down the hall, following his invoker's gaze, where the sounds of fighting were still thick, coming from somewhere below. The enchanter appeared shocked, and it took Rew a moment to notice the woman's robes were splashed with bright crimson. Presumably what remained of her partner.

"Barnaus," called Rew, striding toward the man. "What's happened?"

"Hunters," spat the baron. "Three of them, I'm told. They got in somehow, I'm still not sure how, and they've been slaughtering soldiers and citizens, working their way up the tiers of the city.

We managed to erect a barrier for a moment and evacuated most of the citizens behind it. The soldiers at least are dying with blades in their hands and aren't any use to the hunters. Those common people would have been like oil on a fire. Unfortunately, the hunters were at work before we realized what was happening, and they drained hundreds. It's like fighting... Pfah! Like fighting ghosts. They're fast, and they're dangerous."

"Drained... You said something like that before."

Baron Barnaus looked into Rew's eyes. "These hunters take power from their victims. They leave them empty and worthless. The hunters themselves... They're strong and fast, unlike any mortal man. Ranger, there are hundreds of people below, and three hunters will slaughter them all."

Rew grunted. He asked, "They're using mundane weapons?"

"So far. If they have other capabilities, they haven't shown them."

"They're farther down this passage?"

"So far," repeated Baron Barnaus, glaring at Rew. "It's been a quarter hour since any runners have come back to report. You can hear as well as I how it's going. It's only a matter of time until we see them."

Rew glanced at Cinda, and she nodded, understanding his look. The ranger told Raif, "Watch her, will you?"

The fighter looked confused, but he followed his sister several dozen steps back up the hallway and stood beside her when she sat in a chair against the wall and closed her eyes. Baron Barnaus crossed his arms over his chest and must have guessed what she was attempting, but he didn't comment. Instead, he tapped his foot impatiently and began directing his men as they started to trickle down from above.

It seemed he assumed the barrier they'd fashioned on the lower level was going to fail soon, and he was preparing another line of defense. In the raw stone of the city's corridors, there was little they could do quickly, but the baron arrayed two score of men across the passageway with long halberds pointed down where they expected the hunters to come at them.

"Where are those archers?" growled Barnaus, shouting so that his voice echoed up the hall behind them. "We need the archers!"

While everyone was distracted, Rew sauntered over to Cinda and crouched beside her.

"I see two of them," she whispered. "They're fast and strong, like he said. They're coming up, and—pfah! Hold on. Let me get another vessel. They must have realized I was watching them."

"Valchon will have warned them of your talents after Jabaan," said Rew quietly. "See if you can spy the third hunter that Baron Barnaus mentioned. Then, leave off with the, ah, the spies. Just concentrate on drawing power. Your corpses will be too slow and clumsy for these things, and if they already took out one, they know what to look for. They must have some ability to sever your bindings, or maybe they just obliterated the thing. Filling the hallway with the breath of death will be more effective. No matter how fast they are, they can't avoid it if you blanket the corridor wall to wall."

"Understood," said Cinda, her eyes still closed, a frown on her face. "They got another one. You're right. They've been trained to combat the undead. A precaution against me or the king, do you think? And, Ranger, we might have a problem. I haven't found the third hunter yet."

Rew scratched his beard, wondering if there had been a third. Soldiers were as bad as fishermen when it came to exaggerating what they'd seen. Did running terrified from three men sound better than running terrified from two?

"Ranger," added Cinda. "There's a well of power I'm drawing on. Hundreds have died below us, but… these souls are weak. They're diminished. It's not life those hunters are devouring. It's the very souls of their victims. I don't know what that means."

"Neither do I, but it doesn't sound good."

"What happens if you die without a soul?" asked Cinda rhetorically, her eyes closed, her jaw clenched tight.

"We can't leave here without stopping them," declared Raif.

Rew clapped the fighter on the shoulder. "We'll do our best."

He thought Raif probably meant that as the sort of honorable and foolish declaration young fighters like him made when they were trying very hard to be brave, but whether or not he meant to be, Raif was right. They couldn't leave without dealing with the hunters. The passageways down to the bottom of the city were blocked. There was no way out of Olsoth without going through Valchon's dogs. Whether they wanted to or not, they would have to face the things.

"Let me know if anything changes," Rew instructed Cinda. Then, he moved back to where Baron Barnaus was ordering freshly arrived men into his defensive position.

Raif, realizing now what his sister was doing, placed his greatsword tip-down in front of him and stood on guard, ready to attack anyone who interfered. Anne and Zaine looked worried as Rew explained what the necromancer had said.

"If their souls are diminished, Rew…" hissed Anne. She looked horrified. "If their souls are diminished, then they may be beyond the care of even the Blessed Mother. This is an abomination. It's worse than the king's most despicable acts. At least in time, the king's minions leave his clutches to the Mother's comfort."

"You're sure it's worse than stockpiling crypts—cities—full of corpses to fuel his own immortality?" questioned Zaine. "Because that's pretty awful."

"The king may trap a person's soul, but with these things… the soul is consumed. Who you are ends when you die, who you could be ends when you have no soul. That dead man in the village, the dehydrated one, that's why he died. They drained him. There was nothing left of him to fight. He couldn't even bring himself to stand and stumble a few hundred paces for water to save his life."

Sighing, Rew looked down the hallway, waiting for the arrival of the hunters. He rubbed his hands over the wooden hilt of his longsword, feeling the grains worn smooth from use, distracting himself from what was coming, what he worried he would have to do if they were going to prevail. If these hunters had the strength and speed of hundreds... he wasn't sure he could face them. Not without help.

A scared-looking, blood-stained squad of soldiers came staggering around the bend. They lurched toward their peers, and the halberds rose out of the way to let them past.

"Report," barked Baron Barnaus.

"Overrun, m'lord," gasped one of the soldiers. "We only managed to escape because they were draining the others. I-I know we were supposed to hold, but there was nothing we could do. If we'd stayed, they would have just... taken us."

The baron, his eyes flashing with anger, merely nodded curtly. He glanced at the sixty soldiers holding the hallway. "We cannot fall back again. If they make it past us, they'll reach the juncture outside of the throne room. From there, they can reach most of Olsoth with nowhere we can pin them down. This is it, the last line. Those of you who have families... fall, and your families will pay the price."

The men, grim-faced, nodded and reset their line of halberds. Sixty soldiers, who clearly did not believe they would be enough.

Behind them, Rew grimaced. How many had the hunters cut through below? Now, they would be even stronger. In Barnaus' eyes, Rew could see the man's fear. The baron thought his entire city was going to fall. Tens of thousands of people. If Valchon's new spellcasters drained their victims for power, then they weren't going to let those people survive. Valchon had proven who he was in Stanton. His minions would follow his footsteps.

"Baron—" said Rew, turning to face the man.

He stopped then lunged forward, thrusting his longsword at one of the bloody soldiers who'd just walked through the line of the baron's men. The soldier seemed to bend like wind-blown grass, curving out of the way of Rew's attack then whipping back, swinging a fist at the ranger's head. Rew caught the blow on his bracer and was sent staggering to the side, stunned at the force behind the strike.

The soldier—the hunter—turned toward Baron Barnaus but then paused and spun back to Rew.

"Recognize me, do you?" growled the ranger. He charged again.

This time, the hunter, attired in the stolen gear of one of Baron Barnaus' soldiers, drew its blade and slashed at Rew's face before the ranger could move his longsword to defend.

Rew turned and let his momentum carry him into the hunter, smashing into it with his shoulder then yanking his hunting knife from his belt and dragging the edge across the hunter's hip.

The hunter swung its head forward, catching Rew on the cheekbone, splitting his skin, and exploding a field of stars across his vision.

Instinctively, he ducked and felt the breath of a broadsword cleaving the air a finger-width above his bare scalp. Reeling backward, Rew swung at the hunter, just trying to keep it off of him, but it drifted out of the way and kept pressing him toward the wall. Rew knew once his back hit that stone, he would have nowhere to maneuver.

Around the pair, Baron Barnaus, his men, and Rew's companions stood stunned at the ferocity of the fight and the speed at which it had unfolded.

The hunter moved with the grace and strength of a valaan, but with the knowledge of a man. It'd been trained in combat and knew the use of its sword as well as any elite soldier. Trained by Valchon's armsmen, no doubt, or even by Vyar Grund. Is this what the ranger commandant had been doing for the prince?

Rew's heel hit the stone wall, and the hunter seemed to pause a breath before flowing in and trying to finish him. Lunging forward, Rew feinted to the side with his hunting knife. The hunter wasn't fooled and moved to defend against a strike from Rew's longsword. Dropping the blade, Rew snaked behind the hunter's guard and grappled with it, stabbing a finger toward its eye then twisting out of the way as it recoiled and swung at him.

He grasped the hunter's arm and hauled it close, coming in behind his opponent and wrapping his arm around the spellcaster's neck.

The hunter struggled for a moment, thrown off guard by his attack. Then, it flung itself and Rew toward the wall. The ranger felt his back smack against the stone. Breath exploded from his mouth, and his ribcage threatened to crack from the force, but he held on and wrapped his legs around the hunter's waist, locking himself into the choke.

The hunter spun and tried to stab behind its back with its broadsword, but clearly, it'd never fought like this, and none of the training it had received had prepared it for the brutality of hand-to-hand combat to the death. Eye pokes and chokes weren't the methods of nobility. Rew fought like he'd learned after Mordenhold, in the streets and taverns. He fought ruthlessly, dirty.

The ranger arched his back, tugging his arm tight, and then Zaine was in front of the hunter, plunging both of her daggers into its sides and ripping them away. The hunter staggered, its airway cut off, its lungs filling with blood. Hoping whatever high magic granted it increased speed and strength didn't somehow keep it alive, Rew held on.

The hunter stumbled half a dozen more steps, and then it fell face first onto the floor.

Rew laid on top of it, his arm still wrapped tight around its neck. He didn't let go for a long time, not trusting the thing was actually dead, until he felt its blood under his boots, making the stone floor slick as it trickled down the sloped passageway.

Rolling free, Rew staggered to his feet.

"Blessed Mother," breathed Barnaus.

Putting a toe beneath the hunter, Rew kicked it over onto its back. He pointed to its face, the face of a young Prince Valchon, and demanded, "If anyone sees another man who looks like that, kill him immediately."

"Everyone get a good look," ordered Barnaus, shaken.

Rew met the baron's gaze and understood the nobleman knew what they were looking at. A young Valchon, maybe seventeen winters. For Rew, it was like looking at his brother, when they were still younger, bonded by the common experiences no one else in the kingdom could share. Rew had abdicated his role as a prince by that age but hadn't yet left the creche. It would be years later before he left Mordenhold entirely. He hadn't become Valchon's friend during that time, but he'd become the closest thing the prince ever had to one. There'd been difficult moments but good ones as well. Rew shuddered and looked away from the body. What had Valchon done?

It was as if he'd created simulacra of himself, younger versions, who aped him in looks and ability. The hunter had fought just like Valchon—skilled, confident, but trained in the practice yard instead of the real world. Rew was certain the hunter had never faced, and never expected to face, someone who was better with a blade than they were. The young man—if it could be called a man—had been trained by Vyar or someone just like him. Maybe even the prince himself.

That was a crack Rew could exploit, having sparred with both men throughout the years, but it would do the baron and his soldiers no good. These men wouldn't have Rew's knowledge or his experience. One on one, they'd be helpless against the hunters. King's Sake, even sixty to two, the baron's men didn't have a chance. The hunter had been blazingly fast and as strong as a dozen men. Even with practice-yard skills, it would be enough to slice through Baron Barnaus' men like they were warm butter.

"Ranger," called Cinda. "I don't know how much strength these things can gather from several hundred people, but get ready. They're coming now."

"Do you have any men with ranged weapons?" Rew called to the baron.

Barnaus shook his head, "I do, but…." He waved up the curving corridor. "Wherever they are right now, they're no use to us."

Rew grunted and strode toward the line. "Your spellcasters need to hit them quickly before they can engage your soldiers."

"Of course," responded the baron.

His invoker was already standing at the backs of the soldiers, flexing his fingers, waiting to unleash against the hunters. The baron's enchanter was lurking ten paces behind and babbled a protest, but beneath her liege's stern gaze, she went to join the invoker. It wasn't clear what use the woman would be, but when it came to fighting magic, the spellcasters of the court couldn't be allowed to hide from conflict.

"Do you have any high magic of your own?" Rew asked the baron.

"None that will do us any good."

There was the sound of frantic scrambling, and then around the corner, a lone soldier appeared lumbering toward them. Blood covered half his face, and his mouth was open as if frozen mid-scream. The other soldiers tensed, prepared for a hunter in disguise, but one of them called the approaching man's name.

The halberds parted to give the man space to slip through, but in a blink, two purple-robed figures streaked up the passageway. King's Sake, they were even faster than the one who'd been in disguise! Before anyone realized what was happening, one of the hunters grasped the fleeing soldier by the head and ripped off his helmet. With one hand, it held the man by his forehead, and the hunter's hand seemed to glow.

"Blessed Mother," whispered Anne as they watched the hunter drain the soldier's soul. "Rew, we have to…"

The hunter tossed the soldier aside. The limp man slapped against the wall and slid down it listlessly. He wasn't dead, but he wasn't much alive, either.

The baron's men shifted, pointing their halberds toward the two hunters. The pair of purple-robed men, with the same cold eyes as Prince Valchon, studied the opposition. Then, their gaze landed beyond the ranks of soldiers on Rew. They studied him and looked past to Cinda.

She'd taken Rew's side. The young necromancer whispered, "I can't hit them without catching most of the baron's troops in the blast. I think I can completely fill this passage with death's breath, but none of these soldiers will survive it. Should I..."

The baron's invoker lobbed a pathetic, bubbling ball of liquid fire down the hallway.

One of the hunters laughed and sidestepped the ill-aimed attack. Grinning broadly, the hunter juggled the helmet it'd torn off the soldier's head. Then, it hurled the helmet up the hallway. The invoker didn't have time to squeak with surprise before the steel armor struck him in the face. The man's skull crumpled from the blow, the muffled crack of shattering bone the only sound in the passageway. The invoker reeled backward, blood spraying from his head. He was dead before he hit the ground.

Baron Barnaus' enchanter turned and ran.

Cinda raised her hands, and ephemeral vapor began to collect around her fists.

"I'll handle it. If I fail, you know what to do," said Rew, putting a hand on her arm and then stepping forward. With his off hand, he tapped the shoulder of one of the soldiers. "Let me through, will you?"

The hunters' expressions did not change at Rew's approach, but they waited for him as he slipped through the line of soldiers. Once he was past the tips of the soldiers' halberds, the hunters sprang at him.

The hunters were like flashes of lightning, streaking toward him faster than his vision could follow. They'd been draining hundreds of souls down below, far more than their companion who Rew had faced earlier. They were... brothers, or perhaps something closer? They acted in perfect harmony, as if sharing the same thoughts, both taking optimal angles to prevent Rew from dodging out of the way. Whichever one of them he faced, the second could come at his side. The pair of them were too fast to defend against.

If they'd been in nature, in the wilderness, or some other place where he could tap into the surging life around him, Rew might have had a chance. He could have thrown glamours in front of the attacking hunters, or he could have obscured his form, making them guess where he really was and where he was going. He might have drawn on a deeper well, if they were far enough from civilization, and called upon the ancient magic that lay in such hidden places. That strength would aide him, grant him senses and ability beyond normal men, but they were in a city, and the hunters he faced had pulled the energy from hundreds of normal men.

Olsoth was a monolith, far above the empty plain around them. It had been occupied for centuries. The plants in the place were trained and manicured by the citizens, and they didn't pulse with the life of the wilderness. Rew had no magic within this place.

So instead, he released the magic trapped within his enchanted longsword. It flared alight, a soft white glow along the edge of the steel. He felt the surge of magic fill his limbs immediately, and he felt the surging connection to his attackers, as well.

They were truly of Valchon's blood. Rew knew that now. They were of the same blood as him, the same as the king, and the king's father, whose soul had been entombed in the longsword hundreds of years before.

The soul within the blade hungered for its own blood, and Rew let the weapon drift ahead of him as he lunged. He spun, supernatural energy burning through him as he whipped the longsword around. He felt resistance twice as the blade passed through each of the hunters, and then, he was past, and the cleaved bodies of Valchon's simulacra slapped wetly against the stone floor.

Rew stopped, motionless. He struggled to control the weapon. It keened, though he did not know if anyone else could hear it, and on its own volition the weapon twisted in his hands, the smooth wood of the hilt sliding against the calluses on his palms and fingers. The blade sought its own blood. His blood.

Silently, for a long time or short, he struggled with the blade, whispering to it, to his ancestor. Whether or not Erasmus Morden could hear his words, imprisoned somewhere within that steel tomb, Rew did not know, but the words helped him focus, helped him pacify the grand magician, and then helped him seal the breach that had opened when Rew had activated the magic within the blade. The glow winked out, but he waited, making sure it would not reappear, and only then did he turn.

Sixty soldiers of Baron Barnaus' guard stood stock still, staring at Rew as if they were looking at their own mother after she turned into one of the land wyrms of the plains. The younglings looked much the same. Anne's eyes were knowing, as if she'd just confirmed something she'd already known.

She'd healed him. She'd felt what resided within that blade.

Baron Barnaus was the first to speak. "King's Sake, man."

"I wouldn't mind an ale," said Rew quietly, gripping the longsword tight to hide the trembling in his hands. "Then, we need to talk."

The baron, speechless, nodded, and led them higher into Olsoth. Anne and the others fell in behind Rew, while the baron's men fanned out through the bottom of the city, making sure there were no more intruders and that the gates to the city were resealed. Not even Anne voiced a complaint about drawing an ale before they broke their fast that morning.

Chapter Eighteen

"Is that how you defeated Prince Calb?" wondered Baron Barnaus. "I've heard the man could conjure nightmarish creatures that are far beyond my own meagre abilities. The way you moved..."

"No, that's not how I faced Prince Calb," responded Rew. He shifted in his chair, looking morosely at a half-empty ale mug, his second, and the platter of sausages and biscuits beside it.

He'd forced himself to eat, but the food had no taste. He could barely concentrate on the baron's unsubtle prodding, so he let Anne field most of the questions. Raif had spoken up as well, but the fighter seemed humbled by what Rew had done and barely squeaked out responses to the baron's inquiries. Cinda had withdrawn into herself, perhaps pulling more of the ambient power that lay within Olsoth after the attack, or perhaps her thoughts were simply elsewhere.

Zaine devoured the food on her plate, and then the food on Cinda's. The thief was taking advantage of the hot meal, evidently foreseeing another long journey with travel rations. She took the sausages from Raif's plate when the fighter wasn't looking and then went back for a roasted tomato he'd been pushing around unconsciously with his fork. Rew smiled and tucked back into his own meal.

Whether he could taste and enjoy the food or not, they'd been through a lot, and it was foolish to ignore a hot breakfast when they had one. His motion seemed to break a spell on the party, and they all began eating again, except for Raif, who was staring at his plate, confused.

"Do you think we can be allies?" asked Baron Barnaus.

Rew chewed for a moment then swallowed. "Allies? I already rid your city of three hunters who I believe we can agree would have ravaged this place if I hadn't intervened."

"And I believe we can agree there's no doubt those hunters were only in Olsoth because of your presence," retorted the baron, bobbling his hands as if they were scales. "Hundreds of my people are dead, and hundreds are worse than dead, Ranger. I visited them in the infirmary, and they're just... lying there. We're discussing whether or not killing them would be a mercy."

"Perhaps the hunters struck Olsoth to get to us, but they were already on the plains before we arrived in the region," argued Rew. "Sooner or later, they were going to attack. The balance is in our favor, Baron."

"Boys," said Anne, leaning forward and glaring at the two of them. "Does it really matter what happened in the past? Barnaus, you're hoping we rid you of your liege. It's a dangerous pursuit, and if we're successful, I imagine all of Vaeldon will be waiting breathlessly for what Rew intends next. His support will be a boon for anyone hoping to obtain the throne in Mordenhold, or anyone hoping to keep any land-holding in Vaeldon, I suppose. For his support in the future, what can you offer?"

Baron Barnaus steepled his fingers and smiled at the empath. "No simple woman, are you? I've been wondering why the ranger keeps you in his company."

"She has a fair point," said Rew. "If all you intend is to let us go on our way, that's not enough for me to consider you anything other than another noble. Besides, you saw what happened below. Do you really think you can keep us here if we want to leave?"

Baron Barnaus pursed his lips and dipped his head in acknowledgement. "Of course. I ask much, so I must give much. There are two things I can offer you. One, information. I've spent time in Iyre. I know Heindaw, and I know the people in his court. I can tell you who is dangerous. I can describe his spellcasters and their capabilities, and I can tell you what I suspect Heindaw has been developing as a weapon for the Investiture. I can map out the city for you and describe the protection he's arranged around himself."

"Information is a valuable commodity," conceded Rew.

"I can also save you time," continued Barnaus. "It's a long walk to Iyre. It'll take you at least a week and a half if you left today. While on the road, the Investiture may very well pass you by. Who knows what could happen while you're hiking north, and if you think to portal into Iyre, you should know Heindaw has prepared for it. Of course he has. If he hadn't, Valchon would have already appeared there and cast his maelstrom over the city. You heard about Stanton? Going to Iyre is a long, tiring journey, but I can help. I have access to a portal stone. It's an established connection which Heindaw will not detect, and I'm the only one who knows about it."

"If I show up in Heindaw's basement..." began Rew.

Barnaus shook his head. "You're right. The portal stones in the palace will be more closely guarded than Heindaw's own bedchamber. It'd be suicide, even for you, to attempt strolling into there. I have another way. Heindaw's predecessor in Iyre—the king—is an enchanter as well, did you know? An enchanter who had a mistress who was my mother. When Vaisius Morden the Eighth won over his brothers and took his seat in Mordenhold, my mother went with him, but before she did, she left me the secret of the portal stones she used to visit him in Iyre. As far as I know, the king is the only other person who realizes the stones exist, and because the connection is established, Heindaw will

AC COBBLE

have no idea you are in his city. I've tested it myself several times, and I'm certain the passage is safe."

Rew frowned. "Your mother went to Mordenhold…"

Baron Barnaus' eyes flashed. "When Morden was crowned, I was named Baron of Olsoth and given enough work to keep me busy for years. By the time things settled, the letters had stopped coming. I never saw my mother again, Ranger. I'm not a complete fool, so I've never mentioned her to the king, and I've stopped checking the faces of the women I see on my rare visits to the capital. I asked Heindaw once, and he laughed and changed the subject. I don't know the details, but I suppose I don't really need to, do I?"

"You don't have children, do you?"

"No children," confirmed Baron Barnaus, his voice cold and eager. "No children, just a hope. I know I can't do it myself, but you…" The baron shrugged. "If you are successful, and you see fit to grant me your blessing, I'll do the best I can for whatever people I end up ruling. I swear that to you, Ranger, but if you do not grant me your blessing, I will still do what's in my power to stop the reign of your father, just as you do. Either way, the promises of nobles fade as quickly as an echo, so I will not ask for yours. Instead, I'll offer what assistance I can, and trust that you remember me when all of this is over. Assuming we both survive, of course."

"Of course," said Rew. "Valchon must know we are here by now, so we need to keep moving. I suggest we rest another day while you tell us what you know. After that, how quickly can we access the portal stone?"

"It's right here in Olsoth," said Barnaus, showing a wicked grin. "I agree that speed is important. A day of rest and discussion, and at dawn, you go to Iyre."

THEY QUESTIONED THE BARON ABOUT HEINDAW AND HIS COURT, learning the talents of his spellcasters, the organization of his soldiers, and the layout of the small home the portal stone would take them to. It was much that Rew already knew and confirmation of what he feared. Heindaw had been plotting against his older brother Valchon from afar, and he'd intentionally goaded the invoker, hoping Valchon would move first against Iyre where Heindaw had spent years layering traps around the city and around his palace. The efforts Heindaw had made in Spinesend and elsewhere in the Eastern Province had been to anger Valchon and to spur him into a rash attack. Cutting through the traps Heindaw had laid wasn't going to be easy.

The prince had set a complex network of wards throughout the city, and the palace was nearly covered with them. His entire military force was held close, along with his spellcasters. He'd been training specialty units for the coming battle, with which he hoped to surprise Valchon. He'd enchanted unique equipment, which he would utilize in the final confrontation. Knowing Heindaw, it was much that Rew would have guessed already, but it was good to understand a few specifics.

Unfortunately, while Barnaus related rumors of an elite force recruited and held ready in the Arcanum, he clearly didn't know the whole truth. He didn't know Heindaw had been attempting to raise the dead, and as far as he knew, when the Arcanum had been destroyed, Heindaw's minions had gone with it. Had Salwart been successful raising any of the dead? Were those creations all destroyed in the king's attack, or would they have to face them in Iyre? Or it could be none of that. It could have been a failed experiment which Heindaw had spread rumor of to distract Valchon.

Rew sighed. The baron had even less information about what Salwart and Heindaw had been attempting in Spinesend with Baron Fedgley. The ranger probed as best he could, without revealing his own hand, and came up empty. If he had to guess, that meant the real plot was Fedgley, and the Arcanum was a feint to sow confusion, but guessing Heindaw's intent was a more complicated ball of thread than Rew had time to untangle.

Most disappointing, Barnaus had no knowledge of the nameless woman or the Sons of the Father. He was aware of the cult, as anyone familiar with Iyre would be, but according to him, the temple had never burned down, and the cult had little to do with local politics. Descriptions of the nameless woman made the baron simply shrug. He spent most of his time in Olsoth, but when he'd been in Heindaw's court, he hadn't noticed anyone meeting her description.

"A beautiful warrior woman adorned in enchanted armor? I would have noticed, Ranger. I might not have children, but I have the same desires as all men."

It made Rew nervous, knowing the woman was out there and that, somehow, she'd slipped away from their camp in the hours before Valchon's hunters had found them. Rew assumed she'd been in league with Heindaw, but how had she sensed Valchon's men? Had it truly been recognition of the hunters that spurred her flight? If so, where would she have gone?

When they'd exhausted much of Baron Barnaus' knowledge and the nobleman had left to tend to the damage in his city, the children sprawled out on couches and beds and promptly fell asleep. Rew was eying them enviously, wishing another night wedged in front of the door didn't sound so unpleasant, when Anne came and sat down in front of him, crossing her legs and settling on the floor.

"Do you want to explain?"

Rew rubbed his hand over his head. "No."

"I couldn't see... but I felt a connection between you and that sword, Rew. It's... not just a sword, is it? It's alive. There's an echo of it within you, a hurt. I'd say anger, but it's beyond that. Rage like I've never encountered. Do you feel that always?"

"Alive isn't the right word," he murmured, "but something like it. And yes, I feel it every time I touch the hilt, though its manageable until I release the powers trapped within. Then... I've survived it so far."

Anne waited patiently, sitting at his feet, watching him.

He coughed and looked everywhere but at her.

"Don't tell me it's too dangerous for me to know the truth," said the empath. "You only get to use that excuse once."

Sighing, Rew leaned forward and grasped her hands. "The sword is imbued with the soul of Erasmus Morden, Vaisius' father. I can call upon his power through the blade."

Anne's jaw fell open, and she stared at him wordlessly.

"He's been imprisoned in the steel, entombed there by his own son, for over two hundred years. Using this longsword, calling upon Erasmus, is how I learned of what Vaisius Morden had become and how I learned to defeat him. The king knows his father is trapped within the blade, of course. He used this weapon himself in the early years when he fought the Dark Kind and consolidated Vaeldon. Over time, Erasmus grew in understanding of his prison, and he fought back against Vaisius, making this weapon useless to the king. Later, others picked up the blade, but there is incredible danger in utilizing it fully. From what I've discovered, everyone eventually gives into temptation. They draw too much or too often, and they fail."

"But... the king's father?"

"Erasmus holds great hatred for his son," continued Rew. "That's the rage you felt. It's his hurt as well, hurt at his son's betrayal, maybe, but sometimes I think it is regret he did not act first. For decades, this sword sat untouched in the king's palace. I don't believe my brothers know it is Erasmus entombed within, but they do know the cost the blade exacts. Morden family history is littered with stories of those driven mad by this weapon. The king and my brothers do not believe I have the capability to cast high magic and hence am not able to draw upon the power of Erasmus. They're wrong."

"High magic?"

"I'm a son of the king," murmured Rew. "I chose a different path, but that old path is not closed to me."

"That hatred, how does it not consume you? The hurt, how do you bear it? What I felt through our connection still is an ache inside of me. It's not like any pain I've ever experienced. It does not go away."

"No, it does not," replied Rew with a bitter smile. "I try to avoid utilizing the power of the sword. It's the only thing I can do to combat Erasmus's hunger. It's been years since I last had to draw upon his strength. Today... I didn't think there was a choice."

The empath's expression was clouded with grief, a mirror to his own sorrow. She'd felt it. She knew.

Rew cleared his throat. "Vaisius Morden is his father's son, Anne. Erasmus was not a good man. He's... evil, and when I activate this blade, he is a part of me. I can feel him coursing through my blood and connecting with what is already there. He is a part of me. His thoughts, his memories. You felt that when you healed me, didn't you? It's like filth upon my soul."

"Erasmus is a part of you, but he is not you."

"You felt it?"

Anne looked away and nodded.

Squeezing her hands, Rew continued. "I do not fear I will become him and be compelled to commit the same atrocities he did, or his son, or his sons... my uncles, my brothers. I don't fear I will become them, but I fear Erasmus will become me. He fights me, tries to take control. He seethes, Anne. He yearns for revenge not just against his son but against all. Today, after I killed the hunters, I could feel the blade thirsting for more blood. The sword —Erasmus—would have helped me slaughter anyone I turned the edge against. He would have reveled in the blood if I'd struck down all of Olsoth, but when I stopped, the blade wanted me. The will of Erasmus is a part of me, and it wanted to plunge that sword straight through my own neck. I fought it, and I won, but it's close every time. So close."

"Oh, my."

Rew sat back. "This sword has the properties of any enchanted blade. It's sharp, sturdy, but... I fear to unleash what it can truly do. I fear that one day, it will mean my death. I know that within moments of unleashing that force, I won't be able to stop it—stop myself—from taking the lives of others. Every time, it gets harder to bend Erasmus to my will. It gets harder to sheath the blade. It's a gamble on how quickly I can act against how quickly I can reseal his tomb. Anne, I have not always been quick enough. You... you understand? People have died because I lost the wager against time, against Erasmus."

She freed a hand and wiped the back of it beneath her eye. She cleared her throat and said, "You turned from that path when we went to Eastwatch."

"I've changed, but I'm still me."

"I sensed the connection between you and the blade when I healed you," she admitted. "I'm still tied to you, and today when you fought those hunters, something... traveled between the sword and you. A bit of Erasmus, I suppose, joined you. That is why you find it more difficult to control him after each use. After each time, there is more of him inside of you. Rew, I, ah, I said that you were not him, that you would not become him, but... You're right. The taint is upon your soul. It's not you, but it's there. I think he's... escaping, bit by bit, into you. That's what the king spoke of, in the Arcanum, isn't it?"

Rew nodded. "Erasmus, while not as powerful as Vaisius, was the most powerful spellcaster the world had seen during his era. His talents would dwarf anyone outside of the Morden line, even today. When I began using the blade, before I became a ranger, I wasn't as cautious as I should have been. I learned from him, but he learned from me as well. He's been brooding for centuries, and with me, he found what he needed. You're right. It's me. I'm his way out of this prison. I am his path to revenge."

"I don't think you should..."

"I agree, Anne," said Rew, giving her a small smile. "I won't use the sword again. Not like that. You understand now, why I never allowed you to heal me? This… darkness is always with me. Part of it will be with you, now. I knew if you felt that…"

She brought herself upon her knees and put her hands on his legs. "Rew. I can feel that darkness, but I also feel you. You're fighting it. You always have. You always will."

He tried to smile and did not respond. She spoke of a certainty that he did not share.

Standing slowly, she rubbed her hips. "Now, I don't know about you, but I think I've still got some sleep to catch up on. It's been years since I could hike like we did these last days and not pay for it."

"Me too," said Rew, "but—don't argue—I'm going to sleep in front of the door again. I slept in the chair last night. It was comfortable enough."

She didn't look like she believed him, but she left him there in the chair with one of his feet propped against the door, guarding against anyone coming into their room. He sat there, but he did not sleep.

Chapter Nineteen

T rue to his word, Baron Barnaus showed Rew and the others to a hidden portal stone which took them to the city of Iyre. The portal stone was concealed within a wardrobe in a sumptuous apartment near the baron's own rooms, and it led to a simple townhouse several blocks from Prince Heindaw's palace. Presumably, there were furtive ways one could take from the townhouse to the palace, but Barnaus wasn't familiar with those, and as Rew looked around the small home, he didn't see anything obvious.

Zaine rapped on walls, peeked behind furniture, and finally admitted, "If there's a hidden door or tunnel, I can't find it."

"One of the princes created this and hid it," said Rew. "Maybe there's something we could find if we searched hard enough, or maybe they portaled from here to the palace. If wards were laid around the edge of the city, they could move freely within it. Or who knows? Maybe the prince and Baron Barnaus' mother just walked out the front door late at night, and no one ever noticed."

"However they did it, it's been a long time," remarked Anne sourly.

The empath was standing in the middle of the kitchen, looking disdainfully at the thick layers of dust that coated every surface.

There was some evidence of traffic from the portal stone to the front door, but Barnaus had said he'd used the portal stones several times in the past. He certainly hadn't used the kitchen. It looked as if it'd been decades since anyone had been in there, which Rew supposed was the truth. The prince won the Investiture, but then Vaisius Morden took his soul. This was the prince's place, not the king's. Even if the king had taken knowledge of the townhome from his son's memories, he had no reason to be sneaking about the city.

"We're sure this is Iyre?" questioned Zaine.

"It is," confirmed Rew, peering out a cloudy window at the street beyond.

Drab gray walls braced a drab gray cobblestone street, but the people on the street were a burst of color. Vibrant hues abounded. Even the commoners dyed their thick woolen clothing. Those dyes were the city's primary industry. Berries, roots, and minerals were harvested from the land around Iyre, some of it there naturally, other sources domesticated over the years. Most of the dyes in the kingdom were manufactured in the Northern Province, and even the markets of Carff were stocked with Iyre's products, exporting Vaeldon's colors to the lands across the sea.

Moving the dyes to Carff made them expensive, but in Iyre, dyes were plentiful. If one wasn't picky about the color, dyes were nearly free as merchants raced to respond to a season's changing tastes, adjusting their hues and needing to clear the previously fashionable colors out of their warehouses. It was jarring when one wasn't used to it.

Iyre had a reputation as a cold place, the northernmost capital in the kingdom, and one that was most strongly associated with the Cursed Father and the rites of the dead. That reputation wasn't entirely undeserved, but the common people in the city were just as joyous as they were anywhere. Perhaps more so as the bitter winters forced them inside, and frequently, that meant into a tavern.

Musicians and actors could make their careers in Iyre. During the winter there was nothing to do but drink ale and watch someone on stage. Performers spent months in the city, until the weather changed. Then, they flocked to the south of the kingdom, where those cities were getting unbearably hot and the migration between indoors and outdoors reversed course.

Rew was busying himself with such thoughts until Anne cleared her throat, and he turned to look at the rest of them. The area around Heindaw's palace was layered in a network of traps, wards, and protections. Baron Barnaus had told them some of what to expect, but the baron wasn't privy to Heindaw's inner-most kernel of defense. Even if he had been, from the Arcanum, they knew the prince was exploring realms of magic that were previously undiscovered—or maybe just wisely left alone.

By now, Heindaw must know of Valchon's endeavors in the Northern Province, and he would know Rew and the others had slain Calb. He would be as ready for an attack as he could be. He probably was hoping for one. It was Heindaw's way, to set a trap and to let someone walk into it.

"So, do we climb over the walls of the palace or wear disguises and try the door?" asked Zaine, looking over Rew's shoulder at the profusion of colorful garments passing by the filthy window. "It looks like it'll be easy enough to stay unobtrusive out there. King's Sake, dressed like we are, we'll be invisible on these streets."

"Or we'd stand out like a chicken amongst a muster of peacocks," remarked Raif.

Zaine blinked at him. "A group of peacocks is called a muster?"

Raif nodded.

"Why do you know that?"

Rew cleared his throat, silencing their squabbling. Then, he turned to Cinda. "How are you feeling, lass?"

She shifted uncomfortably at the scrutiny of the others. "I am fine, but I suspect that's not what you are asking, is it?"

"Iyre was the home of Vaisius Morden before he ascended to

the throne and built Mordenhold as his capital. It's the place the cult of the Cursed Father was founded and houses his oldest crypt. There's a well of power here I believe you can tap, and taking it from the king's hands might be just as important as stopping Heindaw, but that's not something I can do. Whatever is here, stored within the temple, is beyond me. Can you feel anything?"

"Maybe. We need to get closer," she said. "Ranger, like you said, the king will have spent centuries building his power base here. You think we can really slip in and just take it?"

Rew shrugged. "On a Kings and Queens board, sometimes the most vulnerable pieces are those that haven't been moved. They've been forgotten, left hanging. Besides, you were able to draw upon that power in Jabaan, weren't you? It's going to be dangerous, but I think we have an opportunity to gain leverage over Heindaw and strike a blow to the king as well."

"I lost every game of Kings and Queens I played against that innkeeper, Bressan. If I had to guess, I'd imagine that the king and the princes are far better players. Surely, Ranger, both the king and Heindaw have considered someone threatening the crypt."

Rew grinned. "I'm not so sure. Heindaw isn't a necromancer. He can't use the power housed here and likely doesn't even know it exists. He wouldn't be able to feel it any more than I can. There hasn't been a necromancer who ruled Iyre since Vaisius Morden himself. Since the first Investiture, none of the princes have been necromancers. It's possible, even if another necromancer was aware of the stored power, they may not be able to take it. I've been thinking about your family and why there are no crypts in the Eastern Territory. I think that's the secret of your blood, Cinda."

"What if Heindaw is aware of the power in the crypt?" interjected Anne. "Could this be what he captured Baron Fedgley for, the reason all of this began? Turning the king's own power against him sounds like something your brother would do, at least the way you've described him."

Rew scratched his beard. "It is something he would do. There's more to it, though. Simply stealing the power from one crypt won't be enough to take down the king."

"He could use it against Valchon," mentioned Anne.

Shaking his head, Rew replied, "Risk the ire of the king to face his brother? Even if he didn't use it against the king, he'd be stealing some of our father's power. I don't think that'd go over well."

"Fair enough," admitted Anne.

"Prince Heindaw might be playing a deeper game than us, Ranger," warned Cinda. "Your family has been plotting for this Investiture since the last one. We don't even have a plan. On a Kings and Queens board, what may look like an undefended piece is frequently a trap, and whoever spends the time planning almost always wins."

Grinning, Rew shook his head. "You're right, but instead of trying to beat them at their own game, we're going to flip the board."

Anne crossed her arms over her chest. "Rew, that sounds like foolishness, and it's definitely not an actual plan."

He laughed and nodded in acknowledgement. "The nameless woman lied to us about the Cursed Father's temple burning to the ground. How about we go there and find out what else she lied about?"

Despite Zaine's assertion they would be nearly invisible in the colorful and crowded streets of Iyre, they wanted to be sure, so Anne, taking the thief with her, went shopping. Rew and the Fedgleys paced restlessly back and forth in the narrow town-house, kicking up clouds of dust and sneezing furiously.

Raif looked eager to get on the move, just happy to have a plan they could try to execute with little care for what the plan was. Cinda looked nervous.

Rew came beside her and said, "You'll do great."

She snorted. "Do great at what? I understand the power that may be housed within the crypt, but what am I to do with it? You don't want a repeat of Jabaan, do you? Ranger, how many people —innocent people—do you think died there? That is a burden I will bear because I must, but I don't fancy shouldering it again. I lost control in Jabaan, lost control completely, and the stakes are too high to gamble with that again."

"I hope it does not come to that," said Rew. He tucked his thumbs behind his belt and continued, "And I can't give you instructions for what we need to do. I don't know. But I know this. You are the heir to incredible talent. Your blood is the summation of centuries of careful breeding and training. Only the king himself is more capable than you, and part of his capability is a part of you. His blood runs in your veins, and here, in the place that was his home, I think we can find opportunity."

"He's a part of me, but I want no part of him," said Cinda. She shuddered and shook her head mournfully. "What happened in Jabaan, binding all of those souls, that's a part of me that I don't want to acknowledge. You cannot understand, Ranger, having that in me, knowing it is who I am."

Rew touched the hilt of his longsword. "I understand that sorrow more than you know."

Cinda glanced at him.

"The king's blood that flows in your veins flows in mine as well."

"Fair enough," replied Cinda, and her eyes flashed green before she looked away toward the doorway where they expected Anne and Zaine to return.

When her eyes left him, Rew cringed. He felt the pull of his blood. Did she feel it too? When the time came, would it pull her, or would she pull it?

An hour later, Anne and Zaine finally returned. Rew had grown quite grumpy, but Anne flightily dismissed his complaints about her pausing to shop by declaring that in a months' long quest, a few minutes to purchase new clothes and perhaps keep them from being noticed, was a small investment to make.

Rew became worried they were going to try to fit in with the denizens of Iyre, wearing loud purples and oranges, but when Anne opened the packages she'd brought, he saw it was somber clothing meant to make people's eyes slide over them without anything standing out. She would not try to hide that they were foreigners to Iyre, but instead encourage everyone to think they were unremarkable foreigners.

They could not hide that Raif was wearing armor, so he tugged on a plain blue tabard over it. It looked like the attire of a minor house which had not yet earned a crest or that of a wealthy merchant who aspired to more but couldn't afford customized uniforms for his men. In short, it gave no one reason for anyone to give Raif a second look. There would be hundreds of armored men in the city just like him.

Anne herself replaced her blouse and skirts with a dress of forest green. It accentuated her red hair and pale skin, and Rew thought it looked quite fetching. She appeared to be a well-off housewife or artisan, dressed for the city, rather than a country wife wearing clothing suitable for the outdoors. Rew scratched his beard. It was a change, but not much of one.

Zaine produced a pair of trousers made of leather and a silken blouse, and when she changed into them, she returned with her hair bound back behind her head. She put her old wool and cotton clothing in her pack then tugged her leather vest back on.

"You look the same," remarked Rew, glancing between Anne and the thief. "You both look nearly the same."

"It's a finer cut than my raggedy old stuff," said Zaine, her chin in the air. "And my hair is in the style of Iyre now. People notice these things, or, I should say, women notice these things."

Rew threw up his hands. "Well, we're not just hiding from

women, and the whole point of this is that we shouldn't be noticed."

"It's all about our persona, Ranger. We'll inhabit a role, and those who see us will believe that is who we are," claimed Zaine. "We figured I could play your apprentice."

Sighing, Rew asked, "All right. What did you get for me?"

"You already look like a forester," said Zaine. "We didn't get you anything."

"I might be recognized."

"We thought you should shave your beard," suggested Anne. "If they recognize you, Rew, it won't be your clothing, it will be your face. Do you have a razor with you?"

He scowled at her and stepped back.

Anne raised an eyebrow.

"If I shave my beard, it will be rather obvious," argued Rew, beads of sweat beginning to form on his brow. "The sun hasn't touched my cheeks in over a decade. It'll look like I'm wearing a mask, or that I'm sick."

Pursing her lips, Anne kept looking at him but did not comment. Finally, the empath turned to Cinda, "We got you clothes befitting a common lass of Iyre. With luck, people will think you're my daughter and that we're simply out running errands. We saw people were carrying weapons, so that's not a concern. Apparently, word of the conflicts around Vaeldon is getting out."

Cinda shook her head. "No, I've been thinking since you were gone. I've decided to keep wearing my robes."

Anne frowned.

Rew said, "Cinda, they may or may not recognize any of our faces, but they will certainly notice your robes. Word of a necromancer strolling through the streets to the temple of the Cursed Father is going to get Heindaw's attention."

"I know."

Rew threw up his hands. "What's your plan, then! You want to give him a warning so he can prepare for us?"

"The palace is layered in traps you said, right? Traps so insidious, so difficult to squirm between that Prince Valchon himself cannot do it. Ranger, what if we can't get into the palace? I've been considering that maybe we don't need to. We can have Heindaw come to us. You think he'll hear about me being in Iyre? Good. Let him find us at the crypt, and we'll face him there, where with luck, I can draw upon its power. We make him move, take away his advantages and his traps."

"And our advantage of surprise."

Cinda smiled coldly. "If I'm able to tap into the power residing within the crypt, I think he will be surprised."

Muttering to himself about that, Rew looked to Anne, who appeared nervous.

The empath shrugged. "We're counting on her to face the king, right? Maybe this will be good practice."

Rew glared at Anne then glanced at Raif, who held up his hands to signal he didn't want to get dragged into it. Clearing his throat, Rew said, "But if he knows—"

"You gave me the idea," interrupted Cinda. "We spread our story, hoping word would get out and slow the princes' plans, hoping it'd keep Heindaw near home. Isn't that what you said, you wanted to keep him here so we didn't have to chase after him? I'm paying attention, Ranger. It worked with Baron Barnaus, didn't it? This is just a twist on what you did."

Uncomfortable with her argument, Rew gripped the wooden hilt of his longsword and tried to come up with a better plan, but he couldn't. Alerting Heindaw to their presence was dangerous, but attempting to walk into the palace could be even worse.

He grumbled, "It goes against my instinct as a ranger."

"It works for me," said Raif, grinning.

"We know that," groused Rew.

"He'll be ready for us at the palace, won't he?" Cinda argued. "We're not giving up the element of surprise if we don't have it in the first place. Isn't it always better to pick the ground for a fight?"

"That's true," chimed Raif. "It's always better to pick your own ground."

"Very well," conceded Rew. "I suppose we should get started, then."

He led them into the street, trying to appear casual as they exited a home which hadn't been occupied in years. Most passersby wouldn't think anything of it, but any neighbors who saw them walk out would be suspicious. But the location of the home had been well chosen. It was near a bustling street where strangers were common but tucked between the backs of two commercial shops on an alleyway. There were people passing in front of it regularly, but there would be few people who had a direct view of the door.

They shut the door and waited a moment, but no one gave them more than a cursory glance. Rew waved down the street, and they joined the jostling crowd, letting it sweep them along the streets of Iyre.

The northern capital was built for harsh winters and for defense. Hundreds of years prior, it'd been the home of Vaisius Morden, and it still retained some of his character. Rew knew the outer walls had been constructed during Morden's rise, when mankind battled against the Dark Kind. Supposedly, the walls had been to protect against the narjags, ayres, and their valaan leadership, but the barriers served a handy defense against the king's old enemies as well once the threat of the Dark Kind was dealt with.

The buildings and the streets of the city were dark granite, threaded with delicate white crystal veins. The roofs of those buildings were black slate. The sky above was thick with clouds. Late winter, it could portend either snow or sleet. Rew sniffed the air, but within the throng of people in the street, he couldn't get a clean whiff to tell for sure.

The people were like a rainbow river, each adorned with brilliant color, the only thing that granted any levity to Iyre. Without them, it would be as dark and bleak as Mordenhold, which Rew supposed made a lot of sense.

It'd been years since he'd visited Iyre, but Baron Barnaus had given them a sketch of which part of the city the portal stone exited into. Anne also had some familiarity with Iyre, and between their recollections of the city and the baron's information, it was an easy trek through the rigid granite matrix toward the old town, which had been there before Vaisius Morden had claimed the city as his capital and expanded its footprint.

There were still stark buildings formed of dark stone, newer constructions replacing older structures that had crumbled or had burned, but there were ancient edifices still standing proud and hardened by the years. Some structures had pale limestone facades, others were of simple wood, grown as sturdy as stone over the centuries. There was a pretentious-looking theatre clad in shimmering marble, and a few humble structures hidden in alleys slathered in stucco. In the old town, the streets were not as neatly laid, and more people wore the dark gray or black of the king and his administration. Rew tried to avoid those men and women when they could, tagging along with packs of brightly attired citizens, looking resolutely ahead and hoping no one noticed.

No one did notice them, until they saw Cinda.

Her crimson robes were like a banner, and there wasn't a person in the king's colors who did not mark her passage. They would feed information of her presence to whatever spies the king kept in the city, and no doubt to Prince Heindaw as well. Rew guessed they had half an hour before that information reached the prince's ear. Longer, he hoped, until the king found out. After that, maybe another half hour for the prince to gather his spellcasters and his armsmen. Would he portal, or would he come on foot, expecting an ambush?

Rew couldn't guess. Heindaw, though the youngest, was the deepest thinker of the princes. Even as a child, he'd guessed Rew would abdicate, and Heindaw had already been preparing. The prince hadn't just accepted the idea of a struggle against his older brothers, he'd wanted it. He'd grown up knowing they were bigger, stronger, and more powerful with magic, but he believed that he was more cunning. More so than any of the others, Heindaw would be ready for this moment.

But whatever way the prince came, Heindaw would come after them. Even if he did know of the power within the crypt, he wouldn't allow Rew and Cinda to stroll about his city unchallenged. He would have been envisioning this confrontation since they had faced Calb, if not long before. If anyone had suspected Rew would reemerge and challenge his brothers, it would've been Heindaw.

But thanks to Cinda's boldness, they weren't walking into his traps. The prince would have to adjust. That gave them an hour to set their own trap. They just had to come up with one, first.

Chapter Twenty

꧁꧂

They arrived at the vast, imposing structure of the temple for the Cursed Father. It was a bleak place and not only because it was purported to be a temple for the god of death. The building had been designed to keep people away, and people did stay away unless they absolutely had to be there. The grim facade of the temple shouted the message clearer than words. Carved from the same dark granite as the rest of Iyre, it was festooned with tableaus of death.

Frescos depicted murders, executions, suffering from illness, accidents, and dozens more horrific scenes of the citizens of Iyre meeting their ends. Just looking at the place sent a chill down Rew's spine, which only got worse when he considered the size of the temple. It had the breadth of one of the princes' palaces, but he knew the living occupants only numbered several score in the priesthood. The rest of the building was dedicated to the dead.

Two massive steel doors, striated with patterns of ancient rust, barred the entrance. The doors had stood there for centuries and had overseen the gateway between one world and the next. The rust, spilling down in broad streaks, gave anyone approaching an uncomfortable reminder of blood pouring from a wound. It might not have been intentional when they first hung the doors, but Rew imagined the priests of the Cursed Father enjoyed the effect now.

He put a shoulder against one of the huge doors and shoved. The door swung open easily on silent hinges. Rew stumbled inside. He coughed and muttered to the others, "I, ah, I thought that was going to be a lot harder than it was. Those are big doors."

Cinda stepped around him. "The front is meant to turn away the casual passerby, but the gates to death are always open to those who seek it."

Rew wasn't sure what she meant by that. He didn't think she was being literal. He was pretty sure. He shivered and followed Cinda inside.

The foyer of the temple was a long, broad corridor that extended to the height of the building, though the ceiling high above was lost in gloom and shadow. Huge, polished granite columns rose into that murk and marched down the length of the room to where a simple, giant golden block sat bathed in the low light of a pair of torches. The torches and the light from the open door were the only illumination in the cavernous room. Only in this place could such a wealth of gold be left unattended.

Rew gripped his longsword. Gold. That was just a show. Down below, within the crypt, the true altar of the Cursed Father was made of copper, and it was used to collect and trap the souls of the departed.

The expansive foyer was the receiving hall where family and friends would make a pilgrimage, carrying the body of their lost loved one. It was the only room in the temple any outsiders would see. In a ritual unique to Iyre, the families of the departed would place the body upon the golden block, an altar to the Cursed Father they assumed, where the priests would take over and anoint the body with oil, wrap it with fine linens or silks if the family could afford them, and then inter the body in the crypts. It was a solemn place, quiet, as whatever words that would be said over the dead were said before arriving at the temple. The temple was not a place for remembering what was lost, but for forgetting.

The Cursed Father took all comers into his embrace, but the priests did not describe a kind god. They described a ravenous hunger which could never be sated. In that respect, the public face of the Cursed Father and Vaisius Morden were one and the same.

The room appeared empty, which was typical. When one had business in the temple, you did it quickly, and then you left. The Cursed Father was meant to be a god you rued the day you ever saw, and you could either make your peace with that or not. The god did not care either way.

Rew snorted.

The god.

His father. Vaisius Morden. The king. For centuries, the king's priests had been telling a lie. Taking the dead of Iyre, and all of Vaeldon, promising the stillness of the grave, but that was not what happened. They took the power from the passing souls and stored the bodies for when they would be needed again.

"This place oozes power," said Cinda, shivering, "but it's like I'm aware of it being there through thick glass. I can see it, get a sense of it, but I can't touch it. It's... There is more strength here than in Jabaan. It's older, I guess, but unlike in Jabaan, I can't tap into this power. I'm being held from it, somehow. I don't know. I wish I understood more about this."

"I suppose it wasn't going to be easy," remarked Rew. "If any necromancer could walk in and drink the reservoir the king has collected, then I guess they would have. Your blood, do you think that is the key? There are no crypts like this in the Eastern Territory. It has to be because the king knows your line is there, watching over the barrowlands."

"Maybe," responded Cinda, her eyes closed, her lips moving even when she was not speaking. "Maybe my blood is the key, but I don't know where to look for the lock."

"If we can find—" began Rew.

The clank and scrape of men in armor echoed through the huge room, and Rew cut off as a dozen figures stepped out into the center of the space in between the party and the altar. They were barely lit from behind by the torches. The spear of fading daylight from the open door fell short of their feet. All Rew could see was the gleam of their armor and the weapons they held in their hands.

He called loudly, too loudly as his voice bounced around the room. "We're not here to fight."

The armed men advanced slowly, taking their time and raising their weapons. Evidently, they were there to fight. Rew frowned. They were slow, stately. Unhurried by time.

"The Sons of the Father?"

The footsteps slowed, but they did not stop.

"Do you know... ah, a woman with no name?"

The footsteps slowed again, but the Sons of the Father kept coming.

"She wore armor like yours. Bronze chain and breastplates, tailored specially for her. It was enchanted. She claimed she was—"

"You speak of Jacquiss," boomed a throaty voice that Rew thought came from a man in the center of the approaching group. "She is dead."

Rew shaking his head, trying to remain calm, kept his hands by his side. If these people had been lied to by someone, then they were not his fight. At least, they wouldn't be his fight if he could convince them of that.

"She—you said Jacquiss?—is not dead. She was traveling with us until, ah, just south of Olsoth."

The Sons of the Father stopped as a group, their leader alone taking another step forward. "Jacquiss is dead."

"She never told us her name, but if we speak of the same woman, she is not dead. At least she wasn't."

"Prove it."

"She left here four years ago," said Rew. "She thought her father was dead, killed by the king for sharing the secrets of the cult—ah, I mean your priesthood, the Sons of the Father. She believed her father was in the thrall of the king, on the other side of life. She was searching for a way to free him."

"Those things are not true." The speaker shifted and raised a bright, bronze scimitar. "We were told to expect your lies. I thought you'd have better ones."

Rew stared at the man's scimitar. It was just like the one the nameless woman carried. Her father? He was supposed to be dead, but that death was supposed to have occurred when the temple burned. Clearly, the temple was still there, which meant maybe he was still there as well.

"Jacquiss said there was no Cursed Father. She said her own father had told her that."

The man was silent, still, but around him, his companions shifted.

Then, one of them laughed, and bellowed, "He almost had me. These fools didn't even know her name. There is no Cursed Father? Pfah. Where does he think he's standing? Let's finish this."

"Yes, let's," agreed the leader.

He spun, and his scimitar flashed in the gloom, taking off the head of a surprised man standing next to him.

Rew, not understanding what was happening but knowing the advantage of surprise when he saw it, charged.

The leader of the Sons of the Father caught a swinging axe on the edge of his blade, turned it aside, and slashed his scimitar across the face of the axe-wielder. He darted at another man, clouting him on the side of the head with his bronze gauntlet.

Rew stabbed between a man's breastplate and helmet. He felt the crunch of chainmail splitting beneath the force of his attack, and his blade plunged into the man's neck. These men wore armor in the style of the nameless woman's, but it wasn't enchanted. It was bronze. It was like thick paper against Rew's enchanted steel.

The Sons of the Father had been prepared to fight, but they'd been entirely unprepared for their leader to turn on them and start slaughtering them. They hesitated when they faced him, and the man took advantage.

Raif joined the fight with a roar, battering a man's raised sword with a series of vicious overhead strikes, but the fight was already over. By the time Raif beat the man down and his greatsword found flesh, only one more of the Sons of the Father was standing, backing away from both Rew and the leader slowly.

"I don't understand, Jacob. What is this?" he babbled. "We were warned by the prince. These people are our enemy, the enemy of the king. What... What have you done?"

"You've been misled," said the leader, Jacob. "Misled by our histories, our priests, the princes, and the king himself. You've also been misled by me."

Jacob feinted with his scimitar, drawing the other man into a defensive posture. Rew struck from the side, sliding his blade easily into the man's ribs. He drew his longsword from the man and looked at Jacob uncertainly.

"Jacquiss lives, truly?"

Rew shrugged. "She was alive a week ago."

"I knew she was alive. I tracked her from afar for the last four years, but months ago, she seemed to vanish," murmured the armored man. "None of my contacts had any word of her. I worried... Tell me what you know."

"Unfortunately," said Rew, "we don't have time for that. In less than an hour, I expect Prince Heindaw to arrive here with every spellcaster he can find and half of his army. He's coming to kill us, and before he does, we need to figure out how to tap the power stored within your crypts."

The man laughed and stepped closer, the light of the doorway finally falling on his face. He was dark-skinned, like the nameless woman, and old. Old enough to be her father, certainly, though he'd moved like a much younger man during the fight.

"Tell me this, and then we'll talk of what you need. Jacquiss, when she left you, where did she go?"

"I'm not certain," admitted Rew. "We were two days south of Olsoth, and she disappeared in the night. She didn't tell us why she left or where she was going. We only found out when dawn broke and her bedroll was empty. You're her father? She was searching for a way to free your soul from the king's clutches. She thought you were dead, taken by him. That's what she told us. She'd devoted her life to... a lie, it seems."

The old man smirked. "Lies abound. But if she told you what you said—that there is no Cursed Father—then I believe you knew her, and you must have earned her trust. I will trust you as well, but we cannot trust her. She has broken her bond with me, you understand? I love her, but..." The man's eyes flicked toward Cinda. "She thought you could face the king?"

Rew shrugged. "To be honest, I don't know what she thought."

"You do plan to face him, though, don't you?"

"If we survive Heindaw," said Rew drolly. He reminded the man, "He's going to come here."

Nodding, the old man turned. "Come with me. I have a book to give you."

"Is it a long one?" muttered Rew.

The man glanced over his shoulder and gave Rew an empty smile. "It was you, the group of you, in Jabaan, wasn't it? When word reached us to look out for you, I wondered. You—the lass here—released the dead from Jabaan's crypt? When I heard, I began writing down what I know. Before that, the risk was too great to commit my knowledge to paper because there was no one who could use it. Maybe you can. Maybe you cannot, but I will be dead soon enough, so it no longer matters. I... I didn't finish, but I will give you what I have. When Heindaw warned us you may come, I understood my time was over. I had to begin other preparations."

Rew cleared his throat, following the man down into the depths of the temple. "Yes, it was us in Jabaan. We tapped into the power stored within the crypts. Ah, something is different here.

They're more difficult to touch, Cind—our necromancer, said so. Can you help?"

"I will not. I've sealed the crypts from you and even the king himself. That is not the assistance I offer. Do you know how many were killed in Jabaan?"

"I can guess."

"Twenty-three thousand," said the old man. "Rounding, of course. In some cases, it was difficult to tell who was killed during the event and who had been killed shortly before. I hate the king, Stranger, and I will do what I can to end his reign, but I love my city. I cannot allow Jabaan to happen here."

Cinda retorted, "I've learned from—"

"You will learn," interrupted the man, "if you survive Heindaw. You will learn from the book I will give you."

"If we survive," called Zaine. "Any suggestions about how to do that? I'm sure this book is great and all…"

"I have no suggestions," said the old man. "I cannot help you face the prince."

"Wonderful," said the thief. She caught up to Rew. "So far, this plan is looking to be one of your best."

"My daughter," said Jacob. "You said she disappeared outside of Olsoth? What happened? You must have speculated about why she left, and you must have some ideas."

Rew scowled at the man's back. He didn't want to share too much information and give away the little leverage they had. He still wasn't sure where this man stood, or where the nameless woman—Jacquiss, it seemed she had a name—had her loyalties, either. King's Sake, even now, all he had were guesses.

"She was hale when she left," Rew said, hoping some vague assurances would be enough to quench the man's curiosity. "I have no reason to believe she's in danger. Well, no more danger than any of us are in these days."

"Was she wearing her armor?"

Rew blinked. "Yes."

"I was afraid of that," said Jacob. "It was a gift from Prince

Heindaw. The other Sons of the Father believed he wanted to take her as a mistress, and I think she believed that as well. She's attracted to strength and was pleased to accommodate the prince. I was suspicious, though. He knew things he should not know. He asked me about them. I found out he'd been asking her while she wore the armor. She never remembered the conversations. He… learned things that are dangerous to know. I was worried."

"Understandable," grumbled Rew, hoping the man would hurry his story. A quarter hour had already ticked by. Or had it been a half?

"She left, and the prince told me he'd convinced her I was dead. He can do that, I had discovered, through her enchanted armor. It allows him to implant suggestions into my daughter's thoughts. I was upset, but I knew there was nothing I could do. I cannot fight the prince, and going after Jacquiss may have gotten us both killed. We only lived while we were valuable to him. She carried out his work in the world, and I convinced him there was information I was hiding and dribbled it to him and that fool Salwart over the last four years."

"Salwart?"

Jacob grunted and gave Rew a fierce grin over his shoulder. "I sent that man on a merry chase, but the prince is smarter. I had to tell him much."

"Such as?"

"It's in the book. We don't have time for me to explain."

Rew scowled at the man's back. "I know we don't have time."

"If Heindaw could control her, why didn't he have her kill us all while we were sleeping?" wondered Raif. "She had plenty of opportunities."

Rew cringed. The only answer was because Heindaw wanted them alive. Near Olsoth, he knew they weren't walking to Carff and Valchon. Did the prince want them in Iyre? But then, that didn't make sense, either. If Heindaw wanted them in Iyre, Jacquiss would have stayed with them to make sure they got there.

The hunters.

Jacquiss disappeared after they'd spotted the purple-robed spellcasters. She must have gone to report to Heindaw. Jacob had said Heindaw could implant suggestions. Perhaps she'd left before the prince intended her to. Or perhaps not. Simulacra of Valchon would be important information for Heindaw to have.

Rew's mind swirled as the old man inserted a key into a lock and twisted it open. Jacob took them into a small study, where on a desk, a leather-bound book sat open, a page half-filled. On the walls of the room were bookshelves and weapons racks. The nest of a warrior-priest.

The old man offered a tired smile. "What my daughter told you is true. There is no Cursed Father. It's the king, Vaisius Morden, but you know that, don't you? I've spent decades trying to find a way to stop him. I shared much of what I learned with my daughter, hoping she could continue my work, and then I spoke with Prince Heindaw when he discovered our intentions. In my heart, I hoped he would use our knowledge to unseat the king and make this kingdom better, but in my head, I worried he would use us and then rule as a worse tyrant than his father."

"Y-You...." stammered Rew. He didn't know what to say.

"Due to Heindaw, my daughter believes that I perished in a fire four years ago. She thinks I did it to save myself from falling into Vaisius Morden's clutches. Heindaw implanted the thought into her as motivation to do his bidding. The only thing she and the prince are wrong about is the timing. I will not grant your necromancer the power stored in the crypts, but I will seal it from the king. That's the best help I can give you along with the research contained within this book. Destroying the temple will be my final contribution to the war."

"What about Heindaw?" asked Zaine, her eyes darting toward the doorway as if expecting the prince to enter at any moment.

"If you cannot defeat the prince, then you have no chance against the king. I wish you luck with both."

Calmly, the old man moved to a cabinet and removed a dusty

bottle of wine. He opened it while they all looked on in confusion. He poured himself a glass and swirled the liquid, watching it run down the sides of the cup.

He raised the glass and said, "When I finish this, I will set this temple afire with a flame hot enough to melt the entire structure and destroy the vessel the king imprisons Iyre's souls within. The crypt will be nothing more than molten copper and ash. Not even Vaisius Morden will be able to salvage materials from what I destroy. I've had my allies set wards. The fire won't reach far past the temple, but for your own safety, I recommend being at least four or five blocks away."

The old man sipped his wine and licked his lips. He sighed. "I bought this months after Jacquiss was born. It's from Vaeldon's finest vineyard. I could not afford it then, but her mother had left us, and it was a promise to her and myself that I would never leave. I am here, but I don't know if I kept that promise. I meant to share the bottle with her one day, but I was always waiting for the right occasion. It was... what we did each evening, drink wine together." Smiling bitterly, the old man added, "If only I'd known the right occasion was then, any time. Any time but now."

He took another sip.

"We, ah, we should go," worried Zaine.

"You should," agreed Jacob. "My daughter... She is in the thrall of Heindaw's suggestions, but that is all that they are. He cannot control her completely. The armor has clouded her eyes and her mind, but those eyes can be opened. Tell her the truth about me. Spare her, if you can, but you must shock her if you mean to pierce the veil the prince laid upon her. She thought she was deceiving me when she left, and I believe still carries that guilt. Tell her I live. Tell her I forgive her. It may break the hold Heindaw has on her, or it may not, but it will give me peace, and I hope her as well."

"Wait—" said Rew, watching wild eyed as Jacob took another sip of his wine.

"Go, now," instructed the old man. "If you're inside of the temple when it burns, you will not survive."

Cinda took the book from Jacob's desk and tucked it away. Rew led them back into the corridor and through the twisting warren of passageways until they entered the entrance hall of the temple. The two torches still burned beside the golden altar, but now, both doors in the front were thrown open wide.

"King's Sake," growled Rew, drawing his longsword. "We waited too long."

The doors were open wide, but little additional light reached them. Standing in the doorway was a massive, hulking shape. Spreading around it were smaller figures, garbed in the robes of spellcasters. Rew couldn't identify the colors in the low light, but he guessed they were invokers. In the center, the giant shape, he didn't know...

Until it stepped forward, blazing alight with infernal lines of glowing red script. It was a suit of armor, a huge suit of full plate armor. The metal mountain was thrice the size of Raif, and it drew a blade that was not much longer than the fighter's but was twice as wide. The sword glowed with the same pulsating red script as the armor. That wasn't a good sign.

From within the bronze helm of the armor, Rew heard a high-pitched cackle and the voice of his younger brother, Prince Heindaw. "You should see your faces right now. I'd thought to save this display for Valchon... but this is worth it. Rew, you look like a fool."

Zaine released an arrow that Rew hadn't seen her nock. The arrow clinked pitifully off the giant mass of bronze. Heindaw laughed again.

"Ranger," hissed Cinda, "the well of power housed within this place is still kept from me. If Jacob is right and the king himself couldn't break the seal, I have no chance. There's an ocean of strength, but I can't touch it. I can cast a little funeral fire at them, but I'm afraid..."

"We don't have time," cracked Anne. "We have to—"

"I'll hold him off," growled Raif, his armor clanking as he stepped forward. He raised his greatsword. "Cinda, gather what you can."

The fighter looked tiny, framed against the giant shape of Heindaw. His sword, a large weapon in any other circumstance, appeared to be a child's toy.

"I meant we don't have time before Jacob ignites this place," hissed Anne. "We have to get out of the temple."

Zaine fired another arrow, which bounced off just as harmlessly as the first.

"If we can trap him inside..." murmured Rew, glancing around wildly. "Cinda, gather what power you can, but don't bother trying to win the fight. Just get everyone out of here."

The exit to the temple was on the other side of Prince Heindaw and his minions. As soon as Jacob finished his wine, he was going to set the place on fire with a blaze strong enough to destroy the crypt and the well of power housed within it. Rew had no reason to doubt the priest of the Cursed Father knew what he was talking about. If they could trap Heindaw inside the temple and escape with their lives... it would be just like how they defeated Calb. It could work.

With groaning clanks, Heindaw's armored form began striding toward them. His spellcasters stayed back, watching the action. The prince must have instructed them to let him finish the fight. Easy to do when encased within fifty stone of enchanted bronze.

Rew studied his brother's movements, watching for chinks in his armor, places a well-aimed blow could slide through, but the joints in the armor seemed as impervious as the plates. Enchanted by Heindaw himself, Rew didn't figure he would have any chance of actually cutting through that pile of metal. Blessed Mother, even if it wasn't enchanted, the stuff looked like solid slabs of bronze, several times thicker than normal plate. No man could even move such weight without the help of high magic. There wasn't—

The visor. In the low light, Rew could see Heindaw's eyes reflecting the illumination of the torches.

Rew glanced around then retreated and jumped on top of the golden altar. To the others, he whispered, "Circle around behind him, but don't charge the spellcasters. They may be a small threat compared to Heindaw, but they're still dangerous. I'd like to avoid fighting so many of them if we can. Distraction, not direct contact, that's our way out of here."

Anne led the children toward the columns that lined the right side of the room. Heindaw's armored head turned, and Rew knew the prince was watching Cinda.

Behind him, his spellcasters shifted. One of them called out, "She won't get by us, m'lord."

Heindaw turned back to Rew, and his voice echoed metallically from within the suit of armor. "Good. This won't take long."

The armor, dark in the dimly lit room except for the whorls of intricate glowing runes, seemed to throb like a heartbeat. Heindaw raised the enchanted sword, and Rew crouched, waiting. Aside from the sheer size of the armor and the fact that it granted his brother enough strength to even move it, Rew didn't know what properties it might endow upon the prince. He was the kingdom's preeminent enchanter. What would he have imbued into his own personal set of plate? Something to face Valchon, he'd said. Heindaw would have prepared the suit for a battle against an invoker, which meant Rew had a chance.

Heindaw showed no fear at all and strode purposefully closer. At three long steps from the golden altar, he raised his sword above his head, preparing to bring it down and smite Rew in two.

Rew sprang at Heindaw, launching himself off the altar the moment before his brother began his stroke down, stabbing at the thin slit in the prince's helm. Rew could see his brother's eyes there, barely visible in the dark, just pinpoints of reflection. Heindaw would have expected Rew to dodge, to run, to—

Rew's longsword nearly jolted out of his hands. The open

space in front of Heindaw's eyes crackled with a spiderweb of white energy. A magical barrier.

Scrambling to hold onto his longsword as he fumbled it from the unexpected impact, Rew bounced off the solid metal chest of Heindaw and fell back onto the golden altar. He stared up in surprise at his younger brother.

"Fitting," said Heindaw. Then, he finished his stroke, bringing his sword down.

Rew rolled away a breath before the enchanted bronze sword cleaved into the golden altar, slicing it in half as neatly as a wheel of soft cheese.

Flopping onto the cold stone floor, Rew scrambled on hands and toes away as Heindaw turned. The prince surged forward, stabbing with his sword with shocking speed. The granite floor cracked where the huge blade thrust into it, shards of rock pelting against Rew as he stumbled to his feet and broke into a lurching run.

He didn't need to look back to judge Heindaw's pursuit. He could hear it. The tremendously heavy footsteps crashed after him, just two steps behind. The armor didn't slow the prince. He was faster than Rew remembered him being without it. Maybe not as quick as Rew, but he was close enough.

All of the king's sons had some training with arms and physical conditioning. They'd spent years in the hands of Mordenhold's weapons masters being sharpened into the blades that would kill each other. They only paused for instruction on high magic. Rew, eschewing his ability to cast spells, had spent more time with the weapons masters. He was a far superior swordsman, but Heindaw was wearing a set of impenetrable enchanted plate armor that gave him the strength of several men.

Rew darted behind one of the towering granite columns on the side of the room, hoping that even if the prince was as fast as Rew, and breathtakingly stronger in the armor, that Heindaw wasn't as maneuverable. It might be the only advantage the ranger had.

Except Heindaw didn't bother to try and round the column.

He simply unleashed a vicious backhand swing, and his huge, enchanted blade sheared through the stone. Rew ducked, the tip of the prince's sword passing a hand-length above his head. Heindaw came smashing through the broken column, rubble exploding, fist-sized chunks of granite battering painfully against Rew's back as he took off sprinting again.

The length of the column collapsed, falling onto Heindaw, but the prince simply shrugged it off. In a frantic glance over his shoulder, Rew couldn't tell if the massive pile of stone had even scratched the enchanted plate armor.

Another arrow bounced off Heindaw, and Rew screeched at Zaine to turn her fire onto the spellcasters instead. The robed men and women were weaving through the columns, headed toward Rew's companions, evidently not content to just keep them in the room. It looked as if they were planning to capture them, now.

Raif took several steps toward Rew then paused. The boy appeared terrified. Cinda stood calmly, the vapor of death's breath trailing from her hands, but without the power locked within the crypt, she couldn't face the combined might of all of Heindaw's spellcasters. In a battle like that, her raw talent would falter against their extensive training. Without a nearly endless well of strength to draw upon, Cinda would be easily outmatched. Anne kept looking back to the narrow doorway that led down below, where even now, the old man was likely preparing to turn the temple of the Cursed Father into one last funeral pyre.

"King's Sake," muttered Rew, slipping and skidding as he darted around the granite columns opposite the rest of the party.

Behind him, Heindaw smashed through the stone, seeming to take perverse pleasure in destroying the temple dedicated to their father.

Surprised and unprepared, Rew had no chance against Heindaw. Their plan had backfired. The prince had anticipated coming out to face them. He'd strategized this very moment and hadn't shown a bit of shock at finding Rew within the temple. Heindaw was ready, and Rew was not. Heindaw had a plan, and the ranger did not, and he wasn't going to make one in the little time they had. Their only chance was to run and hope that the prince was caught within the coming conflagration.

"Anne!" cried Rew. "I'll clear the path."

He didn't need to tell her the rest. He turned and ran straight for the spellcasters, who were halfway into the room now, hiding behind the columns, watching for Cinda's spells.

Heindaw, with the inevitability of an avalanche, came after Rew.

Chapter Twenty-One

T he spellcasters, seeing what Rew was attempting, finally
unleashed their magic. Heaving globs of liquid fire, fists of
solid sound, and jagged spears of ice erupted into reality,
streaking toward the ranger. He slithered between them like a
snake, but the huge armored form of Heindaw was harder to
miss, and blast after blast of magic thundered into the prince. Rew
didn't turn to look, but he heard the footsteps faltering behind
him, but they did not stop.

Protected by the enchanted armor or by his own magic, the
prince kept coming, just as Rew had expected. The ranger
chased into the spellcasters like a dog into a flock of geese, and
the men and women released their spells trying to strike him.
Rew avoided the flames and the sharp tips of ice but was
battered around by other attacks. He tried to anchor himself,
but they were far from the wild world where he drew his
strength. A fist of solid air collided with his mouth, and he spit
blood. A line of fire scorched his shoulder, and he felt warmth
leaking down his arm. He stumbled as thick bands of air tried
to snag his feet. But he'd gotten amongst the spellcasters, and
their aim was hampered by their peers, though the invoker
tossing spears of ice did not let that stop him from viciously

skewering another spellcaster who was on the wrong side of Rew.

Then, Heindaw was amongst them, still chasing Rew, spells crashing off his armor and spraying into his people. Masonry exploded as he smashed through another column. A spellcaster was hacked in two by an errant swing from Heindaw's sword, and as a group, the spellcasters turned toward flight rather than continuing their assaults on the ranger.

An eerie white-green mist billowed up from the floor, bitterly cold, stinging Rew's skin. Cinda had released death's breath, but it wasn't potent. It stung, but that was all. Clouds of it swirled as Rew ducked and dived amongst the spellcasters, avoiding Heindaw and sewing chaos.

Cinda's spell was meant to further that, he realized, so Rew took one last looping spin around a towering granite column then sprinted toward the doors, hoping that the rest of the party had the same idea. In the midst of the exploding spells and irritating mist, it was their chance to slip away, perhaps not unnoticed, but all they needed was a head start to get away from Heindaw.

The air cleared near the doorway, and racing out of the roiling fog of death's breath, Rew blinked his eyes and coughed the acrid fumes from his lungs. He'd been trained to defend against high magic and would be able to weather the spell better than most. He hoped Cinda's casting was enough to do more than irritate Heindaw's spellcasters and that the young necromancer had been able to shelter their companions.

A moment after Rew, Cinda and the others came stumbling free. Rew grasped Anne's arm and led her and the younglings to the two massive steel temple doors. He pushed Anne outside then spun, hauling on one door while Raif took the other. The two of them slammed the giant steel barriers closed, though Rew realized as soon as they were shut that there was no way to lock them from the outside.

There were handles they could slide something between to prevent a person opening it, but Rew didn't fancy leaving his enchanted longsword or Raif's greatsword lodged in the door. If this didn't work, they were desperately going to need those.

"Well, maybe they'll think we—" started Raif. He yelped and jumped back as something exploded against the other side of the door.

The metal cracked and popped. One of the invokers must have flung their liquid fire after the party, hoping to catch them before they escaped. The incredible heat was melting the door. Rew could feel it bleeding through the barrier and see the straited metal beginning to glow a dull orange. The giant doors began to buckle and sag.

"Cinda," cried Rew. "Do you have strength for funeral fire?"

The necromancer nodded and cast her ethereal green flame against the door, the awful chill of the grave cooled the steel, fusing the two barriers together where they'd begun to melt.

She twirled her other hand, her lips pressed tightly together. Rew realized she was drawing the death's breath she'd released into a bank of fog on the opposite side of the door. It'd be a toxic field that Heindaw's people couldn't see through or breathe if they entered it.

"With luck, we just sealed them inside," said Rew incredulously. "Well done, Cinda. I can't believe that... Let's go. Whether or not Jacob ignites the place, we don't want to be standing here long."

"You hear that?" called Zaine. "It's like the wind. Flame is building inside. He's burning it right now. Hurry. Hurry!"

They did, pelting down the empty street, fleeing the blast they knew was coming from behind.

"I can't believe this is working!" crowed Zaine as they got a block from the temple.

Already, billows of red and orange flame could be seen casting a glow in the belfry of the temple. Windows, set high above the frescos that banded the outside of the structure, hidden beneath the eaves of its roof, spilled angry glow, casting the scenes of death depicted along the front in terrible light. They made it two blocks down the wide, empty boulevard that led from the entrance and passed a barrier of cool air that pebbled the skin on Rew's arms.

"Are we safe?" panted Raif, waving his hand as if to touch the invisible line they'd walked across.

"Safer," said Rew, rubbing his hands together to chase away the brief chill, still trying to comprehend what had happened over the last quarter hour. "We should keep moving, though, just in case Jacob's barrier isn't as sound as he expected it to be."

They slowed, falling into the cautious pace of those who'd moments before thought they were going to die but now, shockingly, were somehow spared. Behind them, they heard sharp cracks echoing from the temple as stone began to shatter in the heat of the growing fire.

Rew turned and walked backward, still moving away from the temple, watching as blooms of flame began to sprout hungrily from between the roof tiles. On the street, smoke or steam poured out of the sewers from where he guessed the crypts were being immolated by the worst of the inferno. It would destroy the corpses stored there, he was sure. Would it be enough to destroy the well of power that Vaisius Morden had been accumulating?

"I can feel the deaths, but I cannot draw from them," said Cinda, walking backward just like Rew. "I was able to draw power when the spellcasters died, but it's out of reach now. I think that cool air, the barrier we passed, is sealing the power of those deaths within."

"It seems Jacob knew what he was talking about. Let's hope it keeps the king from accessing the power as well," responded Rew. "You could feel the deaths of the spellcasters? How many were there?"

"I felt the deaths, but not many," said Cinda, shrugging. "The temple was empty except for the old man, so that's no surprise. The spellcasters are too close together for me to count—"

There was an incredible, wrenching screech. The massive steel doors of the temple were flung onto the cobblestones, skidding in a shower of sparks as the metal bumped over stone. Streamers of smoke rose from the glowing doors like flags flapping behind a cavalry charge. The doors were half-melted from the heat of the flames inside of the temple and the spellcaster's fire. They came to a rest a block and a half from the entrance of the burning building. Framed in the doorway, an inferno of brilliant flame forming a wall behind him, stood Prince Heindaw. His armor was black with soot, the glowing red runes barely visible before the fire.

"That's not good." Zaine trembled.

"No… it's not," agreed Rew. "Ah, I think we'd best run."

"Where?" asked Raif. "Can we outlast him?"

"To the palace," said Rew, turning and starting a lopping jog down the empty street.

"Won't all his men be there?" questioned Zaine. "The traps we were worried about…"

"Ranger, maybe we should be going… literally anywhere else," called Cinda.

"There's a bit of a forest behind the palace," said Rew between breaths. "I can use that strength to call for help, though I don't know if there's time for them to get here…"

"Ranger stuff," muttered Zaine, already breathing heavy from the run. "I hope it works."

"What else can we do? My sword bounced off Heindaw like I was poking him with a wet noodle. Raif's greatsword won't fare any better, and I don't know if he even noticed your arrows. Unless an awful lot of people die and Cinda is able to draw the power, we don't have the craft to get through that armor. As long as the suit remains powered, he's invulnerable. King's Sake, even if Cinda does find a well of power, I don't know what we can do to him. He walked right through that fire."

Zaine grunted, and Rew glanced behind them. Heindaw, his massive sword clutched in one armored fist, was running after them.

"Faster now. Run faster. A lot faster."

THE PALACE IN IYRE WAS UNLIKE ANY OF THE OTHER PALACES IN Vaeldon. Those structures had either been built or been expanded upon following the rise of Vaisius Morden. In the years after his ascension, it became less important to protect the cities against foreign invasion but more important to protect against attack from within. The cities were frequently only lightly guarded, but the walls of the palaces themselves were heavily fortified. They were designed to stop small groups of intruders—spellcasters and assassins.

Iyre's palace had a hardened section where the prince resided, but it had also been home to Vaisius Morden before modern concerns like fratricide had influenced architecture, so it still retained outdated features including ample grounds for hunting. Such a large space was impossible to guard and had fallen out of fashion in the other capitals, but it was exactly what Rew needed. Sprawling behind the palace was a thick forest, unused by Heindaw or his father before he'd become king, as they were interested in more dangerous game.

The forest wasn't open to the citizens of Iyre, but it wasn't difficult to access, either. There were no battlements, no ranks of crossbowmen training their weapons on anyone who approached. There was just a wall. The threat of angering the prince was more than enough to prevent most interlopers from considering climbing the thing, but Rew figured they'd already done enough to enrage his brother, so hopping the wall wasn't going to make it any worse.

When they got to it, Zaine sprang at it like a monkey and was at the top in a breath. Raif and Rew knelt, boosting the other women up after the thief. Then, cursing and grunting, Rew helped Raif clamber up, the big fighter barely reaching the top with his fingers before kicking his boots and knocking Rew out from under him.

Leaping back to his feet, Rew saw Heindaw was two blocks

away, his giant armored form clanking and screeching as he ran tirelessly down the street. How long could the prince keep it up? The armor must weigh five or six times what the prince himself did, but the enchanter appeared to have no difficulty moving in it.

Rew spun and jumped, catching the top of the wall then vaulting over it. He landed quietly on the wild grass inside. Raif crashed down next to him. Rew hauled the fighter to his feet and led the party running into the dark forest.

Behind them, Heindaw didn't bother to climb the wall. He simply plowed through it, his armored elbow bursting a path through the mortar and stone like a battering ram.

The others close behind, Rew darted and wove his way into the undergrowth. The children stumbled and cursed, tripping over every exposed root, snagging their clothing on every jutting branch.

"Head west. Keep moving. Don't try to fight. Don't get caught," snapped Rew. He turned east, angling toward an opening in the vegetation.

When he reached it, he burst into view and almost into Prince Heindaw's grasp. The enchanted script etched into the armor flared alight, and Heindaw lunged at him. Rew, having meant to be seen but not so close, darted away with just a pace of room between him and his brother.

But once he got back within the depths of the wood, Rew changed direction and slipped away. Heindaw was just as fast and much stronger, but he wasn't a ranger. He couldn't move as freely and silently as Rew in the forest, and with the vegetation as cover, Rew was able to easily keep out of reach. The crash of breaking trunks and limbs followed, and suddenly, a brilliant golden glow shone from Heindaw's armor.

It made it easier to spot the enchanter, and Rew was skilled enough he could keep out of sight until he wanted to be seen. Drifting away like a ghost, Rew showed himself enough that Heindaw kept after him, but he didn't let the enchanter close the distance between them.

As he moved, Rew consciously brushed against the trees and bushes, the grasses and ferns. He sank his senses into the soil, only half his mind on staying away from the monstrosity looming behind him. For a ranger, keeping track of the brightly lit, screeching mass that was Heindaw was as easy as breathing. The rest of his mind, he turned toward absorbing the energy of the wood. It wasn't as full of life as the wilderness, not by far, but it was something. It was rejuvenating, and as Rew darted and ducked, he felt his lungs filling with clean air, his blood pumping with the rhythms of natural life, and the peace of the land bolstering his soul.

Rew communed with the wild, drawing in and pushing back out. He sent his need out in a wave, following the lines of ancient magic that life inscribed upon the world. He pulsed a call for help and hoped that someone would hear. The wood thrummed around him, echoing that call. The message was on the air, traveling with the vibrancy of untamed space, the clawing urgency of growing life. Rew felt it, but would the others? Ang and Vurcell had enough sensitivity, but few of the others would be adept. Were they ready to respond?

Moving confidently, Rew caught his breath, easily avoiding the well-lit Heindaw, but he still had the problem that the prince was completely invulnerable to Rew's sword. Heindaw hadn't been slowed much by the fire, either. Would another form of magic work against him? Maybe Rew could trick a spellcaster into unleashing something against his master. He'd told Anne he wouldn't call upon the power of Erasmus Morden, but he would if he had to. He wasn't sure it would help. Heindaw appeared invulnerable to enchanted steel no matter how fast and hard it was swung, so the strength in the longsword would be the last resort.

Or could he simply outlast the prince? Eventually, Heindaw would tire, and once he stopped powering the armor, his protections would fail. Rew hoped so, at least.

It wasn't until Rew burst into a clearing at the center of the wood that he realized Heindaw hadn't been trying particularly hard to catch him. The forest had heard Rew's call for help, but the ranger suddenly wasn't sure it mattered. The golden glow wasn't a light Heindaw had cast trying to spy Rew. It was a light he'd cast so that his men could find them, and when Rew burst out into the clearing, they did.

Chapter Twenty-Two

Heindaw, as always, was prepared. Three score soldiers, the only ones Rew had seen not wearing the vibrant colors common in Iyre, stepped out of the gloom beneath the trees. Rew slowed to a trot, walking to the center of the clearing, cursing himself for sinking his senses into the forest but not questing to see who else was out there. It was an amateur error, and it'd cost him. He'd thought no one would have been waiting for them in this abandoned piece of Iyre, but of course they were. Of course Heindaw had anticipated this was exactly where Rew would come running.

Behind him, smashing through the undergrowth, Heindaw broke free and stopped. "Where did you think you were going, Rew?"

"I thought I could lose you in the bushes," claimed the ranger. He scratched his beard. He had kind of hoped that would work.

Heindaw barked a laugh. "You probably could have, but you kept letting me see you. Sacrificing yourself so that the girl can escape, was it? It's no use, Rew. I've embedded wards surrounding this wood to keep all of you trapped within, and I've got a thousand men and a dozen spellcasters converging on this place and lining the walls. She's trapped here. You all are. It's only a matter of time before my people run her down. I've been leagues ahead of you since you left Eastwatch, Rew."

Rew glared at the prince.

"Don't believe me?" asked Heindaw with a laugh.

The prince raised a bronze-covered arm and gestured. Jacquiss emerged behind Heindaw's men. After giving Rew an apologetic look, she joined the enchanter. Rew scowled at her. His suspicions were confirmed, but he didn't feel particularly good about it.

"You didn't wonder how she ended up with such valuable enchantments?" asked Heindaw, as if honestly curious Rew could have overlooked that. "I'm a little offended. Outside of my own armor, this is my best work. I don't think anyone else in the kingdom could have fashioned this armor."

"This entire time, then?" asked Rew, cutting his gaze between his brother and Jacquiss. "You had her waiting for me in Spine-send and then Stanton. You sent her after us in Jabaan, and then accompanying us all of the way here?"

"I've been following her—and you—every step of the way. You should take that as a compliment, Rew. I'd hoped you would take the opportunity we provided to slay Valchon, but I'll settle for Calb. Not every plan works out as we envisioned, does it? Not that you ever planned for anything. You've always acted on instinct despite time and time again seeing where it got you."

Rew shook his head. "I planned to come here and face you, and that worked."

Heindaw snorted, the sound like a blast coming from inside of his helmet. "Aye, you planned to come here, but it only worked because I wanted you to come."

"Why did you take Baron Fedgley?" asked Rew.

"You know why."

"That's why you sent Jacquiss to us," guessed Rew, glancing at the woman before settling his gaze on Heindaw. "As soon as Fedgley was killed, you realized you needed his daughter."

The prince's armor clanked as he nodded. "Aye, I needed the girl, but I couldn't collect her myself. How would it have looked to Father if I'd shown interest in an untrained necromancer? His hackles were raised after the baron died, and I wasn't ready to fight him for her. Not yet. Vyar Grund was watching like a hawk. What other pieces had Father put into play? I knew there was no one else in the kingdom I could count on to bring her to me safely, so I used you. You brought her right to me, and you managed to kill Calb and draw Father's wrath while you did it. The perfect cover, for me. You've been playing my game since you sat down at the table, and it could not have worked out better."

"We don't have to be enemies, Heindaw," said Rew. "We both want the lass for the same purpose. Let me—"

Heindaw held up a hand to stop Rew. "That's Alsayer's line, Brother. He's wrong. We do have to be enemies."

Rew grimaced.

"Alsayer isn't coming to rescue you," continued Heindaw. "He served his purpose, bringing you close to our brothers so you could strike your blow, but that's done, and the next time I see him, I'll kill him. He's smart. Smarter than you, I'll grant him that. I don't think he'll come back to Iyre. He's a fool if he does, but I always tailor my plans to be adjusted. You wanted to talk? Fine. I'll give you time while we see if our cousin makes an appearance. We'll see if he answers the call you issued. You did call for him, didn't you?"

Rew blinked, and Heindaw laughed, the sound sharp and brittle from within the enchanted armor.

"My wards, Rew. They're designed to keep your friends inside the confines of this park, but they detect magic as well, even low magic. I, unlike our brothers, have never underestimated you. You took a different path, not a lesser one, but I always knew you'd come to the same place we did. You had to. It's in our blood."

Rew shook his head.

"He's still communing, m'lord," called a voice from the fringe of men who'd surrounded the clearing. "I can't pick up what was said, but he established a connection. It's-it's to the trees, m'lord. I don't understand. He's somehow casting his magic through the trees. It's a steady beat, coursing out to… somewhere."

Rew gaped at the speaker in surprise. Even if the man didn't understand what Rew was doing, the ranger couldn't believe Heindaw had a minion who could sense it.

"My own ranger unit," explained Heindaw, "a counter to Valchon's use of Grund and Alsayer's use of you. I've planned for everything, but the trees? Why would you talk to a tree?"

Rew did not respond.

Heindaw gestured to one of his men without turning from Rew. "What sorts of things can rangers get trees to do?"

"I'm not sure, m'lord," mumbled the man. "He, ah, he's utilizing magic we're not familiar with. I think he's communicating to someone, but I can't be sure."

"He's the best of you, I'll grant him that," murmured Heindaw. "We'll give it time, Rew, to see what you have done, who you called to. I'll thank you if it's Alsayer."

"I suppose we'll find out if his preparations can match yours," declared Rew. He struggled to keep his face blank. Alsayer? Why did Heindaw believe he was allied with Alsayer? But whatever his brother's thinking, it bought them critical time. Rew just had to figure a way to use it. He turned to Jacquiss. "I saw your father tonight."

"Did you?" asked Jacquiss, frowning.

"He died in a fire."

"I know," she replied, glancing at Heindaw out of the corner of her eyes.

"He died in a fire tonight. Heindaw was there."

Jacquiss shook her head. "My father has been lost for a long time, Ranger."

"Heindaw uses that armor to implant suggestions into your thinking," Rew told her. "He's the one who convinced you that your father is dead."

"Rew—" began Heindaw.

"Why do you think your lover never called you back to Iyre!"

barked Rew, interrupting the prince, hoping he was right and that the woman hadn't returned to Iyre. "He could have portaled you here any time. He didn't because he knew you'd learn the truth."

"Rew," repeated Heindaw, "I see what you're doing, but you've underestimated dear Jacquiss. She joined me because she wanted to, not because of any trickery. She's always known her father lived."

"He's dead now," said Rew, staring into the woman's eyes.

"There is peace in death," replied Jacquiss, her tone flat, "the only peace any of us are due."

"You told Heindaw of your father's research, his mission. You spied on him."

"My father learned secrets too dangerous for us to keep. His soul wasn't in the thrall of the king like I told you, but it would have been. His death tonight is a mercy." Jacquiss sighed and shook her head. "I regret many things, Ranger, but sharing with Heindaw how to defeat the king isn't one of them. My father held his secrets close, but to no purpose. His way, we'd never defeat the king. I'll grieve his death, but at least he passed without Vaisius Morden learning of what he knows. At least my father's soul is free."

"Cinda won't work with Heindaw."

"She won't have a choice."

"You have a choice," growled Rew.

Jacquiss raised an eyebrow.

"Your father was not fooled by your deception. He knew you lived. He said he loved you. He said he forgave you."

"Some things cannot be forgiven, but we carry those sins with us. There's nothing else to do."

"In the end, your father prayed for the Blessed Mother to watch over you," claimed Rew, scrambling to get a reaction from the woman, to find some crack he could drive a wedge into. "Your father thought with the Mother's Grace that there would still be salvation."

"I betrayed him. I betrayed you. I betrayed Cinda, Anne, the rest. There is no grace for me."

"There could be. Your father forgave you. I forgive you. The Mother will forgive you if you repent."

Heindaw looked back and forth between Rew and Jacquiss, his armor rustling loudly as he turned the massive bronze helm. The enchanter was waiting to see if Alsayer would appear or maybe waiting for his men to recover Cinda and the others, and evidently, he was amused enough by the conversation to let it continue.

"Appealing to the Blessed Mother?" chided Heindaw with a laugh. "You're getting desperate, Rew. You've no more faith than I. We've seen and done too much."

Let him laugh. Rew needed time.

And one more thing.

"There is a way to earn your father's forgiveness, Jacquiss."

She snorted. "My father has no idea of the depths I've gone."

"He does."

She raised an eyebrow.

"He wasn't fooled by your lies. He accepted them. Your father has been keeping track of you, and he still loved you. He knows what you've done. I know as well. We forgive you, Jacquiss. You can have grace in the Mother's embrace."

"You're not my father, Ranger. You're not my friend, not my lover. You don't know what I've done. That's a mercy, but you cannot forgive me those things."

"You missed your opportunity there, Brother," said Heindaw, his eyes sparkling within his helmet. "She's right. I don't think her father would appreciate hearing about the things she's done. Maybe you would, though, while we're waiting?" Heindaw laughed, his cackle sounding evil coming from within that helmet.

"You've planned for every eventuality, haven't you?" asked Rew, raising his voice to be heard over his brother's cruel mirth. "All except one. That armor you gave her, the way you've tracked her every move, what other properties did you imbue into that bronze plate and chain? It's akin to your own set, isn't it? You respect low magic, but you never understood how it worked. You aren't good making connections with people, or even things. It was only high magic and the power it could bring that you cared for, but here in the wood, this is my place, and here, connection matters. You granted her the means to kill you."

"What?"

"Her scimitar is fashioned just the same as your armor. It can cut through your protections."

Heindaw raised his own massive blade and took a step closer toward the ranger.

"Jacquiss," said Rew. "Your father loved you. He forgave you. There is grace, if you earn it. We can stop the king, stop all tyrants, but I need your help."

Then, Rew whistled, and the foliage around them burst into life.

Men, clad in the forest green and brown clothing of the King's Rangers, leapt from hiding and fell upon the rangers in Heindaw's personal company. Blades flashed, and men screamed. The king's ranger contingent was led by Ang and Vurcell, and the twins whirled in a frenzy of gleaming steel and blood.

The twins, Ang wielding his swordstaff and Vurcell the paired falchions of Vyar Grund, were terrors amongst the prince's men. They had the advantage of surprise, and while Heindaw might have believed he'd recruited a talented group of swordsmen, they had never faced the full might of the king's rangers. No one had.

The rangers were battle-tested by narjags, ayres, valaan, and the natural monsters of the world. They faced those horrors alone, unsupported except by another ranger or two. If they survived more than a season, they knew their weapons and their use better than some men knew their arms and their legs. Few trained as hard as the rangers, and there wasn't another group in the kingdom that had their experience. Heindaw's group of rangers melted beneath the onslaught of Ang and Vurcell.

Heindaw, seeing the same thing Rew was seeing, elected to

charge. His armor throbbed with pulsating runes, and he held his sword to the side, ready to strike at Rew. His open, gauntleted hand flexed, and Rew knew there was bone-crushing strength in those fingers.

Rew attacked his brother, not waiting for the heavily armored man to fall upon him. He feinted then ducked below Heindaw's sweeping slash. He hammered the edge of his enchanted blade against Heindaw's giant, armored thigh, but the steel of Rew's longsword bounced off, and the ranger was by his brother without doing any damage.

Heindaw twisted, and the knuckles of the gauntlet on his free hand clipped Rew's back. The ranger was sent tumbling across the grass. The blow had caught him on the muscle, and nothing was broken, but he could feel pain radiating from the injury. In hours, the bruise would be so deep and he would be so sore his arm would be useless, but he wasn't yet.

Rew rolled over just in time to see Heindaw closing on him. The prince jumped as if he intended to land on Rew, crushing him into the dirt. Rew rolled clear and sprang to his feet, whipping his longsword across Heindaw's back, but other than a loud ring, there was nothing to show for the blow.

Ang whirled into the fight, the butt on his swordstaff smacking into Heindaw's head, the bladed-end spinning, scraping across the prince's midsection, carving a path just beneath the prince's breastplate where there would be a gap in any normal armor. The ranger backed away, mouth open, as his swordstaff had no effect on the prince.

Heindaw swung at Ang, and Rew launched himself into a tackle, knocking Ang clear of Heindaw's blade a moment before it cleaved the startled man in two.

Rew scrambled away, avoiding a stomp from Heindaw's boot then jumping, the enchanter's huge blade swinging low as Heindaw tried to catch Rew where he couldn't duck under. The ranger landed and delivered another strike to Heindaw's shoulder, which bounced off uselessly like all of his other attacks.

Cackling, Heindaw boomed, "Why don't you activate the blade, Rew? See if the soul of our ancestor gains power over your own. You think I didn't know the properties of that sword? It's why I let you keep it, Brother. I've known for years and always wondered whether you'd foolishly seek the power in that steel and sacrifice yourself like they all do. It would have made things easier for me, but I'll give you respect for not succumbing. You meant it, didn't you, that you wanted nothing to do with our family and the throne? Why are you here, then? If you can resist the call of the blade, you can resist the Investiture as well."

"M'lord!" shouted a man.

Heindaw and Rew turned and saw a group of soldiers and spellcasters escorting Anne and the children. Cinda wore glowing cerulean manacles, the same sort that had dampened her father's ability to cast. She limped and wore a scowl. Raif was unconscious. His hair hung over his face and swung as he was dragged along, but Rew had seen the lad in worse shape. Anne and Zaine had no visible injuries, and they met Rew's gaze with apologetic looks. They all lived, and that was what mattered.

"Take them to the palace," ordered Heindaw loudly. "I'll come for them when I'm done here."

More of his soldiers were pouring into the clearing, drawn from their positions around the walls around the park. They were forming up into a defensive square, keeping the rangers back. They began to move toward the palace. If they got there, Rew suspected Heindaw had laid defenses not even the rangers could slip through.

Nearby, Ang crouched, poised to leap at Heindaw's back.

"I'll handle him," growled Rew. "Free the children. Quick. You can't let them reach the palace."

Still laughing to himself, Heindaw waited and then bellowed. "I thought you'd use the blade, but it'd be no good to you. Nothing is going to work. I've planned for everything. I thought it a sweet touch that I'll kill you with a sword. You, the best swordsman of us all, killed by the blade. Makes your life feel pointless, doesn't it?"

"I'm not dead yet."

Heindaw, stalking toward Rew, shook his armored head. "You can't touch me, Rew. This place is surrounded, so you can't escape. I have your friends. You're going to die for nothing."

Rew shifted his grip, preparing to activate his sword, to open himself to Erasmus Morden, to play his last card even if it wasn't a winning one, but then he saw Cinda's scarlet back being escorted away. He faced Heindaw and said, "Not for nothing. Cinda will play the role you planned. She'll stop our father, and his immortal reign will end. You'll take the throne, but then your reign will end as well. We all die, Heindaw. If I die now, but my mission is accomplished and Father is deposed, then so be it. I never wanted the throne. I just want Father off of it."

Heindaw threw back his head, roaring with laughter, clutching his breastplate with his gauntlet. "You think I wanted the Fedgleys to overthrow Father? You're a fool, Rew! I've known for years how to sever Father's connection to the bodies he inhabits. That man Jacob played right into it earlier tonight. Kick the legs from beneath the stool, and it's going to collapse. Father can't make the transfer without enormous power. Destroy the crypts, and you destroy the man. His spirit will perish when his body does."

Rew blinked at his brother, intent on what he was saying but trying not to be distracted from the fight. Destroy the crypts...

"I shouldn't tell you this, but I can't resist the look on your face, realizing how thoroughly you've failed. I didn't need the Fedgleys to confront Father, I needed them to become immortal myself. I need the talent in their blood. It's taken years, but I've finally finished my preparations. Tonight, Rew, I'll convince the girl she's fulfilling her destiny to stop the king, and she'll use her power to pull my soul into her body. The opposite of Father's own spell. Her young flesh, her power, will be mine! With the talent in her blood and my knowledge, I'll be an equal to Father. I've never cared to depose the man and inherit the headaches of rule. I just want to live forever. If he challenges me, though... I need that sword back, Rew. It's the one thing Father fears. With Erasmus' strength in my fist, the king will wilt before me."

Rew stumbled away as if struck. Heindaw hadn't been trying to destroy Vaisius Morden? He didn't even care for the throne?

The prince stepped closer and reached out to grasp Rew with his armored fingers. He held the ranger tight, not to hurt him but tight enough Rew couldn't wriggle away.

"This is going to be painful, Rew, but I have to take your soul. It'd be easier if I had the mechanisms I designed in the Arcanum, but you managed to get those destroyed, so this is your fault. I understand the theory now, and I can perform the spell on my own. You know too much about what I'm planning, about how to stop me. I can't let Father find you in death. Everyone who knows must stay within my thrall forever. I'm not sorry, but you have my sympathy. This is going to be horrific for you."

Rew began to struggle, but it was no use. He lashed his longsword against Heindaw's bronze covered arm, but like before, nothing happened. He reached up and tried to free himself from the implacable fingers, but they didn't budge. Then, he began to feel something leaking from him, as if his life was draining away. His eyes darted, looking for help, but the rangers were engaged in fighting Heindaw's men. The nameless woman, Jacquiss was standing, watching, her face blank.

"Your father forgave you," croaked Rew.

"What?" muttered Heindaw.

"Everyone who knows... Heindaw said everyone who knows," rasped Rew, struggling against the flow exiting his body. "Your father... knows. Jacob forgave you, but could you forgive yourself if he cannot rest?"

"What are you talking about, Rew?" growled Heindaw.

"You'll trap the soul of her father," accused Rew. "You'll hold it for eternity."

Heindaw shrugged, his heavy bronze shoulders screeching with the motion. "Yes, I suppose I must."

"He loved you. He forgave you. Could you forgive yourself?"

Slowly, Heindaw turned his head, realizing it wasn't him that Rew was talking to but to Jacquiss.

The edge of a bronze blade clanged against the side of Prince Heindaw's head, and his helmet was snapped to the side. The glowing red runes maintained their light, not flaring to meet the attack from the scimitar. Sword and armor, forged of bronze, enchanted by the same hand. There was a connection in all things, and the metal pieces recognized each other, and the magic of the armor was not deflecting Jacquiss' blows.

She struck again and again. Brilliant gleaming scars shone where she'd landed her strikes, but Heindaw shrugged them off. His enchanted suit made him the height and a half of a normal man, and the attacks barely moved him. Jacquiss struck again, landing several vicious blows before retreating.

Heindaw raised his own blade.

"This bronze is as thick as your wrist." He chuckled. "What do you think you're going to do? You could batter me for days, and all you'll do is wear yourself out. Allow me to finish, and we will talk."

"It doesn't have to be a lie," whispered Rew, his voice barely leaking past his lips. "You told me it was all to save his soul. It can be."

Heindaw flung Rew aside and struck at Jacquiss. She leapt out of the way, and the two of them danced across the open grass, bronze blades flashing in the night.

Rew sat slumped. He felt like... like he'd never felt before. Heindaw, whatever he'd done, had taken something out of Rew. A part of his soul.

He watched the prince and the woman fight. She was unable to do more than scar Heindaw's armor, and he was unable to catch her, so far, but she was tiring, and the prince was not. She had years of training, but he had his magic. It would be over soon.

Supposing he ought to care, Rew looked down at his longsword. Erasmus was in there. He could call to the old man, his ancestor, but why? Heindaw's armor was still impervious to Rew's attacks. The longsword, even powered by the soul of a centuries-old ghost, would be useless.

Sighing, Rew let go of the weapon and leaned back, putting his hands down on the soil to prop himself up while he watched the fight. His fingers found the cold dirt, and he dug them into it. He felt the grass brushing against his hands stirred by the night breeze. The trees rustled about the wood, and he breathed in, letting the clean air and the sound of those bare branches spill into him, drowning out the clash of the two bronze-armored warriors.

The woman was faster and more talented. She landed blows with impunity, but they barely seemed to slow Heindaw. The damage she did marred the prince's gleaming plate, but did nothing to injure him. It didn't matter how much more skill she had. No mortal strength could smash through the heap of metal the enchanter was encased within.

Yawning, tired eyes watching the fight, Rew thought it was too bad her scimitar was such a poor weapon for stabbing. The prince's narrow visor was his only weak point. Even the wide blade of the scimitar ought to fit through the gap, but the weapon was designed to slash. It was an awful option against a man in full plate.

Jacquiss leapt at the prince, aiming for his head again, and Heindaw caught her a glancing blow on the leg. She spun, cart-wheeling away, a bright piece of her armor and a stringer of blood flying free before she landed with a thud.

The prince tried to reach her, but she scrambled back. She had dropped her scimitar, but she leapt closer and snatched it. That cost her another raking blow on the back. She fell again. She crawled, sword in hand, the backplate on her armor hanging loosely, only the delicate chain covering her soft skin. Rew thought that if her armor hadn't been crafted by Heindaw himself, she would be dead already. Her gear was as good as any armor Rew had ever seen and had held up shockingly well, but it wouldn't for long. Heindaw's massive blade was the size of her. A direct blow, and no protection was going to save her.

Rew flexed his fingers in the soil, thinking it felt just like it did back home in the wilderness. The trees were different, though they sounded much the same as the wind blew through them. The creak of branches, the rustle of dry leaves, the random, wild music of the forest. He smiled. It sounded like home. Like him. It fulfilled him, being there, smelling it, hearing it.

He blinked.

Drawing another deep breath, he freed his fingers from the soil. He was a part of the wilderness, and the wilderness was a part of him. Heindaw had taken something from Rew, but he hadn't taken that. He hadn't taken who Rew was. It was rooted too deeply, Rew was a part of the world.

Rew grasped his longsword and rose to his feet.

Screaming in pain and rage, Jacquiss stumbled away from Heindaw. Her shoulders were hunched and she limped. Her leg bled freely, and Rew suspected there were broken bones in her shoulder or arm.

The ranger took a step toward the combatants but paused. The forest was filling him, healing him, but he still couldn't do a damned thing about Heindaw. He had no weapons to pierce Heindaw's enchantments, no way to injure the man. He could run, but he wouldn't. He would try to fight. Bellowing a cry, Rew ran at Heindaw's back. He couldn't harm the man, but maybe given an opening, Jacquiss could.

Her sword. That was the way through Heindaw's defense. They had to use the sword, but the woman and the blade were on the other side of the prince.

Heindaw kept stalking Jacquiss, ignoring Rew until the ranger leapt onto his back and smashed the hilt of his longsword down on top of the prince's head. Repeatedly, he rained blows down on his brother. It might not injure the prince, but the clank of metal on metal sure seemed to annoy him. Heindaw spun, and Rew went flying off, landing in a hard roll that knocked the wind from his lungs.

"Ranger, you're an idiot," called Jacquiss. "I forgive you that. You'll have to finish this, though."

She tossed her scimitar toward Rew and rushed Heindaw.

The prince turned back to her, but she was already inside his guard. She jumped, like she was going to strangle the man, though that was about the stupidest thing Rew could imagine. He was an idiot? Rew stood, and Heindaw wrapped his arms around Jacquiss, squeezing her.

The plates of her armor began to buckle, and chains split with gravelly crunches, but she kept her bronze-armored hands on the prince's neck. Rew stepped closer, unsure what he could do, but certain in moments, her torso was going to be crushed like a rotten melon.

With a wild shout, Jacquiss ripped Heindaw's helmet from his head and threw it over her shoulder.

Heindaw snarled at her and squeezed again. Her armor crumpled, and her ribcage collapsed with a muffled crack. The prince dropped Jacquiss at his feet and raised his blade toward Rew.

The ranger could see the prince now, see the gleam in his eye and the smile on his lips. "I've always moved in the shadows, but I'm beginning to enjoy killing with my own hands. Come here, Rew. Let's end this."

Rew smirked and then charged.

Heindaw was as rested as when they'd first begun, and he'd anticipated Rew's attack. He thrust his sword, trying to skewer the ranger, but Rew was faster. He'd been drinking from the well of natural magic in the wood, and he was invigorated. He was as rested as when they'd begun as well, and unlike Heindaw, he didn't need high magic to know how to swing his sword.

Rew jumped, putting a toe on the edge of Heindaw's blade and stabbing with his longsword.

Heindaw caught it with his empty fist, clamping his bronze-covered fingers around the blade and stopping the thrust.

"Nice tr—"

Holding himself up with one hand on his longsword, Rew yanked his hunting knife from behind his back with the other hand and slammed it into Heindaw's face, the wide blade of the knife tearing through the prince's cheek and burying half its length in his head before reaching the back and stopping there, the tip resting against the inside of the prince's skull.

Blood gushed, pouring over Rew's hand, and he fell off Heindaw's sword, landing and collapsing to his knees. He looked up, but his brother was motionless. The bone hilt of the hunting knife protruded from his face, and he still held the longsword in his gauntleted hand. The red glow of the script along his armor throbbed with the pulse of a heartbeat and began to fade.

And then, it stopped, winking out.

Heindaw still stood, his armor supporting him, but he was dead.

Chapter Twenty-Three

Rew pulled his new cloak tightly around his body, glad one of the rangers had a spare which fit him and that it wasn't in the garish colors popular in the city. He rubbed his head and wished they'd had time to see a barber, but that was a foolish notion.

Heindaw was dead, but Valchon wasn't, and the king wasn't. The moment those two found out about Heindaw, Iyre was going to be a very dangerous place for Rew and the others. He hadn't allowed them to rest or even for Anne to tend to the small wounds they'd received. Instead, they'd immediately set off for the gates of the city, accompanied by the rest of the king's rangers.

The rangers were men and women who'd sacrificed everything to answer his call. They'd left lucrative positions all around the kingdom, their friends, and family in several cases. They'd assembled in Mordenhold, right beneath the nose of the king himself. They'd betrayed him and, for that, would have his wrath. From now until it was over, now until forever if Rew did not succeed, they'd be hunted by Vaisius Morden. They knew that and had come anyway.

Led by Ang and Vurcell, they'd defeated Heindaw's ranger company and then freed Anne and the younglings. If it wasn't for their timely arrival, Rew's victory over Heindaw would have been meaningless. He couldn't have fought through the rest of the prince's men and spellcasters to free the others, but while he was grateful for the ranger's support, he had to tell them to leave. So many remarkable men and women, all traveling together, were certain to be noticed. For the safety of everyone, they had to split up.

They'd arrived by portal stone from Mordenhold where Ang and Vurcell had collected everyone, but all agreed it was far too dangerous to try and flee the same way. The bulk of Heindaw's army was intact, and now, the palace blazed with light as his men and surviving spellcasters tried to figure out what had happened.

Even if they believed they could fight their way through Heindaw's men to the chamber the portal stones were housed in, Rew thought Heindaw might have laid traps on the portals that went anywhere except Mordenhold. That one was protected by the king and only open to those in his service. No one fancied returning to Mordenhold now that they'd helped to kill a prince, and Heindaw was at war with everywhere else.

One ranger, Thaddeous, could manage a little invoking, and he scattered a dozen others outside the city through small portals, but his portals were little things and did not reach far. He wore out quickly, so most of the rangers fled on foot.

Rangers drifted away as the group skulked toward the gates, each taking different paths, hoping to lose any pursuit by going in all directions. They left instructions on where they could be contacted, sharing the information only with Rew, Ang, and Vurcell. They wanted to continue the fight, but they had to get away cleanly first.

Rew tried to memorize where each ranger said they were headed and the secret ways he could reach them. In time, the rangers would assemble again in a safe place, and he could call them if he needed them through the ancient magic of the land, but the messages he could send were primal, little more than instructions to help or to run. He hoped he didn't have to send either.

By the time their party reached the main gates of Iyre, the bulk of the rangers had disappeared. Only Ang and Vurcell remained with them. The gates were open, and the guards were easily distracted by a crackling display of light Cinda set off on a rooftop nearby. Quietly, they slipped outside undetected. They kept walking in the dark, marching down the highway, trying to make good time. Everyone was exhausted, but they all knew they had to get some distance between themselves and Iyre.

Rew would have liked to have disappeared into the woods and hills around the city as many of the rangers had, but Anne and the children couldn't move quickly with stealth, so instead, he opted for speed and distance.

By daybreak, they were five leagues from Iyre, and Rew took them off the road into a thick stand of trees where they could hide during the day when the road would be thick with other travelers. Ang and Vurcell obscured their tracks from the road to the trees. Unless one of the other rangers happened by, no one was going to see the signs.

They made a cold camp, and as they settled down, no one offered anything other than grins and gratitude that they'd survived.

"Two down, one to go," declared Raif, sitting against a tree, stretching his legs out in front of him.

Rew nodded, feeling it was a bad time to point out that after Valchon, they still had the king to deal with. They'd done well, all of them, and it was worth celebrating the victory. Celebrate as much as they could, that was, at a camp with no fire, no ale, no music, and running for their lives.

"We'll come with you," stated Vurcell, squatting on his haunches near Anne. He reached back to touch the wooden hilts of the falchions over his shoulder. "These might come in handy again, and we've got to go somewhere until the dust settles. Might as well be with you, Senior Ranger."

Rew shook his head. "I'm not a ranger any longer."

Ang laughed. "Pfah, you'll always be the King's Ranger. We've just gotta get you a new king. And my brother is right. We can help. We want to."

Rew glanced at Anne, and she frowned, pursing her lips.

"We won't drink all of the ale," offered Vurcell.

"Yes, you will," retorted Rew.

Grinning, the ranger shrugged. He leaned toward Anne. "Maybe we'll drink all of his ale, but after so long, you must want someone to talk to other than Rew, right?"

Anne laughed at that and nodded. "Fair enough. You're not one of us. Don't look at me like that. I mean you're not connected to our party like the rest of us are bound. Not yet, anyway. You don't have to do this. You can leave, find some wilderness, and lose yourselves there. The Investiture has not touched you two. Away from the cities, the king will never find you."

"We're not family," said Ang, looking over the five companions, "but we are friends. We'll come along until we can get you some place safe. Our blades, our woodcraft, it could come in handy. We can be of use until it's safe to gather the others again."

"We'll be glad to have you," said Rew, surprised that he meant it.

He'd been reluctant to involve anyone that he didn't have to, particularly those he cared about. Each moment in his company, they were putting their lives at risk, but it was a comfort to be surrounded by those he knew and trusted. In addition, having the rangers around might make it harder for Anne and the younglings to gang up on him.

"Come with us... but to where?" asked Cinda, her eyes flashing green in the morning light. The rangers saw, and they understood, but no one commented. Cinda continued, "Back to Carff, Mordenhold itself? Now that Heindaw is fallen, will Valchon be named, ah, king? I know Vaisius Morden will inhabit his body, but will they conduct the ceremony? Is there a ceremony?"

Rew shook his head. "Calb and Heindaw are dead, but there's another brother left besides Valchon. Me."

"But you abdicated your title and defied the king," argued Anne. "Surely, after all that's happened, after he knows what we're doing, the king wouldn't... Rew, he knows we're trying to end his reign!"

"He's not inviting us to supper, Anne. He's trying to winnow his sons down so the strongest survives, and that's the body he'll take over. I've killed two of my brothers now. Valchon hasn't killed any. No, I've been thinking about this all night as we walked. It's possible Vaisius Morden will let us go free, for now. He'll want Valchon and I to face each other, and I don't think he'll interfere until we do. If he truly wanted to capture us, he probably could have by now. Blessed Mother, after the explosion in the Arcanum, he could have carpeted the entire province with undead searching for us, but instead, he just sent a few hundred soldiers. I suspect, after two hundred years of rule, he doesn't fear us. We cannot be the first to defy him, and every time, he's prevailed. He might think keeping us alive is worth the risk, or maybe he doesn't see us as a risk at all. We have to watch our backs, of course, but I don't believe he's actively hunting for us. I hope not, at least."

"Blessed Mother," groused Anne. "Maybe he's not, but what if he is?"

"Perhaps a prayer to the Mother instead of a curse?" suggested Rew.

The empath glared at him.

Rew shrugged. "She's your goddess, Anne, not mine. It can't hurt, though, can it?"

"So where to?" repeated Cinda. "If you think Vaisius Morden isn't a threat, do we make for Carff to face Valchon? Or should we try for a surprise and go straight to Mordenhold?"

"Maybe Carff," said Rew, "but first, you need to do some reading—the book you took from the Arcanum and the one Jacob gave us. You need to study those, so we understand what knowledge Jacob sacrificed himself to pass on. There's a place about a week ahead which will be safe from the king and from Valchon. You'll have time there to read and to consider."

"Great. A week," said Zaine with a dramatic sigh. "You know what would have helped getting there? Horses."

Rew laid down, closed his eyes, and did not respond.

Thanks for reading!

My biggest thanks to the readers! If it wasn't for you, I wouldn't be doing this. Those of you who enjoyed the book, I can always use a good review—or even better—tell a friend.

My eternal gratitude to: Felix Ortiz for the breath-taking cover and social media illustrations. Shawn T King for his incredible graphic design. Kellerica for inking this world into reality. Nicole Zoltack coming back yet again as my long-suffering proofreader, joined by Anthony Holabird for the final polish. And of course, I'm honored to continue working with living legend Simon Vance on the audio. When you read my words, I hope it's in his voice.

Terrible 10... Always stay Terrible.

Thanks again, and hope to hear from you!
AC

You can find larger versions of the maps, series artwork, my newsletter, and other goodies at accobble.com. It's the best place to stay updated on when the next book is coming!